DADDY'S GIRL

Josephine Cox was born in Blackburn, one of ten children. She never forgot her own childhood experience of hardship and strongly believed in education as a way out of poverty. Her books have sold over twenty million copies worldwide. Josephine had a long and happy marriage to her husband Ken and was immensely proud of her family and her grandchildren. Josephine said of her books, 'I could never imagine a single day without writing. It's been that way since as far back as I can remember.'

Her legacy lives on through Gilly Middleton who has been a huge fan of Josephine Cox for many years and feels very privileged to have worked with her. Gilly lives in Sussex, where she likes to go to the theatre and to watch cricket.

Also by Josephine Cox

JOSEPHINE COX

with **GILLY MIDDLETON**

DADDY'S GIRL

HarperCollins*Publishers*

HarperCollins*Publishers*
1 London Bridge Street,
London SE1 9GF

www.harpercollins.co.uk

HarperCollins*Publishers*
Macken House, 39/40 Mayor Street Upper,
Dublin 1, D01 C9W8

First published by HarperCollins*Publishers* 2024

1

ISBN: 978-0-00-865071-1 (HB)
ISBN: 978-0-00-865072-8 (TPB)

Typeset in ITC New Baskerville by Palimpsest Book Production Ltd,
Falkirk, Stirlingshire

Printed and bound in the UK using 100% Renewable Electricity
by CPI Group (UK) Ltd

PROLOGUE

IT WAS A Sunday afternoon and the little terraced house in Keele Street, Scarstone was quiet, with just Sarah and her mother at home. Sarah put three spoonfuls of tea in the warmed pot. As she poured over the boiling water, she heard her mother scraping back a kitchen chair and she turned to see her sinking down onto it, her face very pale.

'You all right, Mum?'

Ava didn't answer straight away and when she did, she sounded a little breathless, although she mustered a brief smile.

'Yes, I'm fine, love. A bit tired, that's all. Came over a bit faint, like . . . but just give me a minute.' She closed her eyes and breathed deeply.

'You don't look so good,' said Sarah, putting the cosy over the teapot, then giving her mother her full attention.

Sarah's older brother, Joe, had gone with their father to watch a local football match. Janette, their younger sister, was round at her friend Lorna's house, leaving

1

Sarah and her mother to enjoy the luxury of a peaceful afternoon together.

'I've made the tea nice and strong,' said Sarah. 'That'll buck you up. But are you sure you're all right?'

Ava nodded wanly. 'Thanks, Sarah. I'll be up and doing in a minute.'

She had been looking a little too tired and listless of late, Sarah thought. Of course, she was always busy, what with her job working as assistant to Evelyn Rowley, whose first-class skills as a seamstress brought in a constant stream of customers wanting their clothes altered or mended. On top of that, Ava was a loving and caring wife and mother, whose home was spotless, even if the things in it were well worn, and whose husband and children never lacked for clean and pressed clothes, even if they were second-hand, nor for nicely cooked food of a plain sort. The Quinn family were not well off, but Ava's domestic standards never slipped below excellent.

'Mebbe you've been working too hard, Mum,' said Sarah, sitting down beside her mother and taking her hand, which felt cold yet clammy. 'I'll cook the tea tonight, shall I?'

'That's good of you, Sarah. Thank you,' said Ava. She looked relieved to be able to delegate. She took a couple more deep breaths and noticeably rallied, forcing a wider smile. 'I reckon you should get in a bit of practice. You could be married in a few years – your dad and I were courting when I was seventeen – and, well, cooking is a skill that you'll need if you want to stick to a budget and feed your family decently.'

Sarah laughed. 'I can see no fella on the horizon for me, Mum, but you're right, I expect I'll have to cook for a family one day. But I'd also like to learn a few skills that aren't domestic and put them to good use first. I've been thinking about this; thinking about my future . . .' She looked a little uncertain, being not one to push herself forward, but then she plunged in. 'It'd be grand to learn typewriting and mebbe to study book-keeping, too – what do you think? Girls like me – just ordinary – are learning to do all sorts now, not just factory or shop work, but in offices, using their brains. D'you reckon I could manage that, Mum?'

'Ah, love, I reckon you could do owt you put your mind to – both you and Janette.' Ava had always encouraged her daughters. Joe was disappointingly unambitious about his work – he never lasted more than a few months in any job – and he hadn't paid much attention at school either, but Ava saw no reason why her girls shouldn't do well for themselves.

'Well, Janette is the clever one, but I'd like to see what opportunities there are for me if I work hard.'

Ava smiled. 'I'll always be proud of you, whatever you do, and I hope I see my girls doing better than I ever did. "Reaching your potential" – isn't that what Miss Hurst calls it?'

'Aye, our headmistress is certainly keen on girls getting educated. I know staying on at school means I'm not working, except at the hardware shop with Dad on a Saturday. I know money is tight—'

'Don't worry, love. Your dad and me – and even Joe

at the moment – are working, so we manage. I'm glad you're staying on. I . . . I hope you'd still be able to get your Highers . . . if owt happened.'

Sarah felt a niggle of unease. 'What do you mean, Mum?'

'Oh, just . . . if things changed . . . you know – weren't quite as they are.'

Sarah had stood up to pour the tea, but now she put down the pot and resumed her seat beside her mother, taking her hand.

'What do you mean, Mum? What kind of changes? You'd tell me if there was owt wrong, wouldn't you? There *isn't* owt wrong, is there?'

'No, love.' Ava reached out and stroked a lock of Sarah's fair hair back behind her ear. 'There doesn't have to be owt wrong for me to tell my lass that I want the best for her. But, love, you're the one I can rely on, so I'm just saying, if owt *did* happen, you'd look after your dad, wouldn't you? Even if you're still studying? He's a good man, but I reckon he'd not be much use on his own—'

'On his own! Mum, what are you saying? You're not ill, are you?' Sarah felt panic rising in her stomach. She could not imagine this home without her mother at its heart.

'No, love. I told you. Please, just listen. Your dad's never learned to look after himself – why would he? – and Janette is still only twelve. Joe . . . well, he's a good lad, but it's taking him a while to find his feet. He's not yet learned that you only get out what you put in – and sometimes not even that, truth be told. And he is *only* a lad, so you couldn't expect owt much doing around the house . . . I'm just saying, I know I can rely on you. Your dad . . . well, he thinks the world of you. I know parents shouldn't have favourites – and he's never said in so many words – but it's plain to me that you're the centre of his world and he'd be lost without you—'

'Lost without *you*, you mean. Mum, please! You claim there's nowt wrong, so why are you saying this?'

'Now, Sarah, love, don't get worked up. Pour us a cup of that tea, and let's each have a spoonful of sugar in it, eh? There's nowt in life that can't be made right with a good strong cup of tea.'

By the time they had drunk the tea, Ava's colour had returned, and Sarah had been half persuaded that there was nothing to be alarmed about. Or, at least, not just now. And Ava had extracted a promise from her to look after her father and her siblings, 'just in case I need you to, so I don't have to worry'.

Within weeks, Ava was dead of heart failure and Sarah, broken-hearted and burdened by her promise, left school immediately and went to work for Miss Rowley, taking over what had been Ava's job as her assistant, and earning her first proper wages to help keep her family. It was a sacrifice, but she needed to contribute financially at home, and she knew there were far worse jobs than working for the kindly seamstress.

But alongside that, she took on the role of running the Quinn household. It no longer felt like the happy family home it had been, but four sad people feeling isolated in their misery, and struggling to see how on earth they were to fill the gaping holes in their lives that Ava had left.

One evening, Sarah found her father just sitting in his chair, staring ahead blankly. Joe was not yet home from work, which was currently with a painter and decorator, and Janette was in the rather gloomy little dining room at the back of the house, doing her homework.

'You all right, Dad?' Sarah asked gently. 'Shall I make you a cup of tea while I get cooking?' She knelt down beside him and took his hand.

He squeezed hers in return but could not raise even the slightest smile. He looked so desolate she wanted to cry.

'I doubt I'll ever be all right again, our Sarah,' he said. 'You're a good lass – the best – but, by heck, I never thought I could miss anyone like I miss your mother.'

She understood.

She rose and put an arm around his shoulders. 'We'll cope if we stick together, Dad. There may be just the four of us now, but we've got plenty of love to go round. Let's never forget that.'

Fred nodded, but it was just a token gesture. Sarah saw only despair in his face. Ava had been dead three weeks, and already Sarah felt out of her depth.

CHAPTER ONE

Early Summer 1930

SARAH MET HER friend Rachel outside Scarstone Library, where Rachel worked as an assistant, and the two young women strolled home in the golden early evening light, their sturdy heels tapping along the dusty pavement, their arms linked. Both wore well-worn cotton summer dresses, Sarah's blue, to match her eyes, while Rachel's was primrose-yellow, which looked striking against her dark hair. Sarah carried a bulging cloth bag on her free arm.

'Bringing your work home, Sarah?' asked Rachel. 'It's not like Miss Rowley to crack the whip, is it? What's got into her?'

'Oh, it's not Miss Rowley, Rachel. She's always considerate, but if I can get these repairs done by tomorrow morning and deliver them to the customer early,' she lowered her voice, although there was no chance of being overheard, 'the lady said she'd pay me a bit extra. Mrs Hutchinson, her name is, and she likes things done snip-snap; doesn't like to wait for owt.'

Rachel gave her friend a careful look. 'And does Miss Rowley know this?'

'She knows I'm working on them and that I'll take them round to Mrs Hutchinson first thing. She's pleased I said I'd do that and she trusts me to make a good job of them. The extra is just a private agreement between me and Mrs H, who said not to mention it.'

Rachel raised a questioning eyebrow. 'And you think that's all right, do you?'

'I don't see why not. Miss Rowley will still be paid what she's asked for, I get a bit extra for my effort, and Mrs Hutchinson is pleased to have her blouses made over quickly, so it's good news all round,' Sarah smiled.

'Aye, well . . . just be careful,' said Rachel. 'It's Miss Rowley's business and she might not like you making a deal on the side.'

'Hardly "a deal". And certainly nowt illegal. Plus it's good for her reputation if her clients know she's fast as well as reliable.'

'Mm. There may be two ways of looking at this, that's all I'm saying. Anyway, here you are, Sarah,' Rachel said as they reached the Quinns' front door, 'and as you've work to do this evening, you might want to ask Janette or even that useless article Joe to cook the tea. You can't do everything.'

'I doubt Joe will think the tea's owt to do with him, except when it's on the plate and in front of him,' said Sarah, with a roll of her eyes.

'Aye, probably . . . Right, well, I'll be seeing you. Don't stay up working too late.'

With a lift of her hand, Rachel continued on her way to her own, almost identical house, a couple of streets away, where she lived with her parents, the youngest of three siblings and the only one still at home.

Sarah turned to her front door, noting the grubbiness of the doorstep. Why did she never find the time to keep the step spotlessly white, like Mum had done? It hadn't been donkey-stoned for weeks. She didn't want to be ashamed of her own doorstep . . . to feel as if she was somehow letting down her mother by allowing stand-ards to slip. Still, there wasn't time to do anything about that now.

Inside, the house was stuffy and a little oppressive.

'Janette?' Sarah called, kicking off her shoes with some relief.

'What?' came her sister's loud voice from the back.

Sarah padded through to the kitchen, enjoying the coolness of the hall tiles against her hot feet, her indoor shoes in her hand.

'Good, I hoped you'd be home, love. I've got some blouses to retrim and I want to get on while the light is still good. Please, would you mind cooking the tea?'

Janette, who was just finishing her homework, her exercise books spread on the kitchen table, raised her eyebrows challengingly.

'What's it worth?' she asked with a saucy smile.

'A clip round the ear if you don't. How does that sound?'

'No need to get shirty. I was always going to agree anyway.' Both knew this, just as they knew that Sarah was not the sort to be clipping anyone's ear. Janette held up a finger to indicate she needed a moment, added a final sentence to her essay, then got up, flicking back her blonde plaits, and tidied her school books away into her satchel, which hung on the back of her chair. 'Why the homework? I thought folk waved goodbye to homework once they'd left school.'

'Just summat I said I'd do by morning, that's all,' Sarah said evasively. She was saving up, hoping to buy Janette some shoes for her birthday – a shiny new pair, not second-hand or handed down – and didn't want to mention the extra money.

While Janette crashed around the kitchen, making a big show of being helpful, Sarah took her work into the sitting room, where her mother's treadle sewing machine was set up ready to use on its heavy black stand. The low sun shone through the sooty window, and Sarah began quickly unpicking the frayed lace from Mrs Hutchinson's blouse collar before the light dimmed.

Sarah had been taught to sew by her mother, just as an interest, a skill Ava had been pleased and proud to share, and now, in a completely unforeseen turn of fate, Sarah had inherited her mother's job, working for Miss Rowley.

With Ava's sudden death, leaving Janette, now thirteen, still at school, and Joe – who was twenty, but sometimes acted as if he was thirteen – occasionally getting into the kind of trouble that meant he had to look for another job, there was little hope that Sarah would be trying to find her own chosen place in the world any time soon. Dad was becoming unrecognisable as the caring father he had once been. He was cast adrift without his wife to anchor him, lost and purposeless, sometimes moody, evermore uninterested in his home life and his children. Ava had been the heart of his home and the queen of his heart, and without her he was utterly lost. However hard Sarah tried to rise to the challenge of taking up her mother's domestic role (and it was proving to be hard work for a girl of just eighteen, employed full time and now running the house too), she never could take the place of her mother for any of them, but, of course, most especially for Fred.

As for her sewing job, Miss Rowley was very appreciative of Sarah's talent, and Sarah knew she was well up to the job, but she was beginning to feel she had been coerced into it by circumstances; that she had had neither choice nor control.

Still, just think of the extra Mrs Hutchinson was paying, she thought. Janette was growing taller by the day and her shoes were beginning to pinch. She would be thrilled to have some brand-new ones . . . if Sarah could save up enough to buy them for her.

The front door slammed.

'Dad?' called Sarah. 'In here.'

Fred put his head round the sitting-room door and Sarah explained that Janette was cooking, and why, and that she might need a little supervision.

'Oh, I expect she'll manage,' he said vaguely, brandishing the evening newspaper. 'Someone left this in the shop so I've summat to read while I wait for my tea. Then I'm off to the Lamb and Flag.'

The Lamb and Flag was becoming her father's home from home, Sarah reflected. She understood he liked the distraction of folk to gossip and grumble with, but it seemed to her that he was seeing the pub as a place to escape to and would far rather be there than here.

'But I've got these blouses to finish, Dad – I told you – and I haven't time to keep an eye on Janette as well. Couldn't you just help out this once?'

'I know nowt about cooking, and I have been at work all day, you know,' he said, as if Sarah hadn't; as if she was leading a life of leisure. 'Oh, mebbe in a bit, love,' he added, possibly seeing the expression on her face. But then he sat down in his armchair with the newspaper, shook it open and raised it like a screen in front of him.

Sarah tried to shrug off her annoyance and, conscious of the fast-fading light, continued with her task, splicing a new length of lace between the two collar edges. She ignored Janette's increasingly loud crashing about until she could stand it no longer.

'Dad, can't you hear her? *Please* would you go and just see if she's managing?' she begged, looking up from her sewing machine.

'What are you saying? Can't be much – I've heard nowt.' He carried on reading.

'Oh, honestly . . .' Sarah got up and stomped off, muttering, to the kitchen, where Janette was just putting a cottage pie in the oven. The pie looked delicious, but she had clearly used every single pan in the place to make it.

'All done,' Janette smiled. 'What do you want with it – carrots?'

Sarah looked at the heap of pans, the deposits already beginning to dry on in the heat; at the array of jugs and knives and plates; at the soil-encrusted potato peelings on the draining board and in the sink; at the packet of Bisto on its side, the contents spilling onto the floor.

'Yes, please, carrots . . . but, Jan, you'll have to clear up this lot first. There's no room to do owt.'

Janette gazed around as if noticing the mess for the first time. 'But I've just done all that cooking. I can't be doing with clearing up too! Not all by myself. That wouldn't be fair.'

''Course you can. You made the mess, you side it up.'

'Oh, *Sar-raah*! Is that what you've come in here to do, boss me about but not help?'

'I could hear you crashing pots. I came to see if you were all right.'

'Well, I'm not all right, am I, if I've got all this to clear *by myself?*'

Sarah took a deep breath. There was only one way forward. 'All right, I'll wash, you dry.'

It was when she went to unhook her pinafore from behind the door that it occurred to her that Janette, who was still in her school uniform, should have been wearing the pinny herself.

Sure enough, there was gravy soaked into the lower

sleeve of her school blouse and, now she looked closely, a splodge of mashed potato on the front of it.

'Give me strength! Jan, look at you! Why didn't you . . .? Oh, never mind, it's too late now. Just go and put your old togs on and then come and help. And be quick about it.'

Janette brushed the mashed potato onto the floor and sped away to do as she was asked.

The cottage pie was just about cooked when their brother, Joseph, appeared. It was as if he had some inner clock that told him the exact time when his food would be ready so that all he had to do was eat it and be thankful. He greeted his family cheerfully. The girls, rushing around and dishing up, replied brightly, while Fred grunted and sat down at the head of the table to wait for his food. Fred didn't always have a lot of time for Joe and what he called his 'unsteadiness'.

Having washed, Joe also sat down at the kitchen table. However, he was grinning.

'All right, Sarah? You look a bit heated.'

'I'm fine, thank you, Joe. Apart from—'

'Smashing-looking pie, though,' he said appreciatively, reaching over for the salt and pepper pots.

'Jan made it.'

'Aye, lass, you've done all right,' Fred conceded. He looked at Sarah. 'Told you there was no need to fuss, our Sarah.'

'Clever girl,' Joe said, winking at Janette. 'Been a busy day. I was supposed to scrape the peeling paint off some window frames. I hate that job, but the old biddy where we were working, Mrs Thomas – her cat got stuck up a tree and she got in a tizzy about it. Mr Blake isn't agile enough to get his bulk up off the ground, so I volunteered to rescue it. Took a long while, I can tell you,' he laughed. 'By the time I'd got that cat down, Blake had had to scrape most of the windows himself. Then the old lass made us tea and brought out a cake to thank me for rescuing the cat, and she slipped me a little tip, too.'

'You daft bugger,' muttered Fred.

Janette's eyes were wide. 'How high up was the cat, Joe? Was it very dangerous?'

'No, not dangerous at all – easy-peasy, really – but I had to make a show of the rescue, didn't I? Mrs Thomas might have thought it was nowt if I'd done it in a couple of minutes, so I reckoned I should entertain her a bit, like, with some near-falls and pretending to get stuck. Proper grateful for the tea and cake, I was – and the tip.' He smirked. 'I reckon we're friends for life.'

'Shame on you, Joe, taking an old lady for a ride,' said Sarah.

'Oh, sis, don't you start. It was bad enough Blake bending my ear when Mrs Thomas was out of hearing. A fella's got to get on in this life and it pays to make the most of any opportunities.'

'You'll not be so pleased with yourself if you lose that job, Joe,' warned his father.

'Yes, all right, Dad.'

They ate the cottage pie, while Joe entertained them with an exaggerated description of Mrs Thomas's run-down house. Then he helped himself to seconds before Sarah could stop him, although she had planned to eke out the leftovers with some extra vegetables the following evening, and then it was time to clear away. It was the closing of the front door that told Sarah her father had left for the pub without even removing his plate to the sink.

'Put the kettle on, Joe, would you, while I just side these plates off the table? Then if you and Jan could wash up—'

'No, you're all right, Sarah, I'm off out. Said I'd meet Dora Burgess.' He grinned, looking pleased with himself. 'There's a bit of a dance on at the town hall. Summat tells me that Dora is a good little dancer. I'll not stop late, what with work tomorrow, but I've got to have a bit of fun to set me up until the weekend.'

'But, Joe, I've got some blouses to trim by morning. I hoped you'd be here earlier to give Jan a hand with the washing-up, just this once. I think she could do with some help now while I get on.'

'Oh, sorry. Another time, mebbe. Can't keep a lady waiting outside in the street, can I? Especially one like Dora Burgess. Right, I've just got time to change into my decent bags and pullover and then I'm off. I'll see you later,' he called over his shoulder.

They heard his size nines thudding up the stairs.

'Do you think he's really taking *Dora Burgess* out?' Janette asked.

'I don't know and I don't care,' snapped Sarah.

'She's like a film star, with her golden hair and her pouty lips.' Janette made a little moue in imitation.

'Cupid's bow,' said Sarah, distractedly.

'And, honest truth, Sarah, she wears white silk stockings!'

'Good grief, are you sure? . . . I mean, look, Janette, I'm sorry but you know I've got that sewing to do, and Dad and Joe will never be persuaded to help, however busy I am. Can you just manage by yourself this once . . . please?'

Janette sighed as if from the bottom of her soul. 'All right. If I must. Miss Rowley never used to have Mum working all evening, though. I think she's taking advantage. I might have to have a word.'

'Janette Quinn, if you ever say more than "Good day" to Miss Rowley, you'll have me to answer to. Now, to work!'

They set about their tasks, hearing Joe's thudding return downstairs, his cheery ''Bye, girls' and then the front door banging behind him.

How had it come to this, Sarah asked herself as she returned to her sewing: all this running just to keep up with what needed doing? It hadn't been like this for Mum when she was alive . . . had it? Somehow everything had been clean – even the front doorstep – and Mum cooked and Sarah helped, and everyone tidied up, even if it was just to take their plates to the sink. And there was no nagging or raised voices, or anyone taking umbrage about shouldering a small part of the burden.

How far this current situation had fallen below that ideal! Now Dad went to the Lamb and Flag most evenings, and Joe was out as often, as if they were washing their hands of home life now that Mum was dead. Perhaps that was it: perhaps they couldn't face being here without her.

Well, thought Sarah, crossly, it's not my fault. I wish Mum was here, too. And I'm doing my best.

The trouble was, her best was obviously nowhere near good enough.

The next morning, the kitchen smelled vaguely of cigarettes, although Ava had been very strict in forbidding smoking indoors because Janette had once had bronchitis and cigarette smoke made her wheeze. Joe was undoubtedly the culprit – Sarah had heard him coming in late the previous night, about half an hour after she'd finished the sewing – but she couldn't find any evidence, and he'd already left for work. She opened the windows and the back door for a few minutes to air the place while she made sandwiches for packed lunches and a fresh pot of tea.

'Morning, Dad. Let me know if you're in a draught, won't you?'

Fred, sitting at the table, grunted noncommittally. Maybe he had had a merry time at the Lamb and Flag. But then again, perhaps not.

'Here you are, Dad.' Sarah handed him some cheese sandwiches wrapped in greaseproof paper, secured with string.

'Thanks, love.' He barely looked up from his boiled egg and toast.

'I didn't really see you when you got back from the Lamb and Flag – was it a good evening?'

'Not that I noticed. Sarah, please, can you just stop your chatter over breakfast? Early mornings are bad enough without you chirping around me like a sparrow.'

Sarah duly kept silent while she put eggs to boil for herself and Janette.

'Did Joe have owt to eat?' That wasn't chatting, it was asking.

'I don't know and I don't care. He's old enough to do for himself.' Fred picked up the parcel of sandwiches without a trace of irony. 'Right, I'm off to work; get some peace and quiet. I'll see you later, love.' Thankfully, he put his plate and cup on the draining board.

'Have a good day, Dad.'

'Aye . . .'

Fred worked in a hardware shop on the High Street, where he had a reputation for being extremely know-ledgeable about the correct ways to do small plumbing and joinery jobs and the right sizes of screws, nails, and tools to use. 'Ask Mr Quinn. He knows everything' – Sarah had heard that said. Once quite recently, she now remembered, she had overheard, 'Ask Mr Quinn at Scarstone Hardware. He's a miserable old sod, but he does know how to fix stuff.' Sarah was sorry her father was getting such a reputation, but a part of her acknow-ledged that, these days, he deserved it.

When Janette came down dressed for school, Sarah

realised that she'd forgotten all about the gravy and potato stains on her sister's blouse. Janette had her sleeves rolled up now to try to hide the gravy, but that only drew Sarah's attention to it.

'Oh, no, Janette . . .'

'Leave it. It doesn't matter,' Janette muttered. 'Lots of the others have their dinner down them.' She sat at the kitchen table and started eating her egg as fast as she could.

'But, love, I can't send you off like this. What would Mum have said?'

'Mum wouldn't have forgotten about the stain,' said Janette quietly, then immediately regretted it when she saw Sarah's face was shot through with anguish. 'Oh, Sarah, I didn't mean it was your fault. I forgot, too.'

'Yes, well, you're old enough to wash your own blouse.'

'I know, I know. I said it wasn't your fault,' Janette fretted, knowing there would be sarcasm, or worse, from the teachers. Worn clothes were perfectly acceptable, but slovenliness – the kind of carelessness that could be avoided – was called out, to shame the offender into doing better. 'Look, I'll just have to wear next week's.'

'I haven't ironed it yet. I'm sorry, I just ran out of time.'

'Doesn't matter. I'll wear it crumpled.'

She unbuttoned her blouse, threw it onto a chair and, pale and skinny in her liberty bodice, went to rummage through the ironing basket in the scullery, returning with a hideously creased and slightly damp replacement.

'That looks awful,' said Sarah, wishing she'd thought to iron it when she was doing Mrs Hutchinson's blouses the night before. It was too late now.

'Well, never mind. You won't be looking at it in a minute.' Janette swallowed her tea down in great gulps. 'Now, where's my satchel . . .?'

She left for school and Sarah followed her out soon after, Mrs Hutchinson's neatly pressed blouses all retrimmed and folded carefully into her bag.

The streets of Scarstone were at their busiest, with people going to work, to school or delivering goods to the shops. Sarah walked quickly, crossing the High Street at the end, dodging a handcart of vegetables and then a little brown van with the name of the hardware shop where her father worked painted on the side.

Beyond the High Street and back a couple of roads was where Mrs Hutchinson resided, in a terraced house with a tall front window and shrubs in the little front garden. This area was regarded as a bit smarter than the other end of town, where the Quinns and the Frasers, Rachel's family, lived.

Sarah went up the black-and-white-tiled front path and knocked on the door.

After a little wait, the door was opened by a skivvy. That was the only word Sarah could think of to describe the thin and shabby-looking girl, probably no older than Janette. She was wearing a cross-over pinny that was slack and too long on her, and her hair was covered with a grey scarf that was knotted at the back, a lank pigtail poking out from under it.

'Yes, miss?'

'I've brought Mrs Hutchinson's blouses. She's expecting them.'

'I'll go and tell her. Please wait,' said the girl, and indicated the doormat just inside with a shy smile.

Sarah stepped in, the girl closed the door and then went off along the hallway, knocked on the door of a room at the end and went in. Almost immediately she came out and back to Sarah.

'Mrs Hutchinson says thank you and if you leave them with me, she'll settle with Miss Rowley at the end of the week.'

'Miss Rowley expects me to bring her the money this morning,' Sarah said, but gently so the girl wouldn't think she was arguing with *her*. 'Her terms are cash on completion.' Oh dear, this wasn't looking very hopeful for the promised tip.

The skivvy looked uncertain. The situation was not of her making and she clearly wanted no part in it.

Seeing this, Sarah said, 'May I speak to Mrs Hutchinson, please? I'm sure she's just forgotten and it will be easier if I remind her.' Again, the girl looked anxious so Sarah added, 'I'll say I insisted. I don't want you to be in any trouble.'

'I ought to ask her if she'll see you first, miss.'

The girl went back to the room at the end, knocked again, and disappeared inside. Soon she was back out, looking unhappy, and beckoned to Sarah with a flap of her hand.

'Thank you,' Sarah said, and she went into the sitting

room, gathering her courage, hoping she was up to persuading the woman to pay. The room turned out to be light and very warm with the sun already slanting through the big window.

Mrs Hutchinson was a middle-aged lady whose abundant hair was dyed almost black. Even at half past eight in the morning, she was fully made up, her face pale with a thick layer of powder and her mouth bright red, although she had yet to dress and was wearing a dressing gown with a fashionable jazzy pattern to the silky fabric, and a pair of pink mules with little heels. She was sitting in an armchair with her broad feet up on a pouffe, a cup of tea on a little table beside her.

'Ah, Sarah, my blouses at last. Thank you. If you leave them there,' Mrs Hutchinson pointed to another armchair, 'I'll send Miss Rowley a postal order at the end of the week.'

'Miss Rowley's terms are the same as usual, Mrs Hutchinson,' said Sarah. 'Cash on completion. She's expecting me to bring the money this morning.'

'Is she? Is she really?' said Mrs Hutchinson, looking mystified; as if that hadn't always been the arrangement. 'Well, I don't suppose she'll mind if I pay later this time. Just this once.' She flashed a hard, lipsticky smile at Sarah.

If the intention was to win Sarah over, she failed, because Sarah now recognised the woman for what she was, and she didn't care for her one bit. Mrs Hutchinson had been all soft smiles, compliments and promises when she'd wanted her clothes repaired quickly. Now she didn't even want to pay promptly what she owed.

'I'm afraid she will mind, Mrs Hutchinson. Also, you . . . you mentioned paying me extra if I did the blouses by this morning and brought them round. Otherwise it would have been next week. I worked late, specially.'

'I don't remember that at all,' said the lady, standing up and looking astonished. 'When did I say that?'

'When you asked for the job to be done in a hurry, Mrs Hutchinson,' said Sarah, quietly, fixing her with narrowed eyes.

She could see the way this was going. It would be unfair not to receive the promised tip to put towards Janette's birthday present, but forgoing the bonus was the price of learning her lesson: Mrs Hutchinson was not to be trusted. She put herself before everyone else and rode roughshod over other folk because, in her eyes, they simply didn't matter. Her sole concern was to get her own way. Well, she would not be getting any preferential treatment in future.

'May I just wait here for the money, Mrs Hutchinson?' Sarah asked, and went to stand in front of the window, feeling the warmth of the sun on her back as she blocked some of its light from the room.

'Oh, if you must,' huffed the woman. 'I shall have to fetch my handbag and see if I've got any change. Have you any idea how much it is?'

Sarah produced a book of invoices from her own handbag, the kind with carbon paper to make a duplicate copy. Mrs Hutchinson's invoice was already written out. 'This is for you, Mrs Hutchinson,' Sarah said pointedly. 'When you've paid, I shall write "Paid with thanks" at the bottom, sign and date it. Miss Rowley is very organised, as I'm sure you know by now.'

'Is there any way you could leave my blouses and come back later . . . just this once?' the woman wheedled then.

No sign of the promised tip, and now asking for more favours! Sarah struggled to compose herself as her anger increased. She wanted to slap the spoilt, selfish woman's face. For one wild moment she imagined what would happen if she did: a great cloud of face powder would rise into the air like flour from an exploding bag, enveloping them both, snowing pale pink over Mrs Hutchinson's dark dyed hair.

'Well, if you need to go to the bank or the post office to get the money, I do understand,' said Sarah, managing to sound patient and reasonable, although she was seething and her heart was pounding with the upset of this confrontation. 'In the meantime, I shall take the blouses back to Miss Rowley to keep safely for you. Then you can collect them any time during business hours when you're ready to pay.' She put the invoice book carefully back in her handbag, bent to gather the bag of mending and made to go.

'Oh, all right. If Miss Rowley really can't manage until the end of the week . . .' Mrs Hutchinson said. She left to fetch her bag, taking tiny steps in her fancy mules, and Sarah heard her footsteps fading as she went upstairs.

While she waited, Sarah, breathing deeply to calm herself, looked around the room. It was comfortably furnished, with lots of squashy-looking cushions on the chairs, and pretty, slightly faded curtains. The furniture looked what Sarah's auntie Irene would call 'good', although old-fashioned, but there was a pile of dog-eared fashion magazines spilling out of a rack, and some books with cheap paper jackets on a side table. Sarah stepped over to look and saw a racy illustration on the front of the top one: a pretty young woman in an old-fashioned dress, which was dangerously slipping off one shoulder, and the shadow of a man in a tricorn hat behind her. *The Price of Her Honour* was the title, by someone with the unlikely name of Marie-Antoinette Armstrong.

Soon Mrs Hutchinson returned with her bag and rudely thrust some coins into Sarah's hand. 'I think you'll find that's correct,' she snapped. It was, of course, but the tip was a lost cause.

Sarah stowed the money in her bag, signed the invoice as paid, then gave the top copy to Mrs Hutchinson. She was anxious to get away now. She knew if she pursued the matter of the promised tip she would get upset and so have neither the tip nor her dignity. Then Mrs H would have the upper hand . . . even more than she did already.

'Well, goodbye, Mrs Hutchinson,' she said. 'I'll see myself out.'

But the skivvy was hovering by the front door to open it for Sarah. Sarah guessed she had been listening. She opened the door and wished Sarah, 'Good morning, miss.' Then, so quietly that Sarah almost thought she had imagined it she added, 'Faced her down, the old cow.' She smiled angelically and gently closed the door.

For a minute or two, Sarah was buoyed up by the thought of the mutinous young girl, who undoubtedly sought to get even with her unpleasant employer in some mini battle every day of the week, but then she reflected that she hadn't actually faced down the selfish and mean-minded woman. Otherwise she'd have come away with her tip. And it had been rather too confrontational a start to the day for it to be a good one.

As she did countless times every day, Sarah wished her mother was still alive. Nothing was right without Ava, and there were days when trying to fill her role was too much. Everyone she had to deal with was older, more experienced, better at . . . better at life, really. Mum would have got the promised tip out of Mrs Hutchinson. No, that wasn't right: Mum would have recognised the woman's wheedling for preferential treatment for what it was and would never have agreed to take on the extra work in the first place.

However hard she tried, Sarah thought, events – work, chores at home, life in general, it seemed – just slipped away from her control. She wasn't ready to run the house and do her job, and organise Joe and Janette, and Fred, too. Where would it all end?

CHAPTER TWO

JOE WAS LOOKING forward to another evening in the company of Dora Burgess. They had met up several times lately, to go dancing at the town hall, or to a social at the working men's club, and they had a laugh together, but today Joe was planning to take Dora out for supper.

Scarstone didn't have much of a choice of places to eat in the evening, at least that Joe could afford. There were two fish and chip shops, but you couldn't sit down to eat inside, and Dora wasn't the kind of girl who would happily stand around in the street, eating chips from a newspaper. That left the two nearby public houses, both of which were known to Joe.

The Lamb and Flag was popular, but not the kind of place to take a woman like Dora for a treat. It didn't serve hot food, for a start. It was primarily a place where men went to drink together, grumble over pub games, and to put the world to rights.

As if that wasn't bad enough, Joe knew his father was at the Lamb and Flag most evenings. Fred had become gloomy and moody since Ava had died, and the Lamb was where he went to mope and drown his sorrows. Joe always got the impression that the customers of the Lamb vied with each other to see who could be the most miserable. Certainly, Fred never came home any more cheerful for an evening spent there. Anyway, Joe wasn't ready to introduce Dora to any of his family; to give his burgeoning romance with her any status just yet. Sarah knew her a little, of course – they'd been at school at the same time – but Dora was older, Joe's age, and he was aware that Sarah and Janette were rather in awe of her glamour. As he was himself.

The other place, the George and Dragon, was the obvious choice. It was an old coaching inn, built centuries ago, where stage coaches would change horses before continuing on the main road through town and then out east beyond Great Edge and across the moors. It had a warren of cosy dining rooms, provided good food all day, and with its character and its bit of class, it was, Joe thought, the perfect place to take Dora. Or maybe just the only place. He'd set himself a budget and intended to be generous to Dora even if he had to be thrifty with himself.

Joe collected Dora from her parents' home, not far from Keele Street. She was an only child and her mother and father clearly doted on her, which might explain why she seemed to have more money to spend on herself than most young women did, even in these straitened times; possibly her parents didn't expect her to pay her way at home from her wages as an assistant at a dress shop.

The Burgesses had come north from somewhere on the south coast several years before, and the way Dora's parents spoke marked them out as incomers to Scarstone.

Dora stepped out of the little house looking . . . well, lovely, Joe thought. Her hair was always perfectly in place and in a grown-up style – short and 'done' – unlike that of his sisters, who both had plaits, although Sarah's was pinned up behind. And although Sarah and Janette had blonde hair, Dora's was somehow blonder and shinier. She was wearing a pale pink dress with a sailor collar trimmed in navy blue.

'Ahoy, there!' said Joe, thinking it a witty and cheery greeting.

'Funny,' smiled Dora, who liked to have her clothes noticed.

The George and Dragon, in the central square of Scarstone, was welcoming when they arrived, which took rather longer than Joe had anticipated because Dora was wearing high heels – smart navy-blue shoes that fastened with buttoned straps – which meant she couldn't stride out. Still, they did make her legs look very slim and her feet dainty, he thought. He felt proud to have Dora on his arm, a girl who was pretty and certainly better dressed than most around here.

He led her into one of the rooms at the back, where he found a table for them in a nook behind a wooden pillar, where they wouldn't have to raise their voices to hear each other and could spend their evening flirting in privacy. Then he went to the bar to order drinks while Dora read the menu chalked on a blackboard.

It was a very pleasant evening. The pies, for which the George and Dragon was renowned, were good, the conversation was easy, and really, Joe thought, Dora was so very pretty, with her big blue eyes and shiny hair. They swapped amusing stories about their families and people they both knew in Scarstone. Eventually Dora excused herself to go to powder her nose, while Joe went to get more drinks.

It was as he was returning from the bar that he saw his father sitting at a window table a little further along, on the other side of the room, his back to Joe. Joe had to look twice to see if he wasn't mistaken, but he'd recognise that bald patch, the greying hair and that sleeveless pullover, knitted by Ava, anywhere. This wasn't Fred's usual stamping ground – in fact he tended to disparage the George and Dragon as 'a bit too pricey' – so what was he doing here now?

Joe put the drinks down on the table and peered round the pillar to see who his father was with. The answer was astonishing. It was a woman: a middle-aged woman with abundant dark hair shot through with silver, a thick white stripe at the front. She had rather a hard-looking, jowly, pink face with very dark eyebrows. Joe had never seen her before.

Joe couldn't hear what his father and the woman were saying to each other, of course, but they were sitting at a table for two, so he thought they must have planned to dine together. The conversation between them went back and forth, the woman smiling or laughing loudly and leaning in, Fred replying eagerly; from what Joe could see, he was behaving quite unlike his now habitually grouchy and taciturn self. More like how he used to be in the old days. When Ava was still alive. What was going on?

Dora came teetering back, all dimples and smiles, but by now Joe was distracted.

'Thanks for the drink, Joe,' beamed Dora, lifting her glass to clink with his. 'Cheers.'

'What? Oh . . . yes,' Joe replied, barely looking at her, then gazing across at the pair to his left, by the window. If he sat back, he could get a good view of them. He racked his brains to think who the woman could possibly be. Not some relative, that was for certain. This woman was cut from quite a different cloth from Ava's sister, Auntie Irene, whom the Quinn siblings adored, and she was the only relative Joe knew of.

Dora was saying something, but he hadn't heard.

'Sorry, Dora . . . what?'

'I said, who've you seen? Someone you know?'

'Oh, no, no one,' he said, turning his attention back to her, but within moments resuming his surreptitious observation of his father and the mysterious woman with sidelong glances. By now he was wondering if he ought to go over and say hello, but then if his father had done that to him, he'd have been furious. No, he needed to be cleverer than that . . .

Dora continued to chat, but Joe was hardly listening.

'. . . going home now,' she finished.

Just at that moment, Fred sat back in his seat and laughed loudly at something the woman had said. Joe was amazed. He couldn't remember when he'd last seen his father laugh, and so . . . *carefree* a laugh, too. Even as he was wondering about this – thinking he must be mistaken and this man wasn't his father after all, just someone who resembled him from behind – Dora pushed her chair back and made much of gathering up her handbag.

'Oh, are we going?' Joe asked.

'*I* am. I don't know what you're doing,' she snapped. 'Perhaps you'd like to go and join them, whoever it is who's more interesting than I am?'

Joe coloured and jumped to his feet. 'Oh, sorry, Dora, I . . . I've just been a bit distracted this evening, that's all.'

'You have, that. Thanks for the drinks, and the pie, Joe,' she said, standing and sidling out past him. 'I can see myself home.'

'No! No, I'll walk you,' he said. He'd never let a girl walk home by herself.

'It's still light. There's no need.'

'There is.' But he couldn't help but glance in the direction of the middle-aged couple as he turned to follow her. Yes, it was definitely his father with the woman.

Dora, seeing the direction of his gaze, looked over, too.

'Know her, do you?' she asked with a raise of her eyebrows.

'Er, who?'

'That woman you've been staring at since I came back from the ladies. Who d'you think?'

'Never seen her before. Just noticed her 'cos she's a stranger, like.'

'Lives out by Great Edge,' said Dora. 'Her name's Mavis Swindel.'

'Oh, yes?' said Joe, trying to sound casual while desperate to find out more. 'How do you know her?'

'I don't,' said Dora, slamming the door on that conversation. 'Right, well, I'm off and you can come with me or not, as you like.'

'Oh, don't be like that, Dora.'

'Like what? Bored of sitting with someone who isn't even listening to me? I'd rather have spent the evening with Mum and Dad. At least they show an interest.'

She tip-tapped out in her dainty shoes, while Joe pushed his way to the bar to pay the bill, which took a couple of minutes. By the time he emerged into the High Street, Dora was a good distance along it and he had to run to catch her up.

'Dora . . . Dora,' he panted. 'Don't go off in a huff, please. I'm sorry I got distracted. I'll see you to your door.'

'You can do as you like, Joe,' she said, and continued on as fast as her shoes would allow, pointedly ignoring Joe all the way home.

At her parents' front door, she paused to find her key.

'I'll see you tomorrow evening, Dora? We can go dancing, if you like? I'll call for you at seven?'

'Don't waste your time, Joe. I'll be washing my hair,'

she said, put her key in the door and in two seconds was inside and the door closed firmly in his face.

Damn.

'Mavis Swindel . . . Mavis Swindel . . .' Joe muttered under his breath so he wouldn't forget the name as he mooched home, hands in pockets, slightly ashamed of himself. His thoughts were partly on Dora and her bad mood, which he knew he deserved, and partly on the bold-looking woman sitting in the George and Dragon with his father. He was consumed with curiosity and determined to find out more about her.

Back at home in Keele Street, he found Janette had gone to bed already, and Sarah was sitting listening to the low murmur of a discussion on the wireless and working on some complicated knitting.

Joe wanted to mention the name of Mavis Swindel to Sarah, to see what she knew, or maybe to relieve himself of the burden of the news that his father had dined alone with this woman, but Sarah had taken their mother's death harder than any of them, and he felt he couldn't cope if she got upset about their father seeing another woman. There might not be anything to be upset about either, but it was odd the way Dora had cut off his enquiries about the Swindel person. As if she didn't want to be associated with her in any way. As if the woman wasn't quite . . . nice.

But, then, if Mavis Swindel had a reputation for . . . something, it wouldn't be impossible to find out about her.

'You're back early, Joe,' said Sarah, putting down her knitting. 'Did you have a good time?'

'Not really,' he said. 'I think I've blown it with Dora.'

'I'm sorry to hear that. She's a good sort, what I know of her.'

'Well, she doesn't think I am.'

'Don't fret. She'll come round, I expect.' She looked up and read his hopeless expression. 'Were you a complete idiot?'

'Probably . . .' He bit his lip and hunched his shoulders. 'Shall I make us a hot drink?'

'Yes, please. Cocoa. That's kind of you. I'm trying to get this cardi finished for Jan for her birthday, working on it in secret. I wanted to buy her a new pair of shoes, but I don't think I can afford them, for all she does need some. I don't want to give her second-hand ones for her birthday. She'd love summat nice and new.'

'I could go in with you on the shoes, if it'd help. I'll pay half if you can see about getting them. Don't go for owt dear, though.'

He thought of Dora's pretty navy-blue shoes with the heels. Sarah never bothered with things like that, or fashionable dresses, or smart hairstyles. Their mother hadn't either, or at least not in those last years. There were some photographs of her and Auntie Irene, when they were little, with Grandma and Granddad Mayhew, and they all looked very smart in their best clothes, Grandma with a feathered hat and a long skirt, and Granddad with a shiny watch chain across his broad stomach. And Ava and Irene looking rather doll-like in dresses with sashes, and their hair in corkscrew curls . . .

Suddenly Joe felt his eyes stinging. Strange how his grief about losing his mother could just rise up from nowhere and assault him in a totally unprovoked attack. Mostly he thought he was all right and then suddenly he wasn't, even now, more than a year after her death. What had brought this on? Seeing his dad dining with that woman in the George and Dragon?

Soft bugger.

Sarah was speaking. 'That's good of you, Joe. Thank you. I've been trying to save up for brand new but it's hard work. We'll go window-shopping for fun on Saturday, Jan and me, and I'll see if I can find out which she likes best that we can afford.'

Joe was just going to boil the kettle when he heard his father come in. Astonishingly, he was whistling what might have been 'It's a Long Way to Tipperary'.

'Hello, Dad.'

'Joe.' Fred sounded very chipper.

'I'm making hot drinks – do you want owt?'

'No, thanks. I'll just go out back – ' he referred to the privy – 'and then I think I'll go up.'

'Where have you been?' The question was out before Joe could think it might sound suspicious. He never usually asked his father where he had spent the evening because, he had thought, there was only one answer. Now it seemed that was not so.

'To the Lamb and Flag, of course,' Fred replied straight off. There wasn't a trace of guile in his face.

'Oh, aye. Who did you see?'

Now Fred was looking at his son a little harder. 'Usual folk. Reg'lars, like, same as always. Why? What's it to you?'

'Nowt, Dad. Just wondered.'

'So where have you been, then?'

'Took Dora Burgess for fish and chips. We sat out and ate them in the churchyard.'

'Well, that would be quiet, anyway,' Fred said.

So they were both liars, thought Joe. This was an unexpected turn of events, especially when Sarah, having overheard, asked him, while they drank the cocoa, why he hadn't taken Dora somewhere where she could sit inside – the George and Dragon, maybe – instead of offering her a bench in the churchyard. Then Joe had to lie to her, as well, and he went to bed wondering whether the evening could possibly have been worse.

Over the next few days, Joe reminded himself frequently of the name Mavis Swindel, so that he wouldn't forget it. He asked a couple of his friends, Ed and Dave, at the working men's club, making light of his enquiry – 'just a name that came up, like' – but they hadn't heard of her. But then Dora had said she lived out near Great Edge, so perhaps she wasn't known around this side of Scarstone.

About a week after the disastrous evening with Dora, Joe and Mr Blake began work repainting the interior of the Scarstone Public Library. They started in the little reading room, with its big, bossy notice: 'Silence please!'

Joe was securing dust sheets around the bookshelves when he had an idea. This was a public building in which people told the staff their names. If Mavis Swindel used the library, someone might know something of her, or even where she lived. And, as luck would have it, one of those library staff was Rachel Fraser, who was Sarah's best friend. Rachel was a good sort, a kind friend to Sarah, who had needed Rachel's thoughtfulness and support this last year, although Rachel always gave the impression that she thought he was a bit of a joke, a lightweight. Not a man to be taken seriously.

Still, returning a tray of tea cups and saucers provided the perfect excuse for Joe to ask Rachel if she'd heard of the Swindel woman.

'Thanks for the tea, Rachel,' he began.

'Keep your voice down,' whispered Rachel. 'It's all right, Joe, I said to leave the tray. You'll want to get on with your work.' She looked at him in a way that suggested she had already realised he didn't want to get on with his work at all.

'Well, I, er, wanted to ask you summat, Rachel.'

'Oh, yes?' She raised one eyebrow. 'Usually when someone says that, they're hoping to be excused a fine. Which I'm not allowed to do.'

'Oh, no, borrowing books isn't my kind of thing at all. I've never read a book in my life,' he laughed. His remark came out quite loud and several people looked round to see which philistine was confessing to this, and in a public library, of all places.

'I guessed that,' murmured Rachel, deadpan, and,

leaving the tray behind her desk, she led Joe to the foyer where the silence wasn't quite so heavy. 'So what is it?' she asked.

'I . . . I . . . er, that is, I'm wondering if you've heard of someone I came across the other day. Her name is Mavis Swindel. She might come here to . . . well, to borrow books, like.'

'That's often why people come to a library, Joe,' smiled Rachel. 'No, I don't know her. But if you met her, why do you need to know if I have?'

'Oh, I haven't actually met her, only heard the name. Just wondered . . . about her.'

By now Rachel was looking at him quite hard and he felt a little foolish.

'No, Joe,' she said. 'I don't know the name. I don't remember hearing it.'

'Right . . . Well, sorry to bother you.'

'It's no bother,' said Rachel. 'Now, please excuse me, Joe, but I have to get back to work.'

She strode quickly back inside the main room of the library, leaving him alone in his paint-splattered overalls, just standing there, doing nothing, feeling silly. He often felt like that with Rachel Fraser, although she wasn't mean so he couldn't work out why, in her company, he should feel disappointed in himself. Women – so hard to fathom, he thought.

He was no further forward in learning about Mavis Swindel, and he wondered whether he should ask his father outright about her, never mind that he himself had lied about being at the George and Dragon; but something told him to wait, to tread carefully. He thought of her painted-on eyebrows and striking hair, her womanly figure in her too-close-fitting shiny blouse, her loud laugh . . . and how she had made Fred laugh, too. And he knew – just *knew* – that he would meet her in time. It wasn't a very comfortable thought.

CHAPTER THREE

SARAH WAS WORRIED about Joe. He was out of sorts, not his usual cheeky, exuberant self at all. Of course, he was still grieving over their mother's death – that was understandable – but time had taken the edge off his grief, and whatever else the matter was, it seemed to have arisen only the previous week. Surely he wasn't taking the break-up with Dora Burgess that hard? They had been seeing each other for only a short while, and Joe was frequently taking out one pretty girl or another so that it was hard to keep track sometimes. But he refused to be drawn, shrugging away all Sarah's attempts to get to the bottom of his troubles and to offer a listening ear.

'Joe, can I ask – you've not lost your job, have you?' Sarah questioned him one morning, after Fred had left for the hardware shop and Janette hadn't yet emerged for school. 'It's just that you've been a bit . . . odd recently and—'

'No, I'm still running myself ragged for Mr Blake,' said Joe. 'Now, it's time I went—'

''Cos I remember that time when you lost that

window-cleaning job and didn't let on, and pretended to go to work for days before you told us. Really, Joe, if you're out of work I need to know, so I can budget for it until you find summat else.'

'No, really, sis, it's not that.'

'So it is summat? What, then?'

'It's nowt. Now, I need to get off. We're back at Mrs Thomas's house today – the lady with the cat – so perhaps I'll be spending most of the day up a tree.' He laughed, took the sandwiches she'd made for him and left, whistling.

Sarah had the distinct feeling that this good humour was an act he was putting on. But what could she do? She'd tried.

Janette's birthday was a school day, and she got up a little earlier than usual, full of excitement to open her presents before she left, but not so early that Fred hadn't already gone to work.

Sarah needn't have bothered to wrap the new shoes up neatly in their box – Janette ripped off the paper before Sarah could save it to reuse, and was buckling on the shoes in seconds.

'Oh, thank you, thank you, Sarah and Joe.' She stood up again to kiss them each on the cheek. 'They're grand. They're just what I wanted!'

'If you think they'll be comfy all day you can wear them to school,' said Sarah.

'Yes, they're a perfect fit.' Janette held up one foot in front of her to admire the shiny shoe. 'Like Cinderella's glass slippers!'

They all laughed, as these smart but sensible school shoes were very far from any fairy-tale fantasy. Sarah thought it was sweet that her little sister was still young enough to be pleased with any shoes that were new, and didn't require fashion or glamour.

Then Janette was opening her other presents: a green leather purse from her aunt Irene, and an intriguing squashy parcel that turned out to be a cardigan Sarah had knitted.

'Two brilliant presents!' she exclaimed, putting on the cardigan to admire the perfect fit and Sarah's patient skills. 'Oh, Sarah, you're the best sister ever! Shame I can't wear my new cardi to school, too, but I reckon Miss Hurst would notice that it's lilac.'

There was a lot of hugging then. Janette put aside the cardigan, then gulped down her tea and toast while she opened her cards.

When she hurried through to the sitting room to set them up on the mantelpiece, Sarah took advantage of her absence to say quietly to Joe, 'What, no present or even a card from Dad? He can't have forgotten, surely? He went out before I noticed and could say owt.'

'Did you remind him before today?' Joe asked.

'Well, not as such. Did you? Neither of us should have to. But he saw the preparations I was doing after Jan had gone to bed last night. I've been knitting the cardi for weeks and I'd said it was for her birthday. He's never forgotten our birthdays before. He's just not interested in owt that's going on here, these days.'

'Mebbe he's got other things to think about,' said Joe, quietly.

'What do you mean?' Sarah looked sharply at him, wondering if she was about to learn what had been bothering Joe this last couple of weeks. Then: 'Shush, she's coming back. You can tell me later,' as Janette burst back in, bouncing and grinning in her new shoes.

'I expect Dad'll have summat for you this evening,' said Sarah, not wanting Janette to be disappointed. 'Now off you go. I've asked Miss Rowley if I can come home a bit early, so I'll be here when you bring Lorna back with you for your birthday tea.'

'Thank you, Sarah. Right, I'd better go.' Janette grabbed her satchel from the back of a chair and went off with a smile and a wave.

'Good work with the presents, Sarah,' said Joe, gathering what he needed to take to work. 'Damn,' he started searching his pockets, 'I left my cigarettes . . . left them somewhere.'

'I know when you're being sly, Joe. Where exactly did you leave them?'

'I, er . . . I think I might have put them in Jan's satchel.'

'What!'

'Well, it was just hanging there on the back of the chair and I was having a quiet smoke and . . . I knew you'd mind, so I just slipped them out of sight when I heard you moving about upstairs, in case you came down.'

'So you've sent a fourteen-year-old off to school with a packet of Capstan Full Strength in her satchel *on her birthday*?'

'Oh, Jan'll be all right. Last time she sold them to her classmates and came back with some extra pocket money. She didn't share the loot with me, either.'

'Last time? Well, Joe, please, please can there not be a *next time*? She wants to stay on at school and I don't want owt getting in the way of that. It'll be only a matter of time before she gets caught, if that's what she's up to.'

'I wouldn't bet on it, but, yes, I'll be more careful, sis. She'll be costing me a fortune in cigarettes at this rate.'

'That's not my concern. And don't smoke in the house again either. I've told you before, and you know Mum never allowed it.'

Mention of Ava was the trump card, and Joe looked contrite.

'Sorry. You're right, of course. Now, I really need to go.'

'You couldn't pop into Scarstone Hardware, as you'll be passing, and remind Dad to get summat for Jan, could you?'

'Hardly, sis. You're the one Dad thinks the sun shines out of. He takes no notice of owt I say. And Mr Blake is expecting me promptly. We've a big job on today: walls *and* ceiling to paper. I'll see you later.'

Joe strode out, leaving Sarah to tidy up, the joyful birthday atmosphere dissipating already and her worries crowding in. Really, was she the only one who could take any responsibility?

*

Sarah knew she wouldn't get to work on time if she went via the hardware shop, so she would have to go out at midday, when she took a break, to remind her father of his obligations then.

Miss Rowley had given over the front room of her house, not far from the centre of town, to her work as a seamstress and, although Sarah still had other ambitions, she had to admit that Evelyn Rowley was a kind and considerate employer, a pleasure to work for. The room was always light and airy, warm enough, or cooled with window blinds, if necessary, and sometimes Miss Rowley had the wireless on in the background as they worked.

That morning, Miss Rowley had news.

'I've got summat to tell you, Sarah. I hope you'll think it's good news, but it's certainly a big change, for both of us.'

'Yes, Miss Rowley?' 'Good news' was hopeful, but 'big change' implied disruption; something else to think about, when Sarah felt she already had so much on her plate.

'I had a letter from my sister about a month ago, asking me if I'd like to go to live with her, down south. She was widowed in the war and she's struggled on alone ever since. Actually, I reckon she's managed very well – she's a seamstress, too – but she's older than me and now neither of us is young, of course. She thinks we'd be wise to "struggle on together", as she puts it, and I can see her point. We've always got on, and it makes sense to prop each other up in our advancing years and not be by ourselves.'

'Yes, I can understand that,' said Sarah, her heart thudding as she guessed where this was heading. 'So you've decided to go and you're closing your business?' She felt almost ill just saying it aloud. This would be the end of her job.

'Yes and no,' smiled Miss Rowley. 'I am going, and I shall have to part with the business, but I was wondering if, mebbe, you would like to take over my customers. We've worked closely together – just as I did with your mother – and so they know already what a good job you do. I see no reason why any of them shouldn't be keen to employ you, with your talent. But the workroom will go when I sell the house, of course, so you will need to find new premises: either set up in your father's house, or mebbe rent somewhere else, although that will cost. You'll have to think very carefully about that. Also, Sarah, if you do decide to carry on, you will need to take over the books and keep records, but a sensible lass like you won't have any difficulty with that, I'm sure.'

Sarah felt her stomach churning with nervous anxiety, but also with excitement. Her own business! Such a big responsibility, yet Miss Rowley was pleased to bequeath it to her, and it wasn't like Miss Rowley not to think things through.

'Oh, Miss Rowley! I don't know what to say. I mean, thank you for your faith in me, for offering me this opportunity. But I'll need to talk to Dad about whether there's room at home and decide if I can manage the work by myself . . . if I want to.'

'Of course. I'm not going to my sister's just yet, and I'll have to sell this house, which might take a while, things being how they are these days.'

Sarah nodded. Everyone was feeling the pinch.

'Anyway, you've got plenty of time to think about what I've said. Now, we need to get on this morning, especially as you'll be off a bit early to do young Janette's birthday tea . . .'

It was like Miss Rowley to remember that it was Janette's birthday, but it made Sarah crosser than ever with her father for his apparent forgetfulness. At midday she hurried out, promising to be only a few minutes, and ran along to Scarstone Hardware to find Fred.

The large hardware shop, on the High Street, tended to be at its busiest on Saturday mornings. Today it was fairly quiet, with only one customer. The assistants, of which there were three, each in charge of a counter, wore brown cotton coats. Old Harold, who, it was rumoured, was aged about eighty, and Young Harold, his grandson, who was sixteen, and was often referred to as 'the lad', were talking together quietly. There was no longer a Harold in between these two. Like so many men, he had been killed in the war. Fred was in the corner, serving someone who looked from behind like a middle-aged woman, with a well-rounded figure. Sarah saw, to her surprise, that her usually taciturn father was chatting away with the woman in a very friendly fashion – as if he knew her; as if he liked her. He smiled and leaned in to her, and she laughed raucously at something he said, and then – good heavens! – lightly slapped his hand in a playfully arch way.

Sarah realised she was staring and, worse, her mouth was gaping in astonishment.

Old Harold, behind his own counter, cleared his

throat to catch her attention and then beckoned her over.

'Hello, Sarah. What can I do for you?'

'Hello, Mr Podger. I just came to remind Dad . . .' she looked over and he was still talking animatedly with the voluptuous, dark-haired woman, '. . . to remind Dad . . .' She lowered her voice. 'Mr Podger, who *is* that woman?'

Old Harold leaned forward and murmured, 'Goes by the name of Mrs Swindel. She lives out by Great Edge. Your dad took a delivery over to her a couple of weeks ago. That's how I know.'

'It sounds as though she's having a lot of maintenance done, what with a delivery, and now back here.' *And why shouldn't she be? And why do I feel so cross?*

'I expect so, love. Now, do you want to wait while your dad's free or shall I tell him what you came for?'

Fred must have noticed Sarah standing talking to Old Harold by then because he was looking her way, and Mrs Swindel turned round and looked, too.

'Thank you, Mr Podger, but I'll just say hello and tell him quickly myself,' said Sarah with a smile, and went over to Fred's counter.

Close up she could see that Mrs Swindel wore quite a lot of makeup of a shade that wasn't quite the right one – too dark, too pink against her neck – but that her luxuriant dark hair was threaded through with silver and had a lock of white at the front, which was dramatically attractive. She looked at Sarah in a way that was far from light or fleeting, but rather interested and assessing, as if forming an opinion. She smelled quite strongly of a very heady perfume, which Sarah thought was something containing lily of the valley.

'Hello, Sarah. Are you wanting to see me?' asked Fred.

'Hello, Dad. Sorry, I don't want to interrupt, but—'

'You're not interrupting, dearie,' said Mrs Swindel. 'I was just saying to Fred, I said, ask the girl to come over. Don't leave her wondering who I am.' She held out her hand, on which she wore several heavy gold rings with coloured stones set into them. 'Mavis Swindel, pleased to meet you.'

Sarah was shaking her hand out of good manners, but wondering what grounds this woman had for needing to introduce herself. And for referring to her father by his name as if they were close friends. She sounded a lot more familiar with Fred than one might expect from a delivery of hardware to her house. However, perhaps this was just her usual manner.

'Hello, Mrs Swindel,' said Sarah, smiling politely, then turned back to her father. 'Sorry to interrupt, Dad, but you haven't forgotten it's Janette's birthday, have you? Only I just wanted to be sure.'

'I have,' said Fred. 'Completely forgot. Damn it, I suppose I'll have to go out later and get her summat.' He made it sound like a terrible chore he'd rather avoid. 'What d'you reckon she'd like?'

'Dad!' Sarah couldn't find it in herself to hide her disappointment in him. 'You're supposed to have put some thought into it before now, asked her in a

51

roundabout way to find out what she wants, not just ask me when you've forgotten. I only came to remind you.'

'Perhaps I can help you both out,' volunteered Mavis. 'How old is Janette?'

'Fourteen today,' said Sarah, wondering what this had to do with her. 'Really, Mrs Swindel, it's not for you to go to any trouble.'

'No trouble to me, dearie. And does she like pretty things? I expect she does. Don't most young women like to be treated to pretty things?'

'Janette's not really a young woman, Mrs Swindel, more of a child still. But yes, she isn't much of a tomboy.'

'Well, then, don't you two worry,' said Mavis. 'I'll nip along the High Street and see if I can find the perfect present. I'll be back later. Put those screws and hinges to one side for me, Fred, would you, and I'll collect them then?'

Before Sarah knew what was happening, Mavis had linked her arm through Sarah's and walked her to the shop door.

Sarah extricated her arm as gently as she could. She didn't want to be rude, but, really, this woman – whoever she was, however she fitted in with Fred – was unusually familiar. Sarah felt crowded by her overfriendly attention and by her cloying perfume, too. She longed to get back to the fresh air and quiet industry of Miss Rowley's workroom.

Outside Scarstone Hardware, Mavis untied a quivering and pathetic little dog from a pole provided for customers to tether their dogs. The dog didn't look pleased to see her, Sarah thought. There was none of the delighted barks and fuss most dogs made when their owners were gone for even a few minutes.

'Come along, dearie,' Sarah heard the woman say to it.

Sarah waited only long enough to see which way Mavis was going, before she called 'Goodbye' cheerfully over her shoulder and turned in the opposite direction. It wasn't the way to Miss Rowley's, but she was desperate to put a distance between herself and this woman. She would have to double back and hurry down the parallel street. She had already been longer than she had intended, and her mind was now overwhelmed with Mavis Swindel: her voice, which sounded as if she might be from somewhere down south, her face, even her smell. For the few minutes in which Sarah rushed back to work, thoughts of the encounter in the hardware shop eclipsed even Miss Rowley's momentous news.

Janette was delighted with her modest birthday celebration after school: her friend Lorna invited round to tea, tinned salmon and cucumber sandwiches as a treat, and a sponge cake, which Sarah had made and iced, with fourteen candles.

Janette's eyes were shining when Sarah brought the cake to the table in the little-used dining room at the back of the house, the dim light of its north-facing aspect brightened by the candles.

'Quick, make a wish and blow them out before they set the house on fire,' she joked. 'I think next year you might have to have just one token candle.'

'Or a bigger cake,' said Lorna, giggling.

'The cake's already huge,' said Janette. 'It's lovely. My favourite. Thank you, Sarah.'

She made a wish, which Sarah could see by the briefly serious expression that passed over her face was a heartfelt one, and then instantly recovered her birthday joy and blew out all the candles.

'Imagine when you're forty – you'll need a cake this big, with all the candles,' said Lorna, stretching out her arms.

'And when I'm a hundred, I'll need one as big . . . as big as the *Titanic*,' laughed Janette. 'As big as the iceberg!'

She cut pieces of cake – 'You've got to have yours now, Sarah. Don't wait for Joe and Dad to get home' – and when they'd all eaten them there was a noisy game of Ludo, which went on until Lorna's father came by to collect her.

Joe and Fred appeared after Lorna had left, Joe with a box of Liquorice Allsorts for Janette, and Fred with a small, flat box wrapped in pink paper with a large pink bow tied around it, as big as the box itself.

Sarah, of course, knew that the source of this showy and overdressed parcel was Mavis Swindel, and she felt anxious just looking at it.

'Here you are, Janette,' said Fred, handing it to her, accompanied by an envelope. 'Happy birthday.'

Sarah thought he looked smug, as if he'd made a big effort and was sure his present would be a success, which was a bit rich after he'd completely forgotten. Still, gaudy though the present looked, at least Mavis had ensured there was something for Janette to unwrap.

Janette opened the card first, delaying the pleasure of unwrapping the parcel.

On the front was a collage: a sketch of a pretty young woman, her dress, made out of yellow satin, glued to the drawing, the skirt full and the waist impossibly small. 'Happy Birthday to a Darling Daughter!' gushed the curly lettering. 'All Grown Up Today!'

'Oh, how lovely,' said Janette, beaming. 'Thank you, Dad.'

Sarah saw the hand of Mavis Swindel in the choice of card, too: the brash colour, the inappropriate wording. She thought of the simple pleasure of Janette's choice of birthday tea to entertain her schoolfriend: tinned salmon sandwiches, sarsaparilla to drink, and then a sponge cake with butter-cream icing, raspberry jam and a candle for each year because, at fourteen, Janette was still young enough to be excited by this tradition. Not 'All Grown Up Today' at all.

Now Janette was untying the bow on the little parcel. She opened the paper to reveal a cardboard box with gold lettering on the front and removed the lid to find a powder compact. It was gold coloured, scalloped around the edges like a cockleshell, and the lid was decorated with a painted garland of red roses and blue ribbons.

'What's that you've got?' asked Joe. 'Looks like the kind of thing Dora kept in her handbag.'

'I'm not sure,' said Janette. She pressed the catch and opened it to reveal a tiny mirror on the inside of the lid and a little circle of stiff, thick cloth, then under an inner lid with a little hinged fastening, a layer of compressed face powder. 'Oh! Thank you, Dad. It's lovely. It's so pretty,' she said, clearly not overjoyed but still liking her present: its glamour, and perhaps the thought of one day being old enough to make up her face.

'I'm glad you like it,' said Fred.

Sarah was looking daggers at him but he seemed not to have noticed.

'P'raps put it away somewhere safe until you're a bit older,' she advised. The last thing she needed was Janette going to school with her face powdered. She'd never shown any interest in cosmetics, and this introduction today felt like an intrusion.

'Right, let's think about what there is for tea,' said Sarah to turn everyone's attention away from the wretched powder compact.

'Shall I go and get fish and chips?' asked Joe. 'It'll be a treat. And I'm looking forward to a piece of that cake.'

Sarah agreed, although Janette was too full of sandwiches and cake to want anything, and Sarah was pleased she herself had eaten a very small slice of the cake.

Janette grumblingly admitted to having homework to do and took herself back into the dining room, and Sarah went to make a pot of tea. While the kettle came to the boil, she decided she simply had to mention Mrs Swindel and the unsuitable birthday present to her father. It would be ludicrous to keep quiet, as if it was all right, and she was curious to learn more about Mrs Swindel, too.

'I take it that was Mrs Swindel's choice of present?' she said, following Fred into the front room, keeping her voice down but determined to find out what was going on.

'It was,' said Fred, disregarding her tone. 'She couldn't have been kinder, choosing summat so pretty, and having it wrapped up nicely, too.'

'But, Dad, Janette doesn't powder her face. She's only fourteen.'

'Well, she seemed pleased enough, and she'll grow into it.'

'That's not the point, Dad. Can't you see that it isn't really *suitable*? That your little girl has been given such a thing by someone she doesn't even know?'

'She was given it by me,' said Fred, with a hard edge to his voice. 'Mavis spent a good while choosing. Nowt was too much trouble.'

'But you're Janette's dad – you're the one who should be choosing her birthday present. Choosing summat for *Janette*. Mrs Swindel doesn't know her.'

'Aye, well, what do I know about what young women want? I haven't got your mother to help me and you're worse than useless.'

'Dad!' The accusation felt like a slap.

'I asked you what I should get and you said I should choose. What help was that to me, eh? Then Mavis offered to help, out of the goodness of her heart, and now you're grumbling. If you weren't prepared to help me out then, you can keep quiet now.'

'But, Dad, you know Jan's only fourteen. She isn't a "young woman" so much as a child, still. I told Mrs Swindel that.'

'And I'm telling you that I'm fed up with you and your carping at everything I try to do. Nowt I do is right in your book, and now you've got it in for Mavis, too.'

Tears sprang to Sarah's eyes at the injustice of that. 'Dad, I'm sorry if that's what you think, but it isn't so. I only met Mrs Swindel today. I'm really trying to keep everything going without . . . without Mum, and sometimes it's all too much for me . . . such a lot to do, to worry about . . . and I don't want Janette getting all dolled up and vain, and thinking about her face when she's so young.'

'Don't talk soft, Sarah. It's just a present. If she wants it, she'll use it; if she doesn't, she won't. Now, are you making that tea, 'cos Joe'll be back soon, and I only hope he's thought to bring us some mushy peas.'

Sarah understood her father was drawing a line under the argument and she nodded in agreement, dried her eyes and went to scald the teapot.

Had she overreacted? Maybe she had. Perhaps Mrs Swindel really was just a kind woman, a customer of Scarstone Hardware, a slightly blowsy and brash customer who had done her best and had just misjudged the choice of present for a girl she didn't know.

As Sarah hurriedly put the plates to warm and stirred the tea, she tried to think of Mrs Swindel in a favourable light. Probably she had regretted offering to find a present for Fred to give his daughter. Maybe she had even combed the High Street, getting anxious about the task and dithering as she walked that little dog between shops. She'd had the present wrapped and chosen a card, too, and then taken them back to the hardware shop where she'd handed over the shiny trinket and bought herself some hinges, and gone home alone to attend to her sagging doors.

Sarah was even beginning to feel sorry for Mrs Swindel when Joe arrived back with the fish and chips. Janette appeared immediately and said she'd help Sarah eat her chips as she was hungry again after all. Even Fred seemed satisfied as Joe had thought to bring some peas, and salt and vinegar were passed around, and tea poured.

It was only as she was washing up, and Joe, for once, was drying the dishes, that Sarah remembered the conversation she'd had with Miss Rowley that morning. Fred had already gone to the Lamb and Flag, so there was no telling him the news and asking his opinion. And, anyway, after their argument, Sarah didn't feel she could air the possibility just yet of taking over space in the house to set up a sewing business.

The subject she did broach, however, was Mrs Swindel. Janette was out of earshot, finishing her homework in the dining room, so Sarah felt it was safe to find out if Joe had heard of the woman.

'Joe, you know that powder compact Dad gave Jan?'

'What about it?'

'Well, it was chosen by a customer in the shop, a woman who seems to know Dad. I just wondered if you knew owt about her. Mavis Swindel, she's called.' She looked at Joe's face. 'You *do*, don't you?'

Joe looked even more uncomfortable. 'I wasn't trying to keep her a secret from you, Sarah. It was more that

I didn't want you to get upset; to think Dad is trying to replace Mum . . .'

'He can't replace Mum. Mum is irreplaceable.'

'That's exactly what I thought you'd say and the reason why I haven't said owt.'

'Well, it's too late now. The secret's out, if it was a secret. The woman herself wasn't at all secretive. I met her in the hardware shop this morning and she was a bit pushy. Very keen to jump in over Jan's birthday present. And then look what she came up with! Then I asked Dad while you were getting the fish, and he was cross, and I thought mebbe I was being unkind. And now I don't know what to think, but you obviously think she's upsetting.'

'I didn't say that, Sarah. I saw her with Dad at the George and Dragon one time, and she was making Dad laugh. It seemed to me that we never see Dad laughing these days.'

'And?'

'If this woman, whatever she's like, makes Dad laugh, then is that a bad thing? I know he can be hard work, not what you'd call the life and soul these days, but that's because he misses Mum. Some fellas can't cope without a woman to manage their life for them – I've seen that in one or two I've worked for – and . . . mebbe Dad sees summat in the woman.'

'For all she's pushy and brassy?'

'Well, I think so, too, but mebbe we're not seeing what Dad sees. P'raps she's all right when you get to know her.' Joe didn't sound very convinced.

'So you think Dad knows her?'

'Well, better than we do, obviously.'

'You don't think he's serious about her? Oh, Joe, Mum's been dead for only a year and a half, and he's surely not thinking of taking up with that woman?'

Joe flung the teacloth down on the kitchen table. 'I knew you'd start on like this. That's why I never said owt.'

'But, Joe,' Sarah started to wring her hands in the hot, soapy water, 'I couldn't bear it if he did. I can't take to the woman. Mebbe she has a heart of gold, but . . . it's her manner. Her way clearly isn't our way, and it wasn't Mum's way. And why would we want owt to be any other way than Mum's?'

Joe passed Sarah the hand towel and then gave her a brief hug.

'Don't take on, our Sarah. Mavis Swindel may just be a passing fancy. You're probably worrying about nowt. We may never see her again.'

Sarah nodded and dried her hands. 'I expect you're right,' she lied.

CHAPTER FOUR

FRED HAD HUGGED his daughters goodbye before he left for work. It was the school holidays, Sarah had arranged a week off, and she and Janette were going to stay with their aunt.

'Have a good time, lass,' Fred said to Sarah, as he let her go. 'Give my love to Irene.' This sounded a mite more dutiful than sincere, but never mind.

'You'll be all right on your own – well, you and Joe?' said Sarah, digging a little to see if Mrs Swindel would be mentioned, but not wanting to bring her directly into the conversation.

'Oh, aye, I expect I'll manage,' said Fred, with surprisingly cheerful confidence.

So if she is a passing fancy, she hasn't yet passed.

Fred left the house for work and now it was time for the girls to go for their bus to Blackburn, from where they would take the first of five trains to the little East Anglian town where their auntie Irene lived.

'Now, Jan, are you sure you've got everything you

should have . . . and nowt you shouldn't?' Sarah asked as Janette lugged her suitcase down the stairs.

'I think so, Sarah.'

'I hope you know so,' Sarah said. 'I still haven't got over you selling those cigs around your class.'

'Well, I don't know anyone to sell owt to at Auntie Irene's, do I?' said Janette, setting her case down heavily in the way and exhaling loudly with the effort.

'That isn't entirely true, and you'd better not be trying it. Auntie Irene has invited us to stay with her for this little holiday and I, for one, could do with the peace and quiet to have a think about Miss Rowley's business, and not take any other worries with me. And you know Auntie Irene trusts us to behave responsibly. I don't want her to wish she hadn't invited us.'

'That's not fair, Sarah. It was only that one time – well, and the other – and I got clean away with it,' Janette said, flexing her hand, cramped just from bringing her case downstairs. 'Plus, I made a bit of pocket money for the holiday. But then you got cross, and Joe said—'

'Enough! We're going on holiday, it's just a week, and I want it to be all lovely – for us *and* for Auntie Irene: no worries and no arguments.' Sarah handed Janette her coat and started to put on her shoes.

'So do I. Oh, Sarah, I was counting the days from my birthday till now, but I wish Joe was coming with us.'

'Me, too, but Mr Blake won't pay him if he's not working, and Joe says he can't afford to go on holiday and forgo a week's wages.'

'He'd be able to afford it if he wasn't taking Heather Latimer out every evening.'

'If that's how Joe wants to spend his money then that's his choice, Jan. Right, I've got the bus fares, and then the money for the train fares from Blackburn in my purse.' Sarah hefted Janette's case to the front door. 'Crikey, what have you got in here?'

'Well, there are a couple of books I want to read . . .'

'Take them out now and be quick about it. That case is going to feel heavier by the time we get there, and I can't carry yours as well as my own.'

'All right, Sarah. Just keep calm. It's the holidays, remember? "No worries and no arguments."'

Sarah couldn't help but grin. Oh, it was going to be perfect!

As the girls sat on the train, heading south and east, Janette read her *Schoolgirls' Own*, while Sarah looked out of the window and daydreamed, and thought about how she'd manage if Miss Rowley's business became entirely her responsibility.

It was ten days since Janette's birthday, and Sarah had left it three days for the argument with her father to be put behind them before telling him about Miss Rowley's retirement and the opportunity it presented to her. Fred didn't want Sarah to lose her job – that is, lose her pay – and, something of a pessimist, he showed little excitement at this chance or pride in Sarah for the trust Miss Rowley had, both in Sarah's ability as a seamstress, and as a person worthy to take over her business.

'You'll need to be careful. It could end badly,' was all the advice he could offer.

In the end, and after much begging and wheedling from Sarah, he had offered her the use of the gloomy little dining room at the back of the house, next to the kitchen. It wasn't ideal, but Sarah was grateful. She knew it was both generous and the best she could possibly hope for. It was out of the question for her to try to commandeer her preferred space: the family sitting room, with its sunny aspect. Equally out of the question was to rent separate premises until she had settled into self-employment and knew whether she would be able to afford it. Still, she had almost decided that, on her return, she would be telling Miss Rowley that she would be pleased to take over the business. She was looking forward to discussing it with Auntie Irene, who would undoubtedly have advice that was useful and who was certain to be kind and supportive.

Irene Mayhew was Ava's older sister. She had never married, although she had been engaged to be married twice. Both engagements had ended in tragedy. Her first fiancé, James Fellowes, had been killed in a horse-drawn carriage accident, and her second, Gilbert Wagstaffe, had been one of the hundreds of thousands of men killed in the Great War. Now in her early forties, Irene was one of that generation of women described as 'spare': they far outnumbered the men available to marry them, and their chances of having husbands and children, which might once have been a reasonable expectation, appeared to have vanished. There was nothing pathetic or pitiful about Irene, however.

Irene was waiting on the platform as Sarah and Janette's train pulled in. When the clouds of smoke and steam from the engine cleared, there was their aunt, looking so very like their mother that Janette, leaning through the carriage window to catch first sight of her, turned a momentarily grief-stricken face to Sarah and squeezed her hand.

'C'mon, sis, let's get these cases down,' said Sarah bracingly, instinctively understanding. For Sarah, even the proximity of Irene instilled a bracing effect.

And there Irene was, smiling, reaching to take the cases down onto the platform with ease. Then she embraced both her nieces together, each with a generous one-armed hug.

'Lovely lasses, thank you so much for coming to see me.'

Close up, she didn't look quite so much like Ava. She earned her living as a gardener, and her face had the healthy tan of someone who spent a lot of time outdoors, fine lines now visible around her blue eyes, and she was taller than Ava, with strength and real substance. But her hair was still as fair beneath her straw hat.

She picked up the larger of the girls' cases as if it was merely some light shopping, while Sarah took the other and they all went towards the station exit. The station-master, Mr Ellis, touched his cap to Irene in a most respectful way and smiled at Sarah and Janette.

'Glad to see you again, ladies,' he said, which made Janette giggle. 'I hope you have a good holiday.'

Sarah thanked him and said she was sure they would. Did everyone in the little town of Fettling know everything about everyone else?

But then, having inspected their tickets, he took the cases, quickly strapped them on a trolley and insisted on wheeling it out to the station side, where Irene's vehicle was parked. Sarah saw that that was now a van that said 'Mallinson's Market Garden' on the side, and not the Austin 7 that Irene had been driving in previous years.

'Let me stow these for you, Miss Mayhew,' Mr Ellis insisted, while Irene let him get on with it and the girls enjoyed the fuss.

When they were on their way, all sitting tightly together on the front seat, Janette said, 'I think Mr Ellis has a soft spot for you, Auntie. Do you think he wants to marry you?'

'I hope not,' said Irene, her eyes on the road. 'I reckon his wife would have summat to say about that . . . and his nine children.'

'Nine?' gasped Janette. 'That's . . . quite a lot.'

'At least eight too many, in my opinion,' said Irene, deadpan. 'Still, his choice.'

'I like the van,' said Sarah, wriggling on the hard seat. 'What is Mallinson's Market Garden?'

'It's what Mrs Mallinson is making of her garden now,' Irene said. 'She wants it to be useful, for her to earn some money from it, instead of it just being ornamental. I'll show you later. We've only been going since the spring, but we're making progress.'

'So where does the van come in?' asked Janette.

'I deliver the produce around town and to places nearby, while Mrs M keeps the accounts and generally manages the little business. We decide between us what we grow, but I do the planting, of course.'

'That's interesting,' said Sarah, thinking of the prospect of her own little sewing business. It sounded as if both Irene and Mrs Mallinson might well have some useful advice to give.

Sarah sat back, viewing with a thrill of excitement the long straight road before them, which was characteristic of this eastern part of England and so much a part of the holiday scene. Then there was the windmill on the left, which she and Janette always looked out for, and the prospect of a whole week to rest her tired eyes from the sewing and to enjoy fresh air and, above all, the company of her wonderful aunt, and she felt her worries, big and small, start to ease.

'How's your dad?' asked Irene, as she put delicious-looking plates of hot food in front of the girls that evening.

Fred was not invited on holiday here and never had been. He wouldn't have come anyway. Long walks and country air were not for him.

'He sends his love,' said Sarah.

'Please say I send mine to him.' Irene beamed a twinkly smile at Sarah, who understood the subtext. Both her father and her aunt acknowledged they hadn't a lot in common.

'He's been a bit less grumpy than usual lately,' said Janette.

'Well, that's good,' said Irene. 'Mebbe he's feeling a bit more settled. Everyone comes to terms with their loss in their own time. I know having you girls and Joe is a comfort to him.'

Sarah said nothing. The image of Mavis Swindel crashed into her mind: her voice, her brash laugh; the hard look in her eyes, as if she'd seen a lot of things in her life, many of them nasty; the painted-on eyebrows and her overly pink face . . .

'You all right, Sarah?' asked Irene. 'Aren't you hungry, love?'

'Starving, Auntie,' said Sarah, firmly putting the Swindel woman out of her mind and tucking in to the chops and tender little vegetables. Really, she must stop being so mean about Mavis.

'We'll go over to the House after dinner, if you like?' offered Irene. Fettling House, Mrs Mallinson's home, was just the length of the front drive away from where Irene lived in the Lodge by the main gates. 'Mrs Ramsden would love to see you. She's been talking of extra baking in your honour.'

'Oh, I wish Mrs Ramsden was my cook-housekeeper,' laughed Janette.

'So do I!' said Sarah and Irene in unison.

'Her son, George, is staying with her for a few days,' Irene went on, 'although he doesn't live all that far away. He works as a blacksmith – started out as an apprentice to his uncle, but now he's set up on his own and has taken over the forge in Saxham Ash to be nearer here. He's building up a nice business for himself, I gather.'

'I didn't know Mrs Ramsden had got children,' said Janette. 'I suppose her husband was killed in the war, same as everyone else.'

Sarah kicked Janette under the table and tried to give her a 'Shut up!' look but she wasn't taking any notice.

'You're right, Jan,' said Irene, no change in her expression. 'And she's only got the one child.'

'Unlike Mr and Mrs Ellis,' said Janette, grinning.

Irene knocked on the kitchen door of Fettling House, then opened it and called, 'Betsy? Are you there, love?'

'She's with Mrs M at the minute, but she'll be back shortly,' said a voice, and the door was opened wide by a young man of about twenty-five. 'Hello, Miss Mayhew. I'll put the kettle on. She never lets me do anything, but I don't suppose she'll mind if I make a pot of tea.'

'Hello, George,' said Irene. 'I've brought the girls over.'

'Come in, come in,' said George. 'Sarah? I thought so; your aunt has mentioned you. So you must be Janette. George Ramsden.'

He extended his hand to each in turn in a charmingly formal way – as if we're people worth meeting and not just girls on holiday, thought Sarah. His hands were large and strong-looking, but the backs of them were a little scarred with what looked like burns, and there was black ingrained around his nails.

As they chatted about the weather, the garden, their plans for their holidays, Sarah's eyes were drawn to George's open smile. She watched as he pushed his thick dark hair out of his eyes, but unconsciously, not in an affected gesture. He looked strong, genuine . . . kind.

'Auntie Irene said you're not staying long; that you live close by,' ventured Sarah.

'That's right,' George replied. 'Moved back to these parts last autumn, to set up my own place. I've been busy and I've neglected my mum, so I thought I'd take a few days away now and enjoy her company, while there's a lull in my work. There's plenty of room here for me, that's for sure.'

'Mrs Mallinson's house is enormous,' said Janette, nodding.

'It is, that. I don't know how Mum copes with it, all by herself.'

'Well, I do have Daisy Ellis from the village to help three days a week,' said Mrs Ramsden, coming in to hear the end of this exchange.

'Ellis?' asked Janette. 'One of the nine?'

'Janette, shush,' murmured Sarah.

Mrs Ramsden produced a tin of homemade biscuits to go with the tea, and everyone sat round the table and chatted about the big plans underway for the garden.

'It's a bit late to show you round the changes we've been making this evening, girls,' said Irene.

'But why don't we just go for a quick walk round the

71

old part?' suggested George. 'It's not too late to admire Mrs Mallinson's roses.' He was looking at Sarah when he said this.

'Lovely,' she replied. 'If that's all right, Auntie?'

'Go where you like, but not too near the house. It's Mrs Mallinson's garden, don't forget, not a public park, and you have to respect her privacy.'

''Course.'

George, Sarah and Janette got up to go out, but Mrs Ramsden said, 'Janette, you haven't drunk all your tea – would you like another of these biscuits to help it down?' and offered the tin. 'I was a bit heavy-handed with the chocolate on that one so you'd better eat it to cover up my mistake,' she added with a twinkling smile.

'Betsy, you're incorrigible,' said Irene, laughing, which Janette didn't think was quite the right word for an unintentionally chocolaty biscuit.

Sarah knew the way to the rose garden as well as George. High hedges divided Mrs Mallinson's vast garden up into manageable areas. The sun was now low and cast long shadows, but where the light was allowed to fall, it was golden and beautiful.

'I'm so glad Mrs Mallinson hasn't got rid of the roses,' said Sarah, as they entered the rose garden, which comprised formal square flowerbeds with paths crossing in between. 'Oh, I can smell them already. So beautiful! I think they would have been even better last month, but even so . . .'

'Yes, you're right,' said George. 'I hope she won't

have to have your aunt growing cabbages here instead.'
There was an edge to his voice: sadness, or maybe fear.

'Oh, I think the decision was entirely Mrs Mallinson's
about giving over some of the flowerbeds elsewhere to
vegetables,' said Sarah. 'I reckon it's good that she's
taking on summat new to do, and getting to earn some
money from it, what with her being . . . not young any
longer.'

'Oh, so she's old and poor, is she?' asked George,
with a raised eyebrow.

Sarah's hand flew to her face. 'No, I didn't mean
that. Oh dear, I hope I wasn't being rude.'

George smiled. 'Not at all. I'd say you're tying yourself in knots to be polite. But sometimes you just have
to come out with what you want to say.'

'I just meant that she has courage and energy, and
she's doing summat to help herself. She's a widow but
she's not moping about.'

'Mrs Mallinson must be over sixty and, like a lot of
people, I suspect she's finding her money doesn't go as
far as it used to. She's got this house to keep up. When
Mr Mallinson was alive, apparently they had all manner
of servants, but she's gradually lost them: at first to the
war, and then because they left for better-paid jobs with
better prospects, or because she can't afford them or
doesn't need them with just herself here. Now she's down
to a cook-housekeeper, a gardener and a char. I just
worry that she'll decide to sell up and buy somewhere
much smaller, where she can manage everything for
herself – but where will Mum and Miss Mayhew work

then? Their homes are tied up with this place. In fact, Daisy Ellis, the lowliest of the workers, is in the best position, because if she has to leave she'll still have her home and it won't be difficult for her to find another such job. Not everyone wants a cook-housekeeper or a gardener these days, or can afford them if they do want them.'

Sarah was horrified. She had been visiting Irene here for many years, since before Mrs Ramsden arrived – Ava used to bring all her children to visit her sister for a little summer holiday – and somehow Sarah had never thought that, in this heavenly place, there could be the worries or the kinds of difficulties ordinary people in Scarstone endured. It sounded as if there was a very real danger it might all just disappear.

'I couldn't bear it if Fettling House was sold,' she said. 'Summat else gone wrong and changing for the worst.'

'Well, you might have to, if it is,' said George. 'I'm sorry, it's mean of me to load my worries onto you like that so soon after you've arrived, and so soon after we've met. It's just that this place means the world to my mum, and so does Mrs Mallinson. And it is bliss here, isn't it?'

He bent to inhale the scent of the rose beside where they were standing. Sarah thought he was merely trying to change the subject.

'Well,' she said, channelling Irene's bracing attitude, 'if the House is sold, I can't imagine Mrs Mallinson, Auntie Irene or your mother making a to-do about it. They'll always look to make the best of everything.'

'Quite right,' said George. 'I'd say they're quite a

courageous trio. And I should have more backbone and not worry about what may never happen.'

'You don't look like a man with no backbone,' said Sarah. 'You look like a tower of strength.' She smiled shyly. She'd meant it as a friendly compliment but somehow it sounded a little too forward.

'Only in some ways,' said George. 'It's my work that's made me physically strong.'

'Auntie Irene said you are a blacksmith. That sounds dangerous, what with the horses mebbe being nervous. Don't they kick if they get upset?'

George laughed loudly. 'Yes, dealing with horses takes a special skill, but fortunately I don't have to do that. I'm not a farrier. A blacksmith's different. I do metal-work. Sometimes it's just small stuff – door knockers, coat hooks, weather vanes – but sometimes I make gates.'

'Gates?'

'Ornamental ones, like that big pair at the drive end, right by the Lodge where your aunt lives.'

'Let's walk over here where we'll be in the sun and you can tell me all about it,' said Sarah.

'There, Mavis, strong new catches firmly fixed. You can't be too careful these days,' said Fred, collecting up his tools.

'Quite right, Fred,' said Mavis. 'A woman like me, alone, needs to be extra cautious. I don't want strange men breaking in during the night.'

'I reckon that's unlikely now. I'm hoping you'll be quite safe.'

'*Are* you, Fred? I'd like to think you'd care if I was ravished, then robbed by a stranger, and in my own home.' She clutched a hand to her breast, as if this had been a distinct possibility, from which only the new window catches had saved her. 'Living at the last house along Great Edge – well, a woman needs all the help she can get to keep herself safe. It can feel a little isolated out here, you know. Big house, set back from the road, just me on my own.'

'Really?' said Fred, baffled. The neighbouring house was only the other side of the garden wall, albeit a high wall, on one side, and a bus ran the five-minute journey to the centre of Scarstone from the end of the road. 'But you keep a boarding house, Mavis. Of course you want your property secure, but if an intruder did get in, all you'd have to do is yell out and at least four men living here would surely come to your aid. Plus you've got Basil.' Fred bent to look at the skinny little mongrel, hiding under Mavis's dining-room table. 'Although I'm not sure he would be much use.'

'Nor the men.' Mavis laughed, giving the dog a gentle prod with her foot. 'Silly animal,' she murmured. 'Mr McCain is getting on for seventy-five, I'm sure, and is deaf, or pretends to be. Mr Armstrong wouldn't care if I ran through the house naked with my hair on fire, provided I let him use my telephone and the meals were served on time. Mr Cornwell is away a lot, selling . . . whatever it is he sells. He's prone to nightmares and the shakes, and I can't see his nerves standing up to taking on a burglar. And Mr Lavelle . . . well, there's no knowing with theatrical types.'

'I thought he was a pianist. Didn't you say it was him playing your piano when I was here putting up that shelf in the larder?'

'I did and he is, but he has a theatrical way with him, if you know what I mean. I always thought that with just male residents I'd be saved from having to impose the old "No gentleman callers" rule, but with Mr Lavelle I might have to introduce it.'

Fred looked taken aback and cleared his throat noisily. 'Anyway, you'll be all right now.' He picked up his tool bag to go.

'What this establishment lacks is a real man about the place,' said Mavis, sighing. 'I can't think how I've ended up with a houseful of no-hopers. Someone good-looking would be nice, to brighten the place up.' She looked Fred up and down appreciatively. 'Perhaps a widower, looking for the next chapter in his life to unfold?'

'Ah, go on with you, Mavis. I'm too old to be flattered.'

'No flattery intended,' said Mavis, brightly. 'No offence either. Just speaking as I find. The food's good – I can say that in all modesty as I don't cook it myself – and there's plenty of hot water, most days.'

'Sounds very comfortable.'

'Could be to the advantage of both of us if you were to set up home here,' said Mavis, smoothing her dress down over her curvy hips. 'I mean it, Fred.'

'I'll think about it.'

'You do that. In a way, this place is wasted on me, running it all alone. A big house like this really needs a family in it. I could do with some friendly youthful faces; bring a bit of life to the place, which would make it more homely for the lodgers; less rattling around, more lively conversation.' She paused for a moment, thinking. 'Of course, Fred, it must be so hard for you, bringing up the two girls by yourself. While I would never presume to take the place of their mother, I could perhaps, if you'd like, offer a mature woman's guidance when they're both so young. A kind of friend who's seen a bit of life and can just show them the way forward.'

'Yes, I reckon I'm a bit out of my depth about female advice,' said Fred.

'I liked the look of young Sarah when I met her in the shop. Pretty girl. Nice manners, too. What's the other one called – Janet?'

'Janette.'

'Of course. Oh, I'd love to meet her. Remind me how old.'

'Fourteen. She wants to go back to school after the holidays, but I don't know . . . What's the use of all that learning? It's who you know that gets you where you want to be these days, not what you know, and we don't know anyone.'

'Well, you know me, Fred. And *you* know all sorts. Look at those catches. Safe as houses.' Mavis laughed. 'Do you know, I think we'd do well together. Oh, what am I saying? But, you know, a woman can dream her dreams. You see, Fred, there's so much potential in a house like this, so much *scope* for someone like you, who knows how to bring that potential out. It could be a goldmine if I had a little help to make it so. It will be a struggle for me to realise its potential on my own, but it's my ambition to make Over the Edge the most comfortable boarding house in the whole of Lancashire. I'd be able to charge plenty then . . . Still, we all have our dreams, and mine are a way off while I'm still finding my feet.'

'Over the Edge – is that what you call it? I didn't know. I thought it was just number thirteen.'

'It's what it was called when I bought it, for the view from the back, over Great Edge, I expect. The name's on the gatepost. Got it for a song because the previous owners were bankrupts, which sort of explains a few things. It needs work, as you know all too well, but, as I say, there's so much potential . . .'

'Yes . . . yes, I can see that,' said Fred, thoughtfully.

'Now, I've got my accountant coming shortly,' said Mavis, suddenly shrugging off her dreams and becoming businesslike and efficient. 'Nice man, good eye for business and so helpful; coincidentally, he's a widower, too – so I'll say bye-bye for now.'

Mavis showed Fred to the door, enveloping him in a cloud of lily-of-the-valley scent in the vast hallway.

'Thanks so much for fitting those catches, Fred. You really are a man in a million. I'll pop into the shop on Friday and settle the bill.'

'You've already bought the catches, Mavis. I'll give you the fitting for free.'

'Oh! Oh, thank you, Fred. As I say, a man in a million. I'll see if I can think of a way of showing my appreciation . . .' She gave him a very direct smile, then gently closed the door.

Passing the mirror in the hall, she stopped to make sure her hair was looking as striking as she hoped it was, and grinned at her reflection. And, damn, there was lipstick on her teeth. She hoped Fred Quinn hadn't noticed.

Sucking her teeth, Mavis went back to her dining room and opened one of the windows with its shiny new catch. It was stuffy inside today, but the perpetual breeze blowing from the Edge brought an instant breath of fresh air to the room. She went to the vast oak sideboard and took out a tablecloth and some placemats, which she set out on the table. The smell of a cheese and onion pie cooking was already wafting through from the kitchen.

'Come along, Basil,' she said, and the dog emerged from his hiding place and slunk reluctantly after her as she went back into the hall, and then through a door at the end into the kitchen.

A very thin young woman, her hair tied up in a scarf knotted at the front like a turban, was peeling potatoes.

'Nancy, those are not for lunchtime along with the pie, are they?'

'Yes, Mrs Swindel. And cabbage.'

'Best make it just the cabbage, dearie. Roll the pastry thick enough and there'll be no need for potatoes as well.'

Nancy, who prided herself on making light, crisp, flaky pastry, looked mutinous. 'I've made a right good pie, missis, and I don't want to spoil it with lumpen pastry when I can do better. I thought you employed me because I can cook well.'

'And I do, Nancy, I do. No one said anything about lumpen pastry. But I've got to turn a profit and this is a boarding house, not the Savoy.'

'Do they serve cheese and onion pie at the Savoy?' asked Nancy.

Mavis looked taken aback. 'Don't be insolent. You do as I say in future. Cheese and onion pie is an onion pie with a bit of cheese in it and a good thick crust. All right? No potatoes necessary. Do extra cabbage for if the gentlemen want it, but don't be lavish with the butter. You'll have me bankrupted with your extravagance.'

'Yes, Mrs Swindel,' said Nancy, knowing when to back down.

Mavis had thought when she first employed her that Nancy – unworldly, enthusiastic and in desperate need of a job – would be exactly the right cook for her lodgers. Nancy had turned out to be brilliant – far too good for the position – but it hadn't been long before her willingness had turned to sullenness in the face of Mavis's economies and the limited range of dishes Nancy was expected to cook. She was starting to become sarcastic and even to answer back.

It was beginning to cross Mavis's mind that she ought to get rid of Nancy and bring in someone more suitable, more inclined to fit in. Someone who would do as she was told and not answer back. Sarah Quinn – she might well be the right person to take over the job, even if she could only cook basics. How good it would be to be able to offer a role to Fred's daughter.

Mavis had already formed a view of the kind of person Sarah was, gleaned from Fred's occasional mention of his older daughter, and also from her briefly meeting Sarah at the hardware shop. Mavis had seen a very young woman struggling to do the right thing for everyone and to keep Fred in line, and trying hard to fill the shoes of her mother. Perhaps what Sarah and Janette really needed, the poor motherless girls, was a step-mother.

That afternoon, as Nancy – having cooked and served the lunch to Mr McCain and Percy Lavelle – washed and dried the dishes, Mavis put her feet up on the chaise longue in the room she called her 'office' and lay back for a little snooze. There was and never had been a meeting with an accountant. That had been a story to focus Fred Quinn's attention. It would do him no harm to think there might be rival interest in both Mavis and her boarding house business.

As she settled into her nap, Mavis reflected that although she was not at all the naturally motherly kind, she was very much a woman made for the guiding role of stepmother.

CHAPTER FIVE

SARAH AND JANETTE were enjoying every moment of their holiday. The weather was perpetually sunny, which made the days seem to merge together into one glorious stretch of just messing about outside, doing very little. They spent a little time at the windmill, which was owned by an old couple known as Old Tom and Mrs Tom, who never tired of showing visitors the huge cogs and wheels, the chutes and hoists. Then the girls explored the lanes on Irene's bicycle – Janette sitting on the saddle, Sarah standing on the pedals in front – or wandered aimlessly around Fettling on foot, sucking gobstoppers bought at the little sweetshop there, while enjoying the clean air, the quiet roads, the birdsong, and admiring the pretty gardens and the topiary hedges, shaped into birds and animals, for which Fettling was renowned. On the first afternoon, Janette borrowed a book from Irene, which she took to Mrs Mallinson's garden, to sit among the flowers and read in the sun, while Sarah sat out with her and darned the elbows of Irene's jumpers, as a thank-you to her for the holiday.

Soon after their arrival, George Ramsden took to wandering about with the girls, showing them new walks, spotting a woodpecker, finding an old blackbird's nest, pointing out quietly grazing rabbits on the edge of a field, and a pair of fallow deer hiding in the dappled light of a spinney.

'I wish we could stay here and never go back to Scarstone,' said Janette, after the deer had moved away. 'I want this holiday to go on for ever.'

Sarah smiled and reminded her they only had the week, but she secretly agreed.

That following afternoon, George found some tennis rackets in Mrs Mallinson's attic, having asked permission to use her tennis court. It was weedy around the edges, in need of sweeping and tidying, and the net-winding mechanism was stiff from disuse, but he, Sarah and Janette managed to put the net up in the end and have a game of sorts, even if the balls were a bit old and squashy. Sarah and Janette were hopelessly outplayed, although they had joined forces to try to defeat George, either both of them leaving the ball so that it dropped between them, or both going for it and colliding and then missing it anyway. The hilarity got quite out of control, and Sarah had to sit down and hold her aching side, she was laughing so much.

Then, to everyone's delight, Mrs Mallinson herself came out, dressed in a white knee-length tennis dress with a scarf around her hair. Julia Mallinson was tall and held herself very straight. Sarah admired her style with a seamstress's eye, but there was nothing unfriendly or starchy about the elegant lady. She was very much up for teaching the girls a killer backhand, and when she was satisfied they'd made progress, she and Janette played against George and Sarah, and won. The mood was light and easy, the presence of Mrs Mallinson restraining the silliness and mayhem that had been threatening to overtake the sport, but in no way spoiling the fun. Irene came over to keep the score, and then Mrs Ramsden appeared with a jug of lemon barley water to complete, thought Sarah, a perfect afternoon.

She vowed to try to remember it after the holiday was over, as an antidote to the frequently glum and stressful atmosphere in the house in Keele Street.

How had her home become so joyless, a place from which this holiday felt like an escape? It wasn't only the shocking and sudden death of Ava, although that was a major part of her own and everyone else's low spirits of the past months, it was . . . oh dear, the relentless responsibility for *everything*: trying to step into her mother's shoes but without the benefit of the respect that the others had so naturally afforded Ava. Or maybe Ava had just made working for Miss Rowley and running the home look easy because she was a wonderful mother, and Sarah was not up to the job. Now she had to decide about taking on more responsibility at work, too.

'You all right, love?' asked Irene quietly, while Mrs Mallinson listened to Janette chatting about her favourite books, and George and Mrs Ramsden talked about him going home the next day.

'Yes . . . yes, I'm fine, Auntie.'

'You look sad.'

'I was just thinking about how I'll manage if I take over Miss Rowley's business, along with everything I need to do to keep us going at home.'

'*When* you take over, you mean? I thought you'd made up your mind.'

'Sort of. But I'm afraid I won't be able to cope.'

'Of course you will,' said Irene, breezily. 'Why would Miss Rowley set you up for failure? It doesn't make sense. She has every faith in you; your sewing skills and your ability to run the little business. Isn't it what you *want* to do?'

'Yes . . . yes, but . . .'

'Believe me, Sarah, you'd be daft not to go ahead. You'll earn more money than you would working as Miss Rowley's assistant, and why would you not want that? The others should help around the house more. I'll have a word with Jan.' Irene reached over and squeezed Sarah's hand. 'Courage, love. That's all you need. Nowt more than that.'

Eventually it was time to tidy away the tennis equipment and bring the idyllic afternoon to an end. George would be going home to his cottage behind the forge in Saxham Ash, a village about ten miles away, very early the next morning, so that he could get in a whole day at work.

'Goodbye, George,' said Janette. 'I'm so glad we were having our holidays at the same time. Thank you for showing us the walks and everything.'

He leaned down and gave Janette a bear hug. 'Ah, such

a long way down . . . I had fun, too, Janette. See you next year?'

'I hope so!'

'Yes,' said Sarah. 'It's been lovely – thank you.'

He leaned in to Sarah in turn, but his hug was less the brotherly embrace of a big man for a short and skinny girl, and more tender, somehow.

'Yes,' he said quietly so that only she could hear, 'it has, hasn't it?' Then: 'We can keep in touch, if you like? I'll leave the address of the forge with Mum.'

Sarah beamed and blushed. 'Yes, please.'

The following morning was Mallinson's Market Garden delivery day. The girls got up early to help Irene pick vegetables.

They started work in the long, ornate greenhouse, once full of exotic houseplants, now given over to rows of tomato vines and cucumbers, enjoying the fresh, green, compost smell as they found the first ripe fruits. Then they went outside into the bright air to walk the rows of runner beans and spot the ones that were hiding, dig tender young carrots and pick slender courgettes. Although there was a need to 'get on quickly', as Irene said, 'to deliver the vegetables with the dew still on them', to the girls it felt like fun rather than work.

They all three squeezed into the van and set off, Janette in charge of today's list and ready to tick off each order as it was delivered.

'Well, we make a great team,' said Irene, as she drove back towards Fettling House at the end of the morning.

'We even sold all those runner beans, which slightly surprised me.'

'Stop, stop!' said Sarah suddenly, seeing a familiar figure, carrying a bag, at the side of the road, his thumb out in the hope of cadging a lift. 'It's Joe. What's he doing here?'

Irene pulled up just ahead of him and Sarah opened the door.

'Joe!'

He leaned in. 'Thought I'd come for my holidays,' he grinned, 'if that's all right with you, Auntie?'

'Of course it is,' said Irene, taking this in her stride. 'Get in the back, lad.'

It turned out, as Sarah had feared the moment she saw him, that Joe had been given the sack by Mr Blake. Fred had been furious and the atmosphere at home had been 'unbearable', in Joe's opinion. He'd wisely decided that as there was now nothing to stop him taking up Irene's invitation to stay with her for a holiday, he'd do just that and put a distance between himself and his angry father.

'Why did Mr Blake give you the sack, Joe?' asked Janette, as the Quinns and their aunt sat around the kitchen table. Irene had made some sandwiches and Sarah was passing round cups of tea.

'I don't think we need to know the gory details, Janette,' said Irene. 'Just tell me, Joe, that it was a misunderstanding or some foolishness, rather than owt you did dishonest. That's all I want to know.'

'Yes, Auntie. But I'll tell you the whole of it otherwise Janette will badger me to death. There was a bit of a mix-up over some wallpaper . . . some very expensive wallpaper for a huge room in one of the smarter houses. The pattern was difficult, and Blake and me – we couldn't agree which way up it should go, and . . .' Joe looked slightly pink in the face and was working his mouth to stop himself smiling, '. . . and we still hadn't agreed by the time we'd finished papering the room!'

He gave up trying to control himself, sat back in his chair and howled with laughter. This, of course, proved infectious, and the girls were soon joining in.

'Ridiculous,' said Irene, mildly. 'Honestly, Joe, you really will have to grow up at some stage. What about the customer, who'd bought the paper and was expecting a professional job, not the painter and decorator version of the Keystone Cops? And wasn't it Mr Blake's job to supervise you?'

'You'd have thought so, but he put all the blame on me,' said Joe. 'I dunno what happened – I'd already been given the push by then – so I went and left Blake to sort it out himself.' He guffawed loudly. 'Not my problem in the end,' he added.

'Right, well, you're more than welcome to stay for a holiday, as you know. In fact, I'm delighted to see you, lad, although I wish the circumstances were different. But while you're here, I suggest you have a think about what you want to do next – a *serious* think – and then, when you go back home, do what you can to bring that about.'

'Yes, Auntie.' Joe looked contrite.

After they'd drunk the tea and eaten the sandwiches, and some buns Mrs Ramsden had made, Janette offered to go in with Sarah, as they did at home, to free up a bedroom for Joe, and Irene took Joe for a walk around the garden and a quiet word while his sisters were organising that.

'So you left your dad feeling furious?' she said, as they went to sit on a low wall around a raised bed of lettuces.

'Him, not me,' said Joe. 'I thought he was going to explode. If he hadn't gone off like a mad bull, everything would have been all right. Why couldn't he just be calm about it, like you are – like Mum used to be whenever I got the sack – instead of behaving as if it's the end of the world every time? As it was, I wasn't going to hang around and take any more tongue-lashings. I left at the crack of dawn this morning. I couldn't face another minute of him going on at me.'

'I hope you told him where you were going.'

'I left a note.'

'You'll have to go back and face him at some stage,' said Irene. 'Although I expect he'll have cooled down by then. Please, stay as long as you'd like to.'

'Thanks, Auntie. Dad's been in a really queer mood lately,' said Joe.

'How d'you mean? He's not ill, is he?'

'No, nowt like that. But he's become very impatient with all of us, as if he wishes we were out of his way. He forgot Janette's birthday and then was horrible to Sarah.

There's this woman that I reckon he's seeing: Mavis Swindel. I know he was being shifty about her. I saw them together one time, but didn't let on. Then when I asked him, he lied; said he'd been elsewhere.'

'Your father is old enough to do as he pleases, Joe. And mebbe he doesn't want to say owt about this person just yet. Or mebbe he only took her out that once and there's nowt to say anyway.'

'If I had my way, he wouldn't need to say owt about her ever,' said Joe, heavily. 'But I know he's seen her since, too. I don't know how he can even look at her after Mum.'

'What do you mean? What's wrong with her?' Irene asked, trying to keep her tone light.

'She's a bit bold,' said Joe. 'I could tell from the way she was looking at Dad that she was being flirty. Primping up her hair, as if she was proper proud of it. And her clothes are bit too tight, a bit, er, low at the front.' He blushed and looked away. She's sort of . . . forward . . . I don't know what the right word is.'

'Bawdy?' suggested Irene, keeping her face carefully neutral.

'More hard-faced, loud.'

Joe then told Irene about how Mrs Swindel had come to choose an inappropriate birthday present for Jan and how that had upset Sarah.

'Sarah never said,' Irene told him.

'She wouldn't. You know how she worries about everything. She told me later that she pretended to have to go the other way back to Miss Rowley's to avoid

Mrs Swindel. You know sometimes when you're just sure you aren't going to get on with someone? Sarah feels the same as I do.'

Irene pursed her mouth. 'But Janette doesn't know about this woman?'

'I don't think so. Sarah and me haven't said owt. Dad's keeping very quiet about her, although he's out every evening and I don't think he always goes to the Lamb and Flag, where he's a regular. Sometimes he comes back later than he's wont to do from there.'

'Thank you for telling me all this, Joe. I think Ava was very special and no one could ever take her place, but then, as her sister, I would think that. But she was a proper lady, which isn't about whether you live in a big house and wear a pearl necklace. It's about being a fine person inside, about good manners and showing consideration for other folk, about appropriate behaviour. This Mavis . . . I'm not sure, from what you say, that she sounds *appropriate*.'

'You've summed her up, all right.'

'Well, I'd like to say it will all blow over, your dad will see the light, but that might be wishful thinking. Whatever happens, you must look out for your sisters, Joe. And if you need to come to me, you know where I am. I can't interfere with your dad, but I'll always be your mother's sister and I'll try to be a proper aunt to her children.'

'Thanks, Auntie Irene.'

'Now, come and see what I've been up to here in the garden. It's a shame you've just missed Mrs Ramsden's son, George, who's had to go back to work. He's good fun – the girls like him – and I reckon you'd get on.'

'I wish I'd got sacked sooner,' laughed Joe.

The Quinn siblings piled off the bus from Blackburn at the end of the last leg of their journey home. Joe was carrying Janette's case as well as his own bag, and Janette was struggling with a cardboard box in a net bag, containing a couple of jars of Mrs Ramsden's strawberry jam, a crusty loaf and some flapjacks.

'You'll be tired after all that travelling and it'll be good to have something to hand to put towards your tea,' the kindly cook had said.

The air in Scarstone smelled sooty and unclean, the High Street seeming noisy after the rural peace of Fettling, although it was late in the afternoon by now and the shops were closed.

'I'm completely whacked,' said Sarah, when they reached their home in Keele Street. She noticed that the step still needed sweeping and washing, and she felt the joyous holiday spirit starting to fade already with the thought of all she would have to do, although Irene had reminded Janette and Joe that they needed to pull their weight around the house. 'It's odd that sitting on a train can be so exhausting.'

'It's the rocking. It lulls you to sleep,' said Janette, yawning.

Sarah opened the door. A strange, heady, dizzying scent hung in the air. The house had never smelled like this before and it took Sarah a moment to remember where she'd encountered this smell before. Then a horrible sinking feeling swept over her and she could feel herself almost wilting.

It was, without a doubt, Mavis Swindel's perfume.

'Dad . . .?' called Sarah, her voice sounding odd and shrill. 'Dad?' while Janette sniffed and said, 'Crikey, what's that scent?'

'Hello, love. Hello, Jan . . . Joe,' said Fred, coming into the hall from the kitchen in an awkward manner, the look on his face almost bashful.

By now Janette had picked up on Sarah's anxiety and was hissing, 'What? *What?*'

'Dad? Is Mrs Swindel here?' asked Sarah. It sounded like an accusation, but she couldn't help herself.

'Who's Mrs Swindel?' said Janette, but no one answered her.

'As a matter of fact, she is,' said Fred. He turned back towards the kitchen and called nervously, 'Mavis, love, come and say hello to my children.'

Mavis appeared then, her hair in extravagant waves. She was wearing a swishy floral skirt, which clung to her hips, and her shiny pink rayon blouse was a little too tight.

'Hello!' she said. 'Shall we go into the sitting room? We've got wonderful news to share.'

Oh, surely not! Oh, please, let it not be . . .

Sarah thought she might faint with the effort of hoping not to be faced with her worst fears. It was bad enough that this woman had even entered the house – the home that Mum had made. We should have been warned, Sarah thought. To come back from our lovely holiday and find Mavis Swindel here, and without any warning, is too much.

'Who is she?' Janette begged quietly. 'How do you know her?'

'I don't really, but I'll tell you later. Please, just don't say owt,' whispered Sarah.

'Well, well, well,' said Mavis quietly as the Quinns filed uncomfortably past her into the sitting room. She was looking at Joe. 'I think you and I might have seen each other before, eh? George and Dragon? I never forget a face, dearie.' She winked heavily at him as if they were co-conspirators; as if, thought Sarah, Joe and she shared a grubby little secret.

Joe looked mortified but he didn't answer.

'Now,' said Fred, coming in last and then going to stand next to Mavis, in front of the fireplace. He was smiling uncertainly and rubbing his hands together, in a way Sarah had never seen him do before, and which made her feel queasy with embarrassment. This felt like some sort of play-acting for which none of them had learned the part. 'This is Mavis Swindel, a lady I have come to know well these last weeks. While you've been on holiday, Mavis – who you've already had the pleasure of meeting, Sarah – well, she and I have made a decision about . . . about our future lives, an important one, which I'm sure—'

'Ah, stop mumbling and blathering, Fred, and just come out with it,' said Mavis, digging him in the ribs with her elbow and laughing loudly. 'You can make your own choices, dearie, and they're not your parents.' She didn't give him the chance to continue. 'Your dad and I are going to get married and you're all coming to live with me in my lovely big house at Great Edge.'

There was a long silence. Janette actually had her mouth open in horrified astonishment.

'W-When?' gasped Sarah. '*When* are you going to get married?' She knew good manners should have meant her offering her congratulations, but her mouth just wouldn't let her do it. It was imperative to ask this now, to find out how long she, Joe and Janette had got left of their present lives before Mavis was imposed upon them.

'As soon as possible,' said Mavis. 'No point waiting, at our time of life. And it's not as if I have to plan a white wedding.' She laughed loudly again and winked at Sarah.

Sarah winced and said nothing.

'Well, congratulations, Dad and *Mavis*,' said Joe. 'I hope you'll be very happy. Thanks for the offer, but I won't be coming to live at Great Edge.'

'Joe?' said Janette, now totally out of her depth. 'What's going on? How do you all know this lady and I don't? Why did nobody tell *me*?'

'Shush, Jan,' murmured Sarah. 'I've met Mrs Swindel once before, that's all. I hardly know any more than you do.'

Fred, however, was intent on resuming his pre-holiday quarrel with Joe.

'So where exactly will you be living, Joe?' he asked, mock-curiously.

'I can take over the rent here – I'm twenty-one in a few weeks and can do as I like about everything then – and the girls can stay too, if they want.'

'And how are you going to pay the rent, lad, when you've got no job? Have you forgotten you got the sack, then went cheerfully off on your holidays?'

Joe looked cornered. 'I'll think of summat,' he said. 'I'll get another job – a good one this time. I've got plans . . .'

'I doubt it,' snapped Fred. 'You've never made much of a success of paying your way so far, have you? How many jobs have you had since you left school, Joe? Six? Eight? More? You certainly can't afford to stay here, and you can't afford to keep your sisters, either. You'll all be homeless and living on the streets within two months, I reckon. I won't have you imposing that on Sarah and Janette when they could be living in a big house with their own rooms and everything.'

'You've never been one to encourage me or believe in me, have you, Dad?' Joe said.

'Give me one reason to do so,' fired back Fred.

If sides were being taken, Sarah was on Joe's. She certainly felt no allegiance to Mavis.

'Joe doesn't need to keep me. I can keep myself, and Jan, and Joe, too, if need be,' she said, lifting her chin. 'I've decided I'm definitely taking over Miss Rowley's business when she retires. I'm going to tell her tomorrow.'

'So you're going to pay the rent and keep the three of you, are you?' asked Fred. 'You're being daft, lass.

I thought you were cleverer than that. Think about it, Sarah: you don't even know if you'll manage to turn a profit yet. What if it all goes wrong and you have no customers – have you thought of that?'

'I mean to be a success. I'm going to do my best,' said Sarah, who'd been silently practising this resolution every night before she went to sleep.

'Now, Fred, no need to put the girl down,' said Mavis. 'I'm sure Sarah's very capable, for all she's so young and lacks experience. But didn't I hear that Miss Rowley is having to give up because she's struggling financially? Putting on a brave face, I gather, by calling it retirement. That's what the talk is about town, although I don't listen to gossip, of course.'

She turned to look at Sarah, to whom this was news. How come she didn't know this if other people did, even Mrs Swindel?

'But you see, Sarah, if you come to live at my house, you won't have to find the rent because the house belongs to me. That will make life a lot easier for you when the sewing business is not exactly a money-spinner, if rumour is to be believed. That would be the wise thing to do, wouldn't it? A lot less of a struggle when you're just starting out, and the perfect solution. Nothing to lose! You, too, Joe. A bit of help around the place would be useful to me, if you're at a loose end until you find a job that suits you. What do you say? I'm offering you a home, all of you.' Mavis spread her arms wide, as if to emphasise the generosity of her offer; as if to embrace all three of them, had she been taller and standing closer.

No one moved towards her.

'What's in it for you, Mrs Swindel?' Joe asked.

'Joe, shut up!' yelled Fred. 'I won't have you being rude to Mavis.'

'No, Fred, my darling,' said Mavis. 'Let Joe speak. He's obviously finding it hard to come to terms with change. And the added worry of not having a job . . . or any money.'

'You just seem very keen for us all to come to live at your house,' said Joe. 'And I'm wondering why.'

'But, Joe, of course I want you to come to live at my house. I'd have a heart of flint if I couldn't take on poor motherless children when I'm marrying their father,' said Mavis. 'Now, some people may like me and some may not, but no one could ever say I have a hard heart. There's room for you all in my house. Your wonderful father will be there anyway, and, of course, Janette is still a child – only fourteen last month, I seem to remember – and is the responsibility of her father, not her brother and sister. Janette will be coming to live at Over the Edge whether you do or not.'

Janette was looking unhappier with every passing moment.

'Please don't leave me there by myself,' she whispered to Sarah.

'No, don't worry. I shan't let you go there alone,' Sarah murmured, then spoke up: 'I'll go with you, Jan, and I think Joe should come with us, too; see how we get on as a family. What do you say, Joe?' She fixed him with a pleading look.

'All right,' said Joe, eventually. 'I'll come, too.' He hung his head and the room was silent for a moment.

Suddenly Sarah saw how her and Joe's reaction to the news of their father's imminent marriage must look from Mavis's point of view, and it didn't reflect well on them at all. In fact, they looked ridiculously emotional, childish and ungrateful. Sarah hadn't taken to Mavis, and nor had Joe, but they didn't know her and perhaps they had been too quick to judge. Maybe she was the kind of person it took time to get to know. Perhaps they were being snobbish and mean when they really had nothing to be snobbish and mean about. After all, who were they to be so high and mighty?

'I'm sorry, Mrs Swindel,' she heard herself saying. 'We were being ungrateful. You're right. If Dad is going to your house – Over the Edge, did you say it is called? – then of course we will come too, and thank you.'

'Glad to hear it, dearie,' said Mavis. 'I'll be your new mother and we'll be a proper little family.' She then hugged each in turn, although none of the Quinns returned the embrace. Mavis either didn't notice or she didn't mind, because she started gushing on loudly about her plans for a quiet wedding and she sent Fred to make some tea 'while I get to know your lovely children'.

At least, thought Sarah, Mrs Swindel had got their father to make a pot of tea for everyone, which was more than she had ever achieved. Perhaps there was some advantage to his marrying her.

Later, however, when Fred had escorted Mavis back

to Over the Edge, saying he would drop in at the Lamb and Flag on the way home, Sarah, Joe and Janette sprawled gloomily around the sitting room.

'I'll give it a try,' growled Joe. 'I promised Auntie Irene I'd look after you girls so at least I'll see how it goes.'

'She's not like Mum,' said Janette. 'I noticed how she bossed us all about, got us to do what she wants.'

'I had to say we'd go,' said Sarah. 'We have no alternative. Mebbe it will make Dad happy again – he's been so miserable since Mum died. And as that place – Over the Edge – is Mavis's own house, there's less of a desperate hurry for you to find a job, Joe, to help towards the rent. And, who knows, it might not be as bad as we think there.'

'Or it might be a damned sight worse,' muttered Joe.

CHAPTER SIX

Miss Rowley was keen to know all about Sarah's holiday when Sarah returned to work the following day.

'. . . It was lovely, Miss Rowley, really fun, and my aunt is so kind,' Sarah said, concluding her account.

'I can see you have a little more colour about your face,' said Miss Rowley. 'I'm hoping I shall look the same when I've been retired for a week or two,' she added, smiling. 'I've been making all sorts of plans with my sister.'

Sarah thought of what Mavis had said the previous evening, about Miss Rowley being in financial straits. She had thought of little else, in truth.

Miss Rowley somehow seemed to pick up on this. 'But, tell me, Sarah, there's nowt worrying you, is there?' she asked. 'Despite your rosy cheeks you're looking a little bit . . . down. Surely the thought of coming back to work isn't so very bad, is it?' Evelyn Rowley didn't look as if she really believed this could be true, but she was always considerate to Sarah.

Sarah felt she had to ask, now that Miss Rowley had raised the subject.

'Actually, Miss Rowley, I need to ask you summat. You see, I heard from . . . from someone . . . that the business isn't doing very well. That is . . . it's doing badly and that's why you're giving up and going to live with your sister. Can that be right?'

Evelyn Rowley looked utterly bewildered for a moment and then her expression changed to one of pure anger.

'Well, I don't know where you heard that rubbish, Sarah, and I don't know why you would believe it. I'd be very interested to know who is spreading around untruths about me and my business like that. When I told you about my retirement plans, I spoke the truth. I've always told you the truth and I see no reason why you would doubt my word or set someone else's false version of what is my business above what I have said.'

Sarah saw at once that what Mavis had told her could not possibly be true. How could she have believed Mavis over Miss Rowley for even one second? She quickly sought to put things right.

'Miss Rowley, I'm so sorry. I should not have thought to ask you, only the person who told me volunteered their information, and in quite a persuasive way. I realise now that of course it had to be some awful mistake.'

'Never mind "mistake",' said Miss Rowley. 'Slander, more like.'

Sarah nodded. 'Oh dear, I understand why you're angry. I should have kept quiet and said nowt.'

'No, Sarah, you did right to tell me. But I wish you

hadn't believed a word of it from the start. I would never try to deceive you. Who was it told you these lies? *Who?* I need a name so I know who is not to be trusted. I'll have to confront whoever it is and put them right in no uncertain terms!'

Sarah had never seen Miss Rowley angry before. She had turned in a minute from the familiar gentle, pastel-coloured seamstress to a flashing-eyed, red-faced fury. Sarah wished from the bottom of her heart that she had confronted Mavis there and then for spreading lies about Miss Rowley. It was just that she had presented them as 'rumours' – as uncertain facts but common knowledge – and she had seemed to know all about Miss Rowley's plans to retire.

But, no, that wasn't true, was it? In fact, she'd said nothing factual at all, just picked up on what Sarah and her father had said about Sarah taking over the business. Surely Mavis hadn't made it all up just to spite Sarah, but then what could be the reason for that? And what had Mavis got against Miss Rowley? Probably nothing at all, and certainly nothing compared to what Miss Rowley would now have against Mavis!

'I think it was a misunderstanding,' said Sarah, trying to calm the storm. 'If I hear owt else I shall put folk right straight away.'

This also proved to be the wrong thing to say.

'So I'm the subject of gossip far and wide, am I?' gasped Miss Rowley. 'The whole of Scarstone is talking about me in the streets?'

'No! Nowt like that, Miss Rowley, I promise. In fact,

I think the person who told me was trying to undermine *me*, not you. The lies were probably made up on the spot and no one else has heard owt at all. I don't think your reputation in Scarstone has suffered because there *is* no gossip. I was the only person lied to, and now it's upset you and come between us, and I really wish I'd . . . slapped that person's stupid face for making mischief.'

'Aye, well . . . I can see that you're sorry. Now, who was it? Is it someone I know? It's not Mrs Hutchinson, is it? That woman has her own agenda and I'm not always sure where I am with her.'

'No, it wasn't her,' said Sarah, wishing she could just go back home to bed and start all over again with a clean slate the following day. Nothing had gone right since she, Janette and Joe had returned from Fettling.

'Well, who then?' Miss Rowley really wasn't going to let this lie.

'It was a woman called Mavis Swindel.'

'Mavis Swindel? I don't know her. She's not a client. I know nowt about her and she certainly knows nowt about me if she thinks I'm struggling with the bills. What kind of a person is this Mavis Swindel, Sarah? Apart from a liar.'

'I hardly know her . . .'

'But?'

'She's . . . She doesn't seem to mind what she says.'

'Well, I've already worked that out. And?'

'She's got quite a bossy way about her . . . confident, interfering.'

'And?'

Sarah felt she was being punished. This was a new side to Miss Rowley – tenacious, almost ruthless – and one she would rather not have discovered. She didn't want to complain about Mavis here, to air her deep reservations and risk finding they sounded all too real, so she fell back on the obvious.

'She's marrying my father. She's going to be my step-mother.'

Miss Rowley was silent at last. After a few moments she said quietly, 'I'll go and make us a pot of tea, Sarah. Now sit down and gather yourself. I'm sorry I've upset you more than you are upset already.'

Miss Rowley disappeared to make the tea, leaving Sarah fighting back tears and wishing with all her heart that she had never even heard of Mavis Swindel.

The wedding was to be at the beginning of September, which was not long before Miss Rowley planned to join her sister down south and leave her clients in Sarah's capable hands. Her house was in the process of being sold and Miss Rowley was beginning to sort through her belongings. Sarah noticed tea chests and boxes had started to appear in the hallway. She worried about where she would continue to work and reluctantly went to look at some tiny shop premises, but paying rent was an expense she knew might break her. She found herself putting off making any commitment, although the need to find somewhere nagged at her constantly.

Mavis had invited the Quinns to tea at Over the Edge one afternoon, 'so you can see my lovely big house, where you're all going to live'. It was a hot Saturday in late August and Fred was working at the shop. None of them wanted to go, but there was no refusing the invitation. Mavis was being very welcoming in arranging the tea party.

'As we're going to live at Over the Edge, it would be better to get the lie of the land first; to be prepared for the worst,' said Joe gloomily.

'I don't want to do my work at Mavis's house, but if it's so big there might be room for me, somewhere out of her way,' Sarah mused. After the upset with Miss Rowley, she considered it a last resort, however.

They set off on their bicycles with low spirits and lower expectations.

By now, Fred had disclosed that Mavis kept a boarding house, which explained why Mavis's home was so big.

Over the Edge turned out to be very tall and old-fashioned looking, with big windows and gables, and many chimneys. Sarah thought it looked like the kind of house a Victorian mill owner might have built for a large family, supported by an army of servants, to live away from the noise and dirt of the industry that had provided their fortune in the first place. The house was the last in the road, set back behind a stone wall with a high hedge on the inside of that, so that it felt cold and secluded in the gravelled, weedy front drive, which curved between two pairs of huge gateposts. The place looked dark and unwelcoming.

Joe rang the bell and they heard it echoing far off inside.

Janette's eyes were large with apprehension. 'Do you think it's haunted? It doesn't feel quite right.'

'Don't be silly, Jan,' said Sarah, snappish because Janette had voiced her own silly fears.

Mavis opened the heavy oak door with a smile. Her hair was very bouffant and, in the gloom, the white stripe at the front stood out dramatically. Her little dog, which Sarah remembered from the encounter in Scarstone Hardware, lurked miserably behind her. It didn't even bark a greeting to the visitors.

'Come in, dearies. Don't stand there like refugees,' Mavis said.

The huge hall had a wide staircase to one side, with a dusty-looking, threadbare patterned carpet and heavy brown banisters. There was wooden panelling to half the height of the numerous doors leading off it, and off the corridor to which it narrowed at the back. Higher up the wall on one side was a moth-eaten-looking tiger's head, its mouth open to show ferocious yellow fangs. The Quinns stood looking in silence and astonishment at such an unusual and gruesome sight.

'Did you shoot that tiger, Mrs Swindel?' Janette asked eventually, her eyes wide.

Mavis gave her loud laugh. 'Not on your nelly. No, Janette, I might have shot one or two things in my time, but I certainly haven't been on safari with the international set. No, dearie, this magnificent trophy came with the house, and I think it adds a little distinction to the place, don't you?'

No one answered. Sarah thought it was difficult to describe quite how repulsive the display of the dead tiger, with its glassy eyes and dusty, age-tufted hair, was. But Mavis didn't seem to notice the silence.

'I like your dog,' said Janette, possibly in polite consolation, eyeing the cowering creature. 'What's it called?'

'Basil,' said Mavis. The dog twitched his ears at the sound of his name. 'Same as my first husband,' she added, deadpan. Then she roared with laughter.

Sarah and Joe exchanged disbelieving glances, but Janette knelt down and called the dog over. He came timidly to her and let her stroke his little head.

'I think he likes you,' said Mavis. 'Which is good, as I don't think he likes me much. I bought him because I fancied a little lapdog to pet and to keep me company, but he isn't at all sociable. I thought he might grow better looking, too, but he only seems to get uglier. Anyway, come on in. Bring that silly animal with you, Janette. I told the lodgers I was entertaining special visitors this afternoon and I booted them out of the dining room early.' Right on cue, the sound of a parlour piano being played with skill started from a room to one side. 'That's Mr Lavelle,' said Mavis. She lowered her voice. 'Not much of a man, but he's harmless.'

Sarah, Joe and Janette looked at each other, bewildered. What could that possibly mean? Was this not a boarding house after all, but some kind of a lunatic asylum?

They followed Mavis into the dining room, which was also heavy with wood – furniture and panelling – all in need of a clean and a polish. The wallpaper was beginning to peel off the ceiling in one corner, and there were threadbare patches in the carpet.

Surprisingly in all this shabbiness, laid out on the table was a very generous and beautifully presented tea, with dainty little sandwiches cut into triangles, scones with butter *and* jam, and tiny chocolate-covered cakes decorated with a variety of piped designs.

'Ooh,' whispered Janette.

They sat down around the table, Basil crept under Janette's chair, and Mavis poured cups of tea from a tarnished silver pot, and passed them round.

Sarah had avoided seeing Mavis since the uncomfortable conversation with Miss Rowley. If Miss Rowley had confronted Mavis, she didn't tell Sarah. It wouldn't have been her way. Sarah, however, had told Rachel what had happened as they'd walked home together one evening after work, and Rachel had warned her to be on her guard.

'It could all have been nowt more than silly gossip, of course, but on the other hand it sounds as if Mavis Swindel might be the kind to make up stories to try to turn things to her advantage. I think you'd be wise not to rely on what she says until you see for yourself exactly how things are,' Rachel advised. 'If I were you, I'd try to keep my own counsel and not be persuaded by her.'

'But she's going to be my stepmother – why would she lie to me?' asked Sarah. 'What has she to gain?'

'Well, she tried to put you off taking over Miss Rowley's work, so I would guess that means there's a reason she doesn't want you to do that,' said Rachel unhappily.

'I don't understand.'

'Well, she must have some other plan for you, wouldn't you say?'

'If she has, I can't guess what it is. Mebbe she just likes making mischief. Or mebbe it's all a mistake and she meant no harm. It's awful, not knowing if I can trust owt she says, wondering if she's trying to trick me.'

Rachel nodded and looked grim. 'Just be careful, that's all.'

They had reached the corner of Keele Street. Sarah stopped walking and stood wringing her hands.

'And, Rachel, there's summat else I'm worried about: where am I to do my work when Miss Rowley leaves? I can't afford premises in town, and if Mrs Swindel *was* trying to put me off Miss Rowley's business, she's hardly going to agree to letting me have space in her house, even if I wanted it.'

Rachel put her hands to her mouth, frowning. 'Mm, I can see your problem. And you haven't long to solve it.'

'*I know!*'

'If I think of owt, I'll be sure to tell you straight away.'

But Sarah wasn't sure that even her clever best friend would be able to help her out.

Now, as she drank the tea and ate the delicious sandwiches, Sarah felt tense with the need to keep alert in case of lies and deceit. The sumptuous spread was at odds with the setting, but unless the food was poisoned and Mavis had embraced the fairy-tale role of Wicked Stepmother, she had to take the generous offering at face value.

'Did you make these delicious sandwiches and cakes, Mrs Swindel?' she asked.

'Blimey, dearie, what do you think I am – a miracle-worker? No, I've got a cook, Nancy, to make all the meals, for me and for the paying guests. I'd never leave that kitchen if I had to do all that as well as everything else.'

'How many people do you have living here?' Janette asked shyly.

'Just four at the moment, but I'm hoping to expand,' said Mavis, posting an entire little sandwich into her mouth in one go.

Sarah's eyes were drawn to Mavis's tight-fitting blouse and she had to fight down a nervous giggle. She dared to glance sideways at Joe and saw that he was looking at Mavis's straining blouse buttons too, and that his thoughts were reflected in his blushing cheeks.

'Yes,' said Mavis, as she chewed the last of her sandwich, 'there's plenty of room here for all of you *and* for a few more lodgers.' She swallowed noisily. 'Let's hope I find some more exciting fellas than the ones already here. I prefer male lodgers – less fuss and trouble. But I could do with a few who aren't no-hopers to bring a little life to the place.'

'No-hopers?' asked Janette.

'Odds and sods,' Mavis explained, then laughed uproariously.

The girls looked at each other, baffled. Joe was frowning now.

'Men who are going nowhere,' Mavis went on. 'You've heard of the "spare women", surely? Well, these are the spare men.'

Sarah tapped Janette's leg with her foot and shook her head a fraction. Janette, thankfully, kept quiet.

Mavis, however, was keen to explain. 'Yes, I've a deaf one, a daft one, a mad one and a queer one,' she said.

By now Sarah was feeling a bit sorry for these strange lodgers, to whom their landlady showed not the slightest respect. Janette looked completely out of her depth, and Joe, Sarah could see, was fighting down anger.

'Ah, don't look so tragic,' said Mavis. 'At least they're not dangerous. Now, when you've finished your tea, I'll show you a bit of the house, if you like.'

'Mrs Swindel, please may I just open the window a little?' asked Sarah. Sitting in close proximity to Mavis and her heavy perfume, and her indelicate line in conversation, Sarah could feel a headache coming on.

'Of course, dearie.'

Sarah got up to open the window behind her. The catch was new and worked smoothly, and the window swung open almost from her grasp to admit a gust of surprisingly strong wind. She leaned out and saw the Edge falling away in a steep escarpment and the moors laid out far below like a quilt of green patchwork. It looked airy and free, in contrast to the strongly scented, stuffy and unclean dining room, where she was beginning to feel trapped. She gasped at the cool fresh air as if she were drowning, thinking she might faint.

Oh . . . oh God, that's better. Oh, thank God for some fresh air.

Mavis was leading the way back into the hall, her footsteps silent, Janette following, with the little dog beside her.

'You all right, Sarah?' Joe asked quietly.

'Mm . . . It's just a bit stuffy in here.'

'Overwhelming,' he agreed.

Sarah took another deep breath of cool air, carefully closed the window, and she and Joe hurried after Mavis.

Downstairs, the house was vast and run-down, with shabby old fittings and drooping curtains, peeling wallpaper and grubby paintwork. Mavis's little 'office' was the smartest room, being at least reasonably clean, although untidy, with heaps of documents and old magazines and newspapers on a side table. There was a chaise longue, and a desk with a lot of drawers and a telephone standing on it, set in the middle of the room.

'I'm a working woman and it's important to be business-like,' Mavis said, which, Sarah thought, didn't explain the chaise and the clutter. Or the state of the other rooms.

Mavis showed the Quinns the lodgers' sitting room. This huge and lofty space at the front of the house contained two sagging sofas and an armchair upholstered in grubby moquette. There was a waste-paper basket full of scrunched-up paper, and an overflowing newspaper rack. Little tables at the ends of the sofas held used glasses and cups, a plate with crumbs on it and a well-used ashtray.

'So much to do, and the residents are an untidy lot,' said Mavis.

Sarah noticed an old man at the end of one of the sofas, not doing anything but just sitting as if he'd been asleep. She hadn't seen him at first because his clothes were the same colour as the moquette: greenish-grey.

'Mr McCain,' said Mavis, seeing where Sarah was looking. 'He's deaf,' she added, as if this was a reason to ignore him.

She went out without addressing a single word to him, and Joe, Janette and the dog followed.

Sarah turned back. 'Hello, Mr McCain,' she said, raising her voice slightly.

'How do?' he responded. 'Who are you?'

'Sarah. I'm going to live here. My dad is marrying Mrs Swindel.'

'Oh, aye? Good luck to him with that,' he said.

'Er, thank you,' said Sarah, unsure of his tone. 'Well, I'll see you again.' She turned towards the door with a little wave.

'Aye, if God spares me.'

She left the room in time to see the others going through a door on the opposite side of the hall, and she hurried after them, conscious of the tiger's head gazing down from the wall behind her.

This room held an upright piano. It was untidy, but cleaner than the residents' sitting room. A very slim young man, probably in his twenties, wearing baggy flannel trousers and a Fair Isle pullover, was sitting at the piano, leaning over to mark on a score with a pencil.

'Hello, hello,' he called in a friendly way. 'Who have we here, Mrs S? Youthful company come to join our merry band?'

'My future stepchildren, Mr Lavelle,' said Mavis. 'I told you I'm getting married very shortly – well, these three will be coming to live here.'

'Really?' said the young man, very interested. 'How marvellous! We could do with a bit of new life about the place.'

'I couldn't agree more, dearie,' said Mavis.

The man stood up and held out his hand, first to Joe, then Sarah and Janette. 'Percy Lavelle,' he introduced himself.

They shook hands and the Quinns told him their names.

'Splendid,' he said, sat back down and played a chord. 'Do you know "Ain't Misbehavin'"? No?' He played a few bars, singing along lightly. 'Right, well, regrettably it's time for me to get back to work. See you soon,' he added with a regal wave, and he turned his attention pointedly back to his score.

Even Mavis could take the hint and they all trooped out.

'Ridiculous little man,' she muttered, which Sarah thought was mean. Percy Lavelle had been very friendly, and certainly promised to be more fun than the deaf and dour Mr McCain.

'Well, you'll meet the other two another day,' said Mavis. 'I expect Mr Armstrong is in the library in town, where he spends a lot of time – he claims to be writing a book – and Mr Cornwell is away selling whatever it is he sells.'

'I'll look forward to meeting them,' Sarah said politely.

'I wouldn't expect too much, dearie. Not exactly the life and soul, those two. I told you, no-hopers the lot of them.'

By now Sarah was wondering if Mavis Swindel ever had a good word to say about anyone. What exactly was her problem with the rest of the human race? Why was she so disappointed in everyone? It occurred to Sarah to wonder what Mavis would say about her, Joe and Janette the moment they left the house. Possibly she'd be describing them to whoever would listen as 'no-hopers', too. Oh dear, perhaps it was just her way and she didn't really mean any of it. It was early days to be leaping to what might turn out to be unfair judgements.

She was just thinking about making their excuses and leaving when she realised she hadn't met the talented cook, Nancy. That tea had definitely been the best part of the visit, and the thought of eating such delicious food every day was looking like it might be the only saving grace about living at Over the Edge.

'Mrs Swindel, please may we meet Nancy, to say thank you for the tea? I mean, it was very generous of you to provide it, but didn't you tell us Nancy made it?'

'That's right. Well, I don't know if it's worth your while, but come and say hello anyway,' said Mavis.

None of them asked her what she meant by that; it was probably just her way of speaking. By now, all three Quinns had got the idea that there was a lot that Mavis said that it was best not to follow up.

Mavis led the way to the door opposite her office, down the corridor at the back of the hall. Janette was holding Basil in her arms by now, like a doll. The little dog seemed not to mind.

'Nancy!' Mavis burst through the door to the large kitchen. 'There's people to see you.'

'What? Oh, hello. You must be the tea party,' said the thin young woman swathed in a large apron. She was up to her elbows in washing-up water, but she dried her hands and came over.

'I'm Sarah, this is Joe and this is Janette. We just wanted to say hello, and thank you for the lovely tea,' said Sarah.

'Thank *you*,' said Nancy. 'It's grand when folk are appreciative.' She looked sidelong at Mavis. 'Nice, too, to be able to make summat decent, special. No corners cut,' she added. Now she was definitely looking at Mavis.

Then she turned back to the Quinns. 'So you liked the sandwiches?' she asked.

'They were my favourite part,' said Joe. 'Especially the thin-cut ham with mustard.'

'Thank you,' said Nancy. 'A sandwich needs a decent amount of butter. But what about the scones? Were they all right?'

'Delicious,' said Sarah. 'I've made scones a few times but mine have never been half as good as yours.'

Nancy nodded. 'Butter again. And practice. I made the jam, too.'

'Far better than shop-bought,' said Joe.

'Thank you. I always reckon it's worth the expense of best-quality fruit,' said Nancy. 'But did you like the chocolate cakes as well?' she asked, giving her full attention to Janette.

'The best ever,' Janette replied enthusiastically. 'Lots of chocolate on top, too.'

This must have been the answer Nancy was looking for, because she then turned to Mavis with a raised eyebrow, although she said nothing. 'Thank you, Sarah and Joe and Janette. I'm right glad you liked the tea,' she finished.

'Well, I think it's time we went,' said Sarah, sensing some subtext here and not caring to be drawn in.

Oddly, Mavis was looking perfectly content, as if whatever was behind Nancy's words, which had to be aimed at her, had gone entirely over her head.

'Thank you again, Nancy. And thank you, Mrs Swindel.' Sarah went out, down the corridor and back into the hall, trying not to look at the horrible dead tiger. As she passed the front rooms, she looked to acknowledge Percy Lavelle and Mr McCain, but the doors were closed and the rooms silent.

Joe caught up with her there. 'No need to run away, sis.'

'I didn't know I was.'

'I could hardly keep up. Here's Janette. Jan, put that dog down. He'll still be here next time.'

'Next time . . .' muttered Sarah. 'We might be here for good, next time.'

'Aye, you're right.' Joe pulled down his mouth.

'Goodbye, Mrs Swindel. Thank you for having us. Thank you for the tea,' chimed Sarah, making a huge effort at the door, and the others joined in.

When they were out on the shadowy gravel, Sarah breathed a huge sigh of relief. The atmosphere in the house had been very strange, as if everyone's dislike of each other and their bad feelings were living beings, residing there and poisoning the air. No wonder the poor little dog, Basil, looked as if he were failing to thrive.

'I saw a lane to the far side of the house,' said Joe. 'I think we should just take our bikes down there and have a think about this.'

Glad of their cardigans and pullovers up here on the Edge, the three of them rode down the rough lane until it started to drop away too steeply for them to go any further safely. Then they set their bikes down and went to sprawl on the tussocky grass of the open field that must lie beyond the garden of Over the Edge. If they looked back, they would probably see the house roof looming distantly behind them, but they made a point of not looking.

'Well, what did you make of that?' asked Joe.

'The tea was lovely, but the rest was awful,' said Janette. 'I could tell it wasn't nice even when I didn't know what folk were on about. What is the matter with Mrs Swindel? She hasn't a good word to say about anyone.'

'You're right,' said Sarah. 'But we don't know owt about the others yet, and Mrs Swindel has an unusual way of speaking about folk. Nancy was nice to us, but there was summat going on between her and Mrs Swindel. And Percy Lavelle was friendly, but Mrs Swindel was horrible about him behind his back. She seems to hate everyone, and yet she invited us for tea and was kind to us. I don't know . . . mebbe it was her idea of being amusing, and we're being a bit hard on her.

She's not like anyone we've known before, is she? P'raps she takes some getting used to.'

'She's the most opposite she can be to Auntie Irene,' said Janette.

'You're right about that. She's not a bit like Mum, either. I wonder what Dad sees in her.'

'I expect she's clever with him and tells him what he wants to hear,' said Joe. 'But she probably thinks she doesn't have to bother so much with us.'

'But she bothered with the tea,' said Janette.

'Thing is, once she and Dad are married, we'll go to live there whether we like her or not. It's her house and she's giving us a home. There's masses of room for all of us – your sewing business too, if you want, Sarah – and she says she's bought the house so there won't be the same worry about the rent as there is in Keele Street.'

'And, Sarah, you won't be in charge of seeing that all the chores are done,' said Janette, brightening. 'That will be down to Mrs Swindel. And at least I'll be out at school most days, come September,' she added, 'and you'll be doing whatever job it is you're doing next, Joe.'

'But I won't!' lamented Sarah. 'I'm really worried about this. I need somewhere to work when Miss Rowley goes, and I thought I might have to ask Mrs Swindel if she'd mind if I had some space, but I don't think I want to be stuck at Over the Edge all day.'

'You sure you can't rent some premises?' asked Joe.

'I've looked and I really can't afford it, especially just now, when I've got things I need to buy to get set up on my own.'

Janette put out her hand and squeezed Sarah's arm. 'Don't worry. We'll think of summat.'

They lay there, staring at the sky, thinking of the afternoon and growing more and more unsettled. Eventually the grass started to feel damp and they got up to retrieve their bicycles.

'One good thing – p'raps the only good thing – about Over the Edge,' said Joe. 'The food was brilliant.'

Sarah agreed, but as she pushed her bike up the steep hill, she thought that was not enough to offset her other concerns.

CHAPTER SEVEN

A T LEAST FRED was happy to be living at Over the Edge.

'I actually heard Dad whistling,' said Joe, one evening towards the end of the Quinns' first week at their new home, sitting down on Sarah's bed.

'So did I. I'm so pleased he's feeling more his old self,' said Sarah.

'I am, too, although I don't know what he's got to be so cheerful about,' said Janette, gloomily, leaning against Joe for warmth and hugging her cardigan around herself. She looked pale and cold.

'Well, you're only a nipper so you wouldn't.'

'Shut up, Joe. I don't want to think about Dad and Mavis,' said Sarah, plonking herself down on the only chair.

It was now the middle of September and the 'happy couple', as Mavis coyly referred to herself and Fred, had returned from their honeymoon – a weekend in Scarborough – and were busy showing Fred's children and Mavis's lodgers how pleased about life they were now they were together. Much of Fred's old spirit had returned and he spent his spare time quite cheerfully mending broken hinges and replacing the odd worm-eaten floorboard, painting a yellowing skirting board or replacing a broken windowpane. In the evenings he sat down in what had now become the family sitting room, rather than go to the Lamb and Flag, Mavis laughing loudly and flirting while Fred read his newspaper and they listened to the wireless. His children were pleased to see him more cheerful, although they found the 'happy couple' embarrassing.

The Quinn siblings had left Keele Street when the honeymooners returned to Scarstone. It had been sad saying goodbye to the old house, sadder still because it was so bound up with their childhoods, and their memories of their adored mother. It seemed to all three of them that their father had completely and willingly forgotten about her; that he had moved on and left his first marriage far behind, whereas they tried always to keep alive their treasured memories of Ava.

It didn't help in terms of their settling in that Over the Edge was such a strange and uncomfortable house. The rooms Mavis had given them were in the attic: former servants' quarters. They wouldn't have minded – they each had a room, which was a welcome new experience for the girls, who had had to share a room in Keele Street – but the attic was draughty and inhospitable, with ill-fitting, rattling windows and suddenly slamming doors, even at the beginning of autumn. Like the rest of the house, it was old-fashioned, shabby and run-down. Mavis's 'lovely big house' was far from 'lovely' in reality, and Fred's little bits of maintenance made hardly any difference – like an elbow patch sewn on a completely threadbare jacket, thought Sarah. What Mavis really needed was some builders in to overhaul the entire building from the roof down, and then to have the whole house redecorated.

'I don't like coming up here by myself at night,' Janette confided to Sarah and Joe. 'Once I've passed that dead tiger downstairs, I've got the creeps anyway. Then up here, up all those stairs – that narrow bit where it's not well lit is horrible, what with the shadows and creaking – there are weird moaning noises, and it always feels cold. I keep thinking I'm going to meet some strange person wandering around, haunting the place.'

'Mr Cornwell, you mean,' laughed Joe.

'Joe, that's not funny,' said Sarah, who liked the former soldier turned encyclopaedia salesman. He was friendly but also gentle and polite. 'Poor man, his nerves were wrecked in the trenches, yet I reckon he's doing his very best to put all that behind him and lead a normal life. Please be kind. And about the attic, Jan, I know what you mean, but it's only the wind howling above the Edge. This is the last house, of course, so it'll always get the worst of the wind and weather.' She reached out and squeezed Janette's hand. 'In future, I'll come up with you, if you like. I don't mind going to bed early. In fact, I reckon I'd prefer to be up here with you than spending the evening with the "happy couple".'

They all looked at each other and Janette rolled her eyes.

'Thank you, Sarah. I expect I'll get used to it in time,' she sighed, not sounding as if she expected that at all.

'Last day at Miss Rowley's tomorrow,' said Joe. 'Give the old biddy my love and wish her well.'

'She's not an old biddy and she doesn't want your love,' Sarah smiled. 'But, yes, I'll say you wish her well – we all do. What I do wish, though, is that she wasn't going, but at the same time I wouldn't want to deny her a happy retirement with her sister.'

'And at least Rachel's parents have come up trumps with the offer of their spare room so you won't have to be working here all day.'

Sarah smiled. 'It was such a relief when she told me. Rachel promised she'd think of summat and she didn't let me down. I don't know how long Mr and Mrs Fraser will let me use their boxroom – and for free, too – but I intend to be established in Miss Rowley's shoes as quickly as possible while I'm not having to pay to rent premises.'

'Mebbe I'll come and work for you,' said Janette, jokily. 'Help you along.' She winked at Joe and they all laughed.

'Nonsense. You're the clever one. Not only are you bound to get your School Certificate, but you'll get your Higher, too. It's possible you could even go on to be a teacher yourself, Jan.'

'Do you think so?'

'Why not? Miss Hurst is all for pupils reaching their potential.'

'Oh, I hope so, I really do.' Her face brightened at Sarah voicing her ambition aloud, giving it more validity.

No one in the family had had a profession, but Janette saw no reason not to aim high.

'Yes, you don't want to end up like me, weighing out potatoes,' said Joe, cheerfully. 'There's one good thing about working in that greengrocer's, though: Sally Hardcastle. Looks right pretty in her overall, she does. And her uncle's always generous with any leftover fruit.'

'Which makes *two* good things, Joe,' said Janette, with exaggerated patience. 'But what if you and Sally fall out? Won't you find it awkward to be weighing out veg in her family's shop, with her looking all pretty in her overall –' she batted her eyelashes – 'and hating the sight of you?'

'Jan, that isn't funny,' chided Sarah. 'There's no reason for Sally to hate Joe. And don't use that word – there's enough dislike in the air here, what with Mavis forever grousing about her lodgers and Nancy.'

Janette looked ashamed to have so lightly used the word that the Quinns had come to associate with Mavis since that afternoon when they'd first visited and she had seemed to have such a poor opinion of everyone. 'Sorry, you're right. I didn't think.'

Their conversation was interrupted by the sound of raised voices downstairs.

'Oh, no, sounds like Mavis hating summat or someone, right on cue. I hope Mr Cornwell won't be upset by it,' said Sarah.

'So do I,' said Janette. 'Mavis has such a loud voice, it goes right through me.'

'I'm going to see what's going on,' said Joe, getting up off Sarah's bed.

As he opened the door, the sound of the shouting grew louder. He sidled out to the attic corridor then tiptoed down the narrow stairs that led to the first floor. A row, which had clearly started in the kitchen, had now moved to the middle of the hall. The girls crept out to join Joe at his vantage point, but out of sight from below, and they sat down stealthily to eavesdrop.

'. . . I *told* you, you stupid girl, not to use all that neck of lamb in one go. How many times do I have to remind you I'm not made of money? It's about time you learned a lesson, Nancy. I've put up with your wasteful extravagance too often and now I'm going to dock the cost from your pay. *And* for that butter you so lavishly added to the mashed potatoes. *And* that chocolate you put in that pear thing you made.'

'It was a pear and chocolate cobbler – it's got chocolate in it,' said Nancy, speaking slowly and sarcastically, as if Mavis was stupid. 'You can tell that from its name. I only bought a tiny bar.'

'I don't care what size of bar it was. If you're going to make fancy puddings, you need to ask my permission first, not just set out on some . . . some extravagant jamboree all by yourself, with my money. And there was cream, too. Cream! What is wrong with stewed pears and Bird's custard? This is a boarding house, girl, not the bloomin' Ritz.'

Janette looked at Sarah, remembering the wonderful cobbler. It had been a delicious pudding to follow the slow-cooked lamb stew served with buttery mashed potatoes and carrots cooked in an interesting way, which

Sarah thought might have involved some kind of spices and more butter. Nancy, for all her irony and perpetual friction in her relations with Mavis – or maybe because of that, and her cooking skills – was fast becoming a favourite with Mavis's stepchildren.

'You'd prefer it dry, would you, missis?' Nancy snapped at Mavis.

'Don't be impertinent. I'm telling you not to make it in any way, wet or dry. Don't ever, *ever* make that pudding again.'

'I shan't,' said Nancy, raising her voice to match the volume of Mavis's. 'And I'll tell you why. Because I'm not going to be here. You can make your own flippin' puddings, and your own lamb stew, too. I'm leaving! I'm leaving right now, because I'm fed up of you saying I can never do owt right, when I know that I'm the best cook you're ever likely to find – especially for the pittance you pay me – and you're lucky to have me. If you don't know that, then I'm sorry for you, because that makes you stupid as well as mean.'

'How dare—'

'I dare because it's the truth, you stingy old baggage. The only thing keeping your lodgers here is my cooking, and you know it! So I'm off, and I bet they will be soon as well. Shabby old falling-down house, cold rooms, never enough hot water, and dull food, too – what would they stay for? Not to look on your mean and ugly face, that's for sure.'

'Aah . . .' gasped Mavis. 'You little cat! Shut up! Shut up and get out. You're sacked. I can't bear the sight of you, standing there, looking like a reject from the work-house and giving me lip.'

'You can't sack me because I'm already leaving. I don't need you telling me to go.'

'Good. And you needn't expect to be paid either.'

'I don't, as I'm paying for the lamb and the butter and the chocolate. In fact, I'm off before you start demanding that *I* pay *you*. I wouldn't put it past you. You've got the brass neck.'

Sarah could feel her eyes were huge with shock. She leaned forward to see Nancy ripping off her pinafore, and the scarf from her hair, and flinging them to the floor.

'There! I wouldn't bother with them, if I were you,' Nancy snarled. 'They'll never fasten round you!'

Then she left, empty-handed, no coat or cardigan, slamming the front door behind her as hard as she could.

The air vibrated and slowly settled as the echo of the shouting and slamming faded in the huge stairwell.

Janette's eyes, too, were wide with astonishment, and she pursed her lips in a silent whistle. Her heart pounding, Sarah nudged Janette, and all three tiptoed silently back to Sarah's room and closed the door very quietly.

'Oh, my goodness! That was terrible,' said Sarah, breathless and shaking at hearing such vitriol.

'It was, but I'll admit I kind of enjoyed it, too. Nancy was magnificent,' said Joe. '"Stingy old baggage" hit home. Did you see Mavis's face?'

'I did. Oh, but poor Nancy: no job.'

'Mm, and poor us: no more of her wonderful cooking.'

'Do you think she'll relent and come back?' asked Janette. 'Mrs Swindel – I mean, Mavis – will never find anyone half as good as Nancy. And we didn't have a chance to say goodbye to her either.'

'No, she's never coming back,' said Sarah with certainty. 'I reckon I should go after her and see if she's all right. Jan, would you get Nancy's things from the kitchen while I quickly put my shoes on? I'm sure she's left without even her purse.'

They ran downstairs. Fortunately, Mavis had retreated to her office, so Janette was able to grab Nancy's belongings without any awkward encounter, while Sarah fastened her shoes and then hurried out with Nancy's handbag and cardigan.

The light was beginning to fade and the air was damp. There was only one way Nancy could have gone – unless she meant to throw herself off the Edge – and Sarah set off quickly along the road that led towards the centre of Scarstone, praying Nancy had not been desperate enough to take the other route. Soon she could see the skinny little figure ahead of her, walking fast, her head down.

'Nancy! Wait! I've got your things.'

The girl stopped and turned round.

'I couldn't stand her for one minute more,' she said. 'I was keen enough at first, but I soon found out what that one's really like. If she had her way, I'd be cooking nowt but potato soup for every meal.'

Sarah handed Nancy her cardigan.

'Thank you. I was so mad I just had to go. I admit I never stuck to the budget, but to expect me to pay for the food myself! Then when I realised I'd left my stuff, I was too proud to go back: didn't want to spoil a good exit.'

'It *was* a good exit, but I don't know what Mavis will do without you. Mebbe she'll have to do the cooking herself.'

'Aye, mebbe.'

'I'm right sorry you're going, although I do understand,' Sarah went on. 'But what will you do now?'

Nancy put her cardigan on and then took her handbag. 'Thought I might go home via the George and Dragon. They're looking for a cook. They serve a lot of pies and I know what I'm doing with pastry.'

'And with everything else,' smiled Sarah. She gave Nancy a hug. 'We shall miss you. Miss your cooking, too. It won't be the same without you.'

'Mm . . .' said Nancy. 'You take care, Sarah.'

'The George and Dragon would be mad not to hire you. Good luck with your new job.'

'And good luck with yours,' Sarah thought Nancy said as she turned and set off at her determined pace.

Sarah didn't know Nancy knew about Miss Rowley leaving, but the job was hardly 'new'. Still, it was nice to have Nancy's good wishes. Before Sarah could thank her, Nancy was already some distance down the road.

When Sarah got back to Over the Edge, the house was very quiet. Nancy's pinafore and scarf had gone from the middle of the hall floor. Sarah put her head round the door of the lodgers' sitting room. Mr McCain was sitting reading the newspaper and he did not look up. It was possible he hadn't heard a word of the row.

Percy Lavelle wasn't in this evening. He was accompanying some singers in Blackburn, apparently, so the other room at the front of the house, the one with the piano, was unoccupied. Andrew Armstrong tended to keep to his room, and the faint clacking of his typewriter could often be heard in the evenings. Sarah went in to close the curtains and that was when she saw Richard Cornwell, sitting by himself in the gathering dark, his shoulders hunched, his hands over his face.

'Mr Cornwell?' she said softly. 'Are you all right?'

He lowered his hands and she could see he looked red-eyed and disturbed.

'Please, don't be upset,' she said. 'It was only shouting, and they've finished now.'

He nodded. 'It was j-just the sl-slamming of the d-door: so l-loud . . . s-sudden.'

'It was Nancy. I'm afraid she's left. Gone for good.'

'That's a p-pity.'

'It is. She's a very good cook. That lamb stew was delicious, wasn't it?'

Mr Cornwell nodded mutely.

'And the pudding. I think Mavis thought the pudding was the last straw,' confided Sarah. 'She likes to stick to a tight budget.'

'S-so I've noticed.'

'Shall I make you a cup of tea, perhaps with some sugar in?'

'Yes, please, S-Sarah.'

'I'll put on the light and close these curtains. And I'll bring you your tea in a few minutes.'

Mr Cornwell took several deep steadying breaths. 'You're a k-kind girl.'

Sarah saw to the light and the curtains, then turned on the wireless – which had soothing music playing – at a low volume, and went to make the tea.

'Ah, now, Sarah,' said Mavis, bustling into the kitchen, Fred in tow. 'Just the person I've been looking for.'

'Oh, yes?'

'Yes. It's good to see you're taking charge in here because I've had to ask Nancy to leave. I caught her being dishonest with the housekeeping. Now, I've just this moment had the most brilliant idea,' she gushed on. 'You see, I gather you're a simply marvellous cook. Your father tells me you did all the cooking at your old home, and it strikes me that that could be your role here; make use of your talents. How lucky is that for both of us, eh?'

She paused at last, smiling expectantly at Sarah.

'Mavis, I'm sorry, I don't know what you're talking about,' said Sarah. 'I couldn't help overhearing some of what was said between you and Nancy – it was quite, er, loud – and she didn't steal owt.'

'Of course she did!' snapped Mavis. 'Took my money and spent it in ways that I had most especially asked her not to. Several times! She wilfully refused to stick to the budget. Some weeks . . . well, I hardly had two pennies left to rub together. Nigh-on bankrupted!

I'm trying to make this beautiful old house into some-where special for my paying guests, but it needs so much work on it, and how can I afford to have that done when the cook is spending every penny she can get her hands on? How could I allow her to continue to work for me when it was clear she was not to be trusted?'

Sarah could understand this, yet she also saw that a good part of it was untrue. 'But she left . . . resigned.'

Mavis frowned and the atmosphere suddenly turned frosty. 'I think you must have misheard, Sarah,' she said. 'I don't remember you being there when I had to sack Nancy. You see, dearie, eavesdropping is a dangerous game. You could so easily get the wrong end of the stick – as indeed you have – and, well, if I'm not there to put you right, it could lead to all kinds of trouble. Couldn't it?' She gave Sarah a long look, and Sarah began to wonder if she might have misinterpreted the argument.

'I'm surprised at you, Sarah, jumping in and voicing your view when you know nowt about it,' Fred said. 'Eavesdropping, too.'

There was silence. Sarah felt outnumbered.

'I'm sorry if I misunderstood.'

'Well, you did, and you admit you were trying to listen to a private conversation, too. But I'm prepared to overlook it this time,' said Mavis, sounding hurt but magnanimous.

Sarah saw Mavis was going to stick with her own version of events – although the row had been far from private – and there was a more important question to pursue anyway.

'But how can I possibly do Nancy's job here when I already have a job?'

'But you don't, do you?' Mavis said in a reasonable tone, while leading Sarah to a chair beside the kitchen table. 'I thought you would have seen the truth of the situation for yourself by now, dearie, but I can see I'll have to explain it to you. Miss Rowley's business will close tomorrow when the old lady retires and walks away from it and from you. She doesn't care what happens to you or to her customers and their threadbare clothes. She's off to . . . wherever it is she's going, and she won't be looking back. She's even sold her house, leaving you without premises. Now, that rather sends its own message about how much she's bothered, doesn't it?'

'You listen to Mavis, Sarah. She's talking sense and she's only thinking of you,' added Fred.

'But she had to sell her house because she's leaving Scarstone.'

'As I say, leaving you with nowhere to work. I gather from your dear father that you've had to fall back on some old boxroom in a friend's house. So unsatisfactory.' Mavis, sitting down beside Sarah, reached out and grasped her hand in a comforting way. 'Oh, Sarah, I do worry about you. Someone else's house with hardly anywhere to store your things or put anything down. Poky room and a tiny window, I'm guessing . . . yes? I thought so.' She shook her head, looking very grave about the prospect.

'But it's only while I take up Miss Rowley's reins properly and then I'll be able to find somewhere better. It's only until mebbe . . . Christmas.'

'Christmas! Oh, blimey, dearie! That woman really has left you high and dry, hasn't she? There's certain to be no heating in this glorified cupboard and you'll be frozen long before Christmas. No, dearie, you can do so much better than that. In fact, I refuse to allow you to suffer when there's a job for you here. With me!'

'Mavis is very generously offering you a job where you won't even have to leave the house,' said Fred, putting his hand supportively on Mavis's shoulder. 'It's ideal.'

'Ideal for who?' Sarah asked, feeling desperate as the force of Mavis's will threatened to consume her. 'I *want* to leave the house. I want to continue to work as a seamstress. I know nowt about cooking really.'

'Nonsense. You've cooked for us since your mother died. I doubt it'll be much more work, making meals for a few extra folk,' said Fred, who had never cooked anything in his life.

'Don't be so modest, dearie,' said Mavis. 'I'm putting my trust in you. I know what a talent you have.'

'You see, Sarah,' said her father, 'Mavis is giving you this opportunity, right here. There'll be no struggling on alone in someone else's boxroom. You're guaranteed the work, whereas Miss Rowley's setup comes with no guarantees at all. It wouldn't surprise me if the customers all started going to that dressmaker behind the High Street. Why would they stick by you?'

'But I—'

'Ah, c'mon, Sarah, don't be so ungrateful. I didn't bring you up to behave like this, throwing Mavis's generosity in her face.'

'Just give it a go for a month or two,' said Mavis, smiling and patting Sarah's arm reassuringly. 'Go on, what do you say? It would get me out of a tight spot now that I've had to ask Nancy to leave. Surely you can manage just that much for me? It's so little to ask.'

'But—'

'Family comes first, Sarah. You know that,' said Fred, beginning to lose patience. 'I'm sorry if you need reminding, lass, but the right thing to do is to accept Mavis's offer and be grateful for it. I reckon it's a godsend, for which you'll be thankful when you get your head straight. That sewing business is never going to make you any brass.'

'I—'

'Oh, I knew you would see sense,' gushed Mavis. 'I couldn't be happier, dearie. You're a real saviour, you know that? Such a help to me in my hour of need. You won't regret it, I'm certain.'

'You're a good girl, Sarah. I'm glad you're doing the right thing,' added Fred.

Sarah was enveloped in Mavis's strongly perfumed hug, which made her feel instantly queasy and headachy. Somehow it seemed she had agreed. How had that happened? Yet Fred and Mavis both understood she *had* agreed, so she must have done.

'All right. But only for a month or two,' she found herself saying.

The following day it was mid-morning before Sarah had finished cooking and serving the breakfasts to her family, who left early for work or school, and to the lodgers, who, except for Mr Cornwell, appeared whenever they felt like it and sat behind their newspapers in silence. Then she washed up and tidied the kitchen. She wasn't used to having so many breakfasts to make, and everything, in this strange kitchen, seemed to take so long, or not to work very well, or to be big and old-fashioned and almost too heavy to lift. She wondered how Nancy had managed the job, and so brilliantly, too.

Sarah had told Joe and Janette the previous evening that she was now taking Nancy's place.

'How did that happen?' Joe had asked. 'You were excited about taking on Miss Rowley's work earlier – what's going on?'

'Yes, I was. I *am*. But Mavis said the cooking is just for a month or two, and Dad said family comes first. I got the feeling he thought I was letting everyone down if I refused. I don't know how it happened but I'd kind of agreed before I even knew it.'

'Idiot. I thought you had more sense. I reckon Dad means that Mavis comes first. And it looks like Mavis certainly thinks so, from where I'm standing. And what happens when the "month or two" is up, eh? Is Mavis going to hire a new cook? Why doesn't she do that straight away now?'

'I expect she'll have to look around for someone, which will take time. Then when she has a proper cook again, I'll carry on Miss Rowley's work.'

'If it's still there to be carried on,' Janette had pointed out heavily.

Joe had shaken his head sorrowfully. 'I reckon you've been had, Sarah.'

Now, having finished everything to do with the breakfasts at last, Sarah was worried about missing Miss Rowley's departure altogether. 'I really must go and see Miss Rowley before she leaves and say goodbye and get any final instructions about the clients,' she said to Mavis, who had come to see how she was getting on. She began to untie her pinafore. 'I can't just not turn up.'

'Whyever not, dearie?' asked Mavis, sounding astonished. 'I told you, Miss Rowley will get on her train at Blackburn station, looking forward to her new life with her sister or cousin or whoever, and she won't give you and the drooping hems of Scarstone another thought. And I don't think you should either.'

'But I've worked for her for . . . well, since Mum died, and I don't want her to leave without me even saying goodbye to her. She's always been so kind. And she may well have work lined up for me to undertake as soon as you get a real cook.'

'But, Sarah, you can't just go wandering off to the station or wherever. You took so long over the breakfasts that you'll need to be starting on the lunches straight away. Really, there's not a moment to spare. That's the job that you agreed to do – that I'm *paying you* to do. You do know how to make soup, don't you?'

'Yes, I can do that,' Sarah sighed. Miss Rowley had roped Sarah in to help her when Ava died, just as Mavis was roping her in to help now that Nancy had stormed out, but Sarah liked Eileen Rowley, who had always dealt with her fairly, and had grown to love the job. Sarah couldn't honestly see a time when she'd be happy working for Mavis Swindel.

'I'll see what there is and make it from that, shall I?' she said heavily.

'You've got the idea.'

The front doorbell rang then, and Mavis went to answer it, while Sarah went to look in the larder for what she could find to make into soup. The remains of a chicken sat on a big oval plate, but she thought she'd better keep that back for dinner. There didn't seem to be anything else.

The soup took quite a long time, too, what with searching for the right size pan and then finding a dead mouse in a trap at the back of the larder, and having to deal with that, and wash everything down and rebait the trap. Then the soup looked too thin and she had to find some flour to thicken it, and then it wasn't a very good colour and . . . oh dear . . .

By the time she'd served the soup to Mr McCain, Mr Cornwell and Mr Lavelle – Mr Armstrong having gone to the library for the day – and then dished up some stewed apples for pudding, Sarah was worrying she might be completely out of her depth with the cooking.

'So where exactly is the lovely Nancy?' asked Percy Lavelle, as Sarah handed him a bowl of stewed fruit. 'Not been called to work at the Ritz, has she?'

'No, but I'm sure they would employ her if she turned up there,' said Sarah. 'She's left and I'm sort of standing in until Mavis – that is, Mrs Swindel – finds someone else.'

'Ha! She walked out in a huff, didn't she? I knew she would. I had a bet with Andrew Armstrong that Nancy would be gone by Christmas and now he owes me five shillings. So, Mrs *Quinn* has roped you in to help. Now, sweetie, please don't take this the wrong way, but some of us do still have all our teeth, and it'd be nice to have something to chew on – get my meaning?'

'Oh, yes, I suppose it is all a bit . . . wet.'

'Pap is the word. Wouldn't you say, Mr McCain?' Mr Lavelle raised his voice. 'Pap?'

'Delicious,' answered Mr McCain, whose teeth were as bad as his hearing.

'Perhaps some fresh warm bread with the soup and mebbe a bit of shortcake with the fruit, do you think, Sarah?' suggested Richard Cornwell kindly. 'Just a little tweak to make a big difference.'

Sarah could see this would improve the menu and she wished she'd thought of it. She resolved to do better. She realised she had not taken Mr Cornwell the promised cup of tea the previous evening either, so overwhelmed had she been by the turn of events, but he hadn't said anything about that.

Then there was just time for her to eat her own lunch, after serving Mavis hers in the family's sitting room. Mavis was in a bad mood over something, and not keen to talk, which was a blessing. Basil escaped from her presence when Sarah opened the door, then followed her back into the kitchen to be fed. Next there was all the tidying up, and then it was time to start preparing the dinner. No sooner had Sarah finished one meal than the next had to be started. She had had no idea that working in a kitchen could be so tiring, so all-consuming of her time and energy.

'So, there are we five,' announced Mavis, appearing silently mid-afternoon to issue instructions, 'plus all four of the paying guests.'

Sarah was struck for the second time that day that Mavis was now considered one of them, a Quinn: 'we five'. There had been five, back when everything was better, but now there were four. In fact, it felt increasingly as if there were only three and Fred had defected to the Swindel camp. Mavis was not a Quinn. Mr Lavelle had referred to her as 'Mrs Quinn', but she wasn't Mavis Quinn to her stepchildren; she was Mavis Swindel and always would be.

As soon as they had arrived at Over the Edge, Mavis had suggested that the Quinn siblings call her 'Mum' but they had all politely but firmly refused.

'We could call you "Stepmother", if you like,' Janette had suggested innocently.

Mavis had looked at her as if she was undecided how to take this.

'Call me Mavis,' she'd said, narrowing her eyes at Janette.

Now, however Sarah regarded Mavis, there was still dinner to cook for nine people. Sarah had never cooked for so many before. Oh, for goodness' sake, how hard could it be? People with big families did this all the time. The thought of the Ellises, in Fettling, passed through her mind – there were eleven of them altogether – and

Sarah straightened her back and began stripping the meat off the chicken carcass she'd discovered earlier, which Nancy had cooked a couple of days ago.

The Ellis family naturally led her wandering mind to Auntie Irene and the women at Fettling House. How were they getting on? Irene wasn't much of a letter writer, except when she had birthday wishes to send or something important to say. Sarah had George Ramsden's address, but what could she write? She didn't know him well enough to want to send an anguished account of life at Over the Edge. Besides, he might have his own preoccupations. He had been worried that Mrs Mallinson might have to sell up, and his mother and Auntie Irene would lose their homes . . .

Then it occurred to Sarah that she herself was now displaced, her old home gone, and her old job too – at least for the time being. What was she doing here, in this awful house, working at a job she had had foisted upon her and for which she was so ill-prepared?

Looking up from picking the greasy chicken bones, she was startled to see Mavis standing watching her on the other side of the kitchen table. For someone so loud in so many ways, Mavis could move remarkably quietly.

'You'll need to get a move on if we're all to eat this evening,' she said. 'Mr Lavelle has mentioned there wasn't much substance to the lunch, so get plenty of potatoes on to boil.'

Sarah remembered Nancy telling Mavis, 'The only thing keeping your lodgers here is my cooking, and you know it!' Perhaps Mavis was remembering those words, too.

'Yes, Mavis,' said Sarah. 'It's just I've not cooked for so many before, and everything takes ages when I don't know where owt is.' She sounded whingy, even to her own ears. Really, this would not do! *C'mon, pull yourself together and stop being so pathetic.*

'Well, there's only one remedy for that,' said Mavis. 'Keep at it and you'll soon know what you're doing. Oh, but I've just had another brilliant idea!' She held up her hands as if astonished at herself. To Sarah it looked like a theatrical kind of gesture, badly rehearsed. 'You get on with that – no time to mess about feeling sorry for yourself – and I'll go and speak to your father.'

Now what?

Whatever it was that Mavis had thought of, Sarah doubted it would be good news for anyone but Mavis. Sarah had missed saying goodbye to Miss Rowley, she was risking losing Miss Rowley's clients, and she was stuck at Over the Edge for the next month or two, doing a job to which she was quite ill-suited. Surely, though, things could not get worse.

CHAPTER EIGHT

JANETTE WAS JUST finishing her homework at the dining-room table, Basil sleeping under her chair, when Mavis came in and asked her to go to help Sarah in the kitchen.

'But aren't *you* going to help Sarah?' asked Janette. 'They're your lodgers.'

She wasn't deliberately trying to be rude, but she was tired after a day at school and then doing the homework. Cooking for so many people was a proper job, not a bit of 'helping out', and Janette feared that if she was roped in to help now, she'd be expected to do that every evening, when Mavis should be formally employing the staff she needed, or doing the work herself. Janette feared it would be school, then work, day after day, and no time to herself at all.

The Quinn siblings were all starting to wonder what Mavis did all day. She often mentioned her ambitions for Over the Edge, how she wanted her boarding house to be a 'little palace', but she showed no inclination even to request any quotations from builders to repair a rotting gable end or window frames, or replace sagging guttering. The supply of hot water seemed a matter of chance, the pipes clanged and shook, and every tap dripped and had left greenish stains in the washbasins. Sarah thought perhaps Mavis was overwhelmed by the house, that it needed so much work to make it into the 'little palace' of her dreams that she couldn't face starting. What the place needed was some serious maintenance before winter and then a thorough clean from top to bottom.

Mavis employed a charwoman, Ena Hastings, for a couple of hours twice a week, but Ena was elderly and slow-moving, her feet swollen with varicose veins, her breathing alarmingly audible. Each time she came to Over the Edge she laboriously washed the kitchen and bathroom floors, but seemed never to manage anything else. Janette didn't know what the lodgers' bedrooms were like, but the dust on the stair carpet and on the head of that gruesome dead creature on the wall was clearly visible. The two rooms the lodgers used downstairs were often untidy, and the ill-fitting windows meant a constant layer of black dust settled on the scruffy old furniture. Sarah and Janette kept their own rooms spick and span, and Joe's room . . . well, that was up to him.

'I'll have no backchat from you, madam,' Mavis replied to Janette. 'When I ask you to do something, you jump to it. Do you understand?' She casually slapped out at Janette's arm. 'It'll be your ear next if you don't get off your lazy backside and out to that kitchen now.'

'You can't slap me, Mavis. You're not my mother,'

Janette answered. Ava would never have spoken to any of her children like that.

'Who says I can't? Perhaps you'd like to go and ask your father? You can tell him what you said to me. I've never heard such rudeness!'

Well, that wasn't true, for a start, or else Mavis had completely forgotten the row with Nancy. And Janette didn't think she'd been *very* rude.

'So if you don't want a sore lughole, you'd better move yourself. Now.'

Janette got up and mooched out as slowly as she dared, muttering under her breath the words that she'd treasured since she'd heard Nancy strike insult gold the previous day: 'Stingy old baggage.'

When she got to the kitchen, accidentally nearly shutting the door on Basil, who had followed her, Sarah, who looked flushed and harassed, almost fell on her with a hug of gratitude.

'Mavis sent me,' said Janette, 'with a threat to box my ears. Now, you'd better tell me what to do.'

'Oh, Jan, I'm sorry she was snappy, but I'm so grateful you're helping.'

'Why can't Mavis?'

'I don't know and I haven't time to ask. Mebbe she can't cook.'

'Well, you can't either – not like a real cook. Never mind, just tell me what to do.'

Sarah issued a smattering of instructions, mostly about setting the table, dishing up and summoning the lodgers. The family would eat later and rest of

148

'the chicken leftovers thing', as Sarah referred to it, was to be kept in a low oven for then.

When Janette returned to the kitchen for the vegetable tureen, she announced, 'Mr Armstrong wants to know what it is. I didn't like to call it "the chicken leftovers" so I said I'd ask you.'

'Oh, crikey, I've no idea,' said Sarah, sweeping saucepans into soapy water. 'Er . . . oh, tell him it's called Chicken Mavis.'

'So not spring chicken,' said Janette, and went away with the vegetables, grinning.

When she came back, she said, 'How strange: Mr Lavelle made just the same joke.'

Two days later, days on which Janette had spent her time helping Sarah after her return from school, Mavis asked Janette to come into her office room as soon as she got home.

Immediately, Janette was wondering what she had done wrong now. It might just be that she'd answered back that time. Mavis could be very resentful when something or someone displeased her, and she would foster her grudges until such time as she could exact her revenge. Janette remembered that – on the first day at Over the Edge – Sarah had broken a vase when she was drying it and it had slipped out of her hand. She had apologised and offered to replace it, but Mavis, although she gave Sarah a hard look, had said it didn't matter and it wasn't valuable: it was moulded glass and quite ordinary. But then, a couple of days later, a little porcelain rabbit that Ava had given Sarah for her birthday the year before she died – very pretty and very precious to Sarah – had disappeared from Sarah's dressing table. Sarah had got quite upset about it and Janette had helped her search, although they both knew really that that was a waste of time. The only explanation was that someone had removed it. Ena Hastings had never entered the Quinns' rooms before – no one had seen her even cleaning the lodgers' rooms – and Sarah thought it unlikely her father had moved the rabbit, although she asked him to be sure; to cover every possibility until she had to face what she guessed was the truth.

'No, love, I haven't taken owt from your room. Of course not. Why don't you ask Mavis if she's seen it?'

Sarah had been hoping there was another explanation because, if Mavis had taken it, she would never see it again. She remembered the broken vase, the vengeful look on Mavis's face while she said it didn't matter, and she was not surprised when Mavis came straight out with her tale.

'Oh, I'm sorry, Sarah. I knocked it off when I was dusting. Broken beyond repair, I'm afraid. Sorry I forgot to mention it.' And Sarah just knew Mavis had broken it on purpose. After all, there was little evidence around the house that Mavis did much dusting. And even if she did, what business had she to be cleaning in Sarah's room when the rest of the house, where people paid to live, was so in need of attention?

Now Mavis delivered her message to Janette in a way that the Quinn siblings were beginning to see was characteristic.

'I have some very welcome news for you, Janette. No homework for you this evening, dearie. You're excused homework now and for ever! Isn't that marvellous?'

'What do you mean, Mavis?' Janette asked suspiciously. 'I'm supposed to hand tonight's exercises in tomorrow morning.'

'Well, you won't be doing that, because you won't be there,' beamed Mavis. 'You won't be going back to school tomorrow . . . or at all!' She said this with the triumphant air of a conjurer who has pulled off a particularly baffling trick.

Janette could feel a hot and panicky turmoil rising within her. Mavis was overwhelming her, just as she'd overwhelmed Sarah when she'd forced her to take on the role of cook.

'But, Mavis, I can't just leave without letting anyone know. They'll wonder what's happened to me. And anyway, I don't *want* to leave. I want to stay and pass my exams. That's what I've planned.'

'Oh, no, no, no, no, no, dearie,' said Mavis, shaking her head as if Janette were slow-witted. 'It's all in hand so there's no need for you to worry. Your father has written to Miss . . . whatever she's called, and told her that you are leaving immediately. You're old enough to leave, there's a job for you here, and there's no point whatsoever in you wasting your time learning useless facts about . . . square roots and capital cities.'

'But I need my qualifications. I want to go to college and train to be a teacher,' insisted Janette.

'Don't be silly, child,' said Mavis, with an astonished kind of sneer. 'Women like us don't train to be teachers. You're getting way above yourself and it's bound to end in tears.'

'No,' said Janette, sinking down onto the end of the chaise longue with the weight of her disappointment. 'You're wrong, Mavis. Women can use their brains too, you know. I could go to college.'

'Well, you'll have to learn that the world doesn't revolve around you and what you want, Janette. You are far too selfish. There are plenty of other considerations. I've an opportunity here for you, and I think you'll be perfect for it. Most girls your age would jump at the chance of a job, just handed to you as if on a plate, and not even having to apply.'

'But I don't *want* a job. I want an education.'

'Well, tough!' snapped Mavis, possibly in the hope of ending the discussion there.

'Anyway, I have to go in tomorrow. I haven't said goodbye to my friends or owt.' It flashed through Janette's mind that she could go to see Miss Hurst and protest. The headmistress was very much in favour of her pupils fulfilling their ambitions.

'What's that got to do with anything? You can't be sentimental in life, Janette. It'll only hold you back. Look at Sarah: she should have told that old harridan Miss Rowley to go to hell when she swanned off and left Sarah with the hopeless remains of her business, but Sarah wouldn't see it that way. I've rescued her from certain failure and possibly getting into all kinds of debt. And now I'm rescuing you from silly dreams that can never become reality.'

What on earth had Mavis got against Miss Rowley that she could speak of her so crudely? When had Mavis ever even met Miss Rowley? Janette felt she had entered a strange *Through the Looking-Glass* kind of world, where what was said had two meanings, except that this, being a Mavis world, was nasty and smacked of some kind of scheming, even a vendetta.

'But, Mavis,' said Janette, fighting to keep calm, to keep thinking and not just burst into angry tears, 'what is this job? Why can't you employ someone else to do it? Why do I have to leave school and ruin my life and all my plans, to do whatever it is when you could just hire someone else?'

'Really, Janette, for someone who thinks herself so clever you've got an awful lot to learn. Ruin your life, indeed! The only one ruining your life is you, if you think yourself destined for endless and pointless education, just to satisfy your vanity and make you think you're someone special. Well, madam, you're *not* special, you are ordinary, same as the rest of us. And you're also ungrateful and foolish. I offer you a wonderful opportunity and you throw it back in my face!' lamented Mavis. 'I don't know what I've done to deserve such treatment, I really don't.'

'Mavis, what's the matter?' asked Fred, who had just arrived home from work and come in to hear the tail end of the argument.

'I don't like to tell tales,' Mavis said, looking daggers at Janette.

'Mavis says I've left school, that I'm never going back.

But no one asked me about this and I don't want to leave,' said Janette.

'Well, it's too late,' said Fred, standing over her where she sat on the low chaise. 'Mavis and I have discussed this for a week or so now – it wasn't decided in five minutes, you know. Even Mavis was unsure at one point, despite her being so keen to welcome you into the family business . . . just as if you were her own daughter. But by then I could see it was the right thing for everyone. I wrote to Miss Hurst and she'll have the letter tomorrow, explaining that you have a job now. It'll be better for you to be realistic about your prospects and it works out grand that there's work here for you. Many girls are not so lucky and have to go out and look for a job. And you'll be working alongside our Sarah.'

'You mean I'm also a cook?' Jan felt completely bewildered.

'I mean we are a family, and the boarding house is a family business, so naturally there's a role for you here. We're all playing our part.'

'But, Dad, you know I have plans to—'

'Jan, I really think that it's time you grew up,' Fred said, beginning to lose patience with her. 'You're never going to be a teacher. Folk like us don't have a fancy education, because we don't fit in with those kind of folk or know the sort that can give us a leg up in life. That's what it's about, my girl: who you know, not what you know. No matter how many exams you pass, you'll never get anywhere because folk like us never do.' He patted her shoulder, a futile gesture of support.

'C'mon, lass, it's time to forget about school and start thinking about real life.'

'But—'

'It's what's happening so I don't want to hear one more word about it. Now, Sarah's probably peeling taters like a demon, so off you go and help her.'

'Dad—'

'Now.'

'Dad—'

'Shut up and go!'

Sarah was furious that Janette had been forced to leave school against her will, but no amount of arguing would change their father's mind. He had never been very much in favour of education for his daughters anyway, and Sarah knew she had been lucky to have been allowed to attain her School Certificate. Ava had been keen for her daughters to reach their potential at school, which was why Sarah had been able to stay on beyond the minimum leaving age, but now Ava was dead. Mavis had a completely different agenda and she knew just how to bring Fred round to her way of thinking.

'Just be careful, Joe, if you want to keep your job at Hardcastle's,' Sarah warned her brother the following day. 'The Stepmother has a way of getting what she wants, and if she wants you working here, in her house, you can be sure that's what will happen. Dad agrees with everything she says, so it's no use appealing to him. She seems to have him under some kind of spell.'

'Like a witch,' Janette added.

Joe nodded slowly but said nothing. He had become quieter since they had moved into Over the Edge, more watchful.

Over the following week, Mavis kept asking him for a discount at Hardcastle's, but Joe just said he was only a lowly assistant there and she should telephone Mr Hardcastle if she wanted to negotiate on price.

He had the foresight to cover his back by mentioning to Mr Hardcastle that his 'nuisance of a stepmother' kept badgering him for a discount and he'd told her it wasn't his place to offer anything. 'Should she telephone and say owt else, it's 'cos she's trying her luck. She's got enough nerve. She wouldn't mind what blame I'd get if I hadn't warned you. I reckon causing trouble between us would be as much the point as the discount.'

So when Mavis rang Mr Hardcastle and smarmily told him Joe had mentioned a substantial discount for family, Mr Hardcastle feigned absolute outrage, then put down the phone, laughed heartily, and promised Joe a bit extra in his wages that week.

'I know the type,' Mr Hardcastle said, 'and there's no better sport than queering their pitch. Well done, lad. These hard-faced, cheapskate landladies are a well-known breed, but forewarned and all that . . .'

Sarah and Janette were getting used to cooking for up to nine people, although they knew the food fell well short of the standard Nancy had set. Working together allowed them to finish the kitchen chores with a little respite before they had to start again on the next round. They often did the shopping, too, although with a list from Mavis, and instructions not to deviate from it. Despite Mavis's strict orders, however, the days on which the girls went to the High Street to shop almost felt like they had their old lives back, from the time when they lived in Keele Street, and they felt their spirits lift as they set out.

This particular day, early in October, Sarah might have been tempted to buy a cup of tea at the Scarstone Tearoom, or a bar of chocolate they could share on the walk home, but Mavis kept them on a very tight rein financially. She often found some excuse to deduct something from their pay – to cover the cost of items she said had been damaged or gone missing, but about which they knew nothing – or invented a reason why she couldn't afford to pay them in full, so that they were seldom paid what she had originally offered. Any pay seemed a good deal to Janette, who had been used to no more than a bit of pocket money, when Fred remembered to give her any, but to Sarah the low pay meant worry that she was caught in Mavis's web, that when she tried to pick up Miss Rowley's work, she would have no savings left to fall back on, or to meet her initial work expenses.

This led her to thinking about the boxroom in Rachel's parents' house. She had never had the chance to go round and explain to the Frasers that her starting was delayed for a couple of months. She hadn't seen Rachel once since going to live at Over the Edge.

'Let's go into the library and see if Rachel's there,' Sarah decided. 'She knows where we are, but we've been so busy lately . . .'

It was a Tuesday, mid-morning, and the library was quiet. Rachel and Sarah saw each other straight away. Rachel's grin nearly split her face.

'Come into the reference section – there's no one there just now – and we can have a quick chat if we do it quietly,' she suggested.

They went to sit close together at a table at the far end of the room, speaking barely above whispers.

'So, how it is?' asked Rachel. 'I must say, neither of you looks very happy.'

'That Mavis is a tyrant,' hissed Janette. 'She made me leave school and now I have to work in her stupid boarding house, helping Sarah.'

'Oh, no! But doing what, Jan? Sewing?'

'No, I'm cooking,' Sarah explained. 'It's only for a month or two, but Nancy, her marvellous cook, left in a huff, and Mavis needed someone to cook the food straight away so she asked me.'

'But I thought you were taking over Miss Rowley's business?'

'Oh, Rachel, that's what I intended—'

'Just as I intended staying on at school to sit my exams,' interrupted Janette. 'But Mavis has a way of riding roughshod over folk. She pretended that working at the boarding house is a great opportunity for us, but it's nowt but misery and penny-pinching: endless potatoes to peel, cabbage at every turn, eking out the meat to make it go twice as far as it should. She has fists tighter than a duck's eyelid, does that woman.'

'Oh, this sounds terrible,' Rachel said, looking

troubled. 'I can see why the previous cook left. Mum and Dad are still expecting to hear from you at some point about when you'll need the spare room, although they are quite easy about it. But, from what you've told me, I'm afraid you won't be needing it at all.' She looked questioningly at Sarah.

Suddenly Sarah felt tears stinging her eyes. She'd been trying to convince herself that she would resume being a seamstress in a few weeks, and have a nice little business to run, with all the fun and adventure of making her own way. Now she saw she'd been deceiving herself. That possibility had vanished like a beautiful dream the minute Mavis had bamboozled her into taking on the cooking.

'Yes, Rachel, I reckon you're right, and I've just been hoping against all reason that being Mavis's cook is a temporary arrangement. I'm afraid I won't be needing the room your parents so kindly offered me, because I'm never going to be my own boss and run that business!' She gave a little sob and reached for her hanky.

'I don't think Mavis means to employ another cook,' said Janette. 'Why would she, now she doesn't need one? She's never mentioned advertising for anyone and she keeps talking about expanding: taking on more lodgers, although I can't think anyone who goes to view the place will like what they see.'

'Why? What's wrong with it?'

'It's run-down – peeling wallpaper, woodworm in the stairs, clanking plumbing and draughts everywhere. Mavis got the house cheap because the previous owners went bankrupt – that's what she told Dad – but the whole place is in a right state and now she's realised what a job she has on her hands and it's as if she doesn't know where to start. She has a charlady, Mrs Hastings, but she's old and barely makes any difference in the short time she's there. I wonder Mavis doesn't employ an efficient cleaner for a good long time each week, as it's such a big house, but, as I say, she's Scrooge in a frock.'

'And now, of course, there isn't the draw of Nancy's wonderful cooking either,' said Sarah. 'She and Mavis were always at war over the ingredients Nancy bought to make everything delicious, but Nancy won most of the skirmishes, right up until she could stand the fight no longer and left. I know the lodgers miss her cooking. They try to be kind but I can tell they don't really like my food very much. But I'm not a proper cook; I just can't manage . . .'

Sarah mopped her eyes and Rachel put a comforting arm around her shoulder.

'Listen,' she said, 'there's a lot to think about; we can't discuss it all now. Shall I come round this evening? Surely there's somewhere quiet we can sit and talk in private? Mebbe we can work out what can be done. C'mon, Sarah, all's not lost. Remember, there are three of you and only one of Mavis Swindel.'

They made an arrangement, and then Rachel walked to the library door with her friends. As they passed the reading room, Sarah saw Andrew Armstrong sitting poring over a pile of books.

'Of course, this is where he is most days,' she said

quietly to Rachel, pointing him out to her. 'Mr Armstrong is one of Mavis's lodgers.'

'Is he indeed?' said Rachel. 'Well, that's very interesting . . . Right, I shall see you two later.'

Rachel rang the doorbell of Over the Edge at the appointed hour and waited. When Sarah opened the door, Rachel said quickly, 'I've spoken to Mr Armstrong and he's going to help, if he can.'

'He's in the piano room. He said he was expecting someone to come round this evening to talk about summat to do with the library, and Mavis said to use that room. I guessed it would be you, although he made it sound very bookish and serious.'

'Excellent.' Rachel glanced around the hall and her eyes grew wide. 'Heavens, I see what you mean. Show me where to go, and you tell Jan, and Joe, if he's around. Best avoid Mavis seeing us all together, though, or she might suspect a conspiracy.'

'We usually retreat upstairs in the evenings, so we'll not be looked for. Dad will be about the place somewhere with his tool bag, mending summat.'

Sarah had not come to know Andrew Armstrong at all well, as he tended to keep to himself: out at the library all day and typing in his room most evenings. He was very focused on himself and could be quite abrupt. Rachel, however, had struck up an acquaintanceship with him since that morning and filled him in on the situation. As she had suspected, Mavis's faults as a landlady were as evident as her shortcomings as a stepmother.

'Now, I've a lot to do this evening so let's get to the point,' said Mr Armstrong. 'This place needs a complete overhaul – repairing and cleaning – but, *most urgently*, better food, yes?'

Sarah and Joe nodded, but Janette said, 'We're trying our best.'

'I know you are, Janette, but you should be at school and Sarah should be sewing fine seams. Neither of you is a cook. Now, Mrs Quinn—'

'She's Mavis Swindel to us,' interrupted Joe.

'Yes, all right, Joe. I understand. Now, Mavis won't want to lose the four lodgers she has and have to advertise the rooms, so I'm thinking that if we – Lavelle, Cornwell, McCain and I – were to suggest that, should the food not improve, we'll be looking to live elsewhere, she might decide she'd better employ another proper cook. No offence meant, girls. The solution could be as simple as that. Then Janette can resume her education and you, Sarah, can go and sew at Miss Fraser's parents' house. Shame Nancy took a huff and left, but that was hardly surprising. Anyway, we need to get back to the glory days of her style of cooking, and I'm thinking Mavis might need to learn a lesson. There are four people paying her to live in this house – she can't possibly have no money to pay a cook or buy good food.'

'What if she doesn't agree?' asked Joe, gloomily.

'Well, we could always carry out our threat and leave,' Mr Armstrong said. He didn't sound as if he would mind, but then there must be more comfortable boarding houses. 'Mr McCain might not want to go, at his time of life, but I expect Lavelle and Cornwell will make a stand. It won't come to that anyway. Mavis will see reason long before then.'

'But if she doesn't, would you really do that for us?' worried Sarah.

'No,' said Mr Armstrong, 'but I'd do it for some good food. What benefits one, benefits all, see? Right, well, I need to get on, but I'll have a word with the others and no doubt you'll soon learn how we fared.'

'Oh, thank you, Mr Armstrong,' said Janette. 'I might even be able to get back to school while there's still time to catch up.'

'Let's hope so.'

Andrew Armstrong got up and left then.

'I must be off home, too,' said Rachel.

'Not by yourself,' Joe replied. 'It's dark now. I'll see you safely home.'

'No, really, Joe, it's not necessary.'

'Rachel Fraser, for such a brainbox you can be daft sometimes,' he said. 'C'mon, get your coat on and let's get out before Mavis finds us gathered here and suspects a plot.'

'Do you think Andrew Armstrong *will* threaten to leave?' asked Joe, as he walked along in the autumn cold beside Rachel, each clutching a torch as the Scarstone street-lights didn't extend as far as the Edge.

'He said so, but it would be only because he's got his own agenda,' said Rachel. 'He's not the sort to die on the barricade of someone else's uprising, I can tell that

163

even now. But, provided what you want is the same as what he wants, I think he'll be an ally.'

'I hardly know him,' said Joe. 'You seem to have got an idea of him, though.'

'What are the others like?'

'Mavis always sneers about them, but the girls like them,' said Joe. 'Mr McCain is old and deaf, but he's no bother until you get tired of shouting. Percy Lavelle doesn't mind what he says but he takes the sting out by wrapping it up in a funny way. Richard Cornwell is a good, quiet sort, damaged in the war.' Joe touched the side of his head. 'He's a salesman – encyclopaedias, I think – but when he left the army he had very little. He kind of hinted at a family somewhere, but I reckon he doesn't keep in touch. He's doing his best.'

'Shame if it came to a standoff and he felt he had to leave in protest,' said Rachel. 'Sounds as if he's struggled enough.'

'Aye, but he'll want to support the girls. He's got a soft spot for our Sarah. Anyway, Mr Armstrong doesn't think that's likely.'

'And what about you, Joe?'

'What?'

'You seem rather subdued, less . . . buoyant than you were.'

'Wouldn't you be if you lived at Over the Edge with that woman? I first saw Mavis in the George and Dragon in the summer, and I asked Dora Burgess if she knew who she was. Dora seemed to know summat of her and she made it clear she wanted nowt to do with her. I've no idea what she knows in partic'lar, but there's an awful lot to dislike when you live with the woman. Oh, Dad seems happy enough to be married to her – someone to fuss over him and make his life comfortable, to take on all the domestic stuff he knows nowt about – but she's showing her true colours with us now.'

'Why don't you just ask Dora what she knows?'

'We fell out that evening and I haven't see her since. I can hardly turn up at the dress shop and ask her about my stepmother.'

'Mm. Mebbe Mavis was just an awkward customer.'

'Aye, that might be it.'

They walked in silence for a minute or two.

'What does Mavis actually do all day?' asked Rachel with genuine interest.

'I've no idea,' said Joe. 'I try not to think about her. She must keep her accounts – if she thought she'd lost a thrupenny bit she'd be lifting the carpets for it – but as to how she spends her days . . .'

Rachel laughed. 'You're too generous, Joe. From what I hear, she'd be getting you or the girls to lift the carpets for her.'

'Aye, true enough.'

'So she's not managed to get her claws into you yet? I mean, you are still at Hardcastle's, aren't you? She's not bamboozled you into working at Over the Edge?'

'No. She tried to stir things up between me and Mr Will Hardcastle – he's the one that manages the shop – mebbe hoping to get me the sack, but I saw how it might go and I warned him. She'll try summat else, I'm sure of it.'

'Sounds exhausting, waiting for her to pounce.'

'Do you wonder I'm not as chipper as I was?'

'Poor Joe.' She reached out and gave his arm a little squeeze in support. 'Well, we're here, so thanks for bringing me home.'

They stopped outside the Frasers' house, where lights shone out with a comforting glow. For a moment Joe missed his old home in Keele Street so much it was like a bereavement. He gulped away his anguish and hoped Rachel hadn't noticed his weakness.

'It's no trouble,' he said gruffly. 'Thank you for getting Mr Armstrong on our side. We never thought of going to the lodgers for help.'

'It's easier to see the situation more clearly if you're not involved, and I only opened lines of communication, so to speak. But, Joe, do take care. It sounds as if Mavis is quite ruthless in her selfishness.'

'Aye, I will,' said Joe.

He waited while Rachel put her key in the door and gave a little wave as she stepped inside. Then, as she was closing the door, he heard her calling, 'Mum, Dad. I'm back.'

Again, he felt bereft: no Mum, and now Dad appeared to have given up being at all interested in the welfare of his children. It was as Jan had said; as if Mavis was a witch who had cast a spell on him so that he had eyes and ears only for her. And for Over the Edge; he spent much of his free time doing minor repair jobs but it was like trying to hold back a tide of decay.

As he set off back, Joe wondered about the Stepmother's tight-fistedness. He remembered the row, when Nancy had described her pay as 'a pittance', so probably there wasn't much of a saving in employing both Sarah and Janette to cook, even though they were badly paid as well.

Joe didn't know how much the lodgers paid for their rooms, but there were four of them, so Mavis must be making some money. What was she doing with it? Was she saving up to be able to afford to embark on a complete renovation of the house, or just hoarding her income like a miser? Or might there be something else she was spending her money on, something that none of them knew anything about?

Taking over his sisters' lives, treating his father as if he were her lapdog, trying to get Joe himself the sack – Mavis Swindel was a piece of work, of that there was no doubt. Joe felt himself growing angrier. He had to act before the entire Quinn family drowned under the force of that woman's will.

By the time he got back to Over the Edge, Joe had decided, when the chance arose, to have a little look around and see what he could find to help him to stage some kind of fightback. Perhaps he would find nothing but, then again, perhaps he would find something interesting. Mavis Swindel had already shown that she could employ underhand tactics to get what she wanted. Well, two could play at that game.

CHAPTER NINE

IRENE DUG HER hand into the pocket of her jacket and pulled out a slightly soil-encrusted handkerchief. She was suffering with a cold and this easterly wind cut right through her. It was difficult to raise your spirits and battle on when you felt . . . well, just a little bit wretched, but the key, she kept telling herself, was not to give in. It was *only* a cold. There were bedraggled flower borders to tidy and she needed to get on.

She pulled her hand-knitted beret – a present from Sarah – down over her ears and took up her border fork again.

She hadn't been working long when she heard footsteps and looked up to see a man – a stranger – standing on the path, surveying the garden. He didn't appear to have seen her.

'Hello? Can I help you?' she called hoarsely. He must be looking for someone, maybe about a delivery, although his clothes were far too smart for him to be a tradesman. Betsy Ramsden was out shopping and

Mrs Mallinson had taken the early train from Fettling to Ipswich, then on to London for a day out shopping.

'Oh, good morning. No, it's all right, I'm just having a look round.'

'I'm sorry,' Irene said, 'but this is private property. Fettling House isn't open to the public.'

How strange that he should even think it was. This wasn't one of those grand places with massive fountains and architectural features, which people could pay to take a tour round when the owner was away; it was just a largeish house, although rather a lovely one. More to the point, there were gates at the entrance to prevent people wandering in down the drive.

The man approached. Irene could see that he was middle-aged. Over his grey suit, he wore a townie kind of overcoat with a velvet collar. His black shoes were very shiny and his homburg hat shaded his face. He looked completely out of place in this wet autumnal garden set within quiet countryside.

'I know,' he said, smiling. 'I went to the front door but didn't get an answer, so I thought I'd just have a look. I didn't expect to see anyone.'

'Mrs Mallinson is out at the moment. Mrs Ramsden will be back soon,' said Irene, thinking it wise to hint that she would not be alone here for long. This man had a bit of a nerve, in her opinion. 'Can I help, or do you want to wait until Mrs Ramsden gets back?'

He smiled as if Irene were amusing him. 'Oh, I'm just getting the lie of the land.'

The cheek of it! And so evasive, too! 'May I ask why you would need to do that?'

'You may.'

There was a pause he didn't fill. Goodness, this man was annoying. And so pleased with himself, with his shiny shoes and smart city clothes . . . his superior way of looking at her with those twinkly blue eyes.

'Well?' Irene thrust out her chin, but her challenge was marred by having to wipe her nose again. Oh dear, she really did feel as bad as she must look. There was probably dirt on her face now, too.

And why does it matter what you look like, girl? Just because a handsome man turns up . . . And what business does he have here anyway? He could be a criminal, for all you know.

'Actually, Mrs . . .?'

'Miss.' Two could play at that game.

'Actually, miss, I heard that it's a very beautiful house, and that the garden is the best kept for miles around, with an impressive herbaceous border and a remarkably pretty lady gardener to tend it.' He smiled openly at Irene.

'Go on with your nonsense,' said Irene, vexed to find herself blushing, which was ridiculous in a woman of forty-three, and trying not to be charmed by him, trying not to smile. 'If you're not going to tell me who you are and why you're here, I'm afraid I'm going to have to ask you to leave. As I say, Mrs Mallinson is not at home, and I take it that it's her you've come to see. Although it doesn't look like she was expecting you. I reckon that's all the more reason for you to come back another time.'

'Showing me to the door . . . gate, I see,' the man said, not looking at all put out. 'Quite right. You don't want any old Tom, Dick or Hubert wandering about uninvited.'

'Tom, Dick or . . .?'

'Hubert. Hubert Cole.' He held out his hand. 'How do you do, miss?'

Irene found herself shaking his hand, somewhat reluctantly. 'How do you do, Mr Cole? But you still haven't said why you're here. I'm afraid I really should ask you to leave if you can't explain yourself. I mean, you might be a potential burglar, for all I know.'

He laughed heartily then. 'Do I look like a burglar?'

'How would I know? I don't know what burglars look like.' Irene was beginning to feel she was being played with and she was running out of patience. Besides, she wanted to get on. It was cold out here, and the sky foretold rain. 'Perhaps I'll just see you out and I can tell Mrs Mallinson you called?'

'Good idea. Show me off the premises. You can't be too careful these days.'

Irene pursed her lips and said nothing. She led the way back along the path, down some steps and then round to the front of the house.

'I can see myself out along the drive,' Hubert Cole said. 'I promise I won't sneak back in and ransack the place.'

'No, it's no bother to see you out, Mr Cole,' said Irene. 'It's what Mrs Mallinson would expect.'

They crunched down towards the Lodge and the gates in silence.

'Ah, Mallinson's Market Garden,' he remarked, seeing the van tucked round behind the Lodge from this angle. 'Is that your business?'

'No, it's Mrs Mallinson's. I deliver the veg in the van.'

'I see.' He looked thoughtful. 'And I take it that is your house?'

'It is.'

'Very pretty.' He was looking at Irene when he said this. Really, he was a very unnerving man.

'I keep a massive Alsatian for company and protection,' she said.

Hubert Cole nodded slowly, as if he believed her.

Irene opened the small gate beside the Lodge to let him out. 'Well, goodbye, Mr Cole.'

'Goodbye, Miss . . . You haven't told me your name.'

'You haven't told me what you're doing here.'

'I'm considering whether to buy Fettling House . . . if Mrs Mallinson is indeed selling, that is.'

'Oh . . .'

'Just thought, while I had business nearby, that I might take a look. I'm sorry to have missed her, but I'll telephone and make an appointment before I drop by next time. Maybe I'll see you then, lady with the secret name.'

'Irene Mayhew,' murmured Irene, but her head was full of the thought of Fettling House being sold. This was what she had dreaded. It would mean the end of her near-perfect life here.

Irene hardly slept that night. Mrs Mallinson was back late from London; by the time Irene thought it a reasonable hour to go up to the house the following morning, she felt wrung out with anxiety.

'You look awful, love,' said Betsy, cheerfully, kneading some bread on the kitchen table when Irene let herself in, having left her muddy boots on the step outside.

'Ah, it's just this cold, Betsy, but I need to have a word with Mrs M, if she's about.'

'I'll go and see where she is,' said Betsy, rinsing her hands and then disappearing through the door to the hall.

A minute later: 'Go on through to the back, Irene. I'll get the kettle on, if you've time?'

'Thanks, love.'

The flagged stone floor felt icy under Irene's socks. Mrs Mallinson had a merry fire burning in her sitting room, however. She was sitting on the sofa, *The Times* spread out beside her, and she indicated to Irene to take an armchair.

'Oh dear, Irene, you do look a bit peaky. Ask Betsy for some lemons and honey before you go.'

'Thank you, Mrs M. That's kind of you. But what's really the matter is that you had a visitor yesterday when you and Betsy were both out, and he said he was thinking of buying Fettling House.'

'Oh! Oh dear, I'm so sorry you heard it that way. I *am* thinking of selling – you know how difficult times are, and, honestly, what do I need all these rooms for, just me by myself? But I haven't yet instructed an agent formally, and I had always intended to tell you and Betsy before I did so. I did speak to a man whose wife I know from the Fettling Choir, but I thought it was in confidence. Well, it *was* in confidence! Now he's blabbed in someone's ear and – I'm afraid it can be like this, with buying and selling houses – that person is hoping to get in early. But Fettling House isn't for sale yet. What was this man's name?'

'Hubert Cole.'

Mrs Mallinson got up from the sofa and went to write it down on a notepad beside her telephone. 'Right, well, should he telephone, I'm prepared. I'll ask Betsy to bring in some tea and then I'll tell you both exactly how things are so there will be no more surprises. I know it's a lot for you to think about – both of you have your homes bound up with your work here – but I'm not rushing, whatever this Mr Cole thinks. I won't be hurried.'

When Betsy Ramsden had brought in the tea tray and poured each of them a cup, she sat down at Mrs Mallinson's insistence and their employer told Irene and Betsy together what she was planning.

'. . . It's a lot to take in – such a big change for you both – but now you know, you can start making your own plans,' she finished. 'It's a shame I have no children to give the house to, but that's how it is, and it would be foolish to become so sentimental about it that I can't bring myself to do the sensible thing. I'd hate to be lingering on here in my dotage, living alone in this big place, which has to be kept clean and warm, just because I was too silly to take the better way. I haven't yet begun to look for a new home, but I suppose I should start now.'

'Will you let us know how your plans are progressing, please, Mrs M?' asked Betsy.

'I will. I'll spring no more surprises, and I'm only sorry that rumour got out before I'd spoken to you both. Of course, I'll give you the very best references to take to future employers.'

'Thank you,' Irene and Betsy murmured.

They both got up then without finishing their tea, and, muttering something about needing to get on, they went back to the kitchen, feeling anxious and subdued.

'What will you do, Betsy?' Irene asked, sinking down on a chair.

'I don't know. I had thought I'd be staying here for a few more years, but perhaps I might be retiring sooner. It won't be easy to find a new job at my time of life.'

'I'm sure George will be pleased to have you at the forge. He'll be glad of his mum to take good care of him, I shouldn't wonder.'

'If there's room for me. It's only a little cottage and I don't want to intrude on him.'

'I'm sure he won't think that.'

'He might, Irene. Young folk, they leave home and find their own way of doing things. They don't want to return to the role of being their mother's child again, once they've got away from us.'

'Ask him,' advised Irene. 'Mebbe he'll see it the other way round: him looking after you.'

Betsy gave a little smile. 'I knew it couldn't last for ever – this place and our lovely lives here, but . . .'

She sighed. 'But what about you, Irene? I take it you'll look for another job.'

'I'll have to.' Irene blew her nose. 'Unless the new owner of Fettling House wants to keep me on.' The image of Hubert Cole, in his city clothes, passed through her mind. It might well not be he who eventually bought the house. He had been here on a recce and might not even like the place if he had a proper look round. 'Oh, but, Betsy, I just wish . . .'

'So do I, Irene. So do I.'

Feeling despondent and ill, Irene went back to the Lodge. There was a letter on her doormat – she recognised Sarah's handwriting – and, while she waited for her kettle to heat to make a drink of hot lemon and honey, she slit open the envelope, although with little hope of learning some cheery news to offset the worry of these last two days.

Irene knew Fred had married this Mavis Swindel, of course, and that Sarah, Joe and Janette were far from overjoyed to have Mavis as a stepmother. Now it looked as if their reservations about the woman were well founded. Sarah being forced to forgo taking over Miss Rowley's business and Janette being taken out of school – outrageous!

> *. . . But, not being proper cooks, we just couldn't measure up to Nancy's skills. The lodgers complained in the end – said they'd find somewhere better to live if the food didn't improve – and Mavis had to find a trained cook.*

Susan, she's called – not very friendly – and she soon got the measure of Mavis. The food is better now. There's hot water more often, too, which is a bonus.

But this led to another sly move from Mavis. She said that now that I had been sacked as the cook, I could do the cleaning instead. That I could at least manage that. She sacked Mrs Hastings, her old cleaner, who – admittedly – was useless but, I gather, cheap. Of course I said I intended to take up Miss Rowley's sewing business now, but Mavis went on about family and how I ought to play my part and I was letting her and Dad down, but if I really couldn't manage it then Janette could do it instead. In the end, I agreed to the cleaning job, which is paid even less than the cooking I was doing before – but only if she let Jan go back to school. Dad was furious, as Mavis had already agreed with him that Jan's education is a waste of time, and the atmosphere still isn't very good, but Mavis could see the value of the compromise: I work at Over the Edge, but Jan doesn't.

'Oh, but you shouldn't have had to sacrifice your life,' Irene said aloud. 'That's not fair.' She read on.

I know you will say that's not fair, but I'm just so pleased Jan's resumed her education. Plus, it's for the good of all of us if the house improves. Honestly, Auntie, we'll be better able to put up with living here if the place is at least cleaner. And we do have our own rooms we can escape to . . .

'Put up with', 'escape' – as if a home was somewhere to be endured, and to need to escape from. Irene sank down at her kitchen table and put her head in her hands.

After a minute or two she got up and made a conscious effort to pull herself together. It was a practice that had got her through the deaths of both the men she had loved, and of her sister, and it would get her through her current worries too, which were nothing like as severe. Sarah was exercising the same discipline, from the sound of it.

While she drank her hot lemon, Irene reread Sarah's letter. It was reasonably cheerful, considering, and this awful Mavis woman did seem to have been defeated on a few fronts. The bad feeling between Sarah and Fred was a shame. He had been a caring father to all three children, although Sarah had always been his favourite. From what Irene had gathered when the Quinns had come for their holiday, Fred had lost his way in life since Ava's death; he had sunk into misery and self-pity, and failed to see that his children were also struggling and needed his love and support more than ever. Mavis Swindel had evidently provided what Fred needed: a woman in his life and his bed, a home that wasn't filled with sad memories of Ava, and a stepmother for his children.

And what a stepmother, by the sound of it! She certainly wasn't providing anything the Quinn siblings needed in their lives.

By the time she had finished reading, Irene had made up her mind not to tell Sarah about Fettling House being put up for sale. At least not until she had to.

Fettling held such a precious place in Sarah's heart, with its association with her mother and the cherished memories of the summer holidays of her childhood. She had sufficient worries of her own for now. Let her not have her aunt's anxieties weighing her down as well.

Irene wrote back words of encouragement to Sarah, praising her for taking a stand about Janette's schooling, and reminding her she had choices about her own life too. Sarah thought the letter strangely reticent, as if her aunt had little news of her own she wanted to impart. But on the same day she received Irene's letter, she had one from Evelyn Rowley, which was altogether a stronger brew.

Dear Sarah,

I feel I must write, so worried about you am I.

It is likely that your stepmother has not told you what happened on the day I left Scarstone. Having waited for you to come to say goodbye, when I intended to bestow my best wishes for your future and give you any final instructions you might need, and having not had the pleasure of seeing you one last time, I suspected the inter-vention of Mavis Swindel, so I went to her house in the hope of finding you there.

Mrs Swindel answered the door herself. She told me at first that you were out, but when I said I'd wait for your return she changed her tale. She insisted you had decided not to continue as a seamstress and were pursuing a well-paid job in her boarding house kitchen. When I asked to see you, she said I had 'exploited' you for so long that, having your welfare at heart, she thought it fitting that I didn't see you again, even as I was leaving Scarstone.

I remembered the lies this woman told you about my business, and I could see that there is no end to her mischief-making and vindictiveness. I accused her to her face of lying, of being the one to 'exploit' you, and, having seen the state of the house even in the short time I stood on the doorstep, I doubt you are being paid decently. This is a woman who is not going to put her hand deep into her pocket to pay for domestic help. She was clearly intent on making sure you were not to be reminded that you had another, better choice.

She, in turn, made wild accusations about me and took to name-calling of such vulgarity that I can hardly bear to recall it. Then she slammed the door in my face. I could do nothing other than leave. I am so very sorry that our association ended like that.

You have your father to support you, although I realise his foolishness is the cause of your sad circumstances. I hope he will swiftly come to see what he has done and try to salvage the situation. You have also your brother, whom I believe is a good boy at heart, and I pray you will think, before you are forced to make further choices, of the welfare of Janette. Never forget, you are your mother's daughter. Ava outshone Mavis Swindel as diamonds do ashes.

Whatever you are faced with, Sarah, I know you need only gather your courage and you will find the strength to triumph. Remember that.

With my hopes and prayers for you, always,
Evelyn Rowley

Sarah had gone to read her letters in private in the sitting room, and did not hear Mavis approach. Before she knew it, Mavis was standing right beside her.

'What have you there, Sarah?' Mavis asked. 'I see the post has come. Were there any letters for me?'

'No, none for you, Mavis,' said Sarah, shoving Miss Rowley's letter into her pinafore pocket alongside Irene's.

'So who's been writing to you?' asked Mavis boldly.

'Just my aunt,' said Sarah quietly.

Miss Rowley's letter had left her shaken, and she knew she wasn't a good liar. She decided to change the subject and make her escape from Mavis's assessing look.

'I mean to start on the piano room this morning, washing the windows inside. Er, then . . . mebbe you can think about some new curtains. Those old ones . . . they're worn out.' Sarah felt she was gabbling and made an effort to stop talking.

Mavis continued to look at her with a hard, knowing expression on her face.

'I'll go and get started,' said Sarah. She got up and left the room, trying not to hurry, to run away. It felt to her that Mavis not only knew she'd received a letter from Miss Rowley, but what the letter had said as well! Sarah remembered that the doorbell had rung on Miss Rowley's last morning in Scarstone, when Sarah should have been – *had wanted to be* – there to see her off. Then, when she had next seen Mavis later that morning, she had been in a bad mood. This was proof enough of the accuracy of what Miss Rowley said, even allowing for any difference of opinion.

If only I'd abandoned the cooking and insisted on going. If only I'd stood up to Mavis . . .

She felt in her pocket, where the envelope was tucked safely down. *Gather your courage and you will find the strength to triumph* – Auntie Irene had said much the same during that blissful holiday. Courage, yes, but perhaps a little low cunning too. Mavis had deliberately kept from her that Miss Rowley had come to see her, when she had no right to do so. There was clearly no depth to which Mavis could not sink to get her own way. It would be as well to remember that – always.

That evening, when Sarah and Janette went up to bed, Sarah wearily took off her pinafore to hang behind her door and felt in her pocket for her letters, to show Janette. There was the one from Irene, but not Miss Rowley's. Maybe she'd put it in the other pocket . . . but no, it wasn't there either, as she knew in her heart that it wouldn't be.

'Jan, I'm just going down again for summat I left,' she called, and went off along the creaking corridor, where the wind thrummed and whistled, and the doors rattled, to go through the pretence of looking for her letter, on the ludicrous pretext that it had, in fact, fallen out of her pocket, where it had been tucked down next to Irene's, which was quite safe.

Seeing sense before she had even gone down, Sarah sat at the top of the stairs – in the gloomy light from the single lamp below – and considered what to do.

She could storm into the sitting room and accuse

182

Mavis of stealing it, but then Mavis would deny that, and Sarah herself had said that only her aunt had written to her: a lie that would now catch her out.

She wondered when Mavis had stolen the letter. There had been the opportunity on a couple of occasions when Sarah had removed her pinafore to sit down to eat. Mavis must have found both letters and quickly discovered that one was, as Sarah had said, from her aunt Irene, and the other from Miss Rowley, which she would guess told of her encounter with Mavis. Spitefully, she had removed Miss Rowley's, perhaps in the hope that Sarah would not have the address to be able to reply. This was indeed the case. Unless Miss Rowley wrote again, they would be lost to each other for good, Sarah cut off from her previous employer and ally, and Miss Rowley thinking that Sarah had no regard for her at all. That was typical of Mavis, a woman who could never forget a slight, even a justified one.

Of course, there was a chance that Mavis had kept the letter. If she had, she'd probably put it somewhere in her office. Perhaps there would be an opportunity to search and to get it back. It went against Sarah's moral code to go through someone else's things, but she had every right to reclaim her letter, and if she asked for it openly, Mavis would just deny all knowledge of it. From now on, she decided, she'd have to be more watchful, cleverer, slyer in her dealings with Mavis.

'What are you doing sitting there?' said Mr Armstrong, coming up the stairs. 'You look like you've lost your way.'

Sarah smiled sadly up at him. 'Only a bit. I'm resolving to keep on track in future.'

'Glad to hear it.'

'Mr Armstrong, I didn't ever thank you for insisting Mavis get another cook. You were the one who organised the lodgers' protest, so thank you for your help.'

'Just didn't want to die of malnutrition,' he said sardonically. 'No use being a cook if you can't cook.'

'Well, I can a bit,' said Sarah, stung by his bluntness.

'So can I, but it doesn't mean I do,' he said and, laughing rather cruelly, he went off to his room, from where, moments later, Sarah could hear him pounding his typewriter.

Sarah wasn't sure that she really liked Andrew Armstrong, although she knew Rachel admired his focus.

'He's very single-minded,' she'd said, 'so if you need some help dealing with Mavis, if it's to his advantage – or if you can sell it to him in a way that makes it to his advantage – then I reckon you can rely on his help. Just don't expect any altruism, that's all, or you might be disappointed.'

There was, Sarah was learning, something of a life lesson in that advice, especially at Over the Edge.

CHAPTER TEN

IT WAS A cold evening in late October, and Mavis and Fred had gone to the George and Dragon to celebrate Mavis's birthday.

'I think I can say in all modesty that I really don't look my age,' she'd said that morning at breakfast, plumping up her dramatic hair and sucking in her stomach and her cheekbones.

'Not a day over sixty,' murmured Joe.

Sarah looked down to hide her grin.

'You're marvellous,' gushed Fred, giving Mavis's thigh a squeeze while she pretended to be coy, and playfully slapped his hand away.

Fred's children regarded this with disgust. It wasn't just the embarrassing flirting; Sarah couldn't help remembering Fred's lack of interest in Janette's birthday. He hadn't made much effort over Joe's twenty-first, either. A pint at the Lamb and Flag, and a rather loud Fair Isle pullover, undoubtedly chosen by Mavis, and which turned out to be too big, had been the extent of Fred's largesse. Well, he'd certainly not forgotten a present for Mavis. She was sporting a new ring on her right hand, an elaborate filigree setting and a bulbous semiprecious stone within it. He got up from the breakfast table to present her rather showily with a large flat parcel, tied up with a red bow. It was a box of chocolate liqueurs, which she'd been dropping hints she'd like, having seen an advertisement for them in one of her magazines. Fred had gone all the way to Manchester to buy them on an afternoon off.

'Ooh, thank you, Fred. Do you think I need sweetening up?' She nudged him saucily, gave her loud laugh, and opened the box. 'These look so delicious that I can't wait. Shall I have a little taste now, just a tiny one, to see what they're like?'

All the chocolates were identical and all quite large. She reached her hand into the box, the light from the lamp reflecting off her abundant rings so that it appeared that she was wearing more shiny-wrapped chocolates on her hands, clawed out a chocolate with her long fingernails, peeled off the foil wrapping and popped the chocolate in her mouth.

'Mm, so rich and . . . ooh, very, very strong,' she said with her mouth full. 'Just how I like a man,' she added, then crowed with laughter. She pinched Fred's cheek as if he were a plump baby. 'You trying to get me drunk, Fred, you naughty boy?' She wriggled her shoulders flirtatiously, then turned her attention to her appalled stepchildren. 'No liqueurs for you two,' she said to Sarah and Janette. 'You're far too young for such grown-up tastes. But you may have one, Joe.'

Sarah recognised this as the kind of game Mavis liked to try: playing one of them off against the others in an attempt to sow discontent.

'No, thanks, Mavis,' said Joe. 'I've got to get to work.' He stood up and left the dining room without another word.

Mavis watched him go, narrowing her eyes.

Sarah and Janette also left the table then. They looked at each other as they took their crockery to the kitchen, but neither thought it necessary to voice her thoughts.

Now Mavis and Fred had departed for the George and Dragon, Joe had gone to meet Sally, the lodgers had eaten their evening meal and retired to their rooms or their sitting room (Percy Lavelle was working as usual on a Saturday evening, so the piano was silent), Susan had gone home, and it was time for Sarah to implement her plan.

Upstairs in her attic room she briefed Janette.

'I just want my letter back so I can reply to Miss Rowley and explain. If I steal it back then Mavis can hardly confront me, as it was her who stole it from me in the first place.'

''Course not. If she's hidden it somewhere in her desk she might have forgotten all about it anyway,' said Janette. 'It can be of no use to her. The point of taking it was only to prevent you from communicating with Miss Rowley, to spite both of you.'

'Do you have to bring Basil?' asked Sarah as Janette called the little dog to heel.

'Don't worry, he won't tell on us,' smiled Janette.

'He dislikes Mavis as much as we do. Besides, you know he's mute. He's speechless in the face of Mavis's awfulness.'

She scooped up the little dog, and she and Sarah made sure the hall was empty of lodgers, then they crept down and into Mavis's office.

The scent of lily of the valley was powerful here. No wonder Basil, with his sensitive canine nose, preferred to avoid Mavis. As soon as Janette put him down, he turned and went to wait for her just outside the door, which Sarah closed gently.

'Poor little scrap,' she said. 'At least his life's improved now you're here.'

'Mine hasn't,' said Janette. 'If it wasn't for going to school again, I think I might have flung myself off the Edge by now.'

Sarah turned to her in shock, although she'd spoken lightly. 'Jan! Never, ever say owt like that. I mean it. Especially as a joke. You've got me and Joe, and Basil loves you, too.' She didn't mention Fred; it wasn't at all clear whether he cared for his children any more these days.

'I think you mean *especially seriously*,' said Janette. 'Now, where to start?'

'The desk, like you said. You take those drawers and I'll do this side.' Sarah tried to set aside her sister's rash words and concentrate. 'Be careful not to move owt out of place. Just look through as neatly as you can. Soon as we've found the letter, we'll make sure we've covered our tracks and go.'

They set to work in silence.

It was Sarah who found her letter, in the third and

last of the desk drawers on the left. She drew out the envelope addressed to her in Miss Rowley's very neat handwriting.

'I knew it,' she said, furious. 'Stolen from me. Well, she shan't have it. Put that in your pocket, Jan. C'mon, let's check we've not left owt out of place and go.'

'No, just a minute, Sarah. What else is in there?' asked Janette. 'Could be all sorts, if that's where the Stepmother keeps her secrets.' She stepped over and knelt down to examine the rest of the drawer's contents.

A couple of minutes later: 'Who's Mrs Basil Swann?' she asked. 'Someone else whose letters she's stolen, d'you think?'

'Let me see. Didn't she say Basil was the name of her first husband? Mebbe it's Mavis herself and it's an old letter.'

'There's one way to find out,' said Janette. She opened the envelope, and drew out the letter. 'It starts "Dear Mavis", so it's her all right.' She quickly scanned the letter, then put it back where she'd found it. 'It's years old, and just someone writing to say how sorry they are that her husband has been killed. It's dated 1917. Now, you tidy up here and I'll have a quick look through this last drawer.'

The bottom drawer on the right held, among an untidy heap of magazine cuttings, a red leather box, which looked like a cash box. It was locked and there was no sign of a key in the pen tray on the desk. Janette shook it to see if it held coins, but it wasn't especially heavy and there was no rattle of metal.

'We haven't time to search for a key,' said Sarah. 'Better just put it back.'

'Yes, but let's quickly go through these heaps,' Janette suggested, turning to a side table on which Mavis had piled some cardboard folders, muddled up with shop receipts, magazines, old newspapers and lists of things that needed doing. She really was a terrible hoarder.

'Oh, Jan, do you think we ought?'

'No, but we're going to,' said Janette boldly. 'She stole your letter *and* she broke that china rabbit Mum gave you. She bamboozled you into skivvying for her and stopped me going to school until you saved me. She didn't get to be such a horrible person without having some secrets to hide, and it might be useful to know what they are and p'raps to learn how horrible she really is. We owe her nowt, Sarah. We're not on her side, remember.'

Of all this, it was the mention of the precious little porcelain rabbit that hardened Sarah's resolve the most, and, having left the desk as they'd found it, she turned to one of the untidy piles of papers while Janette looked through another.

'If we haven't found owt in five minutes, we'll have to go,' said Sarah after a while. 'We can't risk being caught.'

At that very moment they both heard the door handle turn and they stood frozen, horrified. The door swung slowly open. Basil trotted in, followed by . . . Joe.

'Good grief, you two,' he said quietly. 'Good thing I'm not Mavis or Dad. The look on your faces is a complete giveaway.'

'Joe,' gasped Sarah, 'thank God it's you. Please, don't ever creep in on me like that again. I was about to faint with shock.'

'Sorry, sis.'

'I thought you were out with Sally this evening.'

'I'll tell you about that later.' He didn't look happy, but rallied to join the search party. 'Now, quick, what have you found?'

'I've found Miss Rowley's letter. Now we're looking for owt that we can use against Mavis.'

'I think we should try to find out what she does with her money,' he said. 'She has four lodgers paying her rent, so she can't be that hard up. She's always complaining she's broke although she hardly spends owt. Either she's a miser or she's a secret spender. If she's a spender, I'd like to know what on.'

'I agree. We haven't long, Joe, so don't make a mess or disorder the papers. You take that little heap and work your way through. Be quick, but be careful.'

A few moments later Janette said, 'These look like her accounts. See?'

Sarah cast an eye over the columns of figures set out on loose-leaf foolscap in one of the cardboard folders. 'Yes, this side is out – Hardcastle's, Scarstone Hardware and other places she gets stuff from – and this side is in – the lodgers' rent. You're right, Joe: quite a lot of incomings, considering she claims to be broke. Hold on a minute, who's this on the "Money Out" side? "C", it looks like. What could that be?' She flipped back a few pages and saw the accounts looked pretty much the same every month, with 'C' regularly in receipt of money. Sometimes it was a couple of pounds, then more the following month.

'Well,' said Joe, 'she pays this "C" quite a lot of money, and every month, but there's nowt to explain it, and we haven't time to stand around here wondering. Now, quick, tidy up and make sure it looks like it did before.'

'Do you think Dad and Mavis will be back so soon?' asked Janette, doing as she was told.

'They'd have been back before now if Mavis had found out that Nancy is the cook at the George and Dragon. She'd make a point of complaining over some invented fault, then stalking out.'

Sarah and Janette could envisage this scenario only too well.

'Nearly done. Jan, off you go and we'll follow you up when we've finished,' said Sarah.

Janette ran off to her room, Basil galloping after her as fast as his little legs could move.

It took longer than they had envisaged for Sarah and Joe to restore the untidy heaps to the exact degree of chaos they had been in before. Sarah had just adjusted the last of the heaps on the side table when Joe nudged her with his elbow and held a finger to his lips.

'They're back,' he muttered.

'Kitchen, quick,' she hissed.

'Go in, shut the door and put the kettle on.'

'But—'

'Just do it.'

Joe stuck his head out into the corridor to see his

father and Mavis at the far end of the hall, their backs to him, hanging up their coats. He pushed Sarah across the narrow space into the kitchen, then went out, too, shutting Mavis's office door at the same moment as Sarah closed the kitchen door. Then he came down and into the open hallway.

'I was just making a pot of tea when I heard you come back,' he said. 'Would you like a cup?'

'No, thanks, lad,' said Fred. 'I think I'll have a beer. The George and Dragon is very dear. I can't run to more than a half there.'

'What about you, Mavis?'

'I'll have a beer too.'

'I hope you had a nice evening?' said Joe insincerely. No beer offered to him, he noticed. Not that he'd want to be sitting around drinking with them.

'It was lovely, dearie,' said Mavis. 'We ate the famous pies and they were better than ever. I think they might have put the prices up, but you can't fault the quality.'

'I hope it was Dad who paid,' said Joe. 'But I'm glad to hear you recommend the pies.'

'Weren't you supposed to be out with Sally this evening?' asked Mavis, a little too eagerly. Her eyes shone with interest and, yes – Joe was certain – with mischief.

'Summat like that,' said Joe. 'Now, I'll get you that beer, if you like . . . seeing as it's your birthday, Mavis . . .'

'So what happened? Sally's not ill, is she?' asked Sarah, when she, Joe and Janette were gathered in her bedroom.

'No, not ill at all. The energy of a tempest, in fact.'

'Oh, no. What's happened, Joe?'

'She said a friend of hers told her this afternoon, her afternoon off, that I was out with Deirdre Carson one evening last week, so she doesn't want to see me any more. She got quite heated about it.'

'But that's not true, is it?'

'I walked Deirdre home, but it wasn't how Sally made it sound. She was really het up and wouldn't believe owt I said. I doubt we'll get back together. She's shown she doesn't trust me – possibly doesn't even *like* me very much – and she said things she can't unsay.'

Sarah tutted and bit her lip.

'Will you have to leave Sally's family's employment?' asked Janette, worried now that the awkwardness she had foretold as a joke was real.

'I dunno. I'm hoping not. I like it there and I get on all right with Mr Hardcastle. What I don't like is it *here*.' He raised his voice slightly. 'I reckon it was Mavis told Sally's friend about Deirdre. She had a knowing look on her face when she asked me about my evening earlier. She wouldn't have spoken to Sally herself but, as you know only too well, she has a way of overwhelming folk – persuading them against their better judgement – in order to get her own way. It will have been a remark meant to be overheard, then explained in a certain way, or some comment twisted from a grain of truth to become an outright lie.'

'But, Joe, what were you doing with Deirdre Carson anyway?' asked Sarah.

'I just happened to see Deirdre outside the club one evening last week and we got chatting. She was by herself, waiting for some fella, and he was late. After I'd waited with her a bit, it became clear he had stood her up, so I said I'd see her home safely. I'd only gone there to have a drink with Ed and Dave, as Sally was busy that evening. Someone is making mischief and I reckon that person is Mavis Swindel. The way she couldn't wait to ask me about my evening, all eager smiles . . . I don't know how she's done it, but I'd be prepared to bet it was her.'

'But why didn't Sally believe you when you told her the truth?' asked Sarah. 'It sounds like you were just being kind. That's not difficult to believe.'

'Ha, too kind for Sally's liking,' said Joe. 'She's always looking over her shoulder to make sure she's the prettiest girl in the room, that she has no rivals, that all eyes are on her. For all she's so attractive, she does like to be reminded of it. Truth is, it can be a bit wearing. Anyway, she was more inclined to see Deirdre Carson as her rival than to believe me, although Deirdre isn't half as pretty as Sally.'

He sighed and – for an unguarded moment – Sarah saw real unhappiness in his face. She reached out and squeezed his hand.

'Sorry, Joe. Deirdre Carson is a nice girl, friendly and chatty, and mebbe that's what Sally knows she can't compete with. Good looks aren't everything.'

'Well, whatever it is, after this evening I'm no longer seeing Sally, and on Monday I shall have to go to work with her there, pouting all over the cabbages.'

'Tell Mr Hardcastle what's happened – your side of the story – and mebbe he'll have a quiet word with her. He's a good sort.'

'Mm, p'raps.'

'I'm sorry, too, Joe,' said Janette. 'I reckon Mavis is trying to cause trouble for you at work again, as she did when she told Mr Hardcastle you'd promised her a discount. Just make sure she doesn't succeed with her fibs.'

He nodded, but he didn't look at all hopeful.

They sat quietly for a few moments. Then Sarah said, 'Before you turned up, Joe, Jan said she thought that Mavis didn't get to be such a horrible person without making some enemies. If we have summat to use against her, mebbe we can stop her getting the upper hand all the time. Let's think what we've found out.'

'The first thing is that Mavis did steal your letter from Miss Rowley, just as you thought,' said Janette, pulling the letter out of her dress pocket and giving it to Sarah.

'So we know she's a liar and a thief,' said Sarah.

'We already knew she's a liar,' Janette said. 'We also found out that she used to be Mrs Basil Swann. We saw a letter addressed to that name, Joe, and it started "Dear Mavis". Of course, she did tell us that her first husband was called Basil, and this letter made it clear that he was killed in the war.'

'Yes, but then why was she called Mavis Swindel and not Mavis Swann before she got her claws into Dad?' asked Joe.

They all looked at each other.

'This is very confusing,' said Sarah. 'I was assuming Mavis's first husband was dead – that she was a widow – but if she was Mrs Swann, how is it that she was Mrs Swindel? Can she have had two husbands, and been widowed twice?'

'There's no law against it,' said Joe. 'Lots of women are widows. Look at Auntie Irene: both future husbands killed before she could even marry them.'

'Yes, but we know how lovely Auntie Irene is,' said Janette, 'while Mavis is so awful that you can't think it was all bad luck, her being widowed.'

Sarah couldn't help laughing. 'Jan, Mavis's awfulness has nowt to do with it. What are you suggesting – that she got rid of them? Seems a bit extreme, even for Mavis. No, now I think about it, I wonder if, after Basil Swann was killed in the war, she married Mr Swindel, or didn't marry him and just called herself "Mrs Swindel" to sound respectable. Whoever Mr Swindel was, he's not on the scene now.'

Everyone fell to thinking this through, but there were no conclusions to reach with so little information. Mavis had not lied about being married to someone called Basil – this was all that had been proved.

'And the third thing we learned is that about five pounds are paid every month to someone or summat called "C",' said Joe.

'That's a lot every month for someone or summat unknown,' said Sarah. 'It's more than I earn in a week for all that cleaning.'

'It does go some way to explaining why she is forever

saying she can't afford to improve the house, even though four people are paying her to live here.'

'If we can find out why she's paying "C", we might discover a whole lot of things about the Stepmother,' said Sarah.

'But how we can do that?' asked Janette. 'We can't just ask her.'

Sarah put her hands to her face and tried to think. She looked at her letter from Miss Rowley. Then she thought again about the rabbit ornament Ava had given her, which she'd treasured, not just for its prettiness but for that precious connection. She felt her heart harden towards Mavis – a hardening of attitude but almost a physical feeling, too, as if it were growing a tough shell, an armour against her developing any sympathy.

'I don't know yet, Jan,' she said. 'But I mean to find out all about Mavis Swindel.'

On Monday Joe went back to Hardcastle's, steeling himself to face Sally's sulks and her turned back. He did not have to face them for long.

'A word, young Joe,' said Mr Hardcastle, beckoning him into the storeroom.

They stood there in the cold, their breath slightly misting. Sacks of potatoes and carrots, and boxes of cabbages and apples were heaped all around, creating a pleasantly earthy smell that reminded Joe of the scent of Mrs Mallinson's garden when Irene was working in it.

'I'm sorry, lad, but I'm afraid I've got to ask you to leave. Your job here's done.'

Joe was astounded to hear this in reality. He had allowed the thought of his dismissal to run through his mind, but had refused to engage with it seriously. Now it felt like playing out a bad dream.

'But I've done nowt wrong, Mr Hardcastle,' he said. 'I know this is about Sally, but I can't think she'd really want me to lose my job over a misunderstanding. That's all it was, I swear to you.'

'Thing is, Joe, it's Sally's dad, Jethro, that owns the business. I'm shop front and he's behind the venture – puts up the money so he gets to make the decisions – and Sally's her daddy's little girl. He spoils her rotten, and she's learned just how to get her own way.'

'So she complained to him about me and now I've lost my job?'

Mr Hardcastle sighed. 'That's about the size of it. And I'm the one to have to tell you to leave, although I don't agree with it. Sorry, young fella.' He lowered his voice. 'I gather there was a bit of a scene on Saturday and, with missis no longer with us, well, Jethro only knows one way to keep Sally sweet. He won't listen to me where she is concerned.'

'But it's not fair,' said Joe. He knew he sounded young and petulant, reciting the lament of the unjustly sacked, the exploited and the underpaid down the ages, but it was true! It wasn't fair at all. 'Please, Mr Hardcastle. I really can't afford to lose this job. I like it here and you know I've worked hard. Please . . .'

'Sorry, lad, but there it is. Now, I reckon the best I can do is give you a good reference. You have made an effort here, I've noticed that.' He slipped an envelope into Joe's hand. 'Just show that to your next employer and tell him to telephone me here if he needs to know more. And . . . there's your wages in there, too.'

Joe was finding it hard to think straight, but he thought he wasn't owed any wages. He'd been paid for last week after he'd finished here on Saturday.

'I don't think I'm owed—'

'You are, Joe. Say no more about it. Now off you go and I'll see you around.'

Joe was dismissed. He unbuttoned his overall, hung it behind the storeroom door and went back into the shop. It was early yet and there were no customers. Sally was looking pleased with herself and arranging apples in a pyramid on the counter. She tossed her head when she saw Joe and turned her back.

''Bye, Joe,' said Mr Hardcastle. 'Good luck to you.'

'Goodbye, Mr Hardcastle . . . Sally.'

No answer from her. He went out, closing the door carefully behind him. He owed Mr Hardcastle that respect.

'Right then, miss. You've got your way,' said Will Hardcastle, 'and now I'm getting mine. It may be your dad's business, but it's me that manages this shop and now I'm short-staffed. So I suggest you stop playing with those apples and get yourself into that storeroom. I want two bags of potatoes brought through and in those boxes – now. Then you can go through all those cabbages that came in before the weekend and remove any yellowing leaves. And then you can wash all the muck off those carrots.'

'I'll tell Dad what you're making me do,' threatened Sally, thinking of the dirt and the single cold tap above the storeroom sink.

'Aye, you do that, lass. But I reckon you'll find you've used up quite a bit of goodwill of late, so if I were you I'd pace myself about making complaints, all right? You've lost a good lad his job. It's not some daft game you're playing, Sally, when you take away a lad's way of making a living like that, and you'd do well to bear that in mind.'

Sally went off to do as she was told with a very ill-grace.

By mid-afternoon she realised she'd made a very silly error about Joseph Quinn. It wasn't half so much fun working in the shop without him there. But by then it was far too late. Her pride would never let her admit her mistake to anyone else.

'Got yourself the sack again?' snarled Fred. 'Good grief, lad, you're making being sacked a career in itself. I'd have thought even you could manage to weigh out a few taters without mucking it up.'

Joe had spent the rest of the morning walking the streets of Scarstone, looking for another job, but there had been nothing. Eventually, he had gone to sit in the shelter of a dry-stone wall on the Edge, where he'd remembered the reference and extra wages Mr Hardcastle had given him. He drew the envelope out of his pocket and opened it. The reference was excellent and the two ten-shilling notes were beyond generous. For a moment, Joe had thought he might cry. In truth, the greengrocery job had meant more to him than his relationship with Sally Hardcastle.

Eventually, cold and damp, he'd dragged himself back to Over the Edge and gone to tell his father that he no longer had a job, again. It was late afternoon by then, and he had found Fred, whose half-day this was, in the family's sitting room, reattaching some loose tiles above the hearth. Unfortunately, Mavis was there too, feet up on the sofa, eating her birthday chocolates. She rather firmly suggested that Joe did not sit down but stood and said what he had to.

'There was a misunderstanding, Dad,' muttered Joe. 'It wasn't the job, it was . . . well, it was the folk I was working with.'

'You can't mean Will Hardcastle,' said Fred. 'He gets on with everyone. You can't mean him, can you?'

'No, Dad. Sally and I . . . well, we had a disagreement.' He paused and looked hard at Mavis, wondering if she would say something and give herself away, or if he was going to have to accuse her. 'That is, she—'

'That's right, you blame the woman!' said Mavis, but lightly, almost as if she thought she was making a joke. 'Isn't that what Adam did in the Bible story? "It was the woman's fault"? Really, Joe, can't you do better than trot out those tired old excuses? It's not the first time you've been asked to leave, is it?'

Joe was suddenly furious and took a step towards

her so that he towered over her. For a second he was gratified to see a flash of alarm in her eyes, and she put her feet down and sat up properly on the sofa. 'It wasn't like that, and you know it, Mavis. You know exactly what Sally thought because you as good as told her. It's your fault I've got the sack and it's what you wanted all along.'

'What! I don't know what you're talking about, Joe. How could I have done that? Why would I have got you the boot?'

'Don't speak to Mavis like that,' snapped Fred, but Mavis and Joe were having their own conversation now and they ignored him.

'For the same reason you made Sarah give up the sewing business before she'd even taken it up when Miss Rowley left. For the same reason you took Jan out of school, although you knew because she told you – because she *told* you, Mavis – that she wanted to stay on and take her exams. But no, you just rode roughshod over them both.'

'I did not. I could see the way it was going to go with the sewing—'

'Sarah had a choice, Mavis, and you took it away from her. Jan had made her choice, but you still took her out of school until the lodgers complained about the food and Sarah bargained with you and agreed to be your skivvy if you let Jan return to school.'

'It wasn't like that at all!' said Mavis, looking affronted. 'And what has that to do with your job at Hardcastle's?'

Joe put his hands to his face, as if to hold in an

explosion of temper. Had the woman no shame – getting him the sack and now playing the innocent?

'Because, you stupid woman, you want me to work here, too! It's obvious!'

'Don't you dare call Mavis a stupid woman,' yelled Fred.

'I expect she's been called worse,' Joe retorted, turning his attention back to Mavis. 'You've taken over Sarah's life, and Dad's, and now you're trying to take over mine as well, so that all I have left is Over the bloomin' Edge.'

'What are you talking about?' barked Fred.

'You! Spending all your spare time mending stuff and fixing things.'

'It's my home and it needs fixing,' said Fred.

'It is now. It used to be just Mavis's and it needed fixing and now you're damn well fixing it – for free! Your life has been taken over, just as Sarah's has. You're all Mavis's servants.'

'Ooh, how could you?' gasped Mavis, her bejewelled hand fluttering to her breast. 'Such lies! How can you even think such things about me when all I want is for us all to be together, as a family, in my home? I know nothing about why you were sacked, Joe. How you can even think it had anything to do with me is a mystery. But I can see you're very angry at the injustice of it all and I'm prepared to forget your . . . your accusations. There will always be a home for you here, Joe, and I will always find you paid work here, should you need it. You're my stepson and I love you like my own. I can't do more than that.'

Fred got up and came to put his arm around Mavis.

'You see what a generous woman she is. And there's you, shouting about and slinging accusations and lies—'

'No, Dad. They're not lies. It's all true and you're too blind to see it.'

'How dare you?' said Fred. 'Get out before I throw you out, you waster. Mavis has been nowt but kind, and this is how you repay her. You're behaving like . . . well, it's like you've gone raving mad.'

'It's the shock of losing another job,' said Mavis mournfully. 'I'm not taking it personally, Fred. I can see the poor boy is suffering.'

'I'm going,' said Joe. 'I've lost my job at Hardcastle's because of you, Mavis, but you shan't take owt else from me. I'll never work for you.'

'Get out!' yelled Fred, making a move towards Joe to throw him from the room.

Without another word Joe turned and left, slamming the door as hard as he could.

Sarah was in the hall with Janette, just home from school, alerted by the raised voices.

'Joe, what's going on?' Sarah said, hurrying after him as he took the stairs two at a time, Janette racing behind her. They followed Joe to his room, where he grabbed his duffel bag and started stuffing some of his belongings into it.

'I'm leaving. I can't stand that woman and the way she's taken in Dad any longer.'

'What! Oh, Joe, please. Don't go. Did Mr Hardcastle give you the sack? I know it's unfair but you can get another job – you've always been all right in the past. Please, Joe,' Sarah pleaded.

'No, I won't be all right, not if I stay here. Not if that woman has her way. My life will never be my own if I let her get her claws into me. Look at how things are here. Look at what you've become. You had a little business all lined up and now you're her servant – her skivvy – and that's what will happen to me, and to Jan in the end.'

Tears rushed to Sarah's eyes and Janette was openly sobbing, 'Please don't say that, Joe. Please don't . . . please stay . . .'

'Sorry, sis, but I have to go. Look after each other.' He enveloped them in a hug, both together, then pulled them off as they clung to him. Then he grabbed his bag and bounded out of the room and down the stairs.

Sarah rushed after him, distraught.

'Joe! Please, come back. Please . . . don't leave us.'

For a moment he hesitated at the front door, his hand on the handle, his back to her. Then he opened it, stepped out, and pulled it firmly to behind him.

CHAPTER ELEVEN

NEITHER FRED NOR Mavis mentioned Joe's name in Sarah or Janette's hearing, but his absence loomed large in the girls' lives. Days passed and they heard nothing from him, although Janette, on her return from school, always greeted Sarah with, 'Any news from Joe?' The girls avoided Fred and Mavis as much as they could, sickened that Mavis had engineered his sacking and that Fred had not stood up for him. It was almost as if Joe, and not Sarah, had been the glue that had held the family together since Ava's death, and now the fractures between them were widening with every passing day. Fred tended to be a bit shifty with his daughters these days. Nothing was said, but Sarah thought her father was ashamed of himself. His attention was all for Mavis, as if he had had to choose between his second wife and his children. Sarah and Janette were saddened by this, remembering the happy family they had once been, when Ava was alive. Now Sarah could hardly make the effort to address him or Mavis politely, and sometimes she just pretended she hadn't heard when they spoke to her.

Janette became quieter and sad-looking, and after school she was often at her friend Lorna's house, where they did their homework together and then Janette stayed for her tea. Sarah was glad of Janette's friendship with the funny, giggly Lorna, but with winter approaching, Over the Edge grew quieter, colder and darker, and, for Sarah, quite lonely.

She wrote to Miss Rowley, explaining that Mavis had stolen her letter just to spite them both, and that she deeply regretted not standing up to Mavis on the day Miss Rowley had left.

'I shall always be sorry that I wasn't courageous enough to face down Mavis Swindel and come to see you and give you the thanks and best wishes you deserved,' she wrote.

She wanted to stay in touch with her former employer, but Miss Rowley had now moved into a new phase in her life, and with both of them aware that Mavis was vindictive enough to try to intercept Miss Rowley's letters, Sarah doubted that she would hear from the elderly seamstress again.

Now that she had been relieved of the cooking, Sarah found her role had become, as Joe had said, little more than Mavis's skivvy. The huge, draughty house was a magnet for dust, black filth blowing in down chimneys and through badly fitting windows and doors from the coal fires of Scarstone and Great Edge, cobwebs and fluff collecting in drifts on cornices and along skirting boards that had never been properly cleaned since Mavis bought the house. The taxidermy tiger in the hall, of which Mavis was so proud and which she insisted gave the house some distinction, was a breeding ground for moths.

'Mavis, you'll have to get rid of this disgusting dead animal's head. It's moth-eaten and decaying,' Sarah said one day in November, fed up with finding clothes moths and wondering how she could even begin to clean the shooting trophy without creating a toxic avalanche of loose fur and dust.

'Nonsense,' snapped Mavis. 'If you'd worked a bit harder it would never have got in this state in the first place. There were no moths here before you came. Perhaps, if you can't manage, I'll need to get Janette out of school to help you.'

There was no reasoning with anyone so ridiculously unfair, but Mavis had polished her tactics and had made unfairness an art form.

Mavis hardly lifted a finger herself to help make the place clean – just did a little light dusting in her office – but now that Sarah was tackling the entire house bit by bit, Mavis noticed what needed doing and would regularly inspect progress and voice plenty of criticism, expecting the impossible.

'Is that really all you've done this morning, dearie? If you can't work any quicker than that I might have to reduce your wages,' was a typical observation. Or: 'But I can see cobwebs hanging from that lamp. Really, Sarah, what's the point in doing only half the job? Perhaps I should pay you only half the wage, eh?' Usually the punishment for any imaginary falling short was some reduction in Sarah's pay, which was little enough anyway.

Sometimes Mavis let Sarah get on with what Sarah saw as the next most urgent job, but at other times she would issue instructions, then depart only to come back later with contrary orders. 'I told you it was the kitchen I wanted doing this morning,' or, 'I most particularly asked you to do the bathroom, so why are you wasting time in the ruddy sitting room? You'll have to do the bathroom now. It can't wait for whenever you might fancy tackling it, and you're a fool if you think it can.'

Sarah started to answer back. 'Mebbe you should make a list, Stepmother, if you're so weak-minded you can't even remember what you did say.'

While Sarah recognised Mavis's tactics as an assertion of power, she could see that everything she did in the house was an improvement, and it was only the very obvious progress that made the job bearable. Over the Edge was a wreck, but at least it was a cleaner wreck than it had been.

Mavis was, Sarah had come to realise, quite astonishingly lazy, and she would avoid doing almost anything herself if she could get someone else to do it for her, especially if that cost either nothing or very little. The only exception to this was her keeping of the accounts, which she implied took her many hours a day. In fact, when she wasn't taking slow walks with Basil, or out buying groceries, she spent a good deal of her time lying on her chaise longue, eating chocolates and reading magazines, as anyone going into her office would see for themselves; the management of the boarding house took hardly any of her time at all.

Susan, the cook, was friendly with no one and was at Over the Edge only as long as she took to do her job. The lodgers had their own lives, and Sarah felt it was inappropriate for her to engage with them other than as their landlady's stepdaughter. She feared that in fact they had even forgotten she was Mavis's stepdaughter, who had been treated to a slap-up tea a few months ago, and they now regarded her only as Mavis's skivvy. She cleaned their rooms and took their washing to and from a woman in Scarstone who took in laundry, so she learned a little about them just from their belongings, but the lodgers would never be friends, she knew. They would not want that, and maybe she wouldn't either.

The exception was Richard Cornwell, who was never less than gracious and quietly friendly. Sarah took to playing draughts with him sometimes in the lodgers' sitting room after tea if Janette was at Lorna's house. Fred and Mavis never enquired how she spent her evenings, or came looking for her, so it was possible they never knew. Andrew Armstrong was often busy working on his book, and Percy Lavelle tended to work late at some public hall or theatre, too, so Mr Cornwell was as glad of the company as Sarah was.

Mr McCain never sought the company of Sarah or the other lodgers. He was a retired businessman, Sarah learned eventually, although what the nature of his business had been she never discovered. He liked to read and he owned a lot of books – three-volume novels with elaborate, old-fashioned, leather bindings, which probably dated from the previous century and which always seemed to need dusting. He borrowed from the library, too, although Rachel said she knew him only by sight. Conversations at full volume were forbidden there, of course, which made her speaking to him at all quite awkward.

Apart from the books, which were heaped up around the place, Mr McCain's room was very tidy. Sarah wondered whether he was a widower or a bachelor. It occurred to her that Mr McCain might not have a lot of money left, what with being very elderly and having possibly lived for some years on his savings or his old-age pension, if he had one, and paying rent to Mavis. His clothes were old, but then elderly people often made do with worn clothes rather than buy pristine new ones, as if new garments that might outlast them were not worth the expense. Poor old man, he had an air of resignation, of putting up with reduced circumstances, she thought. Apart from the books, he appeared to own practically nothing.

One day Mr McCain didn't show up for breakfast, even at his usual late hour, and Susan was fretting about finishing her work and getting off to make the most of the morning before she had to come back and cook the lunches.

'Here, Sarah,' she said, putting on her coat. 'I've done the old fella his soft-boiled egg. He can eat that cold, if he ever comes down, but will you reheat that toast?'

'Yes, all right,' said Sarah. Even in Keele Street it had not been unheard of for uneaten toast to be reheated, and Susan was very thrifty. Perhaps that's why Mavis had hired her. It certainly wouldn't be for her charming manner.

It was a weekday and, when Susan left, apart from Mr McCain, only Mavis and Sarah were in the house. Everyone else had gone about their business.

Lately Sarah had noticed Mr McCain struggling to rise from the sofa where he spent most of the day asleep, or reading a book or the newspaper. It was taking an age for him to go upstairs, too, clutching the banister tightly and hauling himself up breathlessly one step at a time. His fingers were swollen with arthritis, and she wondered if, this morning, he was struggling to button his shirt or to tie his shoelaces. Perhaps she ought to see if he needed help. If he did, she would make sure he was aware she wouldn't be telling anyone else he was finding those simple tasks a challenge.

When she tapped on his room door there was no answer. The fear that had lurked at the back of her mind now sprang up to become a certainty. She took a deep, unsteady breath, turned the handle and went in.

Mr McCain was dead. Of this there was no doubt. He was lying in bed, in his thick cotton pyjamas, his sightless eyes staring at the ceiling, his mouth open, his face devoid of colour. Despite this, Sarah instinctively felt his wrist for a pulse, and found him to be quite cold and stiff. He had died alone and she was filled with sadness at the thought of that. Perhaps he'd had a heart attack, or some other organ failure. Sarah hoped his death had been quick and that he had not been in terrible pain.

Superstitiously, she opened the window to make sure his soul could fly free and then she went down to tell Mavis.

'Are you sure he's dead, not just asleep?' asked Mavis, looking impatient at being disturbed, as if this was a minor matter she would rather not be bothered with. She was seated behind her desk as if she was busy, but Sarah could see that the document she was supposedly working on was nothing more than a word puzzle in one of her magazines.

'Yes, quite sure. I'll call Dr Pritchard, shall I, and he can tell us what to do, how to go on?' asked Sarah, although she imagined the steps that had to be taken were exactly the same as when her mother had died.

'I suppose you'll have to,' said Mavis. 'I hope he won't want paying much. Which makes me think: next month's rent is due in a couple of days and I was relying on Mr McCain paying me.' She put down her pencil and stood up, suddenly all energy. 'I think I'd better get this sorted out before I've got McCains up to my ears claiming the old fella's stuff. Here, you telephone Pritchard and I'll go and see what I can find . . .'

She flapped her hand in the direction of the telephone on her desk, then strode out and shut the door behind her.

By the time Sarah had left a message with the doctor's housekeeper and then gone up to find Mavis, Mavis appeared to have ransacked Mr McCain's room. All the drawers were open in the dressing table, the wardrobe doors were agape, and she had his clothes laid on top of his dead body on the bed and was going through the pockets.

'Mavis! Oh, the poor man. Please, have some respect,' Sarah gasped in shock. 'He's hardly dead and I can't believe you're searching his pockets.'

'Dead several hours, it looks like,' said Mavis, not even stopping to look up. 'And I don't know what you've got to be so pious about. It's the rent that keeps a roof over your head, too, Miss High-and-Mighty. Is Pritchard on his way?'

'I left a message for him. But, Mavis, please stop this. It's not right. Mr McCain might have relations who have a claim on his things. He's probably left a will to say who is to get what, and I don't think it will be you who . . .' She saw Mavis had made a little heap of valuables, comprising Mr McCain's gold watch, his tie pin with a purple stone in it and some coins, and she faltered into speechless disgust. Then she gathered herself. '. . . who inherits his cash, his watch and his lovely tie pin,' she finished.

'Never mind about that. I know nothing of a watch and tie pin, and if you're wise, Sarah, you will know nothing of them either.' Mavis paused in her rummaging in pockets to give Sarah a long look, her eyes like flints.

'But it's stealing,' insisted Sarah, really wishing she wasn't standing four feet from Mr McCain's corpse while arguing with her stepmother. 'Please, Mavis, have some respect.'

'And you have some respect for me, young woman or, I promise you, I shall make your life a misery. McCain was a huge financial burden on me, as his landlady. There's been a fire in that sitting-room hearth just for him many a time, *and* up here. And the amount he ate! Twice as much as anyone else, although he didn't pay me any more than the others do.'

'Mavis, *please*,' pleaded Sarah. 'You can't just help yourself.'

'I don't see why not. Now, shut up, with your sancti-monious whinging. And if I have any comeback on this I'll know it was you who blabbed, so if you wish Janette to continue at school I suggest you button your lip, my girl. Now, it might be as well to see if there are any relations in the picture. Here . . .' She took up a worn leather writing case that had been on the dressing table, and flung it in Sarah's direction. 'Go through that and see if you can find any addresses or even telephone numbers. Soon as we've got him shipped off to the undertaker, we can get the relations to come to clear the room and then they can see about burying him. The last thing I need is any kind of expense over McCain's death.'

It was the following day that Mr McCain's cousin Bertram drove over from Yorkshire and arrived at Over the Edge. He was much younger than Mr McCain had been, but probably in his sixties. He looked tired after the journey, and sad but not stricken. Mavis introduced herself as the landlady, expressed regret at Mr McCain's death, which was genuine, although not for the reason his cousin might have supposed, but then left Sarah to look after Bertram McCain, saying she herself was very busy.

Having made him a cup of tea and given him one of Susan's scones, Sarah showed Bertram to Mr McCain's room and helped him carry his cousin's belongings downstairs and out to the car. The books were very heavy and the two of them had to make many trips.

'Oh, you mustn't forget these,' Sarah said finally, pulling a brown paper bag from the pocket of her skirt as Bertram stowed the last of Mr McCain's things in his car, which looked worryingly low to the ground with the weight of the books. 'I put them in a safe place for you.'

Bertram McCain looked at her curiously. 'And did you need to keep them safely, eh, lass? Are there thieves about?' he asked. 'I'd have thought it was sufficient to just lock the room door. I told you I'd be on my way today when you telephoned me.'

'I reckon they would have been safe really, but I wanted to be quite sure,' said Sarah, handing over the watch and tie pin, which she'd surreptitiously retrieved from a bowl of bulldog clips and elastic bands on the mantelpiece in Mavis's office, having seen where Mavis had put them. There would be hell to pay now, but Sarah was disgusted at the thought of robbing the dead, like some battlefield mercenary looting the corpses.

'I'm sorry about your cousin,' she said, shaking Bertram McCain's hand as he prepared to leave, having pocketed the valuables. 'He was a nice man, very . . . polite,' she finished. Now she thought about it, she knew only that Mr McCain was elderly and deaf, bookish and gloomy – nothing else. She wished she had got to know him better, but when conversation had to be shouted, all subtlety of the interchange was lost in the volume and the energy it took. It was too late for regrets now, however.

'His was a sad life,' said Bertram, donning his hat and gloves in preparation to depart, 'but he's with his beloved now.' He leaned back against the car and looked up at the gaunt façade of Over the Edge, as if he couldn't believe his cousin's life had ended in this unprepossessing house, the wind gusting around and Sarah shivering in her indoor clothes. 'For all he was just an ordinary Yorkshireman, he made a fortune by hard work and he married well. Henrietta, his wife was called – a landowner's daughter – and they were madly in love. They had seven children, but each and every one of them succumbed to illness or accident – diphtheria, tuberculosis, the Spanish flu, a fall from a horse, one was drowned . . . Then Henrietta died too, leaving Alastair without wife or children. He decided then to travel light through what remained of his life, although this was a good few years back – sold nearly all his belongings, and went to live in a succession of impersonal establishments. These books may look like a lot to you and me, but he had many thousands at one time and parted with all but his favourites. Eventually he fetched up here, where he lived out the last year of his life.'

'I think Mrs Swindel – that is, Mrs Quinn, as she now is – has been at Over the Edge for just over a year,' said Sarah. 'Mr McCain must have been one of her first lodgers.'

'Yes, and I believe it turned out that Alastair knew of the lady already,' said Bertram.

'Really?' Sarah was astonished. 'I didn't know that. Was that why he came here – because they were acquainted?' She tried to think of an occasion where Mavis had expressed any respect or liking for Mr McCain, but her mind was overwhelmed by the thought of Mavis searching his clothes pockets as he lay dead, and she could not think beyond that.

Bertram gave a hollow laugh. 'Not acquainted exactly. It was a coincidence, but Alastair was convinced Mrs Swindel was . . . But, no, I mustn't gossip. It would be inappropriate, especially after all the kindness the lady has shown over my cousin's death, calling the doctor promptly and putting me in touch with an undertaker of the right sort.'

Sarah could barely believe what she was hearing. Mavis had been robbing the old gentleman of anything she could lay her greedy hands on while his body lay awaiting the undertaker! It was Sarah herself who had made all the arrangements that were necessary.

However, she saw an opportunity had opened up to find out something about Mavis. She must think, and fast.

'Would it be to do with her first husband, with Basil Swann?' she ventured.

It was a long shot but it might somehow keep the dialogue open. As it happened, it was a bull's-eye.

'So he was right – Mavis Swindel was once Mavis Swann,' said Bertram. 'Alastair sat on the jury at the trial. That was when he was living down south. Of course, Mrs Swann was acquitted, and he himself was convinced there was insufficient evidence to show she'd definitely done it. This was years ago, of course.'

Sarah nodded as if she knew. She must not give away her ignorance by asking the wrong questions, but she could feel her stomach doing a swoop, as if she'd just jumped from a great height. A trial with a jury! So possibly a serious crime had been committed.

'Alastair had visited Lancashire years ago and liked this wild area along the moors. When he saw an advertisement for Over the Edge, the name caught his imagination and he came here only to find that his new landlady bore a remarkable resemblance to Mavis Swann. It was her distinctive hair that he remembered most especially – the white stripe at the front – and then the lady's manner, her way of talking, was just the same, he told me in a letter. Of course, she didn't recognise him after all that time, and he never let on he knew about the murder trial. He found it quite amusing to think he knew so much about her, yet she was completely unaware.'

'Yes . . . yes, a private joke,' murmured Sarah, thinking: murder trial! Dared she ask? She had to.

'So remind me,' she said, 'it was the murder of her husband, Basil, that Mavis was accused of?'

Bertram looked at her hard. 'I shouldn't have spoken,' he said, and he was less friendly now. 'It's clear to me that you know next to nothing about it. It was all a long time ago. She was acquitted and has no doubt led an exemplary life ever since. Now, I need to be on the road. I've spent far too long standing here gossiping. I'll let Mrs Quinn know when the funeral is to be once I've finalised the arrangements.'

He climbed into his car and shut the door firmly. The engine started on the third attempt and he drove out to the road very slowly, the car struggling under the weight of Mr McCain's books.

Sarah watched him depart, but he didn't look back and wave. She turned to go inside the house, deep in thought.

The 'Mrs Basil Swann' letter in Mavis's desk had offered commiserations on Basil Swann being killed in the war, so how had she been tried for his murder? Yet Mr McCain had been at the trial and later recognised Mavis because of her distinctive hair. And she had certainly been Mrs Basil Swann, so it was without doubt the same woman.

Mr McCain had known about it all along and never told anyone at Over the Edge – just kept the knowledge to himself, as if it were a private and rather peculiar joke. There was much to think about here.

Another thing Sarah had learned, of minor interest, was that Mr McCain was called Alastair. No one had ever called him that. Sadly, it was possible that no one knew.

Of course, Mavis soon discovered that Mr McCain's watch and tie pin were missing from where she had left them in the bowl on her office mantelpiece, removed from among the dead lodger's belongings, but yet immediately to hand, possibly to cover herself if his cousin Bertram asked about them. Then she could just hand them over as if that was what she had meant to do all along.

'Now, I want a word with you,' she said, as Sarah went to wash up the tea things. Mavis grabbed her by the arm and pulled her roughly across the narrow corridor from the kitchen into her office.

'Where are the watch and tie pin that were in that bowl?' she demanded.

'I gave them to Mr McCain's cousin, of course,' Sarah said. 'Bertram McCain came to collect *all* Mr McCain's belongings, and those were a part of them.'

'But I told—'

'No, Mavis! Those things belong rightfully to Mr McCain's cousin, not to you to take instead of rent for an unoccupied room. That would be his loss, and Over the Edge is nowt to do with him.'

'You'd better not be making a habit of telling me what to do, Miss High-and-Mighty. Next month's rent is due from all the lodgers in a day or two, and I was expecting four payments, not three. I can't manage on less. I'm running the place on a shoestring as it is. What the hell am I supposed to do now?'

'You'll have to get another lodger,' said Sarah, trying to be reasonable, trying to keep calm, not get upset by her stepmother's vicious temper and desperate tone.

'And how am I to do that when it's practically

Christmas? I had the watch and the tie pin right here and I know just who would buy them. Do you ever think before you act, you imbecile?' Mavis raised her hand and delivered a sharp slap to Sarah's face. 'I have expenses to meet . . . bills to pay and I can't manage!' she yelled. 'It's all your fault!' She stamped her foot like a stroppy toddler.

Sarah took a step away in shock, her cold hand to her stinging cheek.

'Mavis!' she gasped. 'That was . . . mean. Mean and uncalled for.'

'It was deserved, more like,' retorted Mavis, bunching her fists and looking fit to explode.

This was a new side to the Stepmother. Usually she was sly and calculating; now she was violent and panic-stricken. If what Sarah had pieced together from Bertram McCain's indiscretion was true, Mavis had been on trial for murdering her husband. Although she had been found innocent, that was a charge so horrible, so serious, that Sarah thought it was impossible simply to brush it aside and forget.

It was time for her to talk Mavis down before she . . . grabbed the paper knife and stabbed Sarah through the heart . . . or brained her with that paperweight . . .

C'mon, lass, pull yourself together. You're being soft now. She's just in a daft paddy because you've thwarted her attempt to steal the valuables.

She remembered the money being sent every month to 'C', and she wondered again who he or she was, or what, and what was behind that. She *must* find out!

These regular and considerable payments had to be a drain on Mavis's budget and now, one lodger down, she was in a panic.

It seemed unlikely there could be a right moment to ask Mavis outright about 'C', but this most certainly was not it. Mavis was flashing her hard eyes, and her already pink face was puce with anger.

'Mavis,' said Sarah, moving her hand up to her temple where her head was beginning to ache with the stress of all this dishonesty, intrigue and drama, 'will you stop shouting and lashing out and just listen? Mr McCain's room is too shabby to rent out. Now it's empty of his things it looks terrible. It needs completely redecorating, but when it's done you can get another lodger. The sooner the room is made decent, the sooner you can get someone new, and mebbe charge a bit more, too. You say you want to make Over the Edge a little palace, but you have to put in the work.'

'What! What are you talking about, you stupid girl? How is spending money on decorating going to make it any easier for me to pay my bills in December? The most expensive time of the year! That's my most pressing concern!'

Sarah sank down on the chaise longue before she knew what she was doing. Mavis was exhausting and hopelessly disorganised. Sarah decided to put the slap and the shouting behind her, or they would never make any progress, what with the panic Mavis was in.

'You need to be professional,' she said after a few moments of gathering her strength. 'List what needs doing, calculate the cost, and balance that with what you have to spend. I'll help you, if you like?' Sarah was pleased to have thought of this. It might be a way to cast an eye openly over the accounts and quite naturally enquire about 'C'. Whatever Mavis said, at least it would be a start.

Mavis paced the room, breathing deeply and working her mouth in temper. Sarah sat tight and waited. After a few minutes, a calculating look replaced her step-mother's fury.

'All right,' Mavis said. 'Thank you for your offer of help. You can do the decorating. And you can run up some new curtains on that sewing machine, too. Nothing fancy, mind. After all, it's you who gave away the old fella's things and that's cost me. Your father can fix anything that needs fixing and Janette can help, too.'

'I can't do painting and decorating *and* clean the house, Mavis,' Sarah pointed out firmly. 'There's a lot of cleaning to tackle – you know that – and it's no sooner done than it needs doing again. It's either the cleaning *or* the decorating, but not both.'

'I'll hold the fort while you're busy in McCain's room,' said Mavis. 'And, do you know, you've given me an idea. "Charge a bit more," you said. Well, perhaps there's a way I might make up for the current shortfall in rent eventually.'

Sarah waited, but Mavis wasn't forthcoming.

'Well, run along and get started,' she said instead. 'No time to waste.'

*

Sarah remembered she had been going to wash the tea things after Bertram McCain's departure. Was that really only twenty minutes ago? She felt quite exhausted and not a little upset.

Janette was in the kitchen, just home from school, having returned straight here, for a change. She was looking whether the tea in the pot was still hot.

'Sarah, you look awful. What's the matter? It's not Joe, is it?' she asked.

Sarah told her about Mr McCain's cousin coming to collect his things, that she'd argued with Mavis, who had got in a violent panic, and that now the room was going to be redecorated for a new lodger.

The girls made fresh tea and then took the cups upstairs to the refuge of Sarah's bedroom, as they so often did. Then Sarah told Janette that the Stepmother had been on trial for murdering Basil Swann. The letter Janette had found said Basil Swann had been killed in the war. But the shameless way Mavis had robbed Mr McCain as he lay dead was so repellent that the woman was clearly capable of anything, Sarah reasoned, even if she had been found not guilty.

Janette could only agree. 'Do you think Dad knows?' she asked, her eyes huge.

'I bet he doesn't,' said Sarah. 'About that or about "C". Dad's never mentioned all this money being paid out. I suspect Mavis keeps the accounts to herself and never shows them to him.'

'I agree. And so that means there's summat about "C" she doesn't want anyone to know,' Janette reasoned.

'Which makes me want to know all the more,' Sarah said.

That night, unable to sleep with the howling of the wind around the house, and the creaking of the joists, and the tension of the argument with Mavis, and the cold of the room, Sarah's mind went over and over what she had learned, trying to work out how Basil Swann could have been both killed in the war and murdered by Mavis, or at least she had been suspected of his murder. Was that in some way connected with 'C' and the money being paid to whoever or whatever that was?

Janette had been right: Mavis couldn't have got to be the person she was today without leaving a trail of secrets and lies behind her. Perhaps today had been the first step in finding out all about the Stepmother.

CHAPTER TWELVE

IRENE HAD ALWAYS enjoyed Christmas-time at Fettling House. She'd worked there long enough to have established her own pleasing rituals about gathering the greenery to decorate the house and supervising Mrs Mallinson's Christmas tree being brought inside, with the help of two of Daisy Ellis's strapping brothers. Betsy, being a little older than Irene, had a Victorian sensibility about the celebrations and started her preparations enthusiastically at the beginning of Advent, with much mention of the way her mother used to do things.

George was invited to come over to see Betsy for Stir-Up Sunday, the day on which the Christmas pudding was traditionally made. There were precious childhood memories evoked for him, and, for his mother, the benefit of a strong arm to help mix the pudding ingredients. Betsy asked Irene to join them for lunch, after which the pudding-making, with its ritual of secret wishes and hidden charms, would take place and the Christmas preparations would be under way.

Irene put on her warm winter frock to go over to

the House. The weather had closed in during the previous week, and since then the flat landscape had been shrouded in a fog that seemed to penetrate indoors, too. Her outdoor clothes were never quite dry and, by the end of the day, her feet were often cold in her boots. Now it was a treat to leave the damp-smelling woollens hanging on the backs of chairs to air, and to dress a little smarter, in respect for Betsy and Stir-Up Sunday.

Irene was just leaving the lodge, her curly hair protected from the damp air by her felt hat, and her 'good' winter coat over her dress, when she heard the sound of a vehicle engine, and there was Hubert Cole's car, pulling up at the big gates. He got out to open them and waved to Irene.

'Good morning, Miss Mayhew. Don't worry, I am invited this time,' he grinned in greeting.

'Mr Cole. Here, I'll take this one . . .'

They each took one of the tall, elaborate gates and swung it open.

'Mrs Mallinson has asked me to have lunch with her. I hope we're going to have the pleasure of your company, too.'

Irene smiled. He was being charming; of course she wasn't invited to lunch with Mrs Mallinson. 'No, not me, although I am dining at the House, with my friend Mrs Ramsden, who is even now making the most heavenly gravy.'

'That's a shame.'

'The gravy?'

He laughed at her joke. 'Then let me give you a lift up the drive.'

'Really, it's no distance.'

'Miss Mayhew, will you please just get in? I can hardly drive off, churning up wet gravel over your best shoes and leaving you to make your own way through the mist.'

Irene thanked him and got in the car, which was very smart and shiny, rather like he was, and an entirely different class of vehicle from her delivery van with regard to the comfort of the seat and the space for her legs. The smell was better too: leather rather than leeks.

'How are you?' he asked solicitously as she tucked her skirt in. 'Is your cold quite better?'

'I'd have been a goner by now if it wasn't,' she said lightly. 'Thanks for asking, but it was only a cold, and that was weeks ago.'

Hubert nodded, put the car into gear and set off.

He cleared his throat. 'I'm sorry to have sprung it on you that the house is to be sold,' he said. 'I could see it was a shock, but by then it was too late to retract the news. I've been kicking myself for my clumsiness ever since.'

Irene thought it was kind of him to mind about her at all. Most folk in his position would probably not have given her another thought.

'It *was* a shock,' she said, 'although it shouldn't have been. Betsy – Mrs Ramsden – and I, we kind of knew this couldn't last for ever.'

'"This"?'

'Our wonderf . . . our lives here. We . . . we've got used to this place.' Irene looked away, anxious not to show how much Fettling House and everyone there meant to her. 'Mrs Mallinson has the good sense to look ahead and she wants somewhere more . . . suitable for her later life. I can understand that. It's a big house for one person.'

'So what will happen to you and your friend Betsy Ramsden when Fettling House is sold?'

'Oh, I expect we'll think of summat,' said Irene, not wanting to confide in a near-stranger that she really hadn't got a clue about her own intentions. She'd been pretending to herself that somehow Mrs Mallinson wouldn't sell up anytime soon, that things would stay as they had been for a while yet, as if merely hoping would make it so. She knew it was foolish and she should face up to the inevitable. Now Hubert Cole was back here, it could be for one reason only. It really was time for her to make proper plans.

Hubert had reached the end of the drive and pulled his car up in front of the House. He turned off the engine and looked straight at Irene in the silence.

'No, seriously, Miss Mayhew, what will you do? The Lodge is part of the estate and will be sold along with the House.'

'I know . . . I know,' muttered Irene. She opened the door and climbed out before he could come round to open it for her. 'Thanks for the lift, Mr Cole,' she said. 'Enjoy your lunch.'

She pointedly walked past the front of the house,

then round to the back door, leaving him to announce himself to his hostess at the front.

Annoying man! Do I have to be reminded on my day off – and when I was looking forward to a lovely afternoon with my friends – that the end is nigh so far as my job and home are concerned? He really is a clumsy oaf, making sure I know exactly how things are.

But perhaps he was trying to be kind, caring enough to ask. And he had remembered that she'd been poorly when they'd first met . . .

Well, let him enjoy his lunch with Mrs Mallinson and have a proper look round. There was plenty for him to consider. Mrs Mallinson's taste was for pale salmon-pink walls and cream paintwork, at least in the downstairs parts Irene had seen, and some might consider that a little old-fashioned in these days of geometric designs and jazzy prints in bold colours. Mrs Cole would no doubt have a view about that. She'd want to make some of the bedrooms suitable for their children, too. Strange she hadn't come along today, but then maybe she was a busy woman, a mother but also the kind who sat on charity committees and devoted her free time to doing good . . . Irene imagined a strikingly beautiful and extremely slim woman with slender ankles, wearing high-heeled shoes, the kind of beautiful shoes for which Irene herself had no use.

By now Irene was round at the kitchen door, where she saw George's bicycle was propped against the wall. She gave a little knock and opened the door, calling a greeting to Betsy.

Betsy was indeed making gravy and George was helping by turning the roast potatoes in dripping with a long spoon. For a moment Irene felt tears spring to her eyes that this would be the last Christmas, the last Stir-Up Sunday, at Fettling House, but she quickly blinked them away and resolved to keep cheerful and not spoil this precious day for anyone.

There was plenty to discuss over the delicious food: plans for Christmas; George's metalwork projects, which were always interesting; and Mrs Mallinson's guest, Hubert Cole, for which subject the three of them lowered their voices.

'I must say, he's a good-looking man,' said Betsy. 'Very charming, too. Introduced himself when I took through the chicken. Asked Mrs M most respectfully if she'd like him to carve.'

'Oh, expect he's used to taking charge of that at home,' said Irene. She imagined Hubert Cole carving thin, tender slices of chicken for Mrs Cole, and the little Coles all clamouring to pull the wishbone.

Betsy looked slightly oddly at Irene. 'He wasn't bossy, love. He was just trying to be helpful,' she said. 'Of course, Mrs M said she'd manage,' she added, smiling. Then she looked down and Irene saw her mouth twist with sadness. Everyone knew this was the last Christmas here. The knowledge was like a presence in the room.

When the food was eaten and the three of them had made light work of the clearing away and washing up, they began making the Christmas pudding.

Eventually the numerous ingredients had all been weighed and added to the enormous, buff-coloured mixing bowl. Then it was a case of each of them stirring until his or her arm ached, then letting the next person take over. The pudding batter seemed to weigh far more than the ingredients that had gone into it, but after a while it came together and smelled glorious.

'Right,' said George. 'We have to do the wishes just like Grandma did.'

'We know!' chorused Betsy and Irene.

Just at that moment there was a little tap at the inside kitchen door and Juliet Mallinson put her head round it.

'I know what's happening,' she said, 'and I'm determined not to miss out. And so is Mr Cole. Betsy, you don't mind our joining in, do you? I hope we're in time to make our wishes?'

Betsy was delighted. 'Better and better,' she said. 'Many hands, and all that, and there are certainly enough wishes to go round.'

Hubert Cole was introduced to George, and then he complimented Betsy on her delicious roast chicken, particularly mentioning the gravy, with a little twinkle of his blue eyes at Irene. He was very relaxed and friendly, genuinely pleased to be part of the Stir-Up Sunday ritual, so that it was possible to treat him as a friend of Mrs Mallinson's and almost forget that this was the person who might buy the house and put Betsy and Irene out of their jobs and their homes.

'I haven't done this for years,' he said. 'Mrs Ramsden, please remind me what I have to do.'

'Well, sir, each of us stirs the pudding and makes a wish for the year ahead.'

'But you have to keep it a secret,' added Mrs Mallinson.

'And when we've all done that, we bury the charms in the mixture.'

They took turns stirring the heavy batter. When it was Irene's turn, she wished with all her heart that she could remain at Fettling House. It occurred to her that each of them was likely to be making a wish on the same subject, and some wishes might well be contrary to others. She hoped that the strength of her wish would triumph over any rivals, and perhaps Betsy's was the same and would reinforce it.

When everyone had done with the hoping and stirring, Betsy brought over the charms, set out on a saucer, little squares of aluminium foil ready to wrap each one.

'The first is a silver sixpence,' she explained. 'The person who finds this in their pudding is guaranteed good fortune – I mean riches, not just good luck.'

'I should like that,' said George, and everyone laughed.

Mrs Mallinson was handed the wrapped-up sixpence and she pushed it into the mixture with the wooden spoon.

'The second is a ring, which means marriage,' Betsy went on.

'What if the finder is already married?' asked George.

'Oh, I expect it all works out for the best,' answered his mother vaguely.

She passed the ring to Mrs Mallinson, who pushed it into another part of the generous volume of pudding batter.

'The last is a silver thimble,' said Betsy, 'and perhaps this is the best of all. The person who finds this on his or her plate will have a life of blessedness.'

'Certainly the best,' agreed Hubert. 'No point being rich and unhappy, or married and unhappy. Being blessed with, say, good health and happiness would far outweigh anything else.'

He looked as if he might say something more, but hesitated and the moment passed, with Mrs Mallinson pushing the thimble into the mixture.

'Right, Betsy, we had better let you get this pudding on to steam or you'll be up late seeing about it,' said her employer.

'Six hours, it takes, and I'll have to have the windows open or the whole kitchen will be running with condensation,' said Betsy. 'Thank you for your help, Mrs Mallinson, and you too, Mr Cole.'

'It was fun,' Hubert said, and he complimented Betsy on her cooking again, bade everyone goodbye and followed Mrs Mallinson back out.

'No doubt Mrs M is now going to show him round and they'll discuss the sale,' said Irene quietly. 'She's definitely got him lined up to buy, and is pleased, or she wouldn't have asked him to lunch; she would just have dealt with him through her agent.'

'Perhaps,' said Betsy. 'But, love, she's going to sell to someone – you know that – so it might as well be him.

At least he seems a decent sort of a fella, and not some . . . *villain.*'

George laughed. 'Mum, what are you talking about?'

'Just being silly, I suppose,' said Betsy. 'Just not wanting the place to change . . . to be spoiled.'

'Well, I've been thinking about that,' said George, bringing over the prepared pudding basin and setting it down beside the mixing bowl, 'and I don't want you worrying about where you're going to live at your time of life.'

'What do you mean, my time of life?' said Betsy. 'I'm not in my dotage yet, I'll have you know. Hold that basin steady while I spoon.'

'Of course not, Mum, but as I say, I don't want you being anxious. There's room for you at the forge and I'll be glad to have you, if that would suit you, too.'

'Oh, lad . . .' She dropped the spoon back in the mixture and turned to hug him. 'Thank you . . . thank you . . .'

Irene saw tears in her eyes, and she almost felt the weight of Betsy's anxiety lifting.

'I should have told you that at the outset, but I thought you might feel obliged, or maybe you'd have different plans. I needed to give you space to decide what you wanted, but then, today, I could see you were worried.'

'You're a good boy, George,' said his mother. 'But I shan't interfere with your life and get in your way.'

'I am rather hoping you might be cooking us our dinner,' said George, laughing. 'Oh, Mum, we'll do all right together.'

Irene was feeling a little left out of this happy scene by now. Alone, and potentially homeless. No loving child to take her in. Of course, she was pleased for Betsy, but she felt a growing sense of urgency about her own situation. Hubert Cole was, possibly this very minute, envisaging himself and his family at Fettling House and deciding where he'd be positioning his bookcases and his sofa. He might already employ a gardener at his current home and, with the Lodge being part of the sale, he would be able to install this person – or anyone else he wanted to – there. This might even happen early in the new year!

She'd better stop hiding her head in the sand and get looking for another job. Christmas wishes might well come true, but she couldn't rely on them.

With the Christmas pudding gently steaming at last, it was time for Irene and George to go home. The afternoon was gloomy, and George was keen to set out before the lanes to Saxham Ash were pitch-dark as well as foggy. There were hugs for them both from Betsy, who was bubbling with joy and thankfulness to know that her future home was settled.

'I'll walk with you down to the Lodge, Miss Mayhew,' George offered, wheeling his bike round ready to go.

They strode along to the front of the House, where Hubert Cole's car was still parked.

'Nice car,' remarked George, quietly. 'You know, Miss Mayhew, I can't quite see him fitting in here, for all he's agreeable company.'

'No?'

'No. City man like him. You can tell at a glance. Mrs M is part of Fettling, singing in the choir, going to the WI, shopping at the local shops and doing business about the place with the veg. But can you see Mr Cole doing that?'

'Well, not attending the WI,' laughed Irene, 'and it's likely he wouldn't want to keep up the market garden. I doubt he'd need to.'

'Mm . . . Not short of a bob or two, going by that car.'

'Well, yes,' said Irene, 'and that's why he's able to afford to buy Fettling House. It's not going to be bought by someone who's on their uppers, is it?'

'No,' said George. 'I s'pose what I'm saying is that I don't understand why he wants to buy the old place. There must be houses in London, or even in Ipswich, if he wants to live hereabouts, that would be more what he's used to.'

'It sounds as if you don't want him here,' said Irene, looking carefully at George.

'Then I'm like you and Mum,' said George. 'You don't want him here either.'

'I've nowt against the man,' said Irene. 'As your mum said, George, better him than some villain.'

They both smiled.

'How are Sarah and Janette getting on now?' asked George. 'I left my address for Sarah so we could keep in touch,' he went on, slightly shyly, 'but I haven't heard from her. P'raps she's not bothered now she's back to her life in Lancashire. Or else she's busy with that sewing business she was taking on, and hasn't a spare moment.'

'Oh, George, I'm sorry you've not heard from her, but I'm afraid things with my nieces and nephew are quite different now from how they were in the summer.'

'Tell me,' he said, picking up on the unhappiness in Irene's tone. 'They're all right, aren't they?'

'Not really, love. The thing is, their father has remarried and none of them likes their new stepmother, Mavis. I don't like the sound of her myself, although at first I tried to see things from both sides.'

George stopped walking and turned to look at Irene, his face very serious.

'What's wrong with her?'

'She's just not a nice person. She stood in Sarah's way over taking up Miss Rowley's business, so that didn't happen, and she made Janette leave school against her will, too. It's clear she wanted them both to work for her in her boarding house, and for very little. Sarah made a deal with her to allow Janette to return to school, but now Sarah's nowt more than the woman's skivvy. She had such hopes, and in a short time she's been reduced to that. I know Sarah's trying to make the best of things, pleased to make the place look better – I gather it is in a sorry state – but this dreadful woman has taken over Sarah's life and it isn't right!'

Irene heard herself raising her voice with indignation. She couldn't help it.

'Why isn't their father putting his foot down with this Mavis? Surely it's his duty to look after his children.'

'I fear she's got him in her grip and he can't see beyond what she wants. He must be besotted with her, and mebbe Mavis has presented herself as the ideal wife for a widower, and the perfect stepmother for his children, keeping them all in check and generously employing them. Because she owns this big house he doesn't have to worry about rent, and with the house come these jobs, albeit lowly ones, for the children. He was never in favour of girls being educated anyway.'

'What about Joe, Miss Mayhew? I was sorry to miss him in the summer. Isn't he standing up for his sisters?'

'No, Sarah wrote to me that Mavis got him sacked from his job, and then Fred got in a fury with Joe about that. I'm afraid Joe hasn't a good record for hanging on to his job, for all he's such an agreeable lad. Anyway, he couldn't stand his father's temper and his stepmother's plotting any longer, so he just upped and left and no one has heard owt from him since. That was nearly five weeks ago. Of course, I said I'd let Sarah know if he fetches up here. I'm trying not to worry, but,' she sighed, 'oh, George, I just wish I knew what to do.'

'Have you told Mum?' he asked.

'Only that Joe's left home. I haven't wanted to worry her, what with the House coming up for sale. I haven't told any of my family about that, either. They've got enough to cope with, with this unfortunate marriage of Fred's, and they have such affection for this place that to think it's going from their lives for ever will upset them terribly. They'll have to know eventually, of course.'

George looked grim. 'So many things to keep quiet about. It's hard to be yourself when you're tiptoeing round the facts, don't you think, Miss Mayhew?'

She was silent for a moment. Then: 'I reckon you're right, lad. In the end you find yourself telling lies just because you're avoiding the truth. Evasions can add up to a completely false picture. You've given me summat to think about.'

They walked on and were soon nearing the bottom of the drive, the big gates in full view.

'I'll get the side gate for you, George,' said Irene. 'Oh!'

'Someone on your doorstep,' said George, peering through the gloom. 'Looks done in, poor fellow. Let me go first and see—'

But Irene was racing over the uneven gravel, regardless of her good shoes.

'Joe! Oh, you poor lad. I'm here, Joe. I'm here, don't you worry . . .'

When Joe, cold, dirty and exhausted, was inside, and Irene had built up her sitting-room fire to warm him, and George had been reassured that Irene could manage, George departed with a promise to look in the next day. Then Joe, cradling a cup of tea, told Irene how he had come to arrive at the Lodge, and why it had taken him so long to get there.

'I worked my way south, trying to save what money I had. I did a bit of this and that, some of it on farms for a few days, where they needed a hand. Sometimes I had only a barn to sleep in and cold water to wash in from an outside pump.'

'Farmwork must have been hard,' said Irene.

'Aye, it was, Auntie. I'm not used to wet feet and mud, and bending down all day in bad weather. Truth be told, I'm not used to outdoors,' he said sorrowfully. 'The window-cleaning job I once had was nowt compared to farming. And I'd to work every minute of daylight.'

'I hope the folks who employed you were good people,' said Irene. She couldn't bear to think of this slight young man labouring at the hands of some hard taskmaster.

'Some were, some weren't,' said Joe. 'I tried a bit of warehouse work too, but after a stint in the fields my clothes were too mucky to make a good impression, so indoor work was harder to come by.' He looked away, then turned back with a grimace. 'I even did a few days of helping a rag-and-bone man.'

'Heavens, Joe. You must have seen some sights there,' said Irene carefully.

'I did, that,' said Joe, then fell silent. After a few moments he added, 'The horse was nice, though.'

Irene squeezed his shoulder. 'Well, you're safe here now, Joe. I know what happened at Over the Edge because I had a letter from Sarah.'

'I'll never forgive the Stepmother for getting me the sack. She denied it, of course, but the whole business had her mean nastiness written all over it. I'd like to get even with her, Auntie. The girls reckon she's that awful she has to have some dark secrets in her past, folk she's harmed, but we haven't been able to find owt much. If we do, we'll be sure to use it against her.'

'Well, it wouldn't surprise me if she has crossed a few folk and made herself unpopular,' said Irene. 'And I certainly don't like her for the way she's treating the three of you. Fred's old enough to sort himself out now he's married the wretched woman, but look at you. This is no start in life! And poor Sarah, reduced to being her skivvy when she was looking forward to running the sewing business. But I don't hold with getting bitter and taking revenge. I've been thinking, p'raps I should go there – to this place, Over the Edge – and just bring the girls back with me.'

'They'd love that, but you can't. You can't take Janette from Dad if he wants her there. When Mavis first got her claws into him, I said I wanted to stay in Keele Street and the girls could live there too. Dad said Janette was too young to decide for herself, and must do as he said. And Sarah's still a minor as well.'

'I reckon if Sarah upped and left, no one would be able to stop her, but I can see I would be kidnapping Janette if I took her against your father's will. I can't do that.'

'And Sarah wouldn't go and leave Janette with Mavis. Mavis would just make her do all the work in the boarding house and she's only little and it would be like the end . . . the end of everything she wants in her life. She deserves better than that.'

Joe put his head in his hands then and cried – with exhaustion; for his sisters, and for himself; for the hard time he'd had getting to Fettling and the awful people he had come across, encounters about which he would never burden his beloved aunt.

The next morning Joe was up late, but feeling calmer, knowing he was safe at the Lodge. George thoughtfully turned up in the afternoon with some clean clothes for him to borrow. They were on the big side, but they gave Irene the chance to wash all Joe's clothes and put them to dry before the fire.

Earlier Irene had gone up to the House and asked to telephone Over the Edge. Joe knew the telephone number, of course, and Irene had to gather herself to face speaking to Mavis politely. Luckily, however, it was not Mavis who answered the telephone, but Sarah. She told Irene that Mavis was out walking her dog.

'Oh, Auntie, thank you for letting us know that Joe's safe. Jan and I, we've been that worried.'

''Course you have, and your dad will have been as well.'

'I don't know so much about that. He never mentions Joe.'

'He'll be anxious, love, so please tell him where Joe is.'

'Is Joe stopping with you? He won't want to come back after the row here. It was awful.'

'I don't know how long he'll be here, Sarah. I'll have to let you know what happens. I've other news, too, but I'll put it in a letter.' Telephone calls were for imparting vital information, not chatting.

'Thank you.'

'I've been thinking, Sarah, would you and Jan like to come here for Christmas? I gather you're working hard and deserve a little holiday.'

'Yes, please! That would be wonderful; summat to look forward to at last! Oh, but what if Mavis won't let us come?'

'I'll work on your dad.'

'He might not allow us to come to you if Mavis persuades him we're needed here.'

'Mm . . . I'll see what I can do.'

Irene sent love to Janette and put the phone down. She'd have to write to Fred and explain this would be the final Christmas at Fettling House, and that she'd like to give the girls one last holiday to remember. Surely he wouldn't deny them that.

As soon as Janette came home from school that day, Sarah told her about Joe being at the Lodge. Janette gasped in delight, did a little dance on the spot, and hugged her sister with relief, then hugged Basil, too.

'Auntie Irene's going to write to tell us everything. She doesn't know how long Joe will stay there, but I doubt he'll want to hurry back here,' Sarah said, keeping her voice down as she didn't want to say anything at all about Joe to Mavis. 'She's going to work on Dad to let us go there for Christmas, too.'

Janette's eyes grew wider. This was good news indeed.

When Sarah managed to get her father alone later on, however, and told him, albeit reluctantly, that Joe was safe and well at Irene's, Fred's reaction was in sharp contrast to Janette's.

'If Joe wants to go off like a refugee, then let him,' he snapped. 'If he had applied himself to his work properly, stuck to it instead of always slacking or messing it up, then he'd still be earning a wage here in Scarstone.'

'I don't think Mr Hardcastle wanted to sack him,' said Sarah. 'When I was in the shop the other day he asked most particularly about Joe; said he was sorry to lose him.'

'Then why did he sack him?' retorted Fred.

'You'd better ask Mavis.'

'What's it to do with Mavis? Sarah, I'm getting proper fed up with you taking an attitude with Mavis. If you can't say owt nice then I suggest you shut up.'

Sarah decided perhaps she'd be wise to take his advice rather than waste her breath, but she was more disappointed in her father than ever. Joe was his eldest child and Fred seemed to have washed his hands of him altogether.

She did not say anything to Mavis about Joe turning up at Irene's. She wanted deliberately to exclude her stepmother. Let Fred tell Mavis what he liked.

Sarah was bone-tired with stripping wallpaper, sanding and getting Mr McCain's former room back to a shell ready to begin decorating it. Preparing the ceiling was the worst job. Now she understood why Joe had grumbled about Mr Blake giving him the ceilings to work on. She felt as if her arms might just fall off with fatigue, and the dirty water ran down into her sleeve, or dripped onto her hair, which was tied up in a scarf but still smelled and looked awful when she'd finished. She wanted to wash it but there was no hot water that evening. Mr Lavelle had had one of his long soaks in the bath, ignoring as always Mavis's rule about the maximum depth the bath was to be filled, and so everyone else had to do without.

Sarah heard Andrew Armstrong complaining about this the next morning at breakfast.

'Really, Lavelle, you're not the only one who likes to get washed, you know,' he huffed.

'Obviously not, Andrew, but I do have to work in the evenings. I can hardly turn up to a recital in my dinner jacket, reeking of Susan's cooked breakfast and Mavis's dog, can I?'

Sarah thought this was unfair: Basil was a very clean dog, and tended to keep his distance from the lodgers anyway, and the smell of Susan's cooked breakfasts was no major intrusion on anyone.

'Well, I shall speak to Mavis about the lack of hot water – again.'

'You do that. But I bet you in a week it's back to enough for one civilised person.'

'How much?'

'Half a crown?'

'You're on.'

These silly and rather cynical bets on the domestic situation seemed to be the only link of friendship between Andrew Armstrong and Percy Lavelle. Richard Cornwell was so often away early in the morning that he was very much the outsider. Whenever he was at breakfast with the others it was almost a surprise to them, as if they had forgotten about his existence.

As the decorating progressed, Sarah began to dread facing the task of hanging new wallpaper, as she had no idea how to do it. In the end this suited Mavis, who didn't want the expense of buying numerous rolls of wallpaper anyway. Instead she went to Scarstone Hardware and bought some packets of distemper at a discount. The colour she chose was pale blue, which Sarah thought would make the room feel colder than ever, but she kept her opinion to herself. At least the walls looked clean and fresh when she'd applied two coats of the mixture.

Mavis came up to inspect the work on the morning Sarah had finished.

'It'll do,' she said grudgingly. Sarah knew by this that she was pleased, Mavis being an expert finder of fault with other people's work. 'If there's any distemper left – and I sincerely hope there is – put it away somewhere the damp won't get to it. Then you'd better measure up for these curtains you keep on about, and go and get the fabric. Choose plain so there's no waste, and try the market and the remnant shop first. I'll give you some money but I'd be grateful if you didn't regard it as the sum to aim for.'

Sarah set out, not taking Basil with her. He was such a small, thin dog and he felt the cold terribly. It was a bitterly cold day, which she suspected was the reason

Mavis insisted she should go to buy the fabric immediately. It wouldn't be like Mavis not to make her stepdaughters' lives deliberately as difficult as she could. These petty advantages over the girls were what she thrived on.

The market was held in the square in the centre of Scarstone, the library and town hall offices on one side and the George and Dragon opposite, set back to make the square.

Sarah was rummaging through the piles of fabrics on the remnant stall, all quality cotton from the mills in Blackburn, when she heard a welcome voice.

'Sarah! I thought you'd left the planet. How are you?'

'Hello, Rachel. All right; better for seeing you. I'd forgotten Thursdays are your day off.'

'C'mon, let's go and get a cup of tea, thaw out, and you can tell me all that's been going on.' She saw Sarah's hesitation. 'My treat,' she added.

They went across to the George and Dragon, which served pots of tea in the front parlour, in the old-fashioned coaching-inn way. Rachel took charge and had them seated at a very pleasant table in the window. 'Any news of Joe?' Rachel asked. 'I'm that worried . . . that is, we all are at home – Mum and Dad, too.'

'He fetched up at Auntie Irene's house in Suffolk earlier this week. She telephoned to tell me as soon as she could.'

'Oh, I am glad. I hope he's all right?'

'He is now he's under Auntie Irene's wing. I was relieved when she told me. Jan was beside herself with joy. Of course, I had to tell Dad, who either doesn't much care, or is pretending he doesn't much care, but I said nowt about Joe to Mavis.'

'Shutting her out because she got him sacked?'

'It's petty, I know, but it's how I feel,' Sarah admitted.

Rachel nodded. Sarah had always had a generous nature, but Rachel couldn't hold it against her that she wanted to score what points she could against the Stepmother.

'It doesn't look to me as if you've been having a very good time of late,' said Rachel. 'You're very thin and pale, and you seem a bit tired . . . and frowny. And just look at the state of your hands.'

Sarah had her hands folded in front of her on the table and now she pulled them away and sat on them. 'Just sore with the decorating, that's all.'

'I hope you're getting enough to eat?'

'Well, Susan isn't in the same league as Nancy, who I understand is working here, on the famous pies,' said Sarah evasively.

Rachel nodded. After a few moments' silence she said, 'Right, it's about midday – shall we see if there are any of those pies ready yet, to go with the tea – how does that sound?'

'Oh, no, I can't . . . That is, I haven't—'

'Enough money? Mavis doesn't pay you?'

'I was going to say I haven't time.'

'No you weren't. C'mon, Sarah, if you don't tell me, that means you're siding with Mavis, against me, and I can't believe you'd do that to your very best friend.

I expect she, er, fines you, or some such, for all kinds of invented shortcomings, am I right?'

Sarah nodded.

'Typical bullying tactics. She's making sure you and Jan don't run away like Joe did. It's her way of keeping you in her power. If you have no money, you can have no independence. Let me put my mind to what you can do . . . In the meantime, we're here, we're warm and dry, and if I can summon that nice man who brought the tea, we can have a pie each as well. With gravy. I'll pay. I know you'd do the same for me.'

Sarah leaned over and hugged Rachel. 'You're such a good friend,' she sniffed emotionally. 'I've not forgotten how kind you were when Mum died, and now this. I'll never be able to repay you.'

'We're friends – I don't need repaying,' said Rachel.

Rachel watched Sarah start to walk back towards Great Edge. Even now, her shoulders were slumping, and, as she turned to give a final wave of thanks, Rachel could see that Sarah's smile was beginning to waver already.

While they were eating the pies, Sarah had told Rachel about Mavis Swindel being Mavis Swann, a woman who had been tried for the murder of her husband, Basil, according to Mr McCain's cousin Bertram, although the letter she and Janette had found indicated that Basil Swann had been killed in the war. Both versions of Basil Swann's death couldn't be the truth.

'It might just be idle gossip, and all a mistake,' said

252

Sarah, 'but I wouldn't put it past her to have done summat bad.'

'Yes, I agree, it might be completely untrue,' said Rachel, 'but that woman has proved herself to be a menace. There's summat not right, summat that doesn't add up. Honestly, Sarah, if I make just one resolution this New Year, it will be to see you and Jan out of that woman's clutches.'

CHAPTER THIRTEEN

'CHRISTMAS IS MY favourite time of year,' said Mr Lavelle, playing a couple of lines of 'Jingle Bells' on the piano. 'I've got work guaranteed until the end of January, what with the pantomime and the rehearsals beforehand. It's great to be in entertainment in the Festive Season.' He looked very pleased with himself.

'It must be lovely,' said Janette, her eyes sparkling. 'All those glamorous actors and actresses, and the beautiful costumes and everything.' She liked to sit and listen when Percy Lavelle was practising, and today being a Saturday, she had the opportunity to do so, provided she didn't come to the attention of Mavis, who was always keen to set her a list of chores to work through at the weekend. Mr Lavelle brought a little much-needed lightness to Janette's life at Over the Edge, even though he could be waspish and selfish at times.

'I'll let you into a teeny tiny secret, Janette,' said Mr Lavelle in a stage whisper. 'The theatre isn't very glamorous behind the scenes, but then what in this life is? Some of the costumes have seen better days – I saw the

Dame leaving a trail of tarnished sequins in her wake
– but in this case the shabbiness doesn't matter for the
lead because the panto is . . . *Cinderella*!'

'I take it you're playing Buttons, Lavelle?' asked Mr
Armstrong, sardonically, his head just visible over the
back of a deep and threadbare armchair.

'No, Andrew, I'm playing *the piano*,' said Mr Lavelle
with heavy sarcasm.

'Perhaps Sarah could play Cinders,' said Mr Armstrong.
'It's a role I think she's familiar with.'

A silence fell on the room.

Andrew Armstrong looked round the wing of the
armchair. 'What?'

Janette gave him a furious stare, her eyes narrowed.
'That was not funny, Mr Armstrong. Please don't speak
of my sister like that again,' she said with all the indignation that only an offended fourteen-year-old could
muster. Then she got up and stomped out of the room,
slamming the door.

'Touched a nerve there,' said Andrew.

'Oh, don't bait the child,' Percy scolded quietly. 'Poor
girls, I don't foresee much of a Christmas for them, with
Mavis's greedy little hands grasping the purse strings so
tightly, and the way she has Sarah working like a navvy.
And it's going to get worse.'

'Why's that?'

'Because – ta-dah! – I'm leaving here!'

'What!'

'Yes, I'm moving into digs in Manchester. More central

for any number of theatres, and I can't afford to keep the room here and rent elsewhere as well. Reluctantly I'm giving up the very obvious draw of the Scarstone town hall and even the metropolitan sophisticates of Blackburn, and going where the lights are brighter.' He grinned impishly.

'Have you told Mavis yet?'

'Had to. Told her last night. She wasn't best pleased, but there it is.'

'You never said.'

'I'm saying now, Andrew. In fact, I'm off early, not staying until the end of my notice period. The hot-water situation has become positively spartan, and I think Mavis must have told the charming Susan to make sure I starve, what with my plate containing half as much as yours at breakfast this morning, I couldn't help but notice. Still, onward, ever onward, as they say in the chorus. So it's bye-bye to Over the Edge, and a Happy Christmas to one and all, ha-ha.'

He played a couple of lines of 'Christmas in Jail – Ain't That a Pain' with exaggerated blues rhythm.

Andrew Armstrong got up and went out, also slamming the door. He'd become very fond of Percy Lavelle, and it was now obvious that his feelings were not one bit reciprocated.

'Right,' said Mavis, going into the dining room where Sarah was clearing the table after the lodgers had eaten their breakfast, 'more bad news, I'm afraid. I don't know how I'm going to manage, in truth.'

Sarah sighed. This would be another of Mavis's schemes to try to save a few pennies while blindly maintaining the fantasy that Over the Edge was a boarding house of distinction.

'What is it now, Mavis?'

'Percy Lavelle is leaving. He's going at the end of next week. So keen to get away is he that he's not even staying out his notice.'

'Oh! Oh, no. I'm sorry he's going,' said Sarah. 'Jan and I like him. But isn't it a good thing for you that he's paid, even though he isn't occupying his room?'

'I suppose so, put like that,' said Mavis grudgingly. 'But it means another room empty. I'm two lodgers down and it's nearly Christmas. The selfish old queen hasn't even thought to consider his landlady, after all I've done for him. I tell you, dearie, I wanted to put on a big celebration, but I'm afraid it's going to be a pretty meagre Christmas this year.'

'I wasn't really expecting owt else,' said Sarah, deadpan. She hadn't said anything to anyone but Janette about Irene's verbal invitation to go to Fettling for Christmas. Irene had said she'd write to Fred, so Sarah thought it wise to wait for that.

She wondered what Mavis had done for Percy Lavelle other than take his rent, and why she was calling him a 'selfish old queen'. Sarah knew for a fact that he was only twenty-seven and he had a girlfriend in the chorus at the Palace Theatre in Manchester, which was probably part of the reason he was leaving Scarstone. But that was typical of Mavis: she would never let reality get in the way of her prejudices and ill-informed opinions of other people.

'Good. Then you won't be disappointed. Now, at least you've finally managed to finish McCain's old room and I have someone coming to view it on Monday.'

'So the news isn't all bad then?'

'He hasn't taken it yet. My point is, the rest of the place is covered in dust since you've been sanding down that paintwork. I don't know how you manage to walk it all over the house. So I suggest you get to work with the dusters and carpet sweeper and make a bit of an effort for once. Tell Janette I said she is to help you.'

It was no use arguing that Mavis had said she'd do the cleaning while Sarah was fully occupied with decorating. She would just deny it, and Sarah would still have the housework to catch up on. With Mavis, Sarah knew it was better to pick her battles, and an argument about Christmas was possibly looming. She'd keep her powder dry for that.

'Oh, and that bath has more tidemarks than a river estuary, and there's mould around the window, so I'd be grateful, dearie, if you would attend to the bathroom straight away. Then, as soon as Lavelle gets out of my hair, you can get to work on his room. Use that distemper left over from McCain's – make do with one coat if there isn't enough – and don't, whatever you do, throw out those curtains until I've had a look at them. I know they came with the house, but they should be good for a few more years yet.'

So, eking out the leftover distemper and rehanging

ancient curtains. Really, thought Sarah, that said everything about Mavis.

On the following Monday, a man who introduced himself as William Weaver arrived at Over the Edge to view Mr McCain's former room.

Sarah had worked hard to make the lodgers' sitting room and the hallway look clean and tidy. Mavis, of course, was showing off Sarah's work on the newly decorated room to Mr Weaver, while giving Sarah no credit, and gushing about the 'distinction' that she imagined the grotesque shooting trophy lent to the hall.

'Mm,' said Mr Weaver, 'not really to my taste.'

He looked at Sarah, who was just coming to retrieve the post she'd heard rattling the letter box, and raised an eyebrow, as if he knew she shared his opinion.

'I'll let you know soon if I decide I want the room, Mrs Quinn,' he said.

'Of course, I have other possible paying guests lined up,' lied Mavis, 'so you are running the risk of being pipped at the post, so to speak, if you delay too long.'

'I'll take the risk,' said Mr Weaver, wished Mavis and Sarah good morning and left.

'Well, I'm not holding my breath over him,' said Mavis, the very second the door was closed behind him. 'Bit pleased with himself, that one. Now, what's the post?'

Sarah handed Mavis her and Fred's letters and bills, and pocketed a letter addressed to herself. She had recognised Irene's handwriting straight away – and among the ones addressed to Fred – and her heart lifted.

'You can read that later, when you've unblocked the kitchen sink,' said Mavis. 'Susan says it's taking an age to drain and it doesn't smell too good either.'

'Yes, all right,' said Sarah, and went into the kitchen to read her letter in peace.

The tone of the last letter from Irene had been a little buttoned up, as if she had news she didn't want to impart. Now Sarah learned why.

Dear Sarah,

It was wonderful to speak to you last week and impart the good news about Joe. He was cold and tired when he arrived, but he's looking better every day now. He's borrowed an old bicycle from a shed at the House and is taking himself off to work with George at the forge each morning. He seems to like the work and it's clearly doing him a lot of good to be useful and learn something new.

I've written to your dad to ask him if you and Jan can come here for Christmas. I think you could do with the holiday, and you'll see Joe. But there's another reason why I'm most particularly asking you this year.

I'm afraid Fettling House is to be sold. I am so sorry. I know this will be a huge blow to you both, as it is to Joe. This lovely place has been such a part of your lives and wrapped up with memories of your mum and the summer holidays we all shared then, and those you have shared with me since. I feel the same.

I have met the prospective new owner, Hubert Cole,

a barrister from London. He's quite a fine fellow, not a countryman, and it remains to be seen how he will fit in in Fettling.

Mrs Mallinson has found a very pretty cottage to buy right in the centre, which she says will suit her very well. I think she's going to keep on Daisy Ellis to 'do' for her. Mrs Ramsden is going to live at the forge in Saxham Ash with George. It's so good to see how happy their plans for this new arrangement are making them. I thought Betsy would be heartbroken to have to leave the House, but she's actually looking forward to going now. Joe plans to continue to work with George for the moment, but he'll have to find somewhere else to live once the House is sold, and the Lodge with it. I expect he'll want to live nearer the forge.

I am looking for a new home and a new job. I was foolish at first and hoped that if I delayed doing anything, then the sale somehow wouldn't happen. Such rubbish, of course. Now it is – in the New Year, although these things can take a while – and I need to get on and find a life and home elsewhere.

Anyway, those of us here are all aware that this is the last Christmas at Fettling House, and a sort of last hurrah. I am hoping with all my fingers crossed that you and Janette can come and celebrate with us. I will send you the money for the train fares so that won't be a problem for you.

I do hope your father and stepmother will agree to your coming here. Please let me know as soon as you know.

With lots of love
Auntie Irene xxx

Sarah sank down at the kitchen table, the letter in her hand. Fettling House sold! Tears sprang to her eyes. It was going to be so difficult to let go of the idyllic old place, to put a lifetime of wonderful holidays with the two best women she'd ever known, and could ever imagine knowing, behind her for ever. In this cold, draughty, ramshackle boarding house, the memories of those country holidays with Ava and Irene had sustained Sarah. Janette often mentioned the last summer holiday, too. Now, unless she went there this Christmas, she would probably never see Fettling House again. Who knew where Auntie Irene would find another job? She might have to move far away; she could end up anywhere.

Sarah pulled herself together at this thought. It was so much worse for her aunt than it was for herself and Janette. Irene was clearly wanting to forge one last holiday memory by her generous invitation, and the girls must play their part and make this a special Christmas for her, too.

'Your aunt's invited you to Fettling for Christmas,' Fred announced that evening, looking up from his letter. 'Says the house is to be sold and it's the last Christmas there.'

The girls, Fred and Mavis were in the family sitting room. Sarah and Janette knew Irene's letter would have to be discussed, and had already hatched a plan to overcome any objections Mavis was bound to make. It was risky, but they launched into it straight away.

'She wrote to me, too,' said Sarah, knowing Mavis

had seen that she'd had a letter that morning. 'It's sad that the old place is to be sold, but, well, nowt lasts forever. It's not like it's our home.' She shrugged.

'And, Dad, it's such a long way to go when the days are so cold and dark,' said Janette. 'Is it worth all that travelling in mid-winter? Last time I felt a bit sick on the train.'

'We've been thinking for a while about Christmas here, and how we'll spend the day together, and whether the lodgers will be here. And there's lots of rooms to decorate – just paperchains, Mavis, nowt too fancy – which we were looking forward to,' said Sarah.

'And a huge tree in the hall,' improvised Janette. She caught Sarah's look. 'Or at least a small one . . . with a few candles,' she added.

'And I can help Susan with the dinner, and make my special stuffing,' said Sarah. 'It's always fun if everyone gets cooking together, especially in a nice big kitchen like yours, Mavis.'

'No, no, no. You can't possibly be decorating trees and faffing about with "special stuffing",' said Mavis, looking up from her magazine and hoping to deny the girls having any of the modest fun they purported to be planning. 'In fact, it might be a charity to go to your poor old aunt, who will otherwise be spending Christmas alone. You'll just have to brave the misery of the train journey.'

Sarah looked again at Janette, and each registered the fact that their father hadn't told Mavis that Joe had turned up safely at Irene's house. So Fred was withholding information from Mavis now: that he knew Joe was there and that the girls did, too. Perhaps the scales had begun to fall from his eyes.

'I don't imagine, in the current circumstances, that Mavis will want to pay you if you're not here working,' Fred said. 'It'll be a saving when you're two lodgers down, Mavis, and it's such an expensive time of year.'

'True,' Mavis agreed. 'But I don't know if I can afford the luxury of the train fares, either.'

'You won't have to,' said Fred. 'Irene has said she'll pay the fares.'

Was that a tiny wink he'd given Sarah, or had she imagined it?

Mavis looked relieved; she'd be saving money on all fronts if the girls were away over Christmas. A sly look crossed her face, which made Sarah think that, although she had been taken in by the deceit, she had a plan of her own, something nasty she was saving to dish up later.

'At least you and Dad can enjoy Christmas together,' said Sarah. 'We won't have to mind too much, being sent away.' She looked solemn, and Janette heaved a little sigh.

'If your father says you are to go, then you must go,' said Mavis. 'It will give me less to worry about if you aren't whining about trees and extravagant food.'

The girls struggled to compose their faces into expressions of regret, but Mavis wasn't interested enough in them to be bothered and had moved the conversation on.

And so it was decided. But Sarah could not put from

her mind that devious look in Mavis's eyes. There was bound to be some kind of underhand retribution, and she spent a nervous couple of weeks waiting for the axe to fall. Nothing nasty happened, however, and the girls set off on their holidays on Christmas Eve with little homemade presents for their aunt and Joe, and a promise to be back before New Year's Eve. Fred had slipped them a few shillings each as spending money. He said the cash was from him and Mavis, but both girls suspected Mavis knew nothing about it. There was no money to pass on to Joe, although his father did say to wish him a Merry Christmas.

As soon as Sarah and Janette were away from Over the Edge, their faces split into wide grins and, despite the weight of their luggage, they almost skipped to get their bus to Blackburn station.

Irene met Sarah and Janette at Fettling station, as she always did, and, as always, the girls presented their tickets to Mr Ellis, who greeted them with a warm welcome, then scooped up their luggage onto his trolley and took it out to Irene's vehicle.

Irene was still driving the Mallinson's Market Garden van.

'Mrs M is giving me the van when she moves to her cottage. It's really generous of her, but it isn't very comfortable, as you know, and the name will be misleading when the market garden business closes, so I'm going to swap it for a car like my old one,' Irene explained.

'Lovely. I liked your old car. But how is Joe?' asked Janette.

'He's very excited about your visit, girls. I don't know how permanent the job at the forge is, but I think while George is busy finishing his decorative pieces in time for Christmas, it's very useful to have Joe's help, even though he's not skilled.'

'It's so kind of George to help him out,' said Sarah. She had seen nothing but kindness in the big blacksmith, and she hadn't written to him even once. Still, the news had been gloomy and no one wanted a miserable letter from someone they hardly knew.

Irene smiled. 'I think it works both ways at the moment. We'll have to wait and see what happens in the new year.'

'But, Auntie, speaking of the new year, what about you? When will you have to leave the Lodge and where are you going to go?'

'The first answer is, possibly as soon as the end of January, and the second is that I don't know yet, but I have an interview for a gardening job soon after the Christmas holiday.'

'That's good news. Whereabouts?'

'Oh, a council parks department up north. I don't mind going north – that is, after all, where I come from – but I'm not sure about the parks department part. Anyway, mebbe it'll turn out to be just what I want.'

Sarah had the chance to observe Irene's face as she watched the road, and she didn't really look as if she thought it would be what she wanted at all. Sarah was about to offer hope and comfort when Janette excitedly spotted the windmill ahead of them and the moment passed.

It was, Sarah thought, one of the best Christmases ever, all the more precious for being her and Janette's last visit to Fettling House.

It was traditional that Mrs Mallinson hosted Christmas dinner for everyone who lived at the House, and she was delighted to have the Quinn siblings join the little household, along with George Ramsden. Daisy Ellis, her cleaner, had been invited, of course, but had, understandably, opted to spend the day with her enormous family instead.

Before the pudding, there were crackers to pull, with paper hats and mottoes and jokes inside them. Janette read her joke silently and then burst out laughing.

'What does Father Christmas do if his elves don't work hard enough?' she asked.

Everyone tried to think of the terrible pun that would undoubtedly be the answer, but soon gave up.

'Go on, tell us, Jan,' said Joe.

'Gives them the sack!' chortled Janette, then had a complete meltdown into giggles while everyone else laughed and groaned.

Irene looked at the happy faces around Mrs Mallinson's dining table and tried to freeze the image in her mind: to make it a sight she would never forget.

The last Christmas . . . Ava's precious children, laughing and having fun . . . dear Betsy, cooking up a feast, and beaming on her fine son . . . Mrs Mallinson, making her own final memories of life in this beautiful house, but with her lovely cottage in the heart of Fettling to look forward to . . .

It was good to see her nieces being young and joyful and a bit silly. Irene had been concerned when she saw Sarah and Janette climbing out of the carriage at the station. Both were thin and pale, and Sarah looked tired and careworn, with deep smudges of weariness under her eyes and the signs of a permanent little frown between her brows. Her hands were sore from using harsh cleaning fluids and decorating the vacant rooms, and she looked older than she had in the summer. Janette looked peaky and had a bit of a cough.

Christmas morning at the Lodge had begun with present-opening in front of the much-loved little old tree with its fold-down branches, which Irene had decorated with once-beautiful but now rather shabby glass baubles.

'These were your grandma's,' said Irene. 'Your mum would recognise them from our childhood, and I don't ever want new and shiny while I still have these.'

'We didn't have a tree at Over the Edge,' Janette volunteered. 'Mavis said it was because Sarah and I weren't going to be there and so she'd "have to do without". It was too much expense for just her and Dad and the two lodgers, although she would have liked to have a proper Christmas.'

'She said that?'

'Yes. But I reckon if she'd really wanted a tree, she would just have got one. We weren't stopping her,' said Janette. 'She kept on about a big Christmas celebration until Percy Lavelle, one of the lodgers, left, and after that she started on about having to forgo all the traditions, but tried to pretend it was our fault.'

Irene nodded. Mavis was clearly a manipulative woman, but the girls had got her measure, at least in this case.

Now, resting their stomachs between the main course and the pudding, neither Sarah nor Janette was letting thoughts of the Stepmother spoil her fun.

George and Betsy had gone to see about presenting the pudding, which had been made with such ceremony.

'I hear they're on their way,' said Julia Mallinson. 'Janette, please would you be a darling and turn out the light so that we get the full effect?'

Janette did as she was asked, and George carried in the pudding, flickering with blue brandy flames and smelling utterly delicious. The flames quickly subsided and then Betsy dished out the pudding; everyone poured brandy sauce to one side and then carefully investigated to see if they were lucky enough to have one of the charms.

'Ah-ha,' said George, digging out a foil-wrapped little parcel. 'What have we here?'

'Let me see,' said Janette, leaning over. 'It's a thimble. What does that one mean, Mrs Ramsden?'

'A blessed life,' said Betsy, smiling gently at her son. 'That is my favourite of the charms.'

Irene thought that very fitting, as the blessing would

fall on the two of them now Betsy was going to live at the forge. Maybe Joe would be included in the blessedness because he was working there, too.

'Have you anything there, Janette?' asked Mrs Mallinson.

Janette carefully dug about in her pudding but found nothing. 'Not a dicky bird,' she said with exaggerated sorrow and a pretend pouty lip.

'Me neither,' said Joe.

'I don't remember putting a dicky bird in there,' Betsy said, and everyone laughed.

Mrs Mallinson elegantly parted her pudding with her spoon and fork and found the silver sixpence, which she was too polite to make much of, although Irene thought it might mean that Hubert Cole was paying her a good deal for Fettling House. How entirely suitable the finding of the charms was turning out to be.

The last charm, the ring, was in Irene's pudding.

'A marriage,' said Betsy. 'Now that is exciting.'

'Ha, I think this one has got into the wrong dish,' said Irene. 'By rights it should be for one of the young 'uns.'

'No, no, Auntie, it's yours,' insisted Janette. 'I don't think I want a husband this next year.'

Irene put it carefully to one side for next year's pudding before she remembered there was not going to be a great big Christmas pudding and this happy gathering again. Who knew where she would be?

*

After Sarah, Janette, Joe and George had washed and dried the dishes, Janette said she was too full to move and would have to go and lie on Mrs Mallinson's sofa, please, if that were allowed.

'I think it would do me good to walk off that magnificent dinner,' said George. 'Would you like to join me, Sarah?'

'Yes, please. If I sit down I'll just go to sleep.'

They put on their coats and slipped out through the back door. It was mid-afternoon now and the light was already beginning to fade. It was very cold, but the sky was clear and the sunset had painted it a beautiful golden pink, so that everything it lit was tinted with the gorgeous colour.

'Oh, look at that,' said Sarah. 'We don't get sunsets like that at Great Edge. The Edge – it's a steep drop to the moors to the north – has a huge sky, but sunsets aren't a feature, of course.'

'Your hair has caught the light and it's as if you're turning to gold,' said George, smiling appreciatively at her. He led her round into the pruned and tidy winter rose garden. 'It's mostly the sunrises that are special here. So early and so perfect in midsummer. With the sky lightening at four o'clock and the birds starting to sing, it's . . . well, it's like magic.'

Sarah thought of her own north-facing attic bedroom with, currently, its small, ice-encrusted window and dismal daylight for only a few hours. It was almost like a prison cell, she felt. There would be sunshine and summer at Great Edge, of course, but she wouldn't see

271

such sunsets as this in the garden of Fettling House again . . .

'Are you all right, Sarah?' George was looking at her, concerned.

Sarah realised she was crying. So silly, on Christmas Day, when she'd had such a happy time and everyone was being so kind. She was letting herself down, being miserable and self-pitying.

'Just being daft,' she said. 'Last holiday at Fettling House and all that. It's much sadder for Auntie Irene, and for your mother, of course. I'm sorry, I didn't mean to be a misery.'

'Big changes – they're a lot to deal with sometimes,' said George, casually handing Sarah his handkerchief. 'Oh, I nearly forgot. I made this for you.' He pulled out of his pocket a tiny object wrapped in plain brown paper and gave that to her, too. 'When I knew I would be seeing you, I thought of something you might like.'

Sarah mopped her eyes and took the little present from him. She unwrapped it and found a small, flat metal charm, the silhouette of a rabbit.

'Oh, it's lovely. Thank you, George.'

'Joe told me that a little china rabbit that your mother had given you got broken, and that you were upset. I can't replace that and all it meant to you, but I thought . . . well, it's just a little thing . . .'

'I love it. It's so clever of you. I shall keep it in my pocket and think of you and this happy Christmas when I'm feeling down.'

'Good. You know, it can be all too easy to feel that

the changes in life are all for the worst, but there are always choices.'

'I expect you're right,' said Sarah. 'Look at Joe. It was so worrying when he was missing after such a row at home, but he came to Auntie Irene and then you gave him a job. It's other people who help make the choices the right ones or not. Dad, now, he made a terrible choice with Mavis. I think mebbe he's beginning to think so too. Sorry, I promised myself I wouldn't mention the Stepmother.'

'I'm sorry you're having a hard time with her. But everyone here wants the best for you, and sometimes it helps to share the problem.'

Sarah gave a hollow laugh. 'I don't think Mavis Swindel is a problem to be solved by sharing her around. I learned summat strange about her, George. It seems that Mavis was on trial for murdering her first husband, Basil Swann. One of the lodgers had been on the jury at the trial. Anyway, she wasn't found guilty, so she was either innocent or she got away with it. But what's really odd is that Joe, Jan and I saw summat that referred to Basil Swann being killed in the war. So one of these versions of events must be false.'

'But even if it's true about the murder trial, Sarah, you have to accept that Mavis was innocent. That's what a jury is there to decide.'

Sarah shrugged and her face hardened. 'Mebbe so, but I would believe owt of that woman. I wish Dad had never met her. Sometimes I think I actually hate her.'

George turned to face the last trace of colour in the sky and breathed deeply. Then he turned back to Sarah.

'Don't be bitter and angry,' he said. 'Don't let her spoil who you are.'

He bent and gently kissed her forehead and then, when she didn't resist, her lips.

'Don't feel you can't turn to me, to Mum, to your wonderful aunt Irene. We're your family too – your Fettling family – and although the house will go, we will always help you. You're one of us. Joe and Jan are too. Never forget that.'

'Thank you, George,' whispered Sarah, and she held the little rabbit charm tightly as she reached up to kiss him in return.

Sarah and Jan turned to each other as they approached the dark façade of Over the Edge. It had been a long walk from the bus stop on the High Street, with their cases to carry. Tomorrow would be New Year's Eve, and all the way back on the train they had been swapping ideas for New Year resolutions and plans about how best to cope with Mavis.

It was nearly dark, but few lights shone from the front windows. The house was silent. There would be no jolly piano tunes played by Percy Lavelle any more.

'I shall miss Mr Lavelle. He'd have been an asset over New Year,' said Sarah. 'I doubt Mavis has let the two empty rooms over Christmas.'

She put her key in the door and turned it. The door creaked as she pushed it open onto the dimly lit hall.

A man the girls had never seen before came out of the lodgers' sitting room on the left. He was not above average height, but quite broad, and he stopped beneath the ghastly tiger's-head trophy and looked at them.

'Hello, hello, what have we here?' he said, grinning confidently. 'Youth and beauty. I can see I've landed on my feet here, all right.'

There was a hard edge to his voice, so that his words sounded self-serving and false, rather than in any way light or complimentary to the girls. To Sarah, this overbearing stranger standing in the cold, dark hall, beneath the dead tiger on the wall, encapsulated the strikingly sharp contrast between Over the Edge and the happy, loving atmosphere of Fettling House. How unlike a proper home Mavis's house was, or could ever be.

'We're Mavis's stepdaughters,' said Sarah, an edge to her voice. 'Who are you?'

CHAPTER FOURTEEN

MAVIS WAS, SURPRISINGLY, very much in favour of her new lodger. She had so few good things to say about most people that it was quite noticeable how she had taken to Major Paget Wilkins, as he had introduced himself to Sarah and Janette when they arrived home from their Christmas holiday.

For a while the girls puzzled about his name.

'Do you think Paget Wilkins is his entire name, or just his surname?' Janette wondered.

'I've no idea. I wish we didn't have to call him owt,' said Sarah. 'There's summat smarmy about him. I've tried to be polite, but when he's in one of the rooms and I'm tidying or doing owt, I always feel that I'd rather not be alone with him. He has a way of looking at me . . .'

'What do you mean?'

'Well, it's quite uncomfortable with him there, like he's having mucky thoughts. I just want to get away. With the others I never feel like that, but Paget Thingy is . . . creepy.'

'He certainly isn't nice like Mr Cornwell,' said Janette, who was becoming good friends with the gentle, damaged war veteran now that the vivacious Percy Lavelle was no longer there to entertain her.

The mystery of the new lodger's name was solved one day when they heard Mavis calling him 'Paget', although the two lodgers who had been at Over the Edge far longer were still addressed as 'Mr Armstrong' and 'Mr Cornwell'.

It was odd that Major Wilkins had arrived at the boarding house between Christmas Eve and New Year's Eve, a time when people might not expect to be moving to new lodgings, but Sarah knew how desperate Mavis had been to find someone to occupy Mr McCain's old room. She said she had discovered Major Wilkins 'by recommendation', and everything had just worked out for her. It remained unclear who had recommended whom.

Sarah tried to avoid him as much as she could. One time he had – accidentally, it seemed – blocked her into a corner in the piano room and she'd had to squeeze uncomfortably by him to get away, although he kept up some inconsequential conversation all the while, as if he was unaware. Another time his hand brushed her thigh as she passed by where he was sitting. She knew that was no accident and she warned Janette to avoid being alone with him and vowed to keep her distance too.

Sarah had resumed her job as skivvy – albeit of a heavy-duty kind – now that the decorating of Percy

Lavelle's old room was complete. Gradually Over the Edge was improving, although she still had a battle over every basic household expense with Mavis, especially as Mr Lavelle's room had yet to be taken by anyone.

One night in early January, a fierce storm blew up, and the howling of the wind was incessant and frighteningly loud. At about one o'clock there was a very loud crash and Janette came into Sarah's room, shivering and pale, her eyes like saucers.

'Did you hear that? I think the whole house is going to blow over Great Edge. We might all be killed.'

'I don't think so, love,' said Sarah, although she, too, was afraid. She reached for the little rabbit charm George had given her, which she slept with under her pillow, and tried to steady her voice. 'It sounds like there has been some damage, but Over the Edge has stood a long time and it must have seen many storms. It'll still be here in the morning.' She hardly believed this herself, such was the noise of storm.

'I think we ought to go downstairs,' said Janette. 'That will be safer, if the roof blows off. Besides, Basil's down there and he'll be terrified all by himself. And what about Mr Cornwell? That loud crash might have reminded him of the war, and his nerves are so fragile.'

'Yes, let's go down and we can see if he's all right, too.'

They both dressed hurriedly as there seemed no point in thinking they would spend any longer in bed that night, then went down the steep and narrow stairs to the first floor and along to Mr Cornwell's door.

Sarah knocked quietly, but the noise of the storm was so loud it was unlikely he heard. In any case, he didn't answer.

'He can't possibly be asleep. I think we should go in,' said Janette, and opened the door a crack.

'Mr Cornwell? It's Janette. Sarah and I are going downstairs, where we'll feel less . . . nervous. We'd feel safer if you . . . if you came with us . . . please.'

There was no answer, although the girls could hear Mr Cornwell muttering. They didn't want to encroach, but he didn't sound at all calm. They looked at each other, Sarah gave a nod and they went in.

At first they couldn't see him. He was sitting on the floor behind his armchair, his hands over his ears, rocking back and forth with fear and talking to himself in a continuous low babble.

'Mr Cornwell?' Janette rushed over.

'Aah!' he cried out in surprise, as if he hadn't heard the girls at all. 'No! No!'

'I don't know what to do,' said Sarah, terrified. 'We mustn't frighten him even more by mistake. I don't think he's capable of coming downstairs with us.'

'I'll stay. You get Mr Armstrong.'

'Mr *Armstrong*? Are you sure?'

'Just go, Sarah, quickly.'

Sarah rushed off to knock at Mr Armstrong's door, half expecting him to tell her to go away. He answered her knock immediately, muffled up to his ears in a very thick woollen dressing gown.

'Cornwell? Yes, of course I'll come,' he said, rather

surprisingly. 'I was just thinking I'd better check on him myself.'

Having seen the state Mr Cornwell was in, he took command of the situation with a calm head.

'Right, Sarah, you're no use here to anyone,' he said in his usual blunt way, 'so go and make us all a strong pot of tea and I'll sit with Cornwell. Poor bugger, this storm is enough to give anyone the shakes. Take Janette with you. This is no place for a child.'

He ushered them both out of Mr Cornwell's room and closed the door, just as a loud crash of thunder seemed to shake the whole house.

As the girls went down to the hall, lightning flashes, visible through the windows, illuminated the snarling tiger's-head trophy in a very sinister way. Janette reached for Sarah's hand and they raced to the kitchen to make the tea. There was a nightmarish feeling about the whole situation.

'Basil, where are you?' Janette crooned softly, although her voice shook. She went to the room that opened off one side of the large kitchen, which had once been a cosy sitting room for the servants. It was here that Basil slept in his basket. The poor little dog wasn't asleep now, but shivering with fear in his bed.

'It's all right, Basil, I'm here, my darling,' Janette said, kneeling beside him and stroking his ears. 'There, there, my lovely boy . . . I don't expect Mavis has given Basil a thought,' she said, turning to Sarah.

'Of course not,' Sarah replied. 'But didn't I see a light under our sitting-room door? P'raps I should go and see if anyone else wants tea while you look after Basil?'

'Good idea.'

Whatever Sarah had expected to find, it was not her father, Mavis and Paget Wilkins sitting round a card table playing cards. They were all wearing dressing gowns over their nightclothes and Mavis's hair was tied up in elaborately knotted curling rags on top. Sarah was astonished that her father and stepmother should have so little care of her and Janette that they hadn't come to see if they were frightened of the storm, or even whether the loud crash had been something falling through the roof onto them. And both Mavis and Fred knew well that Richard Cornwell was damaged by his time in the trenches, and this loud thunder and the fall of whatever had been removed by the wind might awaken memories of his terrible experiences then. How could they not even think to see how he was?

'Ah, come and join us,' said Mavis, overloudly. 'Sleep is impossible, and I'm that worried about the state of the house, but your dad and Paget have persuaded me to have a little drink and a calming game of Brag.'

There was a bottle of Scotch in Mavis's hand, and she waved it in a tipsy kind of way in invitation. Sarah had not seen Mavis or her father drinking Scotch before, but all three card players had well-filled tumblers beside them and the bottle was half-empty. Now Sarah looked closely it was clear that Mavis was genuinely nervous. Still, she had responsibilities here! Poor Mr Cornwell, in the grip of terrifying memories of fighting in the war, and Mr Armstrong rising to the occasion and showing more kindness than anyone might have guessed he was capable of, and then their landlady with no thought for anyone else but herself and her own fears of the storm at all.

'How nice for you,' she said coldly, then shut the door firmly on the three of them and went back into the kitchen, closing the door there, too.

She put her hands to her face. 'Oh God, Jan, I think they've actually gone mad. Dad, Mavis and Major Wilkins are drinking whisky and playing cards, and not a thought for the lodgers, or us, or Basil. I am so ashamed of Dad. That woman has tipped him over the edge and he dances to nowt but her tune.' She gave a mirthless laugh at what she had said.

Janette had scooped Basil up and was gently stroking his head.

'It's like I said before: she's a witch and she has him under her spell,' she said. 'I don't know why she's such friends with Major Wilkins, but mebbe he's under her spell, too.'

Sarah gathered herself. 'C'mon, let's get this tea made and I'll take the tray up. You take Basil. Mebbe Mr Cornwell is feeling better and we can picnic in his room, join him on the floor. I reckon he'd like the company while he's feeling nervous.'

'He and Basil can comfort each other,' said Janette.

Daylight revealed the extent of the damage to Over the Edge. The post-storm light was a strange luminous grey, the wind still gusting, although nothing like as fiercely as it had been in the night.

Sarah was up before anyone else and went out as soon as it was light enough to see what had happened to the house. Several tiles had blown off the roof at the front and some were sticking out of the gravel where they had fallen edge on, angled like javelins. She started to collect them into a pile at the side of the house.

'Good thing you weren't out when that came down,' said Susan, arriving to cook the breakfasts at exactly the same time as usual, seeing Sarah bending to extract a pointy tile from deep within the gravel. 'It might have decapitated you or stabbed you through the heart,' she added cheerfully.

'I hope your home didn't suffer any damage,' Sarah said.

'No, we're lower down, in Scarstone proper. I wouldn't live up here for the world,' Susan answered, looking pleased that she didn't and that Sarah did. 'It's asking for trouble, living on the Edge.' Then she went to let herself into the house without another word.

Having found all the displaced tiles, Sarah went round to the back of the house, from where she could stand at a distance and view any damage to the roof. She saw straight away that one of the many chimney pots had blown off, taking a trail of tiles with it. It lay broken in the long, untidy back garden. Here, the wind was stronger, the garden facing the Edge, the overgrown grass lashing her legs wetly.

How huge that space was beyond the garden wall:

only sky visible from up here, no land at all. Regardless of the wet, she wandered down to the wall and peered over. The ground, which could be seen now, sloped away at a greater angle on the other side and she saw the place where she, Joe and Janette must have left their bicycles on the day they had come here to tea in the summer, and lain on the grass to talk about how awful Mavis was. Well, now Sarah thought Mavis was the most horrible, the most selfish and irresponsible woman she could imagine. Disgraceful, no less. The trouble was, her father, when he followed Mavis's lead, was no better, and he *was* her father, not some latecomer, some add-on to the family who Sarah could try to pretend didn't really count as one of them.

Memory of the Christmas holiday at Fettling was fading already in the face of relentless housework and discontent, plus the uncomfortable new atmosphere engendered by the presence of Paget Wilkins. Sarah thought of her aunt Irene: how she reminded her of her mother, with her open and loving nature, her sense of fun in the everyday. She was the perfect combination of wholehearted kindness and sympathy, with only as much strictness as was absolutely necessary. What a wonderful mother she would have made.

If I could I would take Janette and we'd go to Fettling, to live at the Lodge. But how can I do that when Auntie Irene is leaving there and she doesn't know yet where she will go? It might be anywhere! We can't just turn up and assume she can include us in her plans. That wouldn't be fair at all, burdening her with us when she has the worry of finding a new job and home, her own life in disarray . . . And Joe had said he'd look after us both back in Keele Street, but Dad insisted Janette must stay with him. I couldn't ever leave her here alone.

Sarah trudged back up the garden towards the house. Goodness, but the back view was shabby: paint peeling from the window frames, the roof now damaged. Even minor improvements, like having the windows cleaned, would make a difference, but every expense had to be fought over with Mavis, and Sarah was picking her fights these days. Maybe the back windows weren't a priority, certainly not now that the roof needed repairing.

She cast her gaze over the rear façade and her eyes came to rest on Major Wilkins, standing at his room window. He was watching her. His eyes met hers and, even from where she stood, Sarah thought the expression on his face was calculating and predatory.

What was it Susan had said a few minutes ago? 'I wouldn't live here for the world.'

And nor would I if I had a choice.

Irene had caught the earliest train from Fettling for her journey north to her job interview. The train ride was a long one, and not particularly comfortable in third class. She emerged, after three changes of train, onto the platform of a little station in a small town north of Leeds. By now she was cold, and her legs were stiff with sitting. She felt rather third class herself, but she straightened the skirt of her coat, checked the angle of her hat in her reflection in the carriage window and strode out to find the council offices.

Along the way she saw that the municipal flowerbeds were neat and planted with just-emerging snowdrops. Crocus bulbs were beginning to show a hint of their pointy leaves, too. That looked promising: the council cared to have their gardens looking good. Maybe they were the kind of people Irene could work for.

Mr Grigson, head of the Parks Department, didn't keep her waiting outside his office for long.

'Ah, Miss Mayhew . . . it is Miss Mayhew, isn't it?' He looked her up and down.

'I am.'

'Oh, right you are. I was expecting someone . . . someone . . .' He cleared his throat.

'Else? Younger?'

'Aye, mebbe . . . a bit.' He showed her into his office and indicated a chair.

'I wouldn't have had time for all the experience I listed in my application if I was younger,' said Irene. 'You'll remember I've been in sole charge of the garden at Fettling House for nearly seventeen years.'

'Since the outbreak of the war – yes, I can do the maths,' said Grigson. 'I'm just wondering, if there'd been no war, whether you'd have been in sole charge of owt. Different times then. You can see my point, can't you, Miss Mayhew?'

'No, I can't, Mr Grigson. It's over twelve years since the war ended and Mrs Mallinson has never had any reason to want to employ another gardener – a man, I think you were alluding to – instead of me.'

'Tell me about this Fettling place, then. What acreage?'

He sat back, looking smug, as if he expected her to say it was just a small urban front garden.

'About an acre and a half: rose garden, herbaceous borders and lawns, vegetable garden, a greenhouse, a pergola and pond, an apple orchard.'

She was pleased to see him look impressed that she managed all that alone, although he quickly tried to hide it. But his answer surprised her.

'Sounds a bit yesteryear, Miss Mayhew. These old houses, it's not the real world, is it? Not modern times.'

'I'm not sure what you mean, Mr Grigson. It's still a garden that needs careful tending.'

'I suppose I meant it's a bit of a dinosaur, that kind of setup. Sheltered, genteel, like. We're more grafters up here, out in all weathers. There's no rain like Yorkshire rain,' he added proudly. 'It's not all *pergolas* and "yes, my lady" here, you know.'

Irene gave him a long look until he dropped his eyes. 'Yes, Fettling is a nice place to live and to work, and yes, I like my employer – whose title is "Mrs", by the way – and I'm a northerner myself as I'd have thought you could tell, although from the wetter side of the Pennines, so I know a bit about bad weather. It's real hands-on gardening, Mr Grigson, keeping ahead of a garden that size.'

Grigson was clearly not used to being answered back, but he recovered quickly.

'Well, Miss Mayhew, I need to know if you're right for my team,' he said, looking self-important. 'I run a tight ship and everyone has to fit in. I can see you've got some gardening experience, but here you'll not be the one giving orders, but taking 'em. Do you reckon you can manage that?'

'Yes, Mr Grigson, sir,' Irene answered promptly, just about stopping herself from saluting, pushing to see whether this ridiculous man, this dyed-in-the-wool northerner, this inverted snob with a chip on his shoulder, had one iota of irony or humour in his character as a saving grace.

He hadn't.

'And finally, Miss Mayhew – and this is really important – do you know how to make a good strong cup of tea?'

And thinks he's superior to women, as I thought.

'Right, well, Mr Grigson, you needn't take up any more of my valuable time,' said Irene. 'I'm afraid you've failed the interview and I cannot take you on as my employer. I think you'd be better setting your sights lower. Possibly a tea-person is what you really need. Good day to you.'

And she stood up, turned and walked out, leaving his office door wide open behind her.

What a complete waste of time that had been. Still, it would have been worse if Grigson hadn't shown his true colours so early, and she'd upped sticks to Yorkshire and only then found out how unsuitable the job was and how narrow-minded the man in charge. There was another interview lined up in a few days for the position of gardener to a widowed lady near Diss. Perhaps that might be more in her line. This was only the first job she'd applied for, and she couldn't necessarily expect to find the right one straight away.

It was late afternoon when Irene arrived back at Fettling. After the horrible interview, the wasted journey, the cramped, lumpy and none-too-clean seats on the numerous trains, and the anxiety of getting to each station along the way in time to make the change, it was a relief to see the familiar little station with Mr Ellis's smiling face at the exit.

'Saw that Mr Cole, him what's buying Mrs Mallinson's place,' he volunteered.

'Oh, yes? I expect he was going to the House again.'

'I couldn't tell you. Passed by with a car full of children. Didn't wave.'

A car full of children – that sounded unlikely, especially as an accurate description from Mr Ellis, who, with nine of his own, knew what a lot of children looked like. There must surely be some mistake.

Irene went round to where she'd left the van, parked to the side of the station, and set off for home, resolving to forget all about the ridiculous Mr Grigson and turning her thoughts instead to what she had in her pantry that she could cook for herself and Joe that evening. Their dinner might have to be egg and chips, she thought, but at least there were always green vegetables.

It was growing dark and the air was full of spitting rain. Never mind, home soon, and she'd make a good fire while a pot of tea brewed.

Suddenly there was a horrible dragging sound from

the back of the van and the engine grew immediately noisier. Whatever was wrong sounded serious.

Damn it, now what?

Irene pulled well over to the side of the road and got out to have a look. She lifted the bonnet and propped it open, but she didn't really know what she was looking for, and nothing was obviously broken. Then she went round the back and leaned down to have a look underneath, as far as she could, praying that she hadn't run over a large stone or something that might now be caught underneath the van. In the end she had to get right down and kneel on the road to see. The exhaust pipe was broken, hanging down, resting on the road. It was another mile to the Lodge and she didn't know if she ought to drive on. Would it cause the wretched pipe to snap off altogether? Would the van be damaged beyond repair?

Think, Irene. Just take a breath and think what is the best thing to do.

The answer was to walk home and telephone the garage in Fettling in the morning, explain where the van was and ask Mr Cranleigh, the mechanic, if he could go and either fix it there or take it away to be fixed. Irene herself was helpless to do anything about it this evening.

She took her handbag from the seat, and a torch she kept to hand, locked the van up and set off for home. Her shoes weren't really designed for walking far, but it was only a twenty-minute walk . . . well, possibly a bit longer as the shoes were starting to hurt now that she'd worn them all day. And it was beginning to rain harder.

Fortunately, she had her umbrella so her good hat wouldn't get too wet. What a waste of effort that ridiculous interview had been. Why hadn't Grigson advertised for a young, inexperienced person to make tea and learn the basics of municipal gardening, if that's what he really wanted? Stupid man . . .

Don't even give him another thought. It's the lady near Diss next week. She'll be lovely. It'll all be fine . . .

Just then a car came towards her on the narrow road, dazzling her with its lights, which highlighted the heaviness of the rain, and Irene had to step back almost into the ditch that ran alongside to leave room. The car pulled up and, even before she heard his voice, she knew it was Hubert Cole. No one else round here had a car quite so big.

He wound down the window and leaned out.

'Miss Mayhew! I thought it was you. What are you doing on foot?'

Irene explained her van was broken down. 'But it's all right, I'll ask the mechanic in Fettling to sort it out for me tomorrow.'

'Get in and we'll give you a lift home.'

'But you aren't going my way. Quite the opposite, in fact.'

'Please don't argue,' he said. 'It's raining hard, and I can see your shoes are hurting, and I expect that's your best hat you're getting wet.' He turned to his left and said, 'Come on, boys, move round and let Miss Mayhew have a seat.' Then: 'Miss Mayhew, will you please get in before you're completely soaked?'

Irene could see the sense, especially now that a little boy of about ten was out in the rain holding the passenger door open for her.

'Thank you,' she said, folding down her umbrella and getting in. 'It's really kind of you.'

'Nonsense. I could hardly leave you,' said Hubert. 'You might have taken a chill, or worse, and I wouldn't want that on my conscience.'

'Me neither,' said a little voice from the back seat, and Irene turned to see the faces of three boys, almost identical, but in different sizes, like Russian dolls.

'You can introduce yourselves while I look for somewhere to turn the car,' said Hubert.

'I'm Christopher,' announced the child who had opened the door. 'I'm ten and I'm the eldest.'

'And I'm Simon, and I'm eight,' said the next. 'And that's Tiddler and he's only six.'

'I wanted to tell the lady myself,' said Tiddler. 'And my real name is Timothy, but I like Tiddler better, 'cos I'm the only Tiddler I know.'

'It's a lovely name,' said Irene. 'You're the only Tiddler I know, too. And I'm Irene Mayhew. Thank you for making room for me.'

'Glad to help. You do look a bit wet,' said Christopher earnestly.

'The feather on your hat is dripping,' Simon pointed out.

Irene laughed as the boys' father executed a neat turn in a field entrance and set off back the way he'd just driven. She was very pleased to be safe and dry in the big car, with these charming children, not limping her sorry way along the lane alone. This was the best thing that had happened today, even though it was as a result of her van breaking down.

On the short journey, the boys told Irene about their visit to Fettling House, and what they wanted to do with the rooms they'd chosen as their own. They were very excited about the prospect of living there. Christopher particularly mentioned the tennis court, and Tiddler said he liked the pond, and Simon said he wanted to be an artist and Fettling House was full of interesting subjects for his work. None of them, Irene noticed, mentioned their mother.

At the Lodge, Hubert pulled up at the big gates. There was a light on: Joe was back already.

'Is this where you live, Miss Mayhew?' asked Simon, excited. 'We passed it earlier and I said to Daddy, I want to live here.'

'It's like a great big Wendy house,' added Tiddler.

'Come in and have a look, if you like?' offered Irene. 'My nephew, Joe, is staying with me and I reckon he'd like to meet you.'

'Yes, please!' said the boys, just as Hubert said, 'Oh, no, we won't bother you both. It's getting late and you'll be tired.'

Immediately the boys were quiet: no begging or whining, just tacit obedience. Goodness, they were well behaved. Irene *was* tired after her long day and her disappointment, but she wouldn't have minded if they just had a look . . . perhaps a cup of tea. She didn't want to undermine their father's authority, however.

'When you visit Fettling House again, you must come and say hello,' she suggested. 'And I'll show you round then.'

'Yes, please,' said Christopher. 'It's Saturday tomorrow – we could come back then,' he suggested cautiously. 'Couldn't we, Daddy?'

'I don't see why not. If you're certain, Miss Mayhew, I'll telephone Mrs Mallinson and make sure that's all right with her.'

'Well, Joe might be at the forge in Saxham Ash, but I shall be either here at the Lodge or you will find me in the garden. If you want to play outside you might want to wear your wellies,' Irene smiled.

'Thank you,' the boys chorused.

Then Christopher got out to open the car door for Irene without even being asked. 'Good night, Miss Mayhew. I hope to see you tomorrow,' he said, offering his hand.

Irene was enchanted. Christopher was the kind of child who would make head boy at his school in later years. She said goodbye and waved to Simon and Tiddler, grinning at her through the car window.

Hubert was already opening the side gate for her, although she was perfectly capable of letting herself in.

'Thank you for the lift,' said Irene. 'It's so good of you to go out of your way to bring me here.'

'It was a pleasure. Now, in you go before you get wet . . . wetter,' he laughed.

Irene waved goodbye, and let herself into the Lodge.

Joe's boots were by the door and he was in the kitchen, making a pot of tea. The fire in the sitting room was burning brightly, Irene could see through the open door. It was so good to have someone to come home to instead of a dark, cold and empty house.

'How did it go, Auntie?' called Joe as she hung up her wet coat and then went to put her hat down carefully on a chair near the fire to dry.

'Disaster, love.' Irene came through to the kitchen, where Joe had taken the initiative about supper and was now peeling potatoes. He'd grown up a lot in the past few weeks. 'The man fancied himself as someone big and important, but in fact he was just an outdated idiot. Still, I had to go to see.'

'A long way only to find that out,' said Joe. 'I wish they'd just be honest on the job advertisements: "appalling pay" or "half-witted boss" or some such. It'd save disappointment.'

Irene laughed. Then she told Joe about the van breaking down. 'But I had a lift from Hubert Cole, who had his little lads with him. I've invited them to see the Lodge and let me show them round the garden tomorrow.'

'Him that's buying the House? He must be well off.'

'Well, yes, I think we may assume that.'

'What is it he does?' asked Joe. 'His name is all I know about him.' He rinsed his hands, then poured Irene a cup of strong tea.

'Barrister, I gather. He works in London mostly, but sometimes in Ipswich.'

'Barrister, eh? Puts the case for folk in court?'

'Or against them. Yes, that's right.'

Joe was quiet for a few moments, his hands to his mouth as he thought. Then: 'Mavis was in court, accused of killing her husband, Basil Swann.'

'Good grief, I didn't know that. When was it?'

'A long time ago – years. Sarah found out. Mr McCain, who used to lodge at Over the Edge, recognised her. He sat on the jury at the trial.'

'Well, I never! Still, Joe, she must have been found innocent.'

'Yes, but here's summat quite odd: we also saw a letter from a friend of hers, sent during the war, saying how sorry the person was to hear that Basil Swann had been killed in battle. So, two versions of his death.'

'That is strange.'

'I'm wondering, d'you reckon Mr Cole might be able to find out about it?'

Irene took a welcome gulp of her tea, then got up to start chipping the potatoes.

'It would be very lucky if he just happened to have first-hand knowledge of the trial, but he might know where to look up the details, or who else to ask. A murder trial is a big event, not summat that doesn't get written down and is forgotten about.'

'D'you think it would be all right if I asked him?'

''Course, Joe. But don't get your hopes up too high, love. It could have happened anywhere in the country. And if Mr Cole is too busy to help, I reckon he'll just say so and you'll know not to pursue it.'

'Right then, that's what I'll do. George won't mind if I'm late to work tomorrow, if I'm trying to find out about Mavis. He thinks a lot of our Sarah, and he'd be pleased for her if owt we found led to her and Jan being free of the Stepmother. We all wish Mavis would just go away.'

'I think, Joe, we all wish she'd never turned up in the first place.'

CHAPTER FIFTEEN

WHATEVER FRED HAD come to lack these days as a father in sympathy with his children, he was certainly excellent at establishing relationships with reliable builders. A new chimney pot replaced the old, broken one, and the tiles were restored to the roof within two days.

But then the following week a part of the ceiling above the first-floor corridor, which no one had noticed had started to sag, fell down, bringing a lot of debris and dust with it. The mess mysteriously spread over the whole of the upstairs of Over the Edge, as well as down the stairs and, of course, it was Sarah's job to clean it up. Bits of plaster were still floating down like occasional gigantic snowflakes the following day; dust was settling all the time.

Mavis got very anxious about this latest damage, and paced about wringing her hands and muttering about the expense. She claimed she couldn't afford to repair the hole straight away, what with the cost of the roof repairs and still having only three lodgers, and so everyone had to skirt nervously round it when going between the bathroom and their rooms. It was impossible not to look up at the skeletal joists, clearly visible, and wonder if another part of the ceiling was about to fall just as you were passing below.

Once, Sarah met Paget Wilkins in the corridor on the other side of the hole, and they dodged and danced as she tried to pass to one side and he decided to choose the same side.

'Excuse me, please, Major Wilkins.'

'Oh, don't mind me, Sarah.'

In the end she turned and went back downstairs until he had gone.

After a couple of days of everyone circling the hole, Andrew Armstrong marched into Mavis's office one morning to complain. He left the office door wide open, possibly so that anyone who cared to listen could hear what he had to say, which was that he considered he and Mr Cornwell were due a reduction in their rent for the danger and inconvenience of the fallen ceiling. Sarah, who was cleaning in the dining room next door, noticed that he didn't mention Major Wilkins. The two established lodgers hadn't taken to the newcomer, which had strengthened the bond between them and placed the major very firmly in the role of outsider.

'I hardly think so, Mr Armstrong,' said Mavis. 'How can I afford to mend the ceiling if you're living here for next to nothing? That doesn't make sense at all, does it?'

'But the rent isn't "next to nothing" at the moment, is it, Mrs Quinn? So I suggest you get that ceiling mended without any more delay,' retorted Mr Armstrong. 'Shabby is one thing, and that's why you couldn't, with a clear conscience, charge more than you do, but dere-lict is altogether another, and that ceiling is a hazard to life and limb. If more of it comes down and someone is injured, Mrs Quinn, you are very likely to be pros-ecuted, do you realise that?'

The threat of prosecution had an immediate effect.

'It, er . . . no, it won't come to that. If you can just bear with me, Mr Armstrong, the ceiling will be mended as soon as I can get someone to do it,' she said, sounding a lot less confident and bossy now.

'I shall give you a few days, Mrs Quinn, and if nothing has been done by then, I shall not only demand a fairer rent for living in a semi-derelict and dangerous place, but I'll be looking for new lodgings, too. And I don't doubt that Mr Cornwell will be doing the same.'

'I very much hope you won't find that necessary, Mr Armstrong. I'm sure Mr Cornwell can speak for himself, however.'

Andrew Armstrong came out of the room, grumbling under his breath, and Sarah was shocked to hear Mavis swearing loudly, imaginatively and fiercely before she slammed her office door and Sarah heard no more.

The word 'prosecuted' reminded Sarah that Mavis had, according to Mr McCain's cousin Bertram, faced a trial for the murder of her husband many years ago. Possibly it had reminded Mavis, too, resulting in the terrible outburst of foul language, which betrayed real fear of prosecution. How strange, though, that there was another version of the death of Basil Swann: that he had been killed in the war.

Sarah had been pondering for many weeks how she could reconcile these two very different versions of Mavis's past life, but she could see no way forward. She could hardly come straight out and ask Mavis. That would be certain to further sour relations between herself and the Stepmother. She was racking her brains over the mystery as she worked on the grubby green baize of the cutlery drawer, when she heard the dining-room door closing. She turned to see Major Wilkins standing in front of it, smiling in his oily way.

'I'm so glad to have found you alone at last, Sarah,' he said. 'It's nice to see a pretty face about the place and, well, I see so little of yours. I'd really like to get to know you better.'

Sarah didn't like the smirk on his face one bit. Not only had he tried to crowd her on a few occasions, but his whole manner was dislikeable, as if his mind was filled with crude and unsavoury ideas. He had no job that she knew of, and spent much of his time loafing about Over the Edge, although he sometimes went out 'to see a man about something'. Sarah tried to avoid him as much as she could.

'I have work to be doing in here, Major Wilkins. If you'd like to go and sit in the lodgers' sitting room, you'll find it more comfortable.'

'It isn't that kind of comfort I want, my girl,' he said. 'It's something rather more *exciting* than that.'

He quickly advanced towards her, round one side of the table in the middle of the room.

'Come now, Sarah, I think a little *mutual comfort* would benefit us both, don't you? Two lonely souls . . .'

'No, Major Wilkins. No, you're quite wrong,' said Sarah, dodging round the other side to get to the door, her heart hammering now. She'd suspected what kind of a man he was – there had been plenty of hints – and now she was proved right. 'Keep away from me.'

But Wilkins could move surprisingly quickly for someone so stout, and he doubled back and had her pinned against the wall, blocking off her escape before she could open the door.

'There's no need to be afraid,' he breathed hotly in her face, standing very close with one arm up, making a barrier so that she was trapped, his other hand wandering over her stomach, her hip. 'Just relax and I think you'll enjoy this as much as I will.' One hand crept lower, brushing her thigh, while he moved the other down to cover her mouth. Any second now he'd be lifting her skirt, she'd be overpowered and unable to cry out.

'Get away from me, you vile creep!' she yelled, just before he could muffle her protest, and stabbed his roving arm as hard as she could with a fork she had managed to take from the sideboard drawer and keep hidden from his view as soon as he had started to advance on her.

The tines of the fork didn't make much of an impression on his arm through his tweedy jacket sleeve, but it

was enough of a shock for him to release her and allow
her to shove him away from her as hard as she could.

'Aah, vicious! What did you do that for, you little—'

Sarah flung open the door. 'You try that again, Major
Wilkins, and it'll be a knife to the throat,' she threatened
recklessly. Then she ran out and straight into Mavis's
office.

Mavis, after her ultimatum from Mr Armstrong, was
lying on the chaise longue, but her eyes flew open when
Sarah burst in and she sat up, looking fearful.

'Oh, my Lord, what's happened? Has more of the
ceiling collapsed? Is someone hurt?'

'No, Mavis,' gasped Sarah, fighting to get her words
out, so breathless was she with shock. 'It's Major Wilkins.
He's just . . . just groped me, and was about to attempt
worse. He came into the dining room and . . . ugh, it
was horrible, all panting and sweaty wandering hands,
and he . . . he trapped me against the wall.'

Mavis relaxed a little and patted her lush hair back
into place. She actually looked relieved that the trouble
wasn't the fallen ceiling. 'Really, Sarah, are you sure?
Just because you're eighteen and pretty, it doesn't mean
that all the men are after you, you know.'

Sarah was speechless for a moment. Had one of them
misheard?

'Of course I'm sure. I'd hardly be mistaken. Mavis,
that awful man came in, shut the door, talked some
filthy nonsense about "mutual comfort" and then
cornered me. If I hadn't stabbed him, he'd have been
under my skirt.'

'Stabbed him?' gasped Mavis, paling. 'Oh my God, you've killed him?'

'No, of course I haven't! I hardly touched him. It was through his sleeve, with a fork from the sideboard.'

'Oh, thank goodness . . .'

Sarah was astounded. The Stepmother was as far from a caring mother as it was possible for a woman to be. Wilkins was a disgusting predator, and the very least Mavis should do was order him to pack his bags immediately.

'Why do you care so much that he suffered some minor injury when I could have been violated?' Sarah demanded, filled with a surge of reckless fury. 'Are you frightened he'd go to the police – that they'd come here and mebbe question you?'

Mavis leapt to her feet. 'What do you mean?' she demanded. 'Why would I be questioned? It's you who hurt him. You're to blame. I wasn't even there. It's nothing to do with me.'

Sarah had spoken wildly, as a kind of test of the truth of what she had heard about Mavis. But it looked as if she had hit on not one, but two truths. The first was that Mavis had a very real fear of the law, which fitted neatly with what Bertram McCain had told her about Mavis having been on trial.

The second was that Mavis already knew what kind of a man Major Wilkins was, and even that he'd set his sights on Sarah as his victim. Her denial of involvement was far too vehement to be sincere. She might even have suggested Sarah to him as his victim. And why would she have done that except for some gain for herself? Payment, most likely.

'Mavis,' Sarah said, her voice trembling with outrage and because she knew she would never be able to retract what she was about to say, 'if Major Wilkins tries to assault me again, I will go to the police and I will tell them *everything*.'

'No,' gasped Mavis. 'No . . . you know nothing.'

'Then you can have nowt to fear. Which makes me wonder just why you are so afraid.'

Neither moved.

Sarah was struggling to be calm. She wanted just to run from the room, but she needed to hold her ground or she would lose all advantage. She must be strong; she must be composed.

Mavis was working her mouth and clenching her hands, her eyes wide with surprise and fear.

'Get rid of Wilkins, Mavis. You have to! Tell him to leave. What if he tried the same with Janette?'

'All right . . . all right . . . But there's no need to go that far. I'll have to have a little word—'

'A little word? The word you want is "Go!"'

'But then I'll have only two lodgers.'

'Well, find someone else. Someone decent. It can't be that difficult.'

'But that will take time and I have Paget here already. It'll be hard times if Paget leaves. There'll be no staying on at school for your sister then, when she could be working. There's a skivvy wanted in Scarstone, I see; one of those houses out behind the High Street. Janette would need to be earning her keep instead of sitting around in a classroom, with all the expense of the work needed on the house and only *two* lodgers.'

'So we're back to that, are we? You know that you agreed that Jan could return to school if I worked here, cleaning the house. You can't go back on your word.'

A sly look came over Mavis's face. 'That was then. Circumstances have changed, my girl. It's different now: fewer lodgers, the cost of repairing the roof, and now the ceiling down and Armstrong kicking up a fuss. Besides, your father and the major enjoy many a card game of an evening after you and Janette have taken yourselves off to bed early like the good little innocents you are. It would be awkward for your father if Paget called in his debts from the card games and word got round to Mr Godwin, he that owns Scarstone Hardware. A strict nonconformist, I gather, and *very* disapproving of gambling. It would cost your father his job, Sarah, do you realise that? Far better not to blab – about anything. It's time you learned that.'

Was this true? Mavis could just be making it up. But Sarah knew she could not afford to risk it. Over the Edge was fast becoming a madhouse, a place of chaos and grubby secrets, and her stepmother was at the centre of the maelstrom, lacking in any kind of integrity. There could be no limit to what she was prepared to do.

Sarah felt tears threatening. Everything she said, Mavis batted it away with some new revelation, some further depth to which someone had sunk.

'If Wilkins so much as looks at Janette, I will kill him. You can tell your good friend *Paget* that, Mavis.'

'I don't think you will,' said Mavis, rallying now she had the upper hand. 'You haven't got it in you, dearie. Now off you go and get on with your work.'

Sarah was feeling very low when she went to meet Rachel outside the library the following afternoon. Andrew Armstrong had sent a message the previous day that Rachel would be there, and Sarah had left Over the Edge to see her friend without even bothering to tell Mavis where she was going.

'What now?' asked Rachel, after one look at Sarah's face. 'Summat's happened, hasn't it?'

'Oh, it's just . . . everything,' said Sarah, flinging her hand in despair.

'Tell me.'

She told Rachel about Major Wilkins and her subsequent conversation with Mavis.

'But that's awful, Sarah. She should have thrown him out. You could go to the police, you know.'

'Who'd believe me? It'd be my word against Wilkins's, and he was an officer in the army whereas I'm nobody. And Mavis won't take my side. I can only think Wilkins is paying her to turn a blind eye and she knew what he intended all along. They might even have plotted together against me in the first place.'

'Disgraceful.'

'I thought I'd found her weak spot, but then she turned everything around and got the better of me; said

Dad is in debt to Wilkins and could lose his job if I made a fuss about the major.'

'Come and have summat to eat at our house. Mum'd be so pleased to see you. And then, when you're warm and safe and fed, we can get our thinking caps on. It's a right old mess, Sarah, but we'll find a way back to sanity.'

Mrs Fraser was delighted to see Sarah. Rachel had clearly already briefed her mother about the horrible time Sarah was having at Over the Edge because, without asking any questions, she offered kindness, warming food and comforting normality.

'How's your Joe getting on?' asked Mrs Fraser when Sarah had eaten. 'I was that glad to hear that he'd turned up safely at your auntie's. I've always had a soft spot for Joe, and I reckon I'm not the only one.' She beamed at Rachel, who looked away, rolling her eyes.

'He's doing grand, thank you, Mrs Fraser. He's working at a forge now, and I gather that suits him. George Ramsden, the blacksmith, is the son of the Fettling House housekeeper and he was around at Christmas. He's a good man, and it's generous of him to find work for Joe while Joe decides where he's going from there.'

Sarah thought of that happy Christmas Day, with the laughter and the golden light, the peace of the winter garden and the comfort of George's arms as he kissed her and tried to soothe her anguish about the Stepmother. She had the little charm he'd given her in her coat pocket now. George Ramsden and Major

Paget Wilkins – they were like men from two different planets. It occurred to her that they perfectly represented the places where they were: the gentle, loving kindness of life with Auntie Irene in Fettling, and the crass selfishness, the dishonesty and vulgarity of Mavis at Over the Edge. And Janette and I, thought Sarah, are trapped in the wrong world.

Suddenly she felt fury rising up. The Stepmother had ruined their lives. If it wasn't for Mavis, Joe would still be in Scarstone. They would all be living in Keele Street, muddling along but contented in the circumstances, and managing because they *were* all together, except for Ava. Now look where they were: Dad in thrall to Mavis and in debt to Wilkins; Joe exiled from his sisters; Janette continually under threat of having her education and her bright future snatched away; Sarah herself nothing but a skivvy, lowlier than that downtrodden child she had seen working for Mrs Hutchinson that day she'd taken the woman her blouses and been cheated out of the promised tip. And now, to cap it all, she was being pursued by that carnal lowlife Paget Wilkins. It was intolerable.

She put her head in her hands and sobbed for what her life had become.

'There, there, Sarah. Don't take on so,' whispered Rachel, coming over to put her arm round Sarah's shoulder after letting her cry a while. 'There must be some way to help you.'

'There's still the offer of the spare room for your sewing, love,' said Mrs Fraser, handing Sarah a clean and ironed handkerchief.

Sarah explained that Mavis would take Janette out of school if she stopped doing all the skivvying, and she would still be living at Over the Edge and dodging the unwelcome attentions of Paget Wilkins. And, worse, Wilkins might even turn his perverted eye on Janette if Sarah wasn't around so much!

Sarah, Rachel and her mother sat miserably over more cups of tea and racked their brains for a solution, but could think of nothing that was certain to work. In whatever way Sarah attempted to confront Mavis, the Stepmother had some means of thwarting her.

Irene was delighted to see Hubert Cole and his sons the next morning. Tiddler had brought a little net with him in the hope of discovering the creatures that lived in the pond, and the boys had, rather endearingly, all turned up wearing wellingtons, as Irene had advised.

First there was tea and lemonade at the Lodge, and some of Mrs Ramsden's flapjacks, and then a tour of the Lodge, with its little arched windows and tiny fire-places in the bedrooms.

'Oh, it's perfect,' said Tiddler earnestly, clasping his hands together reverentially, which made everyone laugh.

'Miss Mayhew, you lack only a lovely friendly dog,' suggested Simon.

'But I thought you had a fierce Alsatian to protect you from intruders,' said his father mock-seriously.

Simon and Tiddler glanced around nervously but Christopher got the joke. 'I expect Miss Mayhew is wise enough to put the rumour about,' he said.

'And anyway, she has me for company,' said Joe, then blushed at his clumsiness, remembering that Hubert Cole was buying Fettling House and the Lodge, and that he himself was looking for a room to rent near to the forge.

Soon it was time to let the boys run off the energy generated by the lemonade and flapjacks, while Irene and Joe strolled at a distance with Hubert Cole.

'Mr Cole—'

'Hubert, please, Miss Mayhew. I think we've met often enough not to be so formal.'

'Thank you, and you may call me Irene,' she said, remembering how silly she had been, avoiding telling him her name the first time they met. 'Now, Joe and I wondered if you might be able to help us solve a mystery. Joe will explain.'

Joe told Hubert what the Quinns knew of Mavis Swann and the two versions of the death of her husband, Basil.

'I don't think that's such a mystery,' said Hubert, gazing distantly at his sons, who were now pond dipping. He raised his voice: 'Christopher, just make sure Tiddler doesn't fall in, please.' He turned back to Joe and Irene. 'I think Basil Swann will have been missing in action, reported dead, as many soldiers were after those vast and chaotic battles. His wife will have had a letter from his commanding officer, and then the news spread and her friends sent kind commiserations. But a while after the end of the conflict, soldiers who had suffered various serious injuries – had even been misidentified or reported dead – were still returning home at last.

311

Imagine if you thought your husband was dead and then he just appeared at the door one day.'

Irene nodded. She thought of Gilbert Wagstaffe, the man she had been engaged to after James Fellowes' tragic death, who had been killed in the war. If only he had come back from the dead. She would gladly have faced the shock, but she did acknowledge to herself what a shock it would have been nevertheless.

Hubert went on, 'So, my theory is that Basil Swann turned up, and then later he died in other circumstances, and his wife, Mavis, was accused of murdering him.'

'That sounds plausible,' said Irene.

'It does,' agreed Joe. 'I'd be very interested to know how that came about – that Mavis was accused of Basil Swann's murder. I know it was a long time ago and afterwards she must have married a man called Swindel. I wonder what became of him. And now, of course, she's married to my father.'

'Mm, not the life of a retiring widow, it would appear,' said Hubert. 'I can see you might be a little anxious about your father if your stepmother has a history of *being widowed.*'

'I hadn't even thought of that,' said Irene. 'But she certainly didn't marry Fred Quinn for his money, so she's not a gold-digger. Joe's father is an assistant in a hardware store in Scarstone, a little moorside town in Lancashire.'

'They're both short of brass,' said Joe, 'and the boarding house she owns is in a right state, with not enough money available to do the maintenance it needs. Oh, but that reminds me.' He looked slightly shame-faced. 'We, er . . . we noticed in Mavis's accounts that she sends what to me and my sisters seems like quite a bit of money – between two and five pounds – to summat or someone every month. She writes it down as "C", but paying this money seems to be leaving Mavis short of funds so it must be important. We don't know who or what it is – summat so vital and yet never mentioned. With Mavis, if it's a secret, that means it's summat bad – I mean dishonest, like, or suspect in some way.'

Hubert raised a questioning eyebrow.

'I'm not sure that need be quite the case,' said Irene. 'Lots of people have business they'd rather keep to themselves. But, Hubert, it's true that she's not a nice person. Joe knows that well by now.'

'So you'd like me to find out what I can about your stepmother?' asked Hubert.

'Yes, please,' said Joe. 'If it's not too much trouble. It's just that you must know lots of important people, working in the law, and we're completely in the dark about Mavis. She's caused me and my sisters a lot of unhappiness.'

'I'll ask around,' said Hubert. 'Give me a few days and I'll see what I can discover.'

'Thank you,' said Irene, grasping his arm in gratitude before she could stop herself. He placed a hand gently and briefly over hers and smiled.

Then Joe took Hubert's hand in a firm handshake, which Irene noticed was a more confident and mature gesture than he would have shown before he went to work for George. 'Thank you, sir. I am most grateful,' he said.

A little while later, when Hubert and his sons had left, after having seen all of the garden – where Tiddler had asked about newts, and Simon had climbed on every seat and wall 'to get the best view', and Christopher had examined the impressive winding mechanism of the greenhouse windows – Joe cycled off to the forge, anxious to share Hubert's answer to the Basil Swindel mystery with George.

'Write to the girls and tell them so they won't be wondering,' suggested Irene, as he was leaving. 'Or I will if you think Mavis will intercept the letter when she sees your writing.'

'You've got her measure,' said Joe. 'I'll write to Rachel Fraser, Sarah's best friend, and enclose a letter for the girls. Rachel's a good sort.'

Irene waved him off and gently closed the Lodge door. What a lovely morning she had had with Hubert and his boys, and Joe, of course.

There had been two mysteries partially solved today. Not only did Hubert's theory about Basil Swann sound likely, but the question of the whereabouts of Hubert's wife, which Irene had kept trying not to raise in her mind, had been answered, thankfully without Irene saying anything.

'Mummy would have loved this flower garden – I mean in the summer when it's got flowers in it,'

Christopher had remarked as he raced past Irene, all three boys enjoying swerving along the crisscross of paths around the rose bushes. By then, Joe had gone back to the Lodge.

'She would,' said Hubert.

Irene turned questioningly to him, walking beside her.

'The boys' mother, Caroline, died when Tiddler was born,' he explained quietly.

'I'm so sorry to hear that,' Irene replied. She felt as if a grey cloud had cast a shadow over the day, although the sky was still as clear as before. Yet Christopher had openly referred to his mother without regret. He must have been very young when she died, of course, over half his lifetime ago. For Hubert, however, that must feel quite recently.

'How do you manage with the three of them?' she asked carefully.

'Oh, they are at school all week most weeks – they got off early yesterday – and anyway, I have Mrs Lofthouse, my housekeeper, who is pure gold.'

'Still, it must be quiet at home in the week, with the boys away . . .' Irene hoped she hadn't spoken out of turn.

'I'm usually so busy I don't notice,' said Hubert, matter-of-factly. Then he called to Simon to unhook Tiddler, who had got his jacket caught on a briar, and the moment passed for Irene to ask anything more.

All this time Irene had imagined a beautiful, accomplished and elegant woman smoothly running Hubert's home life and raising these lovely children, and there was no one but this Mrs Lofthouse. How often we can be so mistaken in our imaginings, she thought.

It would be easy to become fond of Hubert and his children, Irene thought now as she went into the kitchen to make herself something to eat. But that would be ridiculous in the circumstances. Hubert would complete the purchase of Fettling House, and for Irene it would be – must be – a new life somewhere else, and a new home. Joe was looking round for a room to rent in Saxham Ash, and Irene would be wise to take a look at cottages in Diss while she was there, if the job with the widow turned out to be suitable. It would be madness, with the sale of Fettling House now progressing, for Irene not to secure a new job and a new home as quickly as she could.

A few days after Sarah and Rachel last met, Rachel sent a message with Andrew Armstrong that she had news and would see Sarah at the library as soon as she could get away.

It was a Wednesday afternoon, and quiet when Sarah veered off into the big library building in the square on her way to the shops.

As ever, Rachel was delighted to see her best friend. She beckoned Sarah into a quiet corner of the reference section, where she took a few books from the shelves to use as props, should her superiors wonder what she was doing, and produced an envelope from her pinafore dress pocket.

'I have news!'

'That looks like Joe's writing.'

'It is. I thought it only proper to give it to you myself, not entrust it even to Mr Armstrong. Joe has written to me with a letter inside for you and Janette. This way, there's no danger of Mavis intercepting your letter. Anyway, here you are.'

She handed the envelope to Sarah, who opened it eagerly. It was quite short. Joe explained Hubert Cole's theory as to how there were two versions of Basil Swann's death, and that he was going to try to check on this and also find out who 'C' might be. He ended:

Mr Cole is a kind man – I could tell by the way he treats his three lads, and he also clearly respects and likes Auntie Irene, so that makes him a sound fella – so I reckon he will do his best. I'll let you know what he says.

I'm not much used to writing long letters so ask Rachel my other news!

Love to you and to Jan

Joe xxx

Sarah passed the letter to Rachel to read and then asked what Joe had written to her.

'He says he's found a room to rent near the forge and he intends to carry on working for George Ramsden, at least for the time being. It sounds as if he's settled at last.'

'I reckon so, Rachel. Joe could never find work that suited, and now, by chance, he has. Still, I won't be thanking Mavis for that.'

'Awful woman! I hope you haven't had to fight off that Wilkins fella again?'

'No. I think he's avoiding me as much as I've been avoiding him since last week, but Janette and I are putting our chairs behind our bedroom doors these days, in case he's creeping about at night. I just wish I could ask Dad to throw him out, but then Wilkins would call in his debts and mebbe even put it around Scarstone that Dad has a gambling debt. Mr Godwin wouldn't stand for any of his employees behaving like that.'

'Oh, it's such a mess . . .'

'It certainly is, Rachel,' agreed Sarah sadly.

CHAPTER SIXTEEN

If she stood in the middle of the vegetable garden and turned to the east, Irene could feel a little of the heat of the sun on her face, even in January. She closed her eyes and breathed in deeply the clean, cold scent of Fettling House garden. This time next year, this would all be a distant memory. Goodness only knew where she would be then; what she'd be doing.

There weren't many tasks to do outdoors now. And it was no use planting seeds when she wouldn't be here to pot them on, or even to know if they were wanted. While the redoubtable Mrs Lofthouse was running Hubert's home for him, someone equally esteemed would, no doubt, be in charge of his garden.

One thing Irene could do was clear out the greenhouse and potting shed. It was amazing how much stuff had been kept 'just in case' over the years. Now, what hadn't been used never would be. Although, of course, it felt like the end of an era, she decided it was better to regard it as just a job that needed doing, and now was the perfect time.

She had hardly begun on the greenhouse when she heard footsteps on the shingle path and there was Hubert. He was wearing a pristine waxed jacket and some tweed trousers this morning, but his brown boots were as shiny as his customary town shoes always were. Irene wondered whether he owned any old clothes at all.

'Irene, I'm pleased to have found you. I have been able to find out a little about Joe's stepmother, Mavis.'

'Goodness, how clever you are! Thank you, Hubert. I am very grateful for owt you've discovered, and I know Joe will be, too. He's moved to Saxham Ash and is working at the forge today, but I can tell him, if you like?'

'Not clever at all. Just asked the right person. Why don't we go to the forge and I'll tell you both together? I've got the car by the gates, if you can spare the time?'

'Yes, good idea,' Irene replied. The greenhouse clearing could wait. Mrs Mallinson was at her new cottage in the village with Betsy, who was helping her to sort out her curtains, so no one would miss Irene today. 'I'd better quickly go and change my boots and wash my hands,' she added.

'I'll wait for you with the car,' Hubert replied.

Back at the Lodge, Irene rushed to change out of her scruffy work boots. There was nothing she could do about her wrinkled thick-knit stockings, but remove the Fair Isle socks she wore over them and put on a pair of flat shoes. Then she swapped her worn work jacket for her better coat and put a felt hat over her hair, which had started to curl wildly in the damp air.

And why do I even mind what I look like? she asked

herself. It's not as if Joe hasn't seen me looking grubby after a day's gardening. But in her heart she knew it wasn't for Joe that she was making what little effort she could in three minutes flat.

Having locked up the Lodge, she found Hubert waiting beside his car; he opened the passenger door for her with his usual attentiveness. They set out for Saxham Ash, Irene pointing out a short cut and directing him along the lanes.

'How did you get on with your interview?' asked Hubert. 'Wasn't it with a widow near Diss?'

'I'm surprised you remember,' said Irene. 'The van was fixed in time for me to be able to drive there, but, oh dear, that was about the only good thing about the trip.'

'Tell me.'

'No, you don't really want to know . . .'

'Oh, but I do. I thought you might have set your heart on the job as it sounded very like the setup at Fettling House, but no?'

Irene smiled despite her disappointment. 'Oh, it was hopeless . . . ridiculous. Mrs Carey's husband, the one who died, has become summat of a sacred cow, and now she wants a gardener who will restore the garden to how it was when he last tended it eighteen months ago, yet she doesn't want one single thing moved, touched or in any way improved. It would be impossible to work there with her standing over me – "Don't cut that back. You mustn't dig that out. Charles never did it that way." I'd give it a week before I'd had enough.'

'Ah, no doubt she still has his shaving brush on the

bathroom shelf and his favourite roast dinner cooked on a Sunday,' said Hubert. 'The poor woman, it's very sad.'

'Poor woman indeed. I'm sorry for her loss, but she's not helping herself to get over it,' said Irene.

'Well, it can be very difficult and take time, but nothing will bring back the person who's gone, so in the end you just have to grasp the nettle. Ha, a cliché, but an appropriate one in the circumstances.' He gave a crooked little smile.

Irene knew just what he meant. Had fate dealt her a different hand, she would have been married for many years to Gilbert by now. She had made a conscious effort from the start to move on with her life without him, yet these last couple of days, since Joe had moved out of the Lodge and into his rented room, she was suddenly finding her home lonely and cheerless, when it had never been so before her nephew had arrived. And she had been thinking more about Gilbert, too . . .

They were both quiet for a few moments.

Then Irene said, 'I take it you have a gardener who you're bringing with you when you move into the House?'

'I'm hoping so,' said Hubert. 'In fact, I'm interviewing.'

'That's good. With a garden that size it's very important not to let it get out of hand, otherwise it'll be one heck of a job to bring it back under control,' Irene advised. 'Best make sure you have someone in place the moment you move in.'

Hubert nodded. 'I intend to. And I do have Mr Lofthouse, who, while not a gardener, is a very useful man to have about the place.'

'Good . . . good.'

A little silence fell.

'Left at the next turning and then straight on at the crossroads,' said Irene then. 'I very much enjoyed that morning your sons visited.' She thought of Tiddler with his little shrimping net on a long stick, and the enthusiasm for the garden that the older boys displayed, too. 'What delightful children you have, Hubert. They are not just well-mannered but charming and funny as well. Any parent would be proud of such lads.'

'Thank you. I'm so glad you think so.'

Irene thought she might have overstepped the mark, as an employee of Mrs Mallinson, and maybe Hubert's fulsome reply had an element of sarcasm. It wasn't her place to comment on his children. Oh dear, it would be so difficult to find a job where the relationships were as easy as they were at Fettling House.

'I'm sorry,' she murmured. 'It's not my place to say owt.'

He didn't reply, but he was concentrating on the road, and then Irene was pointing out the forge on the left as they entered Saxham Ash village.

Hubert stopped the car beside the forge and, of course, the big shiny vehicle immediately attracted a little crowd of admirers.

Joe came out, his face looking hot and his hands sooty. There was the metallic ring of hammering coming from inside, indicating George was busy.

'Mr Cole, sir. Auntie Irene. What's up?'

'Nowt, I hope,' said Irene, 'but Mr Cole has come to tell you what he's found out about your stepmother.'

Joe grinned. 'That's good of you, sir, to come to tell us yourself. Come in. George will be pleased to meet you, Mr Cole, and to see you again, Auntie.'

George was even grimier than Joe, but he greeted the visitors with a wide grin, laid down his tools and showed Irene and Hubert through the hot forge and into his little cottage across the yard at the back. The yard itself was filled with interesting metal objects: obelisks and arches for climbing plants, weather vanes with attractive designs at the top – a silhouette of a horse and plough; a row of waddling ducks – and a pair of elaborate gates leaning up against the side wall.

The cottage was plainly furnished, and while George showed Irene and Hubert to an upholstered sofa, he and Joe sat on dining chairs, the seats protected by sheets of newspaper.

'Now,' said Hubert, 'I was able to track down a man who was present at the trial of Mavis Swann. It turns out that my guess about Basil Swann was right. He was indeed badly injured in the war and, in the chaos and horror of the conflict, he was mistaken for another man, and so a telegram telling of his being missing in action was wrongly sent to Mavis. Basil couldn't speak for a while – he had terrible injuries to his face – and, of course, no one was trying to locate him because it was believed he was dead. This was in 1917, after Passchendaele. It was months later that Basil Swann made it home and turned up unannounced on his doorstep, to the shock of his wife, Mavis.'

'I feel a bit sorry for her,' said George.

'I don't,' said Joe. 'Let me guess. She had got another husband already and so got rid of the inconvenient first one.'

'Joe!' admonished Irene. 'Be kind. And remember, she was found innocent of Basil Swann's murder.'

'Yes, it wasn't quite as Joe says,' said Hubert. 'She had got an admirer in tow, a rich man name Cedric Chisholm, who owned a chain of drapery shops along the south coast.'

'So all this took place down south?' asked Joe. 'That makes sense: the way Mavis speaks, I thought it might be London.'

'Brighton,' said Hubert. 'Mr Chisholm did the honourable thing and saw no more of Mavis, leaving her to rebuild her marriage with Basil. Then Basil died. The police thought Mavis had shot him. There were service revolvers turning up all over the place in those days, and Basil died from a bullet to the head at close range. Mavis was arrested and tried for murder, but there was insufficient evidence to convict her. It was, rather, concluded that Swann, horribly disfigured, could not cope with the sight of his own ravaged face, nor with the pain he had to endure from that and his several other injuries, and, I'm afraid, shot himself.'

Everyone was silent for a few moments. What a sad story.

'Poor Mavis,' said George.

'Aye, mebbe it's her ill-luck that's made her so nasty,' muttered Joe. 'And I'm wondering if "C" is Cedric Chisholm, although why she should be paying him now if he's a rich man with a string of shops is a mystery.'

'It could be him, and we don't know the reason, Joe, or it could be someone else entirely,' Hubert said. 'I'm afraid I can throw no light on the identity of "C".'

'So what happened then? How did the widow Mavis Swann become the Mavis Swindel who married my brother-in-law?' asked Irene.

'I'm afraid once the trial was over and Mavis was a free woman, the law played no further part in her life, so far as I know,' said Hubert. 'Swindel, it turns out, was her maiden name, so she must have reverted to that at some point, but using the title "Mrs", perhaps to disassociate herself from the Basil Swann trial. Certainly the man who told me this knows nothing else of her except for more thing.'

'What's that?' Joe leaned forward eagerly.

'Mavis and Basil Swann had a child.'

'What! Mavis, a mother? Now I really do feel pity for the bairn,' said Joe. 'She's the least motherly woman a person could imagine.'

'Do you know owt about this child, at all?' asked Irene.

'Nothing, I'm afraid. The child took no part in the trial – which was my associate's only business with Mavis Swann – and there's no record even of whether it was a girl or a boy, nor how old when the child's father, Basil Swann, died in 1919.'

'Well, some of the mystery is solved, but more mystery is presented,' said Irene. 'Thank you, Hubert, for finding this out. What do you think, Joe?'

Joe pursed his mouth and looked undecided. 'Thank you, Mr Cole,' he said. 'You've been right helpful about the Basil Swann puzzle, which has been bothering me and my sisters. Mebbe Mavis's child died – there was that Spanish flu, which killed a lot of folk, or it could have been summat else – but she seems not to be tied in any way to a child of her own now. She's just this awful woman who bought a falling-down house and took over my family to sort it out for her.'

'And she's paying "C", who may or may not be Cedric Chisholm,' Irene reminded him.

'Write and tell Sarah,' said George. 'That's all you can do. If Mavis is in touch with her child at all, then Sarah is on the spot to learn something.'

'You're right,' said Joe. 'And I've just had an idea. Dora Burgess.'

'Who is Dora Burgess?' asked George.

'A girl I used to be friends with in Scarstone. I've remembered now that Dora once said summat about Mavis that made me think she knew about her. This was before Mavis even married Dad. And Dora's family come from down south, same as Mavis.'

'It sounds a bit unlikely,' Irene began gently. 'There are an awful lot of people living on the south coast.'

'Aye, you're right, Auntie. But not all of them have a father who used to work on a newspaper in Brighton.'

*

Hubert opened the car door for Irene and made sure she was seated comfortably. They waved to Joe and George, who then turned back to the forge and their work.

'Would it be so very difficult for your nieces to ask their stepmother a little about her past?' asked Hubert, putting the car into gear.

'I reckon so,' said Irene. 'She'd just lie, or swerve away from the truth if she had a secret, and then find a way of punishing them for asking.'

'Sounds like a bit of a monster.'

'Yes. I've wondered about going to this place Over the Edge to see what's what, but I can't take Fred's children away from him against his will. And Mavis would just either face me down or pretend summat different from reality, and I'm not sure how I'd deal with that, or even know what was real and what was false. Fred chose to marry her and she's provided a home for him and his children. Joe says she got him sacked. I don't know that for sure – I wasn't there – but it sounds like the kind of thing she might do. Anyway, Joe seems to be fitting in very nicely at the forge now, for which we must thank George. Janette is still in school, as she wants to be. Sarah is the one who has had the hardest time at the hands of her stepmother. I reckon Mavis is envious of Sarah, her being young and pretty, and summat of a favourite with Fred. Mavis has clearly elbowed Sarah out of her father's favour.'

'And it could be that Mavis is clever enough to turn that round and say Sarah is bitter because she's no longer the apple of her father's eye. I've seen how an argument can be turned in court.'

Irene gazed out of the side window, wondering what to do. She wasn't in a position to go to Over the Edge and take Sarah and Janette away to live with her. She might not even have a home shortly.

'Where are we going?' she asked, noticing that Hubert had kept on eastwards instead of turning back towards Fettling.

'Well, I thought as we are both free today – ' he raised an eyebrow and Irene nodded in agreement – 'we could go and have something to eat at one of the places along the coast. But not if you don't want,' he added hastily. 'I'm sorry, Irene, I should have asked you first.'

'You should,' she said, 'but you guessed I'd think it a good idea. A treat. Thank you.'

'A treat for me, too,' he said, and the car sped smoothly on towards the seaside.

Andrew Armstrong quietly suggested to Sarah that Rachel was keen to see her at the library the next time she went to the shops.

'What news?' asked Sarah, when Rachel was free to talk and they'd quietly slipped off to the deserted reference section. 'Has Joe written?'

'He certainly has. Here you are . . .'

Sarah opened the envelope with her and Janette's names on the front and quickly read what Joe had written.

'Good grief,' she muttered.

'Not bad news, I hope,' said Rachel, bursting with curiosity.

As before, Sarah handed her the letter to read for herself.

'Heavens, Mavis a mother!' gasped Rachel, a minute later. 'I bet she was a useless one.'

'I wonder what happened to the child,' said Sarah.

'Oh, Sarah, don't start worrying about that. He or she could have died for any reason, years ago, or is grown up and living far away, perfectly happy.'

'Yes, you're right, of course. There's nowt I can do about that. But it's interesting what Joe says about this Cedric Chisholm possibly being "C", although, if he is, it's a puzzle why he would be being paid.'

'Especially if he's well off anyway. Or was.'

'At least we now know that Swindel was Mavis's name before Swann, and we aren't wondering about another husband. We should do as Joe suggests: go and ask Dora Burgess what she knows.'

'I'd forgotten Joe said that Dora might know summat of Mavis. He mentioned it to me one time and I thought nowt of it. Go and get your shopping and then come back here and we'll try to catch Dora at the dress shop as she leaves.'

Sarah was so glad to have the support of her best friend. Rachel really was a girl in a million, she thought. She put Joe's letter safely in her pocket to show Janette and went out impatiently into the cold afternoon, keen to meet up with Rachel again later.

*

Sarah and Rachel timed their arrival at Regal Modes, as the dress shop was called, to coincide with Dora's preparing to leave for the afternoon. The shop was on the High Street, at the 'smart end'.

The girls gazed into Regal Modes' window, which was overlaid with yellow Cellophane to stop the clothes on display being faded by sunlight, but which gave the elegant dresses a jaundiced look. The Cellophane was unnecessary in January, with few hours of daylight and seldom a glimpse of the sun at all, but Beryl Regis, the owner, sold the best women's clothes in Scarstone, and she wasn't going to be careless of her stock. The dresses were modelled on rather sinister-looking mannequins with painted-on, astonished features and arms in unnatural attitudes, the hands round the wrong way. Even with such a lack of finesse in their display, however, it was clear how attractive the dresses were. Sarah was reluctant to go into Regal Modes, looking shabby and worn as she did in her old winter coat, but Rachel gave her an encouraging smile, stepped up to the door and went in.

'Good afternoon. We're just about to close, but mebbe I can help you if you know what it is you'd like to try?' said Beryl Regis, coming over with a smile, her heels tapping on the polished floorboards. She wore a beautifully fitting green wool dress. Sarah eyed it up approvingly with a seamstress's eye. Beryl and her assistant, Dora, made a point of being advertisements for the shop.

'Good afternoon, Mrs Regis,' said Rachel. 'We've just come to meet Dora, when she's done for the day.'

'She's just putting her coat on now,' said Beryl. She raised her voice and called in a fluty way, 'Dora. Dora, dear, you have *friends*.'

Dora appeared, looking gorgeous in a black coat with a velvet collar and a matching hat. Her shoes had black velvet bows on the fronts. Sarah felt even worse now. Her own coat was black, too, or had been originally. Now it looked greenish and threadbare in comparison with Dora's plush new one.

'Hello,' Dora said, puzzled. 'I wasn't expecting you two. What's the news?'

'We'll walk with you and mebbe you can help us,' said Rachel, and they bade Beryl a good night and set out in the direction of Dora's home.

'Well,' said Dora, 'it's nice to have someone to walk with, but I'm wondering why. You all right, Sarah? You're looking a bit pinched around the face. A touch of rouge would mebbe help lift your complexion, if you don't mind me saying.'

'I expect you're right, Dora. But it's not my face I'm bothered about, it's my stepmother.'

Dora, who liked to talk non-stop about cosmetics and clothes with other women, looked disappointed. 'Do I know her?'

'We think you might have heard of her, Dora. She's called Mavis Swindel.'

'Blimey, that name again. I remember your Joe asking me about her ages ago, in the summer, but I was that mad that he was distracted by her – it was an evening when Joe took me to the George and

Dragon and the woman was there – that I wasn't for saying owt.'

'So you do know summat?' asked Sarah.

'Not really,' said Dora.

Sarah and Rachel looked at each other, disappointed. Well, it had been a long shot . . .

'But my dad does. He's the one to tell you. Come home with me now and you can ask him.'

To Sarah and Rachel, Mr Burgess seemed old to have an only daughter of twenty. He had served in the army in the war, when he must have been older than most of his comrades, and he walked with a stick and a bad limp. He had a part-time job writing features for the local newspaper in Scarstone, and Mrs Burgess also worked part time. This was evidently one of his days off and he was, surprisingly, baking scones when Dora showed the girls into her home.

'Hello, girls,' he greeted them. 'Your mum's not home yet, Dora, but there's a stew heating through for when she gets in. These are not long out of the oven and ready for you all to try.' He indicated a cooling rack. 'I've made a pot of tea.'

'Oh, thank you,' the girls said.

'Dad's got right good at baking,' said Dora. 'Some folk seem a bit surprised, but the great French pastry chefs are supposedly men so I reckon my dad's not so odd. Just a bit different round here.'

'I think you're really lucky to have a useful dad,' said Sarah, then felt guilty because her own father was very good at repairs around the house, and giving out advice as he sold hardware; he had, however, become useless at being a caring father since he'd met Mavis.

Dora took off her coat and hung it on – good heavens! – a padded coat hanger, instead of just draping it over a peg, and then she removed her pretty shoes and put a pair of shoe trees in them. Sarah and Rachel exchanged looks of awed admiration. Imagine wearing things that were worth spending such care on.

'I'll give those shoes a brush for you later, sweetheart,' said her father, and the kindness with which he offered to do this simple everyday task so that his daughter's lovely shoes might be kept at their best touched Sarah's heart.

When the tea had been poured and the scones split and buttered, Dora said, 'Dad, Sarah's been asking me about Mavis Swindel. I know you know a bit about her.'

'Oh, yes? And why would you be wanting to know, Sarah?'

'Well, she's my stepmother,' Sarah confessed, hoping this didn't reflect badly on herself in Mr Burgess's opinion, 'and there's summat about her that I don't understand.'

'Can't you just ask her?'

'Not really. It might be . . . awkward.'

Mr Burgess nodded in an understanding way, as if his question might have been a test. 'I see. Well, I tell you what, Dora. Why don't you and Rachel take yourselves off and look at those fashion magazines you've got in the other room, and Sarah and I can work through the "awkwardness" about her stepmother?'

'Of course,' said Rachel, not at all interested in fashion, but wanting Sarah to get her result. Dora was already halfway out of the room with her tea and a second scone.

'Right . . .' said Mr Burgess, and slowly poured another cup of tea, first for Sarah and then for himself.

Sarah felt she might explode with suspense. Or perhaps he knew very little and she'd leave here full of delicious scones and awash with tea, but none the wiser about Mavis.

'I know about Mavis's first husband, Basil Swann,' said Sarah, to prompt him. 'That he shot himself a while after he returned home horribly injured from the war, and that Mavis was tried for his murder, but in the end the verdict was suicide.'

'I believe that's entirely true,' said Mr Burgess, easing his gammy leg. 'I was a journalist on the *Brighton Evening Argus,* but not until a little while later. I only know about Basil Swann because I got the whole story from Mavis's second husband.'

'Her *second?* I kind of forget that Dad might not be her second.'

'He was called Cedric Chisholm and he was quite elderly when I last saw him. He lived near Brighton, where he owned several drapery shops.'

'Mavis was married to Cedric Chisholm! I have heard of him, but only that she had taken up with him when she thought she was a widow. Then Chisholm parted from her when Basil Swann returned from the war. So Mavis and Chisholm were married in the end?'

'Mavis and Cedric Chisholm were intending to get married before Swann's unexpected return. Chisholm had money to spend on her and I suspect she liked living the life of a widow, on the arm of a rich man, in the lively seaside town of Brighton. But it all came crashing down when Basil Swann reappeared.'

'I can see it would be awful,' said Sarah, fairly, 'to have grieved for Basil Swann and to have found a new life for herself, and with a man who treated her well. It would have been difficult for her to put aside what she had seen as her future and just take up her life as it was before her husband left to fight in the war.'

'Yes, but soon after Mavis was found not guilty of Swann's murder, she married Cedric Chisholm in a service with only witnesses in attendance. He was rather an idealistic man, and he thought he would "save" her, make a good woman of this person who had been accused of murder, albeit unjustly, and ensure she was on a respectable path in life as his wife who was above suspicion. When the dust settled, I went to interview Cedric Chisholm for the newspaper. I was a friend of a friend, and the fellow put in a good word for me so I got the story where other journalists were given the cold shoulder. There were some stories written before then that were rubbish, full of sly innuendo to sell papers rather than inform in a fair way, and Mr Chisholm wanted to give his version of events. The newly-weds settled down to a rather quieter life than Mavis might once have envisaged with her well-off husband. She could hardly be seen out painting the town after the publicity over her first husband's suicide.'

'Even Mavis wouldn't act in quite such poor taste,' said Sarah, nodding. Then she remembered that Mavis had named her dog 'Basil' after Basil Swann, so she was probably wrong about that.

'Well, that's the thing, Sarah. Mavis Chisholm didn't really want to live quietly when she could have been enjoying life to the full once she had married money. But Chisholm was determined that she wouldn't be seen about Brighton inciting gossip and rumour while the trial was still fresh in people's minds. You know how tongues wag, and he didn't want his drapery shops to be the kind of places respectable housewives avoided being seen in. He thought he could change Mavis, or she could change her ways, but despite the outcome of the trial, the rumours would not go away. Someone was forever pointing a finger or whispering behind their hand. People like to spice up life and Mavis was the kind who put people's backs up and made enemies, so her past difficulties followed her around like an unwanted dog. In Brighton, despite Chisholm's best efforts to bury her past, she would be forever the woman who had been accused of murdering her husband, but was now clearly happy to have moved on.'

Sarah could well imagine this. 'I don't think she's much liked in Scarstone either,' she said.

'You're right. From what I've heard, she has retained her character, of that there's no doubt – spreading gossip and lies, asking for unreasonable discounts in the shops, putting people's backs up and then exacting some mean revenge when anyone speaks against her. I get to hear all sorts, working on the newspaper, although it's her distinctive hair I recognised, even before I learned she still calls herself Mavis. Whatever her current surname, this is the woman I knew of in Brighton years ago.'

'So what happened? How has she come to be here, so far from the south coast?'

'In the end she left Chisholm. She took a lot of money, which he kept in a safe in the house, and just disappeared with it one day. He came home from work and she'd gone. This is several years ago now – perhaps about 1924. I don't know, but I would guess that this was when she changed her name to Swindel, perhaps so she'd be difficult to trace.'

'It was her maiden name, I've been told, but she called herself "Mrs" the second time round.'

'I didn't know that, Sarah. Only she knows what happened between her leaving Brighton and arriving in Scarstone. She bought that monstrous house, which I gather was very cheap on account of the owners being bankrupts and the house needing so much work doing to it, and started to take in lodgers.'

'I expect she thought it would be an investment and a way to make money,' said Sarah, 'but she has no idea of what's required to be a good landlady, and she's far too lazy and, it seems, short of money to make of the huge house what she could. That's surely why she's roped Dad and me in: to do the work for her. She got my brother sacked from his job at Hardcastle's – we think to try to get him working for her – but he ran away, and she keeps threatening to take my little sister out of school, to work there or for someone else and bring in money. The house is in a terrible state, bits have been falling off it lately, and half the original lodgers have left. She's not making a success of the place and I wonder how it's all going to end.'

'Oh, that sounds awful for you. I suspect the woman is a fantasist and envisages far more than she can ever achieve.'

'Or can afford, or is prepared to work for herself,' agreed Sarah. 'But there's summat more, Mr Burgess. Do you know owt about Mavis and Basil Swann having a child? Someone reliable has found out that they did, but there's never been a whisper of such a person at Over the Edge.'

'No, I have never heard that, Sarah. I wonder if you've been misinformed. You see, Mr Chisholm would surely have known of this if it were true, and he did tell me he was giving me the whole story.'

'Mebbe . . .'

Sarah wondered if Chisholm had known but just didn't want to say anything to the journalist, to protect the child's privacy. After all, anything that had happened would not be the child's fault.

'Well, thank you for your help, Mr Burgess. The more I know about my stepmother, the more colourful and complicated her life seems to have been. This Cedric Chisholm – is he still alive, do you know?'

'I'm afraid I don't, Sarah. He wasn't a friend of mine

in any way, just someone about whom I wrote a profile, so we never kept in touch. He was a lot older than Mavis, however, so it could be that he is long dead.'

Having said goodbye, first to the Burgesses and then to Rachel in the street outside their door, Sarah went slowly home, clutching the shopping, her head full of Mavis and poor Basil Swann, and this second husband, Cedric Chisholm. Could he be 'C', and Mavis was paying him back the money she had stolen from him? That didn't sound like the Mavis Sarah knew. The more Sarah thought about it, the stranger the whole saga appeared. But one thing was certain: with Mavis, there was bound to be something rotten at the core of it.

CHAPTER SEVENTEEN

Sarah was halfway back to Over the Edge when an astonishing thought struck her so suddenly that she had to stop walking, put down her shopping bags and gather herself to address it. What if this elderly person Cedric Chisholm, who had married Mavis some time after 1919, *was* still alive? He might be 'C', although, of course, he might not. Alternatively, after Mavis had disappeared with his money, he might just have let her have it, be glad to be rid of her and never made contact again. And if he was alive, unless he had divorced her, he and Mavis were still married. Which would mean she wasn't married to Fred.

Not married to Dad . . . Not our stepmother at all . . .

The thought made her breathless and her heart felt lighter than it had for months. After a few minutes, Sarah took up her bags and walked on, her shoulders back, her head held high and her mind filled with this one thought. *Oh, please, let it be true.* They could go back and live in Keele Street. Joe would come home. Everything would be as it had been.

No, that was silly. The house in Keele Street was now rented to someone else. Joe had a job at the forge with George, and it was possible that relations between Joe and his father would never be mended. Things could never be the same as they had been before Mavis Swindel came into their lives, for any of them.

Sarah pushed these thoughts out of her mind for the minute and concentrated on thinking up some lie as to why she had taken so long over the shopping and was so late back. There was a time when she wouldn't have dreamed of telling lies, but that time had long passed.

That evening, Sarah and Janette went up to bed early, as they so often did to avoid having to keep company with Mavis and Fred, both pleading tiredness and headaches. Sarah had been bursting to tell Janette her news and air her thoughts. With a big smile, she gave Janette the letter from Joe to read first.

'A child of her own? And not a hint of it. I bet he or she has broken all contact,' said Janette.

'Well, no one knows owt about this child – neither Mr Cole nor Mr Burgess,' said Sarah, 'so I think your bet is a good one. If this person is owt like Mavis, I hope it died in the flu epidemic.'

'We'd like to break contact, wouldn't we, Basil?' Janette hugged the little dog, who snuggled in among her cardigans.

Then Sarah told Janette everything she had learned about Mavis from Dora's father.

'Mr Burgess hasn't been in touch with Cedric Chisholm

since he interviewed him for the newspaper years ago, and he was much older than Mavis then, but I suddenly thought, it's possible that Mr Chishom is still alive. If he's "C" in Mavis's accounts, he must be. I can't think why Mavis should be sending him money, except perhaps to pay him back what she stole from his safe when she bolted. Yet that doesn't sound like the kind of thing Mavis would do. She'd rather try to get away with owt she can, especially where money is concerned.'

'P'raps he's making her pay him. He could be bribing her: if she doesn't pay him back, he'll appear and stir up trouble for her,' suggested Janette. 'Oh, Sarah, what a mess. How do we find out the truth in all this horribleness?'

'I s'pose a starting point would be to try to establish if Mr Chisholm is alive and, if so, whether he's still married to Mavis. If he is dead, then he isn't "C". If he's alive, and he didn't divorce Mavis, then he still might not be "C", but she isn't our stepmother. She's nowt to do with us, just a horrible person who came into our lives and who we don't have to live with any more.'

'But we have to live with Dad, don't we? And Dad, then living with this woman who isn't even his wife but someone else's . . . well, it's not right. Or Dad could be so angry that Mavis has deceived him that he leaves her, but that isn't a happy situation either, especially in a place the size of Scarstone. Oh, Sarah, wherever we look, the Stepmother has spoiled everything.' Janette looked tearful. 'I hope she's not our stepmother, but even if she isn't, she's still ruined our lives.'

343

Sarah pulled her handkerchief out of her pocket and handed it to Janette. 'No, we'll not let her. I don't know what we can do about Dad, but Joe's making a life for himself now he's got away, and as soon as we can, we should leave too. It's never going to get any better here. Let's think what the best thing would be – for us, not anyone else. I'm fed up of us being at the bottom of the heap when it comes to being happy.'

Janette, sitting on Sarah's bed, rearranged Basil, then pulled the eiderdown up to her chin and Sarah got up out of the chair and went to join her.

'Budge up.'

'I'm thinking really hard,' said Janette.

'I bet we're thinking of the same thing,' said Sarah, remembering Christmas at Fettling House . . . how Irene, who had already given Joe a home, had welcomed the girls and made the holiday perfect . . . the little tree with its folding-down branches and its old decorations, which Grandma Mayhew had treasured . . . the pink winter light in the rose garden and George kissing her so sweetly and giving her the little charm, which she kept with her always, to remind her of him . . .

'So do I,' whispered Janette. 'It's Fettling and Auntie Irene, isn't it?'

Sarah squeezed Janette up close. 'Of course. Auntie always wants the best for us. She's the very opposite of the Stepmother. But Fettling House is sold and Auntie Irene's new job could be almost anywhere, when she finds it. We can't be a burden to her now, can we? All the upset of leaving Fettling House will be enough for her to deal with, without us turning up just as she's packing up to leave and expecting her to take responsibility for us.'

They sank into gloomy silence.

'If you agree, I'll ask Mr Burgess if he remembers how he used to get in touch with Cedric Chisholm,' said Sarah. 'At least if I can speak to him, then we'll know the truth.'

Janette nodded.

'Now, remember what I said about putting a chair behind your bedroom door. If Paget Wilkins is creeping about the place, that will give you time to scream the place down before he gets in. I'll be there before he knows it. I've found a walking stick, which Mr McCain left in the umbrella stand, and I've put it just by my bed. I can fend him off with that. Not just fend him off, but give him a proper hiding.'

'Major Wilkins is a hateful man. I wish you'd been able to grab that great big carving fork, not just an ordinary one. That would have made an impression on him he wouldn't forget in a hurry.'

'Mm, Mavis was right, though: I haven't got it in me to kill anyone, even Wilkins. I just wish we felt safe in our own home, even if that home is now Over the Edge. Is that too much to ask?'

'I think we'd both feel less afraid if we moved the beds into one room. Safety in numbers.'

'You're right, Jan. Good thinking. Let's move yours in here.'

They moved Janette's bed with a bit of a struggle.

Mr Cornwell, hearing the commotion, called up the attic stairs to see if they were all right, and Janette went down to reassure him. She was a little while, and by the time she came back, Sarah had got Jan's bed made up again.

Sarah thought she'd sleep better that night, knowing Janette was safely beside her, but neither of them slept peacefully or for long. The news about Mavis overrode everything else, and the thought that at last they might just have found a way to be free of her went round and round in their heads, their hopes rising and then plummeting all night long.

The next morning, early, Sarah said she'd take Basil for a walk. As it was raining heavily, Mavis was pleased to let her do this.

'Sorry, Basil, but after I was out so long yesterday, I need to be seen to be useful today,' said Sarah. 'But I have a plan, little fella.'

Outside, on the front doorstep, she put Basil in a large canvas shopping bag she'd brought out for that purpose, and held her umbrella over them both as she hurried into Scarstone to see Mr Burgess. Basil was only tiny, but he was still quite heavy to be carried around in a bag, and Sarah was glad when the High Street came into view.

Mr Burgess had mentioned he'd be at work the next day. The *Scarstone Herald* office was just behind the library.

She went into the front office, where a receptionist sat behind a big desk. It was quite noisy with the sound of typewriters being pounded in nearby rooms, and people coming and going, clutching long lengths of paper.

'Good morning,' said Sarah, propping her wet umbrella up beside the door. 'I wonder if I might see Mr Burgess, please? I won't take more than a minute of his time.'

'Is it to do with a story for the paper?' asked the woman.

'Er, sort of,' said Sarah.

Just at that moment, Basil started shifting his weight in the shopping bag and the bag rocked back and forth heavily on Sarah's shoulder.

'What on earth have you got there?' asked the woman, looking alarmed.

Sarah put the bag gently down and lifted out Basil.

'Oh, the darling,' cooed the woman. 'What a pretty little dog. Is she yours?'

Pretty? Basil?

'She's a he, and he's called Basil.'

'Ah, he's a fine fella. Come here, Basil, you little angel, and let me say hello.'

The woman called him over and made much of petting him, while Sarah wondered if she was partially sighted, or even if it was all an elaborate joke and in a moment she'd say he was the feeblest apology for a dog she'd ever seen and it was a wonder Sarah wasn't ashamed to be seen out with him. But no, if it was a joke she was keeping it up long past the punchline.

'And Mr Burgess?' ventured Sarah.

'Oh, just go in at that door and you'll find him,' said the woman, hardly turning her attention from Basil now. 'Who's the sweetest little fella I ever saw, eh . . .?'

Sarah did as she was instructed. Mr Burgess, sitting at one of several desks, all occupied, was not surprised to see her.

'I've discussed this with my sister and she agrees. I should try to speak to Mr Chisholm and see what else he can tell me. What if he's still married to my step-mother? Who knows how it ended between them?' Sarah said.

'Heavens, yes. I just assumed as she has married again that she was free to do so. I'd telephone for you, Sarah, but I think you need to do this yourself and hear the truth at first-hand,' said Mr Burgess. 'I have a number here, but I can't tell you if Mr Chisholm has moved house or even whether he's died.' He pulled a battered indexed notebook out of a drawer of the desk and flipped through to a page on which the ink was faded and the edges dog-eared. Then he wrote on a notebook on his desk and ripped out the page. 'This will be at least a starting point for you, and it could even answer all your questions. Good luck, and I hope it all works out the way you want it to.'

Sarah sighed. 'Thank you, Mr Burgess. It was good of you to take the time with me yesterday, and thank you for this now. But I can't honestly see that any way it works out will be ideal. There's no road out of this except via an upset.'

'Then you must do what will bring about the best

outcome for you and your sister. You're only young; let the grown-ups take care of themselves. It seems to me, from what you told me, that it's a pity they didn't take more care of you and Janette before now. And young Joe.'

'Thank you, Mr Burgess. Now, I'd better go and collect Mavis's dog from the lady in the outer office. She does seem unusually keen on him.'

'Ah, yes, Mrs Winterbourne. Another widow. She had a dog of her own until recently, but, well, it went the way of all flesh. I think she's pleased to have something to make a fuss of, poor lady. It's hard to be alone, I should think.'

Sarah, having extracted Basil from Mrs Winterbourne's hugs and put him back in the shopping bag, wended her way home in the rain. What a good man Mr Burgess was: not only a loving father to Dora, but a sympathetic friend to his colleague at work, and thoughtful and encouraging to Sarah herself. How far she felt she had fallen from that ideal. Now she was often critical and intolerant, short with her father, lying to Mavis, and avoiding Major Wilkins to the point of rudeness. Over the Edge seemed to have that effect on people. Or maybe it was just Mavis Swindel.

Hubert Cole was spending more and more time at Fettling House, or so Irene was pleased to think, as she thought she heard his car on the gravel. They had had that very enjoyable lunch just the day before yesterday – he was charming company and had treated her as a person of interest and value, not merely as an employee of the lady whose house he was buying. It had been . . . she searched for the most appropriate word and settled in her thoughts on 'lovely'. It had been lovely – *he* had been lovely. And now here he was again, just as she was trying to finish emptying the greenhouse. She did admit to herself that her heart lifted when she saw him approaching in his amusingly smart country clothes. It was sad and also strangely lonely in the garden of late – last time for this, final work on that – and, in the back of her mind, mulling over the mystery of Mavis Swindel and the child she had never mentioned. And Irene still didn't know what she was going to do next, or even where she was going to live. That, above everything, made her feel alone. The decision rested entirely on her shoulders. She could hardly go to live in Joe's little rented room, nor in the small forge cottage with Betsy and George. She had another interview lined up at a house outside Ipswich, but she wasn't sure it sounded like the right job for her.

'Good morning, Hubert. I was just thinking what a lovely time we had earlier this week.'

'It was my pleasure to have your company, Irene. I hoped to find you here. I thought I'd have another look at my future garden and perhaps ask . . . ask a bit of advice, if that's all right with you?'

'Well, as it's going to be your garden soon, you may look wherever you like, and I'll help if I can. I'm just finishing clearing out here. I don't know if there's owt you want?'

Advice about his garden? What was his interest in gardens and why did he need advice? It sounded like a weak excuse for being here, to Irene, but she couldn't think why he needed to concoct any kind of excuse. The whole place would belong to him before long.

The expression on his face seemed to betray that her simple question had defeated him.

'I'm not sure. Shall I carry these plants, whatever they are, outside? Do you think Julia will want to take any of them with her?'

'They're geraniums,' explained Irene, laughing. 'Good idea. Mrs Mallinson can choose what she wants, then you can inherit any you want and I'll leave the rest outside the front gates for passers-by to take – what do you say?'

'But I don't know anything about geraniums. How will I know what I want?'

'Oh, they're easy to grow. Any gardener will know.' She saw he looked uncertain. 'You are getting a gardener to take over, aren't you, Hubert? Because I think you need to be getting on with it.' Oh dear, had she been too blunt? But really, what was he dithering about?

'Well, I'm hoping so . . .'

They worked together contentedly, emptying the last of the greenhouse. Irene was amused to see Hubert lining up flowerpots on the shingle and earnestly asking questions about the names on the labels.

'Hubert, I mustn't keep you,' she said when the greenhouse was completely empty. 'I'll put some decent plants aside for you, if you like. I'm sure you must have important things to do.'

'Nothing more important than this,' he said. 'Let's go and, er, look at the vegetables. The boys love that part of the garden. Anything to do with food.'

They went over to the rows of cabbages and leeks.

'A lot of food for just three people,' he remarked.

'It's for Mallinson's Market Garden,' Irene reminded him. 'Of course, that'll go when you move in.'

He nodded but didn't say anything for a few moments. Then: 'Irene, have you got another interview lined up? Have you plans in place for the future?'

'Well, yes, although I'm not holding my breath about it,' she admitted. 'But I'll be lucky to find owt as good as this, I realise. I'm not sure that there's quite such a call for this kind of job these days. Folk are wanting smaller houses with smaller gardens. There's less need of staff, both indoors and out. Not many vacancies in my line of work. But I'll find summat. Mebbe I could work for several folk rather than take on one big garden. Or p'raps I'll buy a bit of land and start my own market garden; be my own boss.' She smiled broadly to cover up that this could only ever be a pipe dream. She had few savings.

'Or you could live here.'

'What, you mean stay on at the Lodge? Be your gardener?'

'No, not at the Lodge. At the House. You could live at Fettling House.'

For a moment she was puzzled. Then she realised what he meant. 'I'm afraid, Hubert, that I'd not be much use to you. I don't cook nearly well enough to be employed in that role, and I wouldn't want to step on the toes of Mrs Lofthouse where the housekeeping was concerned. It's kind of you to offer me the role, but I'm only really suited to being a gardener.'

'No, I don't mean work at the House, I mean live there. With me. I want you to be my wife. Will you marry me, Irene?'

For a moment she was so astonished that she just looked at him with wide eyes.

'Oh my goodness, Hubert, I . . . I . . . well, that is a surprise. I don't know what to say.'

'I want you to say yes, but not if you don't want that; not if the thought repels you.'

'No, never. Certainly not that. But, Hubert, it's just such a big thing and I never thought . . . I mean, it never crossed my mind. This is too much for me to take in without having some time to think it all through.'

'For my part, I have thought it through, Irene, and I think I was in love with you by the time you'd shown me off the premises that day we first met. I had heard of love at first sight, but I didn't believe it was possible until then.'

'That's a lovely thing to say. I would like to say all nice things back, but I have to speak the truth, which is that I haven't allowed myself to think about marriage since both the men I was engaged to were killed. The first died in an accident, and the second in the war – as so many others did, of course – and I have just resigned myself since to being one of the great legion of "spare" women. It seemed unrealistic to hope there could be another chance for me, just one woman among so many. It would only lead to disappointment.'

'But am *I* now being unrealistic to hope? Irene, I can offer you my devoted love and protection, and a home that I know you already love. I can offer you three children, whom I think you like already and I hope you will grow to love. I hope in time that you might grow to love me, too. I intend to do everything I can to bring that about and to make you truly happy.'

Irene had to smile. That little speech had made her happy already. But there were more people to consider than just herself, and anyway, although she liked him – liked him a lot – she didn't know if she was really in love with Hubert Cole.

'But what about your boys? Have you consulted them, Hubert? They might not want someone new in their lives who isn't their own mother. They might be quite happy with things the way they are, and that must be respected. I think Christopher, Simon and Tiddler should be asked how they would feel about having a stepmother.'

'But not just any stepmother. *You*, Irene.'

'Nonetheless, if – after I've had a think about it, and got over my astonishment at being asked – I do decide to accept your most generous offer of marriage, I shouldn't want to impose myself on your children if they don't want a stepmother.'

'And I wouldn't want to get their hopes up in advance if, after you've had a think about it, you decide you don't want to marry me. Then there will be four of us disappointed.'

'Oh dear, I think we've reached stalemate,' said Irene, laughing. 'I don't know quite why that's funny – perhaps I just feel light of heart – but how are we to resolve this?'

'A complete impasse,' said Hubert, smiling too, 'although I hope I see the way things are going. At least your heart is light and not heavy with foreboding.'

'No, not foreboding. Just . . . amazement that there could be another life for me; that I have choices again. I just need to be sure that what I choose is the right thing for me but also for you and for your children.'

'Then will you let me know without delay when you've had that think, Irene? I shall be hoping with all my heart that you will feel able to make me the happiest of men so, please, promise not to keep me waiting one minute longer than necessary.'

'I will let you know by the end of the week. That is a promise I can make now, Hubert.'

'Hello, is it possible to speak to Mr Chisholm, please?'

'Who's calling?' asked the man who had answered the telephone in Mr Chisholm's house, nearly three hundred miles to the south of Scarstone.

Heck, these telephones were clever, thought Sarah, excited to have got through to the right place. If there was one thing she'd have in her own home, it would be a telephone. Well, and a comfy bed, and the sewing machine . . .

'My name is Sarah Quinn. Mr Chisholm won't have heard of me, but I have some news for him.'

The man, who must be a servant of some kind, sounded cross when he replied to this. Sarah thought she might have said the wrong thing. There must be some etiquette to telephoning that she didn't know.

'Mr Chisholm is not at home to prank callers and chancers,' said the man.

'Oh, no, please don't cut me off. I'm not a prankster. This is about Mavis Chisholm.'

There was a short silence. Then: 'Just one moment, please, miss. I will see if Mr Chisholm is available.'

Sarah heard the receiver of the telephone being placed on a hard surface, then there was a wait.

Oh, please hurry up, please hurry . . .

Mavis had gone shopping this morning and Sarah was taking the opportunity to use the telephone in the office. She had checked first that Major Wilkins had gone out. She worried, since his bungled assault, about finding herself alone in the house with him, and she didn't know how long she had got to make her call to Cedric Chisholm.

There was the sound of the receiver being lifted and some heavy breathing such as an overweight or unfit person might make.

'Hello. This is Cedric Chisholm,' a man's voice wheezed.

'Mr Chisholm, my name is Sarah Quinn. I have news for you and I also wonder if you can help me. My father is married to a woman who was called Mavis Swindel. They got married last September. There is some mystery about her past life and it has been suggested to me that she is Mavis Chisholm, your wife, and before that she was Mavis Swann.'

The man took two heavy breaths. 'Describe this woman to me, please.'

'About five foot one, pink face, curvy figure. She has very thick dark hair, wavy, with a white stripe through it at the front. She wears a heavy perfume, like lilies of the valley.'

'Yes, much of that description fits the Mavis I knew, who was indeed called Swann, then Chisholm.'

'But, Mr Chisholm, what I need to know is, whether you were married to Mavis and divorced her, or whether you are still married to her. You see, she can't be married both to you and to my father.'

There was a long pause and Sarah wondered again if she'd breached the rules of polite telephone conversation. It was difficult to ask this question in a delicate way, however.

'No, I did not divorce Mavis,' Chisholm said breathlessly. 'I am still married to her. She left me, emptied my coffers and I haven't seen her since. I have, however, learned something of her progress since then: the various cons and swindles, the botched attempts at making an honest living, which she can never see through because she isn't capable of honest hard work. The cruelty and the lies . . . I'm sorry, Sarah Quinn, that you have been caught in the net of this woman's deceit. You sound . . . only young and I don't think you would have traced me and telephoned unless you were very keen to be out of the clutches of Mavis.'

That seemed to have cost him a lot of breath. He was wheezing very heavily now.

'Mr Chisholm, I am very sorry to bring Mavis back into your life, but I need to ask you – is she paying you owt, perhaps paying you back month by month for the money she stole from you?'

'She is not!' panted Chisholm. 'She took my money, but in return I took away her freedom. She will never be properly and legally married to anyone else so long as I live. I'd rather know that she has to live in fear of prosecution for bigamy than have the money back.' He paused to wheeze heavily. 'Now, Sarah Quinn, I think that's all I can do for you.'

'Oh, please, Mr Chisholm, you must help us. My sister – she's only fourteen – and me, we're living in Mavis's lodging house. Our dad thinks he's married to Mavis, but it looks to us as if she married him so he can help her do up her house on the cheap and bring his children to work for her with hardly any pay. My brother ran away rather than work here. Mavis ruined my big chance of making my work a success, and now I'm just her skivvy, and penniless.' Sarah was fighting back tears and she knew she was gabbling, but she was desperate to get across to this stranger, who seemed to know more than anyone about Mavis, how much she needed his help.

'I can't help you further,' wheezed Cedric Chisholm. 'I'm not well – I have . . . have a lung disease. I have been told that I haven't long to live. Where are you?'

Sarah was stricken with disappointment, both for

herself but also for Cedric Chisholm, who was plainly in a bad way but was taking the time to speak to her, even so. 'The house is called Over the Edge, just outside Scarstone in Lancashire. You can get here from Blackburn by bus. Please, do try to come and help me.'

Chisholm sighed a gaspy sigh. 'I'm sorry, I shan't be making that journey,' he said. 'It's too far and I'm too ill. I'm sorry, Sarah.'

Sarah was crying openly now that Cedric Chisholm could do nothing more. It was as if she'd briefly been shown a distant escape tunnel and now, too soon, the entrance was closing over.

'I'm sorry to have bothered you, Mr Chisholm,' she said, wiping her eyes. 'And I'm very sorry that you're so ill. Thank you for listening to me. Goodbye.'

She put down the telephone and sank onto the chaise longue, her hands over her face. She could go to the police, but she had no real evidence, only what Cedric Chisholm had told her, and who knew how long he had left? He sounded very ill and could be dead in a very short while. And if she told her father everything she thought she knew, although he had been deceived, he might still want to continue to live with Mavis. He might even know the truth already, and would be furious to have Sarah stirring up trouble. He seemed to have strayed away from the path of openness and honesty with his children and embraced a murkier way of living to Mavis's standards.

Sarah sighed from the bottom of her soul. How could her dad behave like this – how could he even look at

Mavis Swindel – when he had once been married to the wonderful Ava? It was impossible to understand.

Sarah wiped her nose and looked up, pushing her hair away from her face.

It was then that she saw, standing grinning lasciviously in the office doorway, Paget Wilkins.

CHAPTER EIGHTEEN

'I THINK WE have a little unfinished business, Sarah, don't you?' smirked Wilkins.

He came into Mavis's office and closed the door behind him, leaning on it as if to emphasise that she was helpless and in his power.

'Rubbish! You have no business with me, you disgusting man,' said Sarah, trying to appear bold, while backing around the other side of the desk from him. 'Mavis will be back very soon. In fact, she's probably on her way now.' She hoped this was true, and also that she was mistaken in thinking Mavis and the major were in league. But Wilkins's reply proved Sarah's suspicions to be true.

'What will Mavis care? I'm paying her good money for a little extra besides the room, and it's time I saw something for it. She promised me you as part of the deal. You or your little sister. Or maybe both of you. Too good a bargain to pass up, missy. So I suggest you just lie back on that there chaise and let me take what I've paid for.'

'You disgusting pig! Keep away from me. I'll scream the house down.'

'And who's going to hear you? There's no one here but us, Sarah. I've been planning this since that regrettable little incident in the dining room: make a show of going out, then nip back when I know you are alone. Now, best not make a fuss, my girl. And you *will* be my girl . . .'

'No, I'd rather die,' said Sarah. 'You vile, bloated beast.' She grabbed a paper knife from the desk and held it threateningly in front of her. It wasn't sharp, but it was all she could find to use against him. 'One step closer, Major, and I'll stab you in the stomach. I couldn't possibly miss.'

Immediately, far too quickly for her to anticipate, Wilkins's hand shot out and grabbed the paper knife from her, tossing it into the waste-paper basket where it buried itself in the rubbish.

'Nice try, little girl, but you just haven't got the killer instinct,' he sneered, following her round the desk.

Sarah hastened round to the other side, grabbed a wooden tray on which were heaped papers and letters and hurled the lot at the major's head. Then she turned and rushed out of the door into the hall.

Wilkins was delayed only momentarily by the chaos, the volume of paper preventing the tray making much contact with his face. Moving astonishingly quickly for a large man, he was behind her immediately, before she could close the door on him and gain an advantage. He made a grab for her skirt but she managed to yank it from him by a strength born of total panic, and she began screaming as loudly as she could as she ran down the hall.

'Help! Someone, help me! Help me!'

Her screams did have something of the desired effect on Wilkins, because he hesitated for a moment, perhaps thinking that one of the other lodgers might be at home after all, allowing Sarah to gain valuable distance. She ran into the lodgers' sitting room and tried to close the door on him, but he heaved his weight against it and Sarah was powerless to stop him as it banged against the wall and he was in the room, sweating and panting.

'Enough of your tricks,' he yelled. 'I have been patient for too long.' He advanced menacingly, ugly and angry.

Sarah dodged behind the wing-back armchair and, in misjudged desperation, tried to push it over onto him, but she hadn't the strength to manage it. He grabbed her then, twining his fist in her hair so she could not escape, although all the time she was yelling, 'Help! Help me, someone!'

Wilkins slapped her face hard. 'Shut up or I'll shut you up for good.' He held onto her, pushing her down hard to the floor while she wept and struggled.

Then he was unbuttoning his trousers and kneeling between Sarah's legs, snarling, 'If you struggle, I'll enjoy this all the more. I mean to hurt you now, to teach you a lesson you won't ever forget.'

Completely without warning, a shot rang out and hit the wall beyond Wilkins's head. Had he been unfortunate enough to have raised it at that moment, he would have had his brains blown out.

Immediately, Wilkins froze where he was.

'Get up, you filthy c-coward,' said Mr Cornwell. 'Turn

round and face me, you bastard, because I'm not a m-man who would shoot anyone in the back, *Major* Wilkins. Or should I say *Private* Wilkins?'

Wilkins heaved himself up and hurriedly tidied his clothes in as dignified a way as he could, but Mr Cornwell was impatient. He pointed his revolver straight at Wilkins, and although his hand shook, he was certain not to miss if he fired again.

'P-put your hands in the air, Wilkins. Now, step out into the hall. That's it. I said, k-keep your hands in the air, or I shall feel obliged, for my own safety, as well as S-Sarah's, to shoot you where you stand. That's it, nice and slow, and come away from the door. Sarah, go into Mrs Q-Quinn's office and telephone the police, now. Say it's an emergency and they're to h-hurry. Go now!'

Sarah, her face red and tear-stained, sidled out behind Wilkins, sobbing loudly, and then ran back into Mavis's office, where she was faced with the chaos of strewn papers. She fumbled with the telephone in her distress and could hardly get the words out for crying, but she managed to ask for the police to come at once.

Then she gathered herself to go back into the hall. She could not leave Mr Cornwell dealing with Wilkins alone. Mr Cornwell was standing with his gun trained on Paget Wilkins, who was looking very nervous, but had obviously decided to try to wheedle his way out of the situation.

'It was all a mistake,' he started.

'It was,' said Mr Cornwell. 'The biggest m-mistake of your life, Wilkins. I had my suspicions about you from the beginning. See, if you were going to p-pass yourself off as an army officer, you'd have done better not to do it in front of an a-actual officer. You have been found out.'

'You?' gasped Wilkins, evidently forgetting in his surprise that he had embarked on appeasing Mr Cornwell.

Mr Cornwell didn't answer that directly. Instead he said, 'A m-man who pretends he held an army rank that he never did lacks all integrity. He insults those of us who were officers and led our men – men who we r-respected and who relied on us in return – into battle. He takes up that false title in civilian life because he's a boaster, a liar, the k-kind of man who has no moral code. And that sort of man is just the kind t-to take the most loathsome advantage of a young woman.'

'That isn't true, any of it.'

'You see, when Janette told me that she was moving her bed into S-Sarah's room because they were frightened of you creeping in on them if they were alone, I wasn't even surprised. I'd already tested you numerous times and I knew you were a f-fake and a liar. You are *that kind of man.* And then Janette told me how you'd c-cornered Sarah and she'd only escaped your vile intentions by stabbing you with a fork. Poor girl, defenceless but for the cutlery from the s-sideboard. What kind of man puts a young woman in that frightening p-position? But again, I saw how this fitted in with the kind of scum you are.'

'It's not true.'

'Liar! How can anyone believe a single word you say, Wilkins? I caught you in the act of trying to force your-self on Sarah. I've looked into your army "career" – I enlisted the help of some old pals – and I know you are a liar through and through. Now, the p-police will be here very shortly. We will stand here – me with my gun and you with your hands in the air – until they arrive. Then Sarah will open the front d-door to admit them and you will be l-led away.'

'But it's all Mavis's fault. She was the one who suggested—'

'Shut up! Shut up, Wilkins. I am not interested in your c-cringing attempts to excuse the inexcusable.'

There were footsteps outside on the gravel, and Sarah ran to open the door, thinking it was the police. They had been very quick to arrive. She was afraid that Mr Cornwell might lose his temper and shoot Wilkins, or that, in his shaking hands, his gun would go off by mistake.

It wasn't the police, however. It was Mavis and Fred. Sarah had forgotten her father was not working at Scarstone Hardware today.

'Good grief, Sarah, what's the matter with your face?' asked Fred, stepping into the hall, while Mavis took in the scene, her eyes widening. Basil trotted away to the kitchen as she dropped his lead in surprise.

'Mr Wilkins hit me. He was trying to . . . he tried to rape me, and Mr Cornwell saved me just in time. Oh, Dad, I know you are in debt to Wilkins over the card games, and I'm sorry if this risks you losing your job with Mr Godwin, but me and Janette can't live here for one single night longer if that vile man is creeping round the place, looking for the chance to force himself on us. We just can't!'

Fred looked completely baffled. But, this being Fred, he was much more interested where the news concerned himself than where it concerned his daughters.

'In debt to Wilkins? Card games? Sarah, I don't know what you are talking about.'

'Mr Quinn, Wilkins attacked Sarah. Whatever else is going on here – and I'm f-fast thinking this place has become a den of vice – that is what should concern you above everything,' said Mr Cornwell, not taking his eyes off Wilkins. 'The police are on their way, there will be questions asked and Sarah and I will tell what we know. If you know anything, and if Mrs Quinn does, relating to Wilkins, then it would be b-best if you tell the police that as well.'

'Come now, Mr Cornwell,' said Mavis with a smile. 'I don't think you really know anything, do you? The number of times you've been distressed by next to nothing, dearie – that thunderstorm we had earlier this month, for instance – well, I would say it was you who got a very exaggerated picture of how things really are; of what dangers there *are not* lurking.'

'No, Mavis, that's nonsense,' said Sarah. 'If Mr Cornwell hadn't been here to rescue me, I dread to think what would have happened.'

'Well, you're just as deluded, Sarah,' said Mavis. 'Always thinking all the men have their eyes on you, just because you're young and slim. They're not all looking at your pretty legs, you know.'

'When did I ever—'

'It's true, isn't it, Mr Cornwell? I can see your hand shaking now. You got all upset about something and imagined dangers where there were none. Now, why don't I get Sarah to make us a cup of tea while we all calm down? If any police officers turn up, they can also drink a cup of tea while I apologise for wasting their time and explain it's all been a mistake.'

'What!' gasped Sarah and Mr Cornwell in unison.

Wilkins took advantage of this distraction to try to relieve Mr Cornwell of the gun. Keeping low, he charged at him and rugby-tackled him to the ground. Mr Cornwell was taken by surprise and he fell backwards, the gun going off in his hand as he fell. The shot went clean through the wooden mounting on which the taxidermy tiger's head was displayed, and the whole ghastly thing crashed to the ground on top of the men in an explosion of moth-eaten fur, filthy shredded-wood packing and twisted wire. One of the tiger's large brown glass eyes rolled across the hall and came to rest like a slowly spinning top outside Mavis's office door.

Although Wilkins had taken the brunt of the tiger trophy's fall, he was much bigger and stronger than Mr Cornwell and he quickly leapt to his feet, shedding debris and loose fur, while everyone else was coughing away the dust and trying to see through the enveloping cloud of filth. He pushed Fred aside, and in seconds he was out of the front door and away.

'Quick, Dad, after him,' cried Sarah, who was helping Mr Cornwell to his feet. 'Oh, good grief, are you hurt? Here, let me help.' She led the limping Mr Cornwell to a sofa in the lodgers' sitting room and closed the door to shut out the noise and dust.

Mr Cornwell's nerves had taken a severe shock at the suddenness and violence of the stuffed tiger-head's fall. His leg was badly bruised by the wooden mounting, but he wasn't much concerned with this when the violence of the incident had shredded his nerves. Sarah held his hand and thanked him over and over for saving her from Wilkins, reassuring him in a soothing voice that she was safe now, that the danger was past, until he was calmer . . .

Sarah lost track of time but eventually she heard voices in the hall.

'I'd better go and see if this is the police arriving,' she said quietly. 'I'll show them in here and we can tell them everything, if you feel up to it.'

But when she went out into the hall, Mavis was just closing the front door.

'Where are the police?' demanded Sarah. 'Was that them now? I didn't hear them arrive. They will want to speak to me.'

She made a move towards the door but Mavis locked it and pocketed the key in a casual manner, displaying no hurry.

'Really, dearie, you're getting a very inflated idea of your own importance, you know,' she said. 'That's just typical of you, drawing attention to yourself and thinking you're the most important person here. You've lost me a lodger, that's for certain. I doubt Paget will be back, not with that dangerous lunatic making false accusations and waving a gun about, and you coming on to him like some kind of cheap tart. I try to run a respectable boarding house and end up with a madhouse. Really, Sarah, I thought better of you. Why do you always have to let me down? I honestly think you're as unstable as Cornwell.'

'What? You know that's not true, Mavis. You don't *honestly* think any of that because you don't think *honestly* about owt. I must speak to the police. Give me the key. Give me the key and get out of my way.'

'No,' insisted Mavis, taking Sarah by both her shoulders and giving her a shake. 'I won't have you making a fool of yourself. There's no chance they'll believe anything you say. I told them I had one lodger who wasn't right in the head and had been waving a gun around. They saw for themselves how my magnificent tiger has suffered with Cornwell's rashness. I explained how wonderful your father had been, how he was the hero of the hour and managed to relieve Cornwell of the gun, which is now in the police officers' possession. They rather lost interest in the incident once they had the gun. Poor Cornwell, with his nerves, is too ill to see anyone, he's harmless without the gun; and anyway, I have the whole situation under control. It was all rather regrettable and undignified, but it was only some minor domestic upset, wasn't it, dearie? Not the kind of thing it's worth calling the police out for. By tomorrow morning you'll see that and be glad I saved you the embarrassment of making a fuss.'

'You're the one who's regrettable and undignified, Mavis. You've bamboozled the police just as you bamboozle everyone to get your own way – about everything! You're a complete liar.'

'I have never lied to you.'

Sarah could hardly believe what she was hearing. She wondered if Mavis was such a practised liar that she no longer knew how to tell the truth. 'You're lying now. You lied to me about Miss Rowley's business being in trouble. You stole my letter from her in which she told me she came here but you wouldn't let her see me. You told me she didn't care. You lied that I'd be working here for only a month or two. You never had any intention of finding anyone else to cook, and you only hired Susan in the end because I wasn't very good and the lodgers threatened to leave. Then you got me cleaning. You lied that Janette could stay at school if I agreed, when at every turn you continue to threaten to take her away, as a way of keeping me under your thumb.'

'She's still at school, isn't she?'

'Be quiet and listen. I'll never forget the sight of you ransacking Mr McCain's belongings to try to find some pathetic sums of cash to steal, while he lay there, dead. You even stole his watch and tie pin, you evil old bag, and then got in a temper because I gave them to his cousin. And you lost Joe his job at Hardcastle's with your sly whispers.'

'No! I never—'

'You lied that Dad is in debt to Paget Wilkins, when it is perfectly clear he knows nowt about any such thing. It was you who was keeping in with Wilkins, a pervert and a liar, because he was paying you. Like a madam in a brothel is paid.'

'Huh! No, I never made an agreement. He must have misunderstood.'

'Rubbish, you liar! And he's one, too. Not an army officer at all. All the time you were smarming up to Wilkins, the war hero under your roof was Mr Cornwell, who has given his peace of mind for his country. And you just dismiss him as a lunatic. Well, Mavis, that says everything about you.'

'No—'

'Not only that, but you're a bigamist and a thief.'

Mavis's pink face turned completely puce and her eyes looked as if they were ready to pop out.

'Who says so? Where did you hear that slander? *Who?* Tell me!'

'From your husband, Mavis Chisholm, who else?'

Mavis was speechless for several seconds. Then she rallied. Sarah could almost see her mind working as the astonishment on her face was replaced by a sly look.

'I have no idea what you are talking about. I've never heard of Mavis Chisholm. Have you any evidence for this wild accusation? Have you? Whoever this woman is, she isn't me.'

'You *are* her. I described you and Mr Chisholm said it was you.'

'Where's the proof? Someone told you something – have you even met this person?'

'No, but I spoke to him on the telephone.'

'Which proves nothing. He could be anyone, have said anything, and you wouldn't know if it was true or not.'

'I believe him and I know better than to believe you.'

'You know nothing!' Mavis took a step towards Sarah and grabbed the front of her frock, pulling her close. Although Mavis was shorter, her heels brought her level to Sarah and the look on her face was venomous.

'If you so much as repeat a word of this slander to anyone, I will have you locked away as a lunatic. You know already that the police believe what I say, whereas they regard you as a very silly girl prone to getting overemotional. It would be very easy, Sarah, for me to have you put away for good. Who's to know or care? Janette is just a child with her head in the clouds about an impossible future. Once you've gone she'll soon forget about you, especially if she's busy working for me. Joe doesn't care – he ran away and you don't even know where he is. Your father? He's just pleased to have a woman in his life, a woman who knows what a man needs and isn't coy about providing it. He isn't bothered about a hysterical girl with all her silly problems, embarrassing and burdening everyone.'

Sarah didn't say anything. There was no point. But now, if she had ever had a doubt, it was clear that Mavis Swindel was Mavis Chisholm, a liar, a thief and a bigamist. It was quite possible that she was also a murderess.

After all, she seemed capable of anything.

There was a rattle of the front door, the lock turned and Susan came in, holding her key.

'What's happened to that tiger?' she asked, looking at the mess in the hall. 'Poor old thing, looks like it's been shot a second time. Who'd have thought it?' And she laughed mirthlessly at her own joke and went through to the kitchen, leaving Mavis and Sarah standing in the debris, hating each other.

For three whole days and nights, Irene thought of little else but Hubert's proposal. What a kind man, so gentle and considerate. And surprisingly romantic. He was offering her more than she could ever have dreamed of when she was younger and thought her modest future was mapped out: his love, his delightful children, a beautiful home and a comfortable, settled future. She would not want for anything. It was almost too good to be true.

Of course, this worked both ways. He would have a mother for his three boys, a woman by his side, a mistress for his house and a gardener as well, although he would undoubtedly let her employ someone else to do the digging. And he said that he was in love with her. She had thought never to hear a man say those thrilling words to her again.

The only thing that had stopped her accepting him on the spot was that she didn't know if she really loved him in return. She knew what it felt like to be in love. She had been in love with James Fellowes, her first fiancé, who had shockingly and tragically been killed in an accident in the street. And she had been very much in love with her second fiancé, Gilbert Wagstaffe, who had been killed on the first day of the Battle of the Somme, his body buried in Flanders alongside so many of his comrades.

Perhaps this feeling of regard, even gratitude, was what love felt like now that she was in her forties and had been alone for so long. Not the stomach-flipping-with-excitement-and-lust kind of love, but a more measured, calm pleasure. She did not know. She could not be sure. She had no experience.

Tomorrow would be Saturday, the end of the week, and she had promised Hubert an answer then. He would be moving into Fettling House in a few days, and Irene knew she needed to be gone if she was not going to marry him. She would have to give up the Lodge; in all decency she would not stay then, even if he offered her more time to find somewhere else. The gardening job near Ipswich had turned out not to be suitable, but there was a job coming up in Saxham Ash. Betsy had mentioned it. The position came with accommodation, although the garden was a fraction of the size of this and had been kept for years by an elderly gardener who had struggled with it. Still, the village was pretty and Joe, Betsy and George would be nearby if Irene took the job and moved those few miles.

She was still undecided what to tell Hubert, but it wouldn't be fair to keep him waiting any longer. Perhaps the fact that she hadn't made up her mind was an indication as to what she should answer. If she couldn't marry him with no doubts, then she shouldn't marry him at all.

She sat at her table and thought harder than she'd ever thought about anything. Eventually she got up, put on her coat and boots, and went out into the garden.

Drifts of snowdrops were showing their dainty, teardrop-shaped flowers, and the berries on the holly trees were darkening and wizening. The garden smelled of frost and earth. Irene wandered along by the herbaceous border, seeing the dug and mulched soil, the slumbering plants, the neat labels. All her own work. Oh, it would be so hard to leave behind all this beauty she had cultivated, perhaps to start all over again.

She wished, more than ever, that Ada was still alive. They would have arranged to meet, maybe somewhere between here and Blackburn, as they sometimes had done over the years. Ada would listen and then they'd drink tea and discuss all sides of the matter, and then Ada would say, 'Right, our Irene, now I've given it some thought, I reckon what you need to consider is this . . .' And she'd just say, in a calm, down-to-earth way, and Irene would see that her little sister was right, and then she'd know the way forward.

A robin was hopping along the edge of the border, stopping to peck into the dark earth, its head dipping and stabbing. Irene knew this bird: it had first appeared soon after Ada had died, and Irene had formed a whimsical attachment to it, imagining that it was a messenger from Ada, close by, reassuring. Sometimes this robin followed her as she dug and it would come very close, its confidence growing as she pretended to ignore it and moved in a considered way so as not to frighten it. Now she stood still and the robin hopped very close, regarded her with its head tilted, and then flew up into a bare lilac tree at the back of the border.

It hopped between branches, intermittently hiding from view, then emerging, and then suddenly it was on the topmost branch. There it sang and sang, its voice so pure and sharp and clear in the otherwise silent garden. It was quite alone but it was so strong, so sure, so proud.

'Ada?'

Had she really said her sister's name aloud? So silly. It was just a robin in a winter garden. And yet it was undoubtedly singing just for her. If only she could understand the song.

Don't fret. It's quite simple. Just listen to your heart.

The message flew into her head. Irene stood and listened until the robin had finished his song. Then she knew what she had to do.

Hubert Cole arrived at Fettling House early on Saturday morning. His knock on the door of the Lodge was a surprise as Irene hadn't heard the car or the big gates being opened.

'Hubert, come in,' she said shyly, opening the front door wide. 'You are here very early. I . . . I wasn't expecting you just yet. There is tea in the pot if you'd like a cup?'

She knew she was gabbling and she decided to be quiet and indicated he should go into the sitting room.

'No, thank you,' he said. 'Irene, I have thought of very little but you all week and I could not wait to see you a minute longer. You know why I'm here. Let's not pretend to be mere acquaintances and talk of teapots. Please give me your answer. Will you marry me and make me the happiest of men?'

'Yes,' said Irene. 'I will. I promise I will do everything I can to make us the happiest of married couples, and I intend to love your children and be a good mother to them.'

'Darling girl . . .' He took her in his arms and kissed her, and Irene thought how very nice it was to be kissed by a handsome man, and one who was a very good kisser, too.

Eventually she said, 'But I'm not a girl, Hubert. I am forty-three and am used to living my life alone. I hope . . . I will try so hard to adapt to and make a success of my new roles as wife and stepmother.'

'I shall be sure not to take from you what makes you the essential Irene that I love,' he replied. 'I don't want you to have to compromise. I love you as you are.'

'Thank you,' she said, and she was so pleased she had decided to accept him. She hoped it wouldn't be long before she loved him in return.

'But now you must tell your boys they have a step-mother. I hope they'll take it well, stepmothers being notoriously difficult to like in fairy stories. The very word has developed some unfortunate associations.'

'Let's see, shall we?' said Hubert, smiling widely.

He went to the door, opened it and called, 'It's all right, boys. She said yes.'

In moments the three little boys appeared and came into the warmth.

'Oh, thank goodness,' said Simon, with a theatrical-sounding sigh. 'We had to get up really early this morning to come from London, and it would have been an awful waste of not having a lie-in if you had said no.'

'And we've brought presents,' said Tiddler. 'Daddy, can we give Miss Mayhew the presents?'

He didn't wait for an answer but handed over a little box of chocolates, and Christopher gave her some flowers with a shy pretend-nonchalant, 'I got you these.'

'Thank you. Thank you, both. Oh, they're so lovely. And so are you.'

Then Simon announced he had wanted to give Miss Mayhew a cake to celebrate, but his pocket money didn't stretch that far, so he'd drawn her one instead and he hoped she liked it. He handed over a delicate and beautiful little watercolour sketch of a three-tier cake, framed in a simple mounting.

'Thank you, Simon. It's a grand cake, nicer than any I've ever had,' she said.

''Cept you can't eat it,' pointed out Tiddler. 'Has Daddy given you his present yet?'

'Not yet,' said Hubert. 'I wanted you all here to share the moment.' He pulled from his pocket a tiny ring box, placed it on Irene's little side table, opened it and extracted a diamond ring.

'I hope you like it,' he said. 'It's a family heirloom.'

He tried to slip it onto Irene's finger, but it was too small and wouldn't pass over her broad knuckle.

'It's beautiful,' said Irene, admiring the stones in an old-fashioned but pretty setting. 'Thank you. Oh dear, I'm so sorry not to be able to wear it straight away, but I'm sure it can be made bigger. I'm afraid these are work hands and not designed for delicate jewellery.'

'I'll have it altered to fit,' said Hubert. 'We'll go to a jeweller together and have it made it perfect for you.' He gave what looked like a brave smile, and Irene was immediately disappointed in herself: that her hands, which had never been particularly small, had coarsened with hard work over the years.

It was as she was making a fresh pot of tea for them all and pointing Simon in the direction of a tin of buns that she wondered why Hubert had even thought so tiny a ring would fit her. Hadn't he noticed the size of her hands as they had cleared that greenhouse together? Would he be disappointed when he did notice she was a tall, strong woman with correspondingly long, broad hands and feet?

Irene couldn't help it: the image of his wife, which she'd invented when she'd first met him, rushed into her head. This beautiful woman was very slender, and her feet, in her smart, high-heeled shoes, were tiny. Her hands were smooth, white and graceful. And now, on the ring finger of her left hand, Irene imagined she wore a diamond ring with a pretty, old-fashioned setting. A family heirloom.

CHAPTER NINETEEN

For a few days Mavis went about her business in a much more subdued way than usual, arranging for the collapsed ceiling upstairs to be repaired, and the walls in the hall and in the lodgers' sitting room, pierced by bullet holes, to be repaired and repainted. She cleared Paget Wilkins's room herself, and Fred dumped Wilkins's belongings in a corner of the gravelled front garden, from where they disappeared one night. Whether Wilkins had come back to retrieve them, or whether someone had stolen them, no one cared.

While all this was going on, Mavis avoided speaking to Sarah and Janette if she could, which suited the girls just fine. Sarah suspected that Mavis was ashamed of herself, but she wasn't the kind of woman to apologise, ever. But then, Sarah reflected, on second thoughts, Mavis wasn't really the sort to feel ashamed, either.

Sarah had told Janette what had happened, of course, and Janette was horrified, but hugely thankful to Mr Cornwell for his part in the drama.

'I guessed Mr Cornwell was a real hero,' she said.

'People underestimate him 'cos he's sometimes not well, but if you put his illness to one side and see the real Mr Cornwell behind that, he's just lovely. I reckon his illness has made him lonely, and,' she lowered her voice although they were in Sarah's bedroom, huddling together under the eiderdown to keep warm, as so often they did, 'there's no one else left but Mr Armstrong – Paget flippin' Wilkins never counted anyway – and Mr Armstrong was never *very* good company. He's working hard on his book, as usual, and he seems to think of nowt else.'

'I reckon Mr Armstrong thinks of nowt but himself anyway. In that regard, he and Mavis have summat in common.'

'That's very unfair, Sarah. Mr Armstrong was the only person we could ask for help when Mr Cornwell was unnerved by the storm. I *knew* he would help.'

'Oh, you're right, of course. I am being unfair. It's this place, it's turning me into a horrible person.'

Sarah hadn't known it was possible to hate anyone as much as she hated Mavis. She could hardly bear to speak to her. She felt as if the loathing was clouding her judgement, consuming her, so that she couldn't think straight but was living in a horrible kind of fog of inaction and uselessness. She didn't want to be this kind of person, but it was impossible for her to set aside the depth of her feelings. She knew the answer was to get away and hope the hostility in her mind receded in time, but she couldn't. She wanted to run away from Over the Edge, as Joe had, but she couldn't leave Janette, and they had nowhere to go. They were all but penniless, so escaping was out of the question. Even if they did leave, Sarah would have to find a job immediately just so she could pay for somewhere for them to live, and there was no guarantee she would be able to afford a roof over their heads. She couldn't write to ask Irene for the train fares, as had been arranged at Christmas. Irene was having to find a new job herself and would need all her savings if this took a while. She'd be looking for a new home, too, and Sarah knew it was unlikely that Irene had been able to save up much to fall back on. The situation looked impossible, at least at the moment.

Sarah obsessively thought of how she might escape from Over the Edge, start work and then send for Janette, but she didn't want to leave her little sister alone at the mercy of the Stepmother for even a day, so all her half-formed plans came to nothing. There was no option but to stay and bide her time.

Mavis also appeared subdued with Fred. Fred's feelings about Wilkins's attack on Sarah seemed to be more embarrassment than anything, as if it made Fred uncomfortable to think his daughter was grown up and might attract any kind of male attention. But, sweeping the hall floor outside the family sitting room one day, Sarah did overhear him complaining that Mavis should have vetted her lodger better.

'Look, Mavis, I don't know what was going on with Major Wilkins, but I have my suspicions, and I'm afraid I don't think any better of you for what happened.

Wilkins seems to have caused a lot of trouble for everyone, not least my girls. Yes, the lodgers are your business, and I never interfere, but this must never happen again. Ever! Please, can you make sure in future that the lodgers are at least reputable folk?'

'There is no need to shout at me, Fred. I always do my best, you know I do, dearie. I think that man took advantage of all of us,' lamented Mavis. 'I'm as much a victim of this as anyone. It's as well not to believe a word that man said.'

'I should think not. What was all that about me being in debt to him? Complete lies.'

'Well, there you are then: proof that he is a liar. Why you would believe him over me is a mystery. I don't know what I've done to deserve that.' She sounded tearful, but Sarah thought it was an act, and she thought from his reply that her father did, too.

'Don't you, Mavis?' said Fred, stonily. 'Don't you really?'

For a few days Fred looked angry and he hardly spoke. Mavis took to wearing her shiny blouses more low-cut, her perfume even stronger, and she had her hair done, but Fred appeared unmoved.

Sarah and Janette discussed this and wondered if it was beginning to dawn on their father what a mistake he had made. Perhaps he would soon fully realise it, and do something about changing the situation.

Mr Cornwell quickly recovered from his part in the drama, and, unsurprisingly, he found himself some new lodgings and set a date on which he would be leaving

Over the Edge. When the day came, he said a fond farewell to Janette before she left for school, extracting a promise from her to work hard, and expressing his own belief that she would go far and fulfil all her dreams.

But then, as Sarah was helping him to pack up his belongings, his sister arrived out of the blue. Sarah hadn't even known for certain that Mr Cornwell had any family.

'Piece of luck, finding you still here, just as you are about to move out, Richard,' said Elizabeth Cornwell, a smart, confident woman, some years older than her brother, with a big smile. She stood in the hallway and gazed around at the shabbiness with a slightly raised eyebrow. She was a model of calmness and contained emotion, where many people would have been shedding tears of happiness at being reunited with an estranged brother. 'I wish you'd kept in touch, but I know how difficult Father can be, and why you felt you needed to stay away. I have missed you, you know, silly boy. I wrote to the regiment ages ago, and they said they knew nothing of where you were living. But then, lately, it seemed you contacted them about some chap, and one of them remembered I'd been enquiring and got in touch with me. Extraordinarily fortunate. Come home with me now. Father has mellowed and I know he deeply regrets the rift he caused. He would welcome you home with all his heart.'

Mr Cornwell looked overwhelmed with happiness. 'Thank you, Lizzie,' he said simply.

Sarah left them to their reunion. Later she learned that the cause of 'the rift' between Richard and his father had been the shell shock, and that old Mr Cornwell had taken a very severe and old-fashioned view of his son's mental turmoil, which he came to regret. Now, father and son were to be reunited. It was, Sarah thought, wonderfully ironic that Elizabeth had found her brother at Over the Edge only because he had been enquiring about 'Major' Wilkins. At least, indirectly, some good had come from the bogus officer's lies in the end.

Sarah helped load Mr Cornwell's belongings into Elizabeth's car and prepared to say goodbye to the gentle, damaged former army officer for good.

'I shall never forget what you did for me, Mr Cornwell,' she said. She felt she and Janette were losing an important ally. 'I'm so glad your family have found you. I hope it all works out with your father.'

'I think it will,' said Richard, smiling more widely than Sarah had ever seen him smile before. Until now he had cut a rather sad figure.

'Wouldn't take you home to face Father again if I wasn't certain you'd get the reception you deserve,' beamed Elizabeth. 'But I must say, this place is a bit peculiar, isn't it?' She glanced up at the gaunt-looking chimneys and the dark, empty windows, and shivered. 'Strangely cold, too. Well, goodbye, Sarah. Oh, now let me give you this . . .' She dug in her handbag and pulled out two one-pound notes. 'Don't say anything, just take them. You never know when they might come in useful.' She gave a twinkly little smile and turned to her car. 'You driving, Richard, or am I?'

'Do you know, I think I will,' said Mr Cornwell. 'Bit out

of practice, but maybe it's time to get back to real life. Take the first step now, and all that.'

Sarah waved them off. Mavis had gone shopping, taking Basil with her, and she'd missed Elizabeth Cornwell altogether. Sarah felt Elizabeth and the news she brought was a secret she might share only with Janette, who would be delighted. Sarah didn't want to hear any more of Mavis's disparagement of Mr Cornwell, and she thought her nastiness would also encompass the redoubtable Elizabeth Cornwell, if she got to hear of her. No, let Mavis remain in the dark about Mr Cornwell's happy ending.

Mavis knew Mr Cornwell was moving out, of course, and she was in a very bad mood about that. It was possible she'd gone out shopping deliberately to avoid saying goodbye to her lodger, to show him he meant nothing to her. But now the only resident of Over the Edge apart from the Quinns was Andrew Armstrong.

'At least there's plenty of hot water for my bath,' Mr Armstrong announced one evening, looking pleased with life.

Mavis, however, immediately saw where she could make a saving, 'plenty of hot water' being a phrase that smacked of extravagance to her, and there was very little hot water available to anyone after that.

She was advertising for more lodgers, and a couple of people came to look at the three vacant rooms, but neither of them was interested.

*

All the while the name 'Mavis Chisholm' lurked at the back of Sarah's mind. She even considered going to Brighton to visit Mr Chisholm to persuade him to speak to the police about Mavis, but the poor man had said he had only a short while to live – he could be dead already, for all Sarah knew – and it would be cruel to take up any part of his final time on earth with questions about his estranged wife. If he had hoped to clip Mavis's wings by refusing to divorce her so she was not free to marry anyone else, then he had failed, because she'd just gone ahead and done exactly as she wanted anyway. Perhaps Mr Chisholm had underestimated Mavis's disregard for anyone and anything except herself, despite the fact that she had relieved him of all the cash in his safe.

Sarah was also very afraid of Mavis's threats to have her committed to an asylum if she revealed anything of Mavis's past to anyone else. After all, the Stepmother had convinced the police that Sarah was just a silly hysterical girl, who had thrown herself at Wilkins and then got overemotional. If there was any memory or record of this drama, she would be thought to be unstable already, and perhaps it would take little more for Mavis to convince the authorities that Sarah was actually mad. She would just bamboozle them as she did everyone else. With all the upset, the hating, the poverty of life at Over the Edge, Sarah was finding it difficult to stand back from her situation, think about what she must do and make a sensible decision.

By the beginning of February, however, she had made

up her mind to go to find Mr Chisholm and bring back proof that Mavis was still married to him. Let Mavis put her in a home for lunatics – it could hardly be much different from living at Over the Edge.

Sarah got up early, having told Janette the night before what she intended to do, and that she'd be back as soon as she could. She scraped together her train fare, which she could only afford as Elizabeth Cornwell had given her some money, and put on what she considered to be her 'good' dress and coat. She knew she looked like a poverty-stricken waif, but that couldn't be helped. She tried to channel some of the attitude of Irene, or even of Elizabeth Cornwell, who had made a striking impression on her, but it was difficult to sally forth with your head held high when there were holes in the soles of your shoes and your coat was discoloured and threadbare with age. She was just about to open the front door and go when there was a ring on the doorbell. Sarah thought Susan, coming early to cook breakfast, might have forgotten her key and she hurried to let her in before she roused the entire house.

On the doorstep was a man in his mid-twenties. He wasn't particularly tall, not much taller than Sarah herself; he had thick dark hair and his eyes were very dark.

'Hello. Have you come about one of the rooms?' asked Sarah, puzzled. It was strangely early to be viewing potential lodgings, but probably the man had a job to go to and wanted to get on with it.

His face split with a grin. 'Yes, that's right,' he said.

'Please would you go and tell the lady?' For some reason he seemed to find this amusing.

His arrival just now was a nuisance. Sarah would have to fetch Mavis, meaning her chance of getting away before anyone noticed would be gone.

'And the gentleman, too,' added the visitor.

'Oh, my dad doesn't have owt to do with renting out the rooms,' said Sarah, hanging up her coat.

'Your dad, eh? Still, I expect he'll want to meet me,' said the young man confidently.

Sarah wasn't sure she liked this cocky fella, with his bold smile. She hoped he wouldn't be moving in here. There was something unsettling about his demeanour, as if he were thrumming with a kind of dangerous energy.

'Please wait here and I'll fetch Mrs S . . . Mrs Quinn,' she said, indicating a chair near the front door.

'Good-oh.'

The young man sat down and gazed around at the peeling wallpaper and the parched panelling.

Sarah rushed up the stairs to see if Mavis was dressed yet.

Mavis was doing her hair and not pleased to find she had a visitor so early in the day.

'Well, didn't you ask his name?'

'No, Mavis. He seemed to think you are expecting him.'

'Well, I'm not.' She tutted impatiently.

'I'll ask him to go, shall I?'

'I suppose I'd better see him,' she grumbled. 'If he

takes one of the empty rooms, that will get me out of a very tight spot.'

She went out and Fred slunk after her at a distance, looking as if he expected bad news, with Sarah bringing up the rear. As she got to the top of the stairs, Sarah could see that the chair in the hall was now empty. The three of them trooped downstairs and the visitor emerged from where he'd moved to stand out of sight further away.

'Hello, Mum,' he said, looking pleased with himself. 'I hear there's a room to let. Shall I move in, do you think?'

Of course! The resemblance is unmistakable.

Mavis stopped at the foot of the stairs, her hand clutched to her throat. For a few seconds she opened her mouth but no sound emerged.

'You!' she gasped at last. 'Where the hell did you spring from?'

'Do I take it you're not pleased to see me?' the young man answered with exaggerated surprise. 'And why would that be, I wonder.'

'You're *Mavis's* son?' asked Fred, unnecessarily. He looked flabbergasted, Sarah noticed. So Mavis had not told him that she'd had a child.

'Spot on. Colin Swann, pleased to meet you,' said the young man.

Colin Swann. 'C'.

For Sarah, another tiny part of the mystery of the Stepmother was revealed.

'Well, I've never heard of you. Swann, you say? Not

Swindel?' Fred looked from Colin Swann to Mavis and back, and his frown deepened. 'And why have you turned up now?' he asked. 'Be careful how you answer, young fella. Seems I've been hearing a lot of nonsense lately and I want only the truth.' He turned back to Mavis. 'And that includes from you, Mavis.'

'Oh, she can tough it out, however deep the mire,' Colin answered boldly. 'Mum, *shall* I answer that? Air the truth without further delay? I think we owe it to this gentleman to put him in the picture, don't you?'

'Get out of my house,' snarled Mavis. 'Go on, get out!'

'What, so soon? That's not very welcoming. I've hardly been here three minutes. Nah, I think I'll stay a little longer, have a look around.' He turned to look directly at Mavis, fixing her with dark eyes that were exactly like her own. 'See what my stepfather's stolen money has paid for.'

'Stolen money?' gasped Fred. 'There's been nowt stolen that I know about. Now listen, Colin Swann, I don't know who you really are and what you're doing here, besides causing trouble, but I suggest you sling your hook.'

'Which would be a terrible shame for you, sir, because I came here to see you as much as Mum. I gather you think you're her husband.'

'I am,' said Fred, stoutly, but his face betrayed his growing uncertainty about everything. He was picking his way over shifting sands and he knew it.

'Wrong! Now, perhaps we could all sit down instead

of standing around like we're waiting for a train, and I shall enlighten you. Spill the beans, eh, Mum?' He winked at Mavis in a way that was intended to be annoying.

Sarah had been standing quietly in the background. Now she went across to the lodgers' sitting room and opened the door wide without a word. Colin led the way in and then turned to beckon to Mavis and Fred, completely taking charge of the situation.

'Come along. No need to be shy. Never known you to be shy before, Mum,' he said, then sat down on one of the sofas and made himself comfortable.

Mavis and Fred sat down opposite, stiff with nerves and anger, and Sarah closed the door, then went to sit to one side, in the wing-back armchair. Her stomach was bubbling with excitement, but also with dread.

Stepfather? Stolen money? Colin Swann had arrived with the exact information she had been about to set out for Brighton to find and bring back as proof.

'Your stepfather . . .' she ventured, '. . . that would be Mr Chisholm?'

'Got it in one.'

'Sarah . . .?' Fred was astounded that she seemed to know anything more than he did.

'He's very ill,' Colin went on, 'but he told me that he had had a telephone call from a distressed young woman who had fallen into the clutches of my mother, and that she is the daughter of my mother's husband. Which is very odd, don't you think, Mum, because you are married to Cedric Chisholm and have been for many years. You are not free to marry anyone else because – do I have to spell it out for you? – it is the law that a person can have only one spouse.'

Fred stared at Mavis open-mouthed. Then Sarah saw his face change as he realised this brash young man had to be speaking the truth. Even Sarah knew more about it than he did. Fred knew he had been taken for a fool – bamboozled by Mavis just as everyone else had been, but more seriously – and he didn't like it one bit. 'Is it true, Mavis? *Are* you married to someone else? Are you? Answer me!'

Sarah looked away, hardening her heart. It was her father who had got them all into this mess. Now he must face discovering just how deep the mire was.

'It was a long time ago—' Mavis began.

'That's no excuse!' roared Fred. 'You told me you were *widowed*, Mavis.'

'I was.'

'But it seems she forgot to tell you that she married again, and that husband number two is still living,' said Colin. He rested his arms along the back of the sofa and settled in to tell the story. 'You see, Mum was first married to my father, Basil Swann. Dad went to war and, in 1917, Mum was told that he had been killed. She took up with Cedric Chisholm, genuinely believing herself to be a widow – and she was a merry widow, at that. Cedric was generous with his money, of which he had a great deal at that time, owning some drapery shops and having had something to do with army uniforms. There were days at the races and evenings at the music hall, new dresses and jewellery. Happy days, eh, Mum?'

Mavis did not answer. Fred had his head in his hands by now.

'Basil Swann was not dead, however, but badly injured, and there had been a mix-up about who he was; some confusion with some poor bugger who was actually dead. Eventually he turned up at home, hoping to take up his life from when it had been so rudely interrupted by the war, but his homecoming wasn't a happy reception, was it, Mum? Remind me: didn't I hear you tell the poor man to his horribly scarred face that you wished he had been killed? Something like that.'

Again, Mavis said nothing.

'This was early 1919. Do correct me if any of these details are wrong, won't you, Mum? So, Cedric Chisholm, being the good sort he is, broke off the relationship, intending that Mum should take up her wifely duties and nurse my father back to health. Unfortunately, the siren call of Cedric's money proved too much for Mum's grasping little hands. How easy it was to do away with my dad with an old army revolver and make it look like suicide. Poor Basil, he couldn't cope with the terrible scars and the nightmares, and the pain of the injuries that would never really heal – wasn't that the story you put about, Mum? Goodness me, you seem to have very little to say for yourself about all this. That's not like you at all. Shall I go on . . .?

'So, there you were, widowed, and for real this time. But the shadow of suspicion fell on you, and the police came and arrested you, didn't they? You were tried for Basil Swann's murder, but there wasn't enough evidence for a conviction. 'Course, I could have provided the evidence that would have had you hanged, Mum, because I saw you do it. I was fourteen at the time, and I'd just lost one parent. Not something you can easily forget: seeing your mother shoot your father. Pretty big event, if I'm being truthful. But I also saw the way things were with you and I thought to myself: keep your head down, old fella, and just see where this goes. Fortunately, in this case, my mother never really noticed whether I was around or at school, so conveniently being off the scene was pretty easy.'

'So what happened then?' asked Fred faintly, his eyes wide with horror.

'Cedric Chisholm is too gallant a gentleman to leave a woman to fend for herself, and he welcomed Mum back into his arms, believing her to be innocent, just as the jury in court did. Took her back and married her. Trouble was, this time he thought it would be more appropriate if they kept a very modest social diary, what with Mum having been tried for murder. He was also mindful of his own reputation – and his profits – and needed to keep the drapery shops very respectable, with no hint of any gossip or scandal associated with his wife. It might look a little . . . tactless to be painting the town so soon after escaping the noose, eh, Mum? Needless to say, this didn't suit you one bit. You tried to stick with Cedric, I'll give you that, but in the end you just upped and left, taking the entire contents of his safe with you.'

'What, left that good man who believed in your

innocence and stood by you, when you'd been on trial and everything?' gasped Fred. 'Took his money?'

'He'd got plenty. Besides, he was boring me. It's very boring indeed living in Brighton and not going out on the town, let me tell you. All that gaiety, and there was I, living like an invalid behind closed doors.'

Sarah thought Mavis's path had led her from a vibrant social life anyway, but of course, Mavis was older now, and she had chosen to move north, to a small town where she was not known, in order to spend the stolen contents of her husband's safe on a ludicrous falling-down house that would never be the 'little palace' of her fantasies.

'And so you *are* still married to him? Colin is telling the truth?' asked Fred.

'Every word, although I do think you might have been kinder, Colin. You did get a very nice career in your stepfather's drapery business out of it. And you haven't told the last part of the story, which I don't think reflects very well on you.'

'Don't you, indeed?' said Colin, looking unconcerned. 'Even if that were true, what would you do about it – turn me in to the police?' He threw his head back and laughed loudly.

Sarah kept quiet, although she was very keen to hear the end of the story, which she guessed was about the money Mavis had been paying to Colin, probably to keep him quiet about Basil Swann's murder. Goodness, but Mavis and her son were an unpleasant pair. Poor Mr Chisholm . . .

'Go on, let's hear it all,' said Fred grimly.

Mavis opened her mouth to object, but Fred was having none of it.

'And you can shut up, Mavis. I want no more of your lies.'

'Well,' said Colin, sitting forward now, 'turns out Mum here disappeared for a while, taking up with one fella or another. Chancers the lot of them – and I include her in that. No doubt she relieved some dodgy type of his money a time or two. It so happens that Brighton is a bit of a leery place – always has been – and, being something of a chancer myself, I got to know some scoundrels, who knew some bounders, and then one day I heard news of my very own mother. I knew it was her because my source, who was reliable, at least where knowing what's what was concerned, described her remarkable hair and said her name was Mavis Swindel. It didn't take much effort to discover where I'd find her, so one day I turned up at her place in London, where she was making her way, mostly at the expense of foolish men, from what I learned. I suggested that she might want to consider paying back all the money she had stolen from my stepfather's safe when she bolted. That would be a wise move because otherwise I'd be taking her life story to the newspapers and gossip magazines, which would not only make a bob or two for me, but would rather cut off her future chances of taking in any more fools.

'It must have been a pretty persuasive argument, because she agreed to pay in instalments. I've been receiving these – oh, not a huge amount, but a decent whack – each month for a while now, and putting the funds away so that I can surprise Cedric Chisholm with at least a partial repayment of his stolen money, eventually. The only trouble now is that he won't live to enjoy what there is of that. And lately the instalments have, er, *dried up*. So when I found out from my stepfather where you are living, and he was unable to make the journey himself to bring to Mr Quinn's notice that you were already married, I offered to take a look and see what was going on. And what do I find? A bloomin' ridiculous lodging house on the edge of nowhere, freezing cold, in need of complete renovation and full of shabby second-hand furniture. No wonder you've got empty rooms, Mum,' Colin went on. 'Who the hell would want to live here? How were you ever going to make a success of a lodging house when you haven't an ounce of business know-how? There isn't a lazier person, man or woman, on God's earth, and there certainly isn't one with a tighter fist where spending on other people's comfort is concerned. I'm guessing you bought the place on the cheap, kidding yourself it needed just a lick of paint, and then realised it wasn't so much a bargain as a millstone around your neck, a drain on what money you had left. You know nothing but what makes your life easier, so you were hardly going to start gutting the place, were you?'

'How could I spend anything on the house when I was paying you?' shouted Mavis. 'You've bled me dry.'

'Got yourself into a tight corner then, didn't you?'

sneered Colin. 'You didn't have to buy this monstrosity.' He gazed round at the huge room with its undersized fireplace, no fire in the grate; the crumbling cornices, the ill-fitting sash windows. His eyes roved over the faded lampshades and the worn sofa covers, the ring-stained side tables . . . 'I expect you thought it would be an investment and, in the meantime, make easy money from taking in lodgers. Didn't you think you'd have to put in some work? Heaven knows, that's hardly your style but I can't believe you couldn't see the need for it.'

'No, eventually she realised that, young man,' said Fred, bleakly. 'She thought I would do it, and that my children would do it. She didn't marry me for my money – I'm just a hardware-shop assistant and have never been more than that – but I've come to realise that she did marry me because I'd be on hand to fix up the house, and my children would work here for next to nowt – be her underpaid servants – while she . . .' he turned to Mavis, '. . . while *you* lazed about on your chaise longue in your office, supposedly keeping your complicated accounts and eating chocolate!'

'No, Fred—'

'Aye, aye,' said Colin, brightening. 'A little dickie bird has just whispered in my ear. It's saying, how come there's no money when you have lodgers paying for their rooms? How many of them are there?'

'There used to be four, but now there's just Mr Armstrong,' Fred said. 'I doubt he'll stick around much longer. He's threatened to leave twice already, and I don't blame him.'

'Four rented rooms and no money. Just as that little bird has hinted, that doesn't add up. You should have been making a decent living, Mum. I can see, now that most of the lodgers have left, you might be short of a few bob, and that explains why I haven't been receiving my stepfather's repayments of late, but I'm blessed if I can see where you spent your rents before that. Unless the bedrooms are decorated with hand-painted Chinese wallpaper.'

'Distemper,' murmured Sarah.

Colin nodded. 'So, Mum, where's the rest of it? Saving up for a rainy day, were you?'

'There was a terrible storm and there was some damage to the roof,' said Mavis nervously.

'But that was last month, and it took no time to fix it,' said Fred. 'It wasn't a big job in the end.'

'But I have had a lot of expenses,' insisted Mavis. 'The upstairs corridor ceiling . . .'

'Mavis,' said Fred, his anger clearly barely under control, 'I was blind to a lot of things, the finances of this place being one of them. I was foolish enough to believe everything you told me at first 'cos I had no reason not to. Big house to run, Sarah and Susan to pay, the vast expense of the insurance on this place, the expensive new carpets and curtaining for two of the rooms, you told me. But gradually what I saw and what you said started not to add up, although you always had some explanation for that. And now I can see I have no reason to believe owt you say at all. Why should I when I learn that we aren't even legally married and you knew that all along? Every half-day afternoon, every weekend, I'm rehanging a door or fixing a rotten window frame, or mending some broken piece of furniture. It's too much. The whole place needs gutting and starting again. But I thought: poor lass, she could do with some help. And, I admit, I was happy to be married, to have some . . . some female company again. I believed you 'cos I wanted to, and I put you before my own kids because it made my life easier. I thought you'd be their mother and I wouldn't have to bother with them. I've little talent for being a parent, and after Ada died I found the children a burden I didn't know how to deal with. And now . . . nowt! There's simply nowt here!'

'Mr Quinn, I'm sorry to drop the veil from your eyes, but I rather suspect there's a bit more here than you might guess,' said Colin. 'See, you've taken your mind off the point. Yes, you and Mum are not married, and I'm afraid you're going to have to work out where to go from here between yourselves. I'm here only to tell the truth, and to come away with my stepfather's money. So, Mum, where are you hiding it?'

Sarah felt panic rising.

'Mr Swann,' she began, 'I've worked for next to nowt for months. There's no hot water and no fires most of the time, I've holes in my shoes . . .' she held up her feet to show these, '. . . my clothes are gradually turning to rags and I've no money at all to do owt or have any kind of life. I've no independence because I can't afford it. I've almost given up seeing my friend Rachel because if we want a cup of tea out, she is the only one who can afford to pay for it. Please, Mr Swann, don't take all the money and leave us with nowt at all.'

Sarah knew she sounded like a beggar on the street, appealing to the generosity of a stranger, but she couldn't bear the thought of Colin departing with what money there was and leaving the Quinns destitute. They couldn't all live on Fred's wage and Mr Armstrong's rent, and keep the house going. Susan would leave for a new job, but Sarah now had nothing in the world and nowhere to go. She had, in effect, become Mavis's slave.

'Shame on you, Mum,' said Colin. 'Now, let's go to this office with the chaise longue, where the chocolates are eaten and the complicated accounts are done, and unearth the treasure, shall we? Perhaps, Mr Quinn, you can lead on and Mavis can follow?'

Fred got up and went to the door. Colin looked hard at his mother until she, too, got up and followed.

'Cheer up, darlin',' said Colin quietly to Sarah. 'I can see how things are here and I'll make sure you can get your shoes mended. Something tells me you were about to leave the house very early this morning, just as I appeared. Not making a bid to escape, were you?'

'I was about to set out for Brighton, to see Mr Chisholm and get proof of the truth about Mavis. You've saved me the trip.'

'Ha! An unlikely knight in shining armour,' laughed Colin. 'Seems to me you've no good reason to be fond of our Mavis.'

'I hate her,' said Sarah with such venom that she shut him up, and she followed her father out of the room.

403

In the hall, Mr Armstrong was just coming downstairs. Susan must have arrived quietly because Sarah could hear her crashing pans around in the kitchen.

'Ah, Mrs Quinn, may I have a word, please?' Armstrong asked.

'She's busy just now,' said Sarah. 'I'll let you know when she's free.' *Although it might be wise to wait a while after Colin Swann has left.*

'Oh, but it won't take a minute . . .'

'Didn't you hear Miss Quinn?' snapped Colin, and gave Armstrong a quelling look, although he was nothing like as tall and imposing in stature as the lodger.

Armstrong fell silent, aware, as Sarah was, of the air of danger surrounding the young man.

Colin followed Fred, Mavis and Sarah into Mavis's office and shut the door.

'Now then, Mum. You have a cash box, a red leather thing, about so big,' he indicated with his hands, 'and with an all-important lock and key. Where is it?'

'I . . . er—'

'Come along, Mum, bring it out. Don't keep us waiting.'

'I . . . I don't have that box any longer. I left it behind. At Cedric's. I never brought it out of Brighton.'

'Liar!' Colin smashed the side of his fist down on the desk, making the pens jump in their tray. 'It was undoubtedly that box you stuffed with the cash you helped yourself to from Cedric Chisholm's safe one fine day in 1924. Now, I'll ask you again, Mum, where's the cash box?'

There was a long silence. Sarah saw indecision crossing Mavis's face. She wondered whether to speak out and announce that the cash box was in the bottom right-hand drawer of the desk, but Colin would soon think to look there if Mavis didn't tell him.

'It's in the desk,' said Mavis.

'Well, get it out then,' Colin replied with exaggerated patience.

Mavis knelt down at the desk, which was quite a feat with her figure-hugging skirt, and pulled open the bottom drawer. She brought out the leather box and placed it in front of her on the desk.

'And the key?' asked Colin. 'It's not much use to me locked, is it?'

'I haven't got the key in here.'

'Rubbish! Oh, you are such a liar. Why keep the box here and the key not with it?'

'I *don't* have the key with me!'

'Get it now!' ordered Colin. 'Or I'll smash the ruddy thing open with a poker, and I don't care if you get a whack from it in the process.'

'No!' said Mavis. 'No. I've . . . I've just remembered where the key is.' She went over to the mantelpiece and picked it out of the same bowl in which she'd put Mr McCain's stolen watch and tie pin.

'Now unlock the box.'

Mavis did so, and opened the lid to reveal the box was stuffed with banknotes.

'Sweet,' murmured Colin. 'Makes this trip all worthwhile. Now, give that money to me.' He held out his hand and Mavis reluctantly gave him the cash. Then Colin casually took a manila envelope from the top of the tray of letters on the desk and stuffed in all the money except for a few of the notes.

'Now, I'm going to give those last few to Sarah so she can get her shoes repaired and buy herself and her friend a cup of tea. Owe her quite a lot of wages, I should guess, eh? It's only paying what you owe, Mum, so there's no need to get in a strop.'

He handed the money to Sarah, who found that she was holding her hand out to take it.

'Now stop right there,' said Mavis. She had the top drawer of her desk open now and suddenly there was a gun in her hand.

'Mavis?' gasped Fred. 'What are you doing with that?'

'Found it amongst Wilkins's belongings and thought it might come in useful,' she replied.

'Put it down. Please, just put it down before someone gets hurt. There's been quite enough nonsense with guns around here lately.'

'Quite your style, isn't it, Mum, shooting people?' said Colin, not taking his eyes off the gun. 'But I don't think you'd get away with it twice. It would look rather too much of a coincidence. You'd be bound to be caught and tried – there are witnesses – and then . . . dear, oh dear. Far better let me just leave now with some of the money you owe my stepfather. He will die knowing you partly paid your debt, and I will have no more reason to let slip the truth about your crimes. Neat all round. Happy ending, in fact.'

'Except I'm not happy,' said Fred. 'I'm not happy at all, my lad. My daughter and I have worked damned hard on this wreck of a house and it's not right, you going off with any money from here. We need that to get this place on track. We're living on air as it is.'

'Forget it, Dad,' murmured Sarah. 'Let Colin take the money to Mr Chisholm.'

'That's right,' said Colin. 'Little Sarah has the right idea. So put the gun down, Mum, and I shan't be bothering you again.'

There was a casual knock at the door and Susan came straight in.

'Breakfast's ready—' she began. 'Oh my Lord! Mrs Quinn!'

Colin made a grab for the gun, as Sarah got down low and Susan started screaming. The gun went off and Colin fell against Susan, both of them falling to the floor. Mavis grabbed the envelope and ran from the room, nearly treading on Sarah in her hurry to escape.

'Oh my God, oh my God,' breathed Sarah. 'Dad, quick, Colin's hurt. See to him and I'll get after Mavis.' She saw Mavis had dropped the gun and it now lay beside its victim. At least she wouldn't have to worry about Mavis being armed.

Sarah scooted through the hall, where Mr Armstrong, wide-eyed, was dithering, and Janette was looking over the banister, pale and frightened, and out of the open front door.

Outside there was no sign of Mavis.

Which way? Which way? Towards Scarstone, of course.

But when Sarah emerged out between the giant gate-posts onto the pavement and looked to the right, there was no Mavis in sight.

Surely not . . .

She set off in the other direction, along the lane that ran beside the house, down to the Edge itself. There, ahead, and moving surprisingly fast, was Mavis, clutching the envelope of money. Where she meant to go was unclear. Perhaps she hoped to hide, lie low until Colin had gone and then return up the slope and back along the road into Scarstone. Perhaps she was just panicking.

'Mavis, come back,' yelled Sarah.

Mavis didn't even look round – perhaps she didn't hear – and Sarah started out to catch up with her before she did herself an injury.

Very soon the slope became steeper.

'Mavis!'

Mavis was slowing now, sliding on the steep lane, beyond where Sarah, Janette and Joe had left their bicycles in the summer. Ahead, Sarah could see that the track petered out and the slope was just rough grass, sheep-grazed and ever more uneven and steep.

'Mavis!'

Mavis stopped and looked back, panting, hesitated for a moment, then turned and continued. There were sheep tracks off to the left, which meandered down long, winding routes at a gentler gradient. She would veer off at any moment and take one of those paths down.

Perhaps she didn't see Great Edge coming up so

quickly. Suddenly there was no alternative way down, and the slope became a near-vertical drop.

With a loud, high-pitched scream, Mavis disappeared over the Edge.

CHAPTER TWENTY

IRENE STAYED ON at the Lodge after Hubert moved into Fettling House.

'You can remain here for as long as you like, my darling,' he said, smiling, 'but I do hope you might want to come to live with me in the House *after* we are married.'

'Thank you. I shall seriously consider that,' said Irene with a grin.

'Fettling House will be your home as much as mine and I want you to feel you belong there. Come over whenever you like – I don't need to be there – and tell Mrs Lofthouse how you'd like the furniture arranged. Do whatever you want with it.'

Mrs Lofthouse, Hubert's housekeeper, was a friendly elderly woman. She came as half of a pair: Mr Lofthouse did jobs that involved lifting and fixing things, and he was also in charge of looking after the car. They were devoted to Hubert and the boys, the kind of old-fashioned servants that not many middling people needed or could afford any longer. Both of them had taken to Irene immediately. Irene wondered if they might have recognised her as one of their own, but they trod the path between deference and friendliness in a most professional way, and treated Irene just the same as they treated Hubert.

Mr Lofthouse said he'd volunteered to take on the heavy work in the garden, fitting in with his other tasks, which suited Mr Cole and he hoped it suited Miss Mayhew, too. If Miss Mayhew would be so kind as to direct him, he'd be pleased to do whatever she asked. Irene suspected that Hubert had foreseen this arrangement and hadn't seriously been looking for a gardener, but it pleased her to have the help. After all, she would have other considerations when she was married. She was very much looking forward to becoming a wife and stepmother. That she would also be mistress of Fettling House felt as if reality was merging with a wonderful daydream. Sometimes she had to just stand still and pinch herself to get her mind around all this good fortune.

Once she had got used to the idea that she would be married and was to stay at Fettling House, she had written to Sarah and Janette to share the news. She hadn't had a reply yet, but Irene supposed they were probably too busy to put their aunt at the top of their priorities. She would invite them to the wedding and perhaps they could stay at the Lodge for a little holiday. It certainly sounded as if the girls needed one.

Now that her own future was settled, Irene thought she would be able to help her young nieces. Hubert might well have some ideas . . . He was such a kind man, he would give some time to think seriously about the Quinn girls.

Irene had tried to shrug off her silly notion about the beautiful engagement ring Hubert had given her, but the fact that it was a family heirloom, not chosen especially for her, stirred an uncomfortable thought from the back of her mind to the surface every so often. A precious piece of family jewellery – he would without doubt have given it to Caroline, his first wife, on their engagement. It wasn't so much that the ring had had a previous owner that disturbed Irene, it was that it had had *that* previous owner. Hubert hardly spoke of his first wife, and Irene was aware that her idea of the woman was entirely of her own imagining. She wanted to know more, yet she didn't like picking at a scab that would then open a stinging cut, but she could not just ask him outright. That might turn his thoughts to comparisons, and Irene feared she'd then be found wanting.

The ring had been taken to the best jeweller in Ipswich and had been resized to fit. It had been so very much too small that it had had to be entirely refashioned for Irene. Hubert seemed not to mind about this at all, but Irene felt a little embarrassed at the size of her workaday gardener's hands. The drastic alteration to the ring felt to her much the same as if a high-bred racehorse's shoe had been completely reworked to fit a carthorse.

At the beginning of February there were still tea chests to be unpacked in the drawing room, and Irene was

eager to help Mrs Lofthouse who, having worked for
Hubert for years, knew what there was and what ought
to go where. Soon, Irene was unwrapping a silver-framed
photograph of a very fine-boned young woman wearing
what looked, were it in colour, like a pretty dress. The
fashion was of several years before. The lady's dark hair
was bobbed in the style of that time, and her heart-
shaped face was perfectly made up in a smart and
sophisticated way. She was very beautiful and exquisitely
petite. Irene guessed straight away who she was. She was
strangely like the Caroline of Irene's imagination, and
Mrs Lofthouse confirmed this without her having to ask.

'That's Mr Cole's first wife,' said Mrs Lofthouse. 'The
boys are all in the same mould, but I think young Simon
looks the most like her, don't you?'

'Yes . . .' Irene was astonished at the likeness; Hubert
must be reminded of Caroline every time he looked at
his second son.

'Where do you think Mr Cole would like this placed?'
she asked bravely.

'Oh, I think we should just put it in this drawer for
the moment,' said Mrs Lofthouse. 'Mr Cole will know
what he wants to do with it.'

Irene took this to mean that he might want the photograph in his study or somewhere similar, to look at while
he reminisced in private.

Now that she had seen the photograph of Caroline,
she was surer than ever that the tiny engagement ring
had been worn by her. She had looked carefully to see
if Caroline was wearing it in the photograph, of course,

but her hands were folded in her lap and it was impossible to see.

Now Irene began to worry more. It was bad enough that the engagement ring had been three whole sizes too small; how could she ever hope to compare favourably with that delicate dark beauty?

Soon, she was choosing her bridal clothes for the early March wedding – a stylish navy-blue costume trimmed with velvet and a rather lovely hat with a brim – all the time comparing herself with Caroline, who looked as though her waist would be twenty-one inches and who had no doubt been married, at less than half Irene's age, in white lace and a veil. Never before had Irene thought very much about what she looked like. She knew she wasn't a head-turning beauty, but she had never thought she was plain, which was good enough. Now she felt lumpen and ugly.

One day she lost all patience with herself and went to walk about in the wet grass of the orchard and give herself a good talking-to.

It was late morning. There was a mist down, which muffled all sounds, and the garden was completely silent but for distant rooks calling.

Irene was growing increasingly fond of Hubert – she might even be beginning to fall in love with him – and she was practical enough to see that this marriage would be her last chance. In fact, her entire future was invested in it: in addition to a good man, it came with a ready-made family, a beautiful home and garden, and financial security, none of which she would otherwise have.

But growing ever bigger, day by day, until one day she feared it would be enormous, was the spectre of his first wife, Caroline. Irene couldn't stop thinking about her, and that was because Irene now wore the ring that had once been hers. Caroline had worn it when it had been tiny and perfect. Now it had been refashioned and the precious family heirloom was no longer identical to how it had been down the years. It was compromised, perhaps ruined, to fit a gardener's ordinary broad hand.

What if Hubert wanted to hold some fancy party at Fettling House and Irene wasn't up to being hostess, not having done that before, or been brought up to it? Caroline would, of course, have taken such events in her stride and been brilliant in the role. Then, when Irene fell short, Hubert would begin to see other ways in which his second wife didn't measure up, and soon he would be unhappy, and unable to hide it.

No, it would be better to break off the engagement now, return the altered ring with apologies for spoiling it, and then hope the gardening job at Saxham Ash was still available. They would both suffer in the short term, but it would be better to face that now for the sake of avoiding terrible unhappiness later.

Irene dragged her wellies through the wet all the way back to the Lodge, her heart breaking. She would go up to the House this evening, when Hubert got back from work, and she would tell him she was sorry, but she'd changed her mind.

When she got to the Lodge, sitting on the doorstep was Sarah, a little overnight bag beside her.

'Good heavens, what are you doing here? Oh, my love, what's happened?'

'Never mind me. What's happened with you, Auntie? Why are you crying?'

'Oh, I'm just a bit sad today, that's all.'

'About Mum?'

'Yes . . . yes, about Ada.'

'I think about her a lot too, especially since Dad took up with Mavis Swindel. I don't know how he could even look at Mavis after he was married to Mum.'

Oh dear. Irene fought back more tears, wiped her eyes and unlocked the door.

'Come in, we'll have some tea – have you had owt to eat lately? – and you can tell me what is going on. Where's Janette?'

'She's gone to stay at her friend Lorna's house for a few days. You'll understand why when I tell you.'

'. . . So she just disappeared over Great Edge,' finished Sarah. 'It was awful. I think the sound of that scream will be with me for the rest of my life. I thought I hated her. I've never hated anyone before and I thought I'd turned into the kind of person she was: full of loathing, but when I saw her go over I was sorry . . . a bit.'

'Such nonsense, love. Of course you're not hateful and full of loathing. The woman was very dislikeable. *No one* liked her, from what you tell me.'

Sarah gave a sad little smile. 'Even her own dog disliked her! After Mavis had been gone a day or two, Basil – she gave her dog the name of the husband she had murdered, which I reckon says everything about her – started to bark for the first time and behave much more like a normal dog. He's growing a better coat, too. Janette reckons he was allergic to Mavis because she was so horrible. He's Janette's dog now.'

'A good thing for both of them. But, tell me, what happened to all that money she tried to make away with? Did that go over the Edge, too?'

'No. I think Mavis must have tripped, and that's what sent her hurtling over so far and with such speed. Mebbe that's when she let go of the envelope. Oh, Auntie, I hardly dared to look over, thinking to see her smashed body far below. It was so steep, and felt so high, that I had to go on my hands and knees and creep slowly forward until I was close enough to peer over. But the first thing I saw, caught in the tussocky grass not two feet down, was the envelope. I lay down and stretched out and just managed to save it, although I nearly dislodged it and sent it down after Mavis.'

Sarah put her hands to her face and breathed deeply.

'Oh, I can still feel that swimmy feeling from the height. I had to creep backwards from the Edge, sort of on my front and going uphill, and it took ages until I felt safe enough to stand up again. I never did see where Mavis fell to, but it was an awful long way down.'

Irene got up and hugged Sarah. 'You were very brave. It was more than she deserved that you went after her. You could have been killed too.'

'Mm, but I was careful not to go too fast. I wasn't going to follow her over the Edge.'

'What's going to happen to the house, love? Will you continue to live there?'

'No fear! It's as horrible as Mavis was, and full of bad memories, too. Besides, as Dad and Mavis were not married, and Mavis didn't leave a will, the house will go to Mr Chisholm. But because Mr Chisholm hasn't long to live, I expect Over the Edge will go to Colin really. He's certain to sell it as he disliked it on sight. And when he's quite recovered from the bullet wound to his arm that *his own mother* gave him, he says he's off to live in Germany.'

'Germany?'

'Yes, he says he thinks what he called "the political situation" is developing in an interesting way there. He thinks Germany will suit him.'

'Good grief,' murmured Irene, slowly shaking her head and thanking God her sister's lovely daughters had escaped the clutches of these insane people.

'There was only one lodger left – Mr Armstrong – and it turned out that he's had a change in fortune and was trying to give Mavis his notice on that last morning, but Colin was there so she never got to hear. So after that he just left straight away.'

'It's good that has worked out for him.'

'Yes. I never knew what to make of Mr Armstrong, but I couldn't have guessed the truth. I knew he was writing a book, but it turns out he's written a whole lot of books under the name of "Marie-Antoinette Armstrong"! I even saw one once, and the cover looked very racy. Apparently, they're romances, and

The Price of Her Honour is going to be made into a film. Who'd have thought?'

They smiled at each other, amused to think of one of Mavis's lodgers writing under the name of Marie-Antoinette.

'Joe is nicely established at the forge,' said Irene. 'I don't know if he'll want to return to Scarstone now Mavis is dead.'

'I reckon he and Dad fell out too badly for Joe to want that. That's doubly a shame because it needn't have happened. Dad told me that Mavis had said at the time that it wasn't her who stirred up trouble for Joe with his girlfriend at the greengrocer's shop. It must have been someone else.'

'But wasn't Mavis always telling lies?'

'Yes, but Dad really believed her about this, even now; said she went on about it, whereas usually she didn't like to draw attention to lies she'd told. I don't know . . . It's what happens when someone lies so much: when they tell the truth they're not believed. She told Joe it wasn't her, but why would he think she told the truth then? Anyway, Joe's been writing to my best friend, Rachel – you know, she who was so good to me when Mum died, and she's been a kind friend through all this difficult time with Mavis, too – and I reckon there's a bit of a romance growing there.' She sighed. 'But we'll have to see. Rachel's really clever and so she and Joe haven't much in common.'

'Cruel,' said Irene, smiling. 'If Joe is keen on Rachel, then he's clever enough to have picked a good 'un this time. Let's hope it works out, eh? That's a reason for him to go back north.'

'Well, I'm not saying owt in case it's the wrong thing.'

'Very wise. And your dad?'

'Oh, he wants to try to rent again – somewhere on the south side of Scarstone, where Keele Street is, although I'll be amazed if the old house is available.'

'But you liked it there, so I hope mebbe you'll be lucky.'

'Ah. I reckon I'd rather not be doing with Dad any longer either. Not on a day-to-day basis, anyway. He's proved himself to be a bit hopeless as a father. He should have stood up for us, not been taken in by Mavis. What I'd really like is to come to live in Fettling. I know you're getting married to Mr Cole, and that's the best news ever, but I love it here, and I mean to make my own future now, not have it made for me by other folk. I'll bring the sewing machine and set up in the village. Some of the money Mavis was squirrelling away should have been paid to me as my wages, so now I've got enough to keep myself and Jan for a little while. I'll get a little seamstress business going, just as I was intending to have when Miss Rowley retired. What do you think, Auntie? You wouldn't mind if I came to live nearby?'

'Oh, love, I wonder you should even ask. It's a brilliant idea, the perfect solution, and I reckon you could make a real success of the work. And George Ramsden and Betsy are only a few miles away in Saxham Ash. I reckon he'd be made up if you fetched up hereabouts.'

Sarah blushed prettily. 'I hope so. He's a good man.

I really like him. It's been difficult to be in touch with nowt but horribleness happening at Over the Edge, but it will be different now.' She put her hand in her pocket and felt the smoothness of the little charm he had made her. She'd go to see him tomorrow . . .

'Well, I'm in regular touch with Betsy,' said Irene, 'and I know George will be pleased to see you. But about Jan . . . it wouldn't be your responsibility to keep her. I could do that. We'll find her a good school nearby, mebbe in Ipswich.'

'That sounds good, but Jan's not used to school being owt fancy.'

'Of course. And . . . how's this for an idea? When I get married I'll go to live at Fettling House. I reckon the House is big enough for you and Janette to live there, too, although I will have to ask Hubert. And his boys will be there at weekends. Or, if you wanted a house of your own, you might be able to live here. At the Lodge. What do you think?'

Sarah looked as if she was filling up with joy and she burst out laughing and hugged her aunt.

'Oh, that is the very best news I could possibly hear. Oh, just wait till I tell Janette. She will be nearly exploding with happiness. There is no woman on earth who deserves a happy ending more than you, and it's so like you to spread the happiness around.'

'Thank you, Sarah,' said Irene.

'And what are the boys like?'

'They are lovely, too! I can't wait for you and Jan to meet them.'

'They are so lucky to be having you as their step-mother. Look what Joe, Jan and I ended up with! A monster! Except, in the end, she wasn't a real step-mother at all. That's the only good part, really. Although we had to endure her, thinking that she was, which was bad . . . Oh, I'm so confused about Mavis. I think it's best if I just regard her as a nightmare that's passed, and leave it at that.'

'Well, Sarah, I shall be new to the stepmother job, so if I show any tendency to turn into a monster – or a nightmare – you'll be here to put me right.'

'Daft thing,' said Sarah, laughing.

When Sarah had gone to put her overnight bag in her room, Irene sat quite still and thought about what had just happened. She'd accepted that she would marry Hubert. She'd forgotten her silly wobble and she'd seen the best way forward with no more hesitation. It wasn't just that she was securing her own future, and her nieces', it was the right decision for her and for Hubert. They would be happy. She had made her choice and she was determined on that.

With James Fellowes and Gilbert Wagstaffe, her happy future had been snatched away before she could embark upon it. Not many women had a third chance. Now she could fulfil her destiny at last and be a happily married woman.

That evening Irene took Sarah up to the House and introduced her to Hubert and to the Lofthouses. The talk over dinner was all of the future.

Afterwards, Irene suggested Sarah might want to look round the House with Mrs Lofthouse. When the door had closed on them, Hubert turned to Irene, who snuggled up with him on the sofa, and said, 'Now, tell me what's happened to you. You seem . . . I don't know . . . lighter of heart than you have been lately. Am I not enough for you? Were you waiting for your niece to arrive to make your life complete?'

Irene laughed. ''Course not. Oh, Hubert, I was just getting myself in a silly tizzy, worrying that I . . . that I'm not some swanlike beauty. It was the ring: it made me feel big and clumsy: some peasant of a gardener with straw in my hair and huge feet.'

'Are your feet huge? Do you have straw in your hair? Let me look . . . No, I can't see anything like that. You must be mistaken.'

Irene elbowed him gently, smiling. 'Actually, I must tell the truth, I was worried that I'm not as beautiful as Caroline was. The precious ring fitted her but it had to be altered for me – in fact, completely remade. I saw your photograph of her when Mrs L and I were unpacking your things, and she was very lovely.'

Hubert sat up a little straighter and Irene could feel him becoming less relaxed. 'Very lovely in some ways, but not in others. Oh, my darling, I'm so sorry you misunderstood about the ring. I should have made it clearer. It wasn't hers at all. I would never have given you a ring she had worn. It is a family heirloom, as I said, but the last person to wear it was my grandmother. Caroline was offered it – and yes, it fitted her – but she wanted a ring she'd seen in a shop in London, a brand-new one with a fashionable setting. I was disappointed that she didn't think the Cole family heirloom was good enough for her, and it should have been a warning to me because I don't think she thought I was good enough for her after a while, either. I cannot tell you how happy it made me to slip . . . ha, to *try to slip* that ring on your finger and have you accept it. A lesser woman would have said it didn't fit and you'd have to choose something else, but not you, Irene. I couldn't be prouder to have been able to have my grandmother's ring altered to fit you. She'd have loved you, you know. She was a genuine and loving person and she'd have seen those virtues in you.'

Irene felt the weight of worry lift from her. 'Thank you, Hubert. I've been an idiot, I can see.'

'Well, just don't be an idiot again, my love. That's all I ask.' He kissed her hair. 'No, still no straw. And your feet are still a perfectly normal size.'

Irene laughed. What a dear man he was. Why had she not spoken up before and saved herself all that unnecessary worry? She should have remembered the words she had spoken to Sarah in the summer, words that her sister, Ava, had first spoken to her, and so they passed from sister to sister to niece and now back to herself.

Courage, love. That's all you need. Nowt more.

How true that was. Courage and, maybe, the chance to decide your own destiny as well.